THE CASE OFFICER

THE CASE OFFICER

BY

F.W. RUSTMANN, JR.

REGNERY
FICTION

Regnery Fiction™ is a trademark of Salem Communications Holding Corporation; Regnery® is a registered trademark of Salem Communications Holding Corporation

Cataloging-in-Publication Data on file with the Library of Congress

ISBN 978-1-62157-749-2
eISBN 978-1-62157-739-3

Published in the United States by
Regnery Fiction
An imprint of Regnery Publishing
A Division of Salem Media Group
300 New Jersey Ave NW
Washington, DC 20001
www.Regnery.com

Manufactured in the United States of America

10 9 8 7 6 5 4 3 2 1

Books are available in quantity for promotional or premium use. For information on discounts and terms, please visit our website: www.Regnery.com.

FOREWORD

Although this is entirely a work of fiction, the events depicted in the book could reasonably have taken place, and the players are realistic portrayals of case officers and other intelligence operatives. I have drawn heavily from my experiences and personal contacts as a CIA case officer to write the book. Some of my old case officer friends will recognize portions of themselves in the characters of the book, and all will recognize the clandestine techniques they, as case officers, have used over the years. In short, the tradecraft is genuine, and the people are reasonable facsimiles of the real thing.

I should say a word or two about just exactly what a CIA "case officer" is. He or she is an intelligence officer attached to the operational (clandestine) arm of the Agency. The case officer typically is a college graduate, fluent in one or more foreign languages, and always a fully trusted American citizen with a Top Secret security clearance. He or she is an individual of exceptional intelligence, integrity, and initiative. The case officer "handles" cases—recruits and directs foreign spies, known as "agents." The case officer is not an "agent"—the FBI's staff operatives are known as field agents, but the CIA's are known as case officers.

I have taken the time to describe what a case officer actually is because so few people ever get close enough to the Agency to know, and because so much "James Bond"-type fiction distorts the truth and misleads the public about these unique individuals. Case officers are indeed the Agency's elite corps, and they will remain so for as long as there is a need for human agents deep within foreign governments to provide our policy-makers with intelligence information concerning foreign intentions toward the United States.

CHAPTER 1

The secure "bubble" was located on the top floor of the luxurious, sprawling, state-of-the-art US embassy building in Mogadishu, Somalia. It was a clear Plexiglas conference room assembled within another secure room—a room within a room—located off the hall midway between the ambassador's office and the entrance to the CIA's suite of offices. The room was just large enough to fit the country team—ten senior embassy officials and section heads—executive chairs around the conference table. But today there were another dozen embassy staff employees and Marines crowded into the bubble, standing uncomfortably behind the seated country team members.

The ambassador sat at one end of the table, fidgeting nervously with a pencil. Holding it tightly around the middle with his thumb and index finger, he bounced the eraser end repeatedly against the table's surface.

It was already getting warm in the cramped bubble when an armed Marine security guard dressed in camouflage fatigues, helmet, and flak jacket pulled the outer door shut, secured the bubble door with two heavy plastic levers, and activated the sound suppressor.

The ambassador motioned to the CIA station chief seated at the far end of the table. "Okay, let's have it, Spinelli. What's the situation?"

"Not good, sir. But the evacuation is going as well as can be expected. More than four hundred foreign nationals were taken out on Saturday on our helicopters and Italian planes, and another two hundred fifty or so Americans and some foreign diplomats and their families have been rounded up from their homes in the city and brought to this compound. They'll be airlifted out today to the aircraft carrier *Guam* and the amphibious transport ship *Trenton,* anchored offshore."

Spinelli shuffled through his notes, a drop of sweat, then another, falling on them as he did so. Finding what he was looking for, he continued briefing the country team. "The UN Security Council has said more than two thousand people have been killed and another four thousand wounded since the rebels stepped up their campaign a week ago. Siad Barre has reportedly fled the country for Nairobi, but that hasn't been confirmed. In any event, it's clear that the rebels have made significant advances and now control most of the city. The areas controlled by government forces are getting smaller and smaller, just little pockets of resistance, and their troops are deserting like rats leaving the proverbial sinking ship."

The ambassador was now sweating profusely. Beads of perspiration dripped from his bald pate down his hawk-like nose and onto his notepad. "Can't we get the bloody a/c working in here?" he grumbled to no one in particular.

One of the Marines started toward the door, but Spinelli put an arm out and stopped him. "It's no use, sir. It's turned down as far as it will go. There are just too many people in here. I'll try to make this as quick as possible."

He returned to his notes and spoke rapidly. "The evacuation operations being run by the Italians, French, and Americans are all reporting ground-fire, but thus far there hasn't been any significant damage reported by any of the aircraft. They are delivering their evacuees to Mombassa. The airport is still relatively secure, although rocket and mortar attacks are a worsening problem. A couple of Italian planes couldn't land there today because they began taking ground fire. Fortunately they weren't hit. It's getting harder and harder to move about the city; ambushes are set up everywhere, and the favorite targets seem to be our evacuation vehicles.

"The city is littered with bodies baking in the sun, and no one is making any effort to remove them. The stench is horrible. There was one report of about thirty-five dead Somali soldiers lying in a perfectly straight row on a downtown street, rotting. This was apparently done in retaliation for a similar thing done by Siad Barre to the rebels about a month ago."

The military attaché, an overweight army colonel looking decidedly uncomfortable in his sweat-drenched khaki uniform, asked, "Do you know how much longer the evacuation ships will remain out there?"

Spinelli replied, "That's a good question." His eyes locked onto those of the ambassador and held his gaze as he talked. "As you know, both naval vessels, the *Guam* and the *Trenton*, were detached from the Persian Gulf armada to rescue us and a bunch of our friends, including several foreign ambassadors and their staffs, from this compound. Most of these evacuations have been completed, and we are basically all that remain. There are only a couple hundred of us left, and we're all on the compound, fairly safe for now. The ships are urgently needed for Operation Desert Shield, and the military wants us to complete this evacuation ASAP and get the hell out of here so they can return to their bases in the Arabian Peninsula."

"Sure they do," snapped the ambassador, jabbing his finger toward Spinelli. "They want us to abandon this embassy and leave it to be vandalized by General Mohamed Aideed's filthy bunch of murderers. This embassy compound was dedicated on the 4th of July less than two years ago. It was built at a cost of $35 million to the American taxpayer, and I'm not ready to fold the flag and carry it out of here. It's a veritable fortress . . . the newest and most state-of-the-art embassy in all of Africa. We can stay inside and wait this out. Sooner or later the US government will come to its senses and retake this city, and then we can go on about our business of building a decent government here in Somalia." He slammed his fist on the table. "That's what we're going to do."

The plastic room fell silent. Spinelli averted his gaze, and no one else made eye contact with the ambassador, now red-faced, shaking nervously, and perspiring profusely. He appeared on the verge of a heart ttack.

The silence was broken by a young Marine officer standing erect in a starched camouflage uniform to the side of Spinelli. "Mr. Ambassador, my name is Captain MacMurphy. I arrived yesterday from Nairobi. I'm the officer in charge of the Marine security guard detachments for the Horn of Africa region, which includes this one."

The ambassador surveyed the young officer standing at the end of the bubble. He looked cool and composed, while everyone else in the room looked decidedly hot and uncomfortable, a fact that served only to further inflame the ambassador. "So?" he demanded.

"So, with all due respect, sir, I'm here to evacuate my Marines before Aideed's rabble start climbing over the walls of this compound. Those are my orders, sir. We can't delay, because if we do, those of us who remain will end up either dead or as hostages. We don't want a repeat of the Iranian embassy hostage crisis, do we, sir?" His unwavering laser stare impaled the ambassador.

All eyes in the room turned to the young Marine officer.

The ambassador pushed back his chair abruptly and stood, gathering his papers. "This meeting is adjourned. I want to see you, Captain," indicating MacMurphy, "and you, Spinelli, back here in thirty minutes. That should give the place enough time to cool off. Open the door, Sergeant, and let some of the hot air out of this furnace."

CHAPTER 2

Thirty minutes later, the CIA station chief and the Marine captain were seated across from one another near the head of the conference table. The ambassador hurried in moments later, secured the heavy levers of the bubble's Plexiglas door behind him, and took his place at the head of the table. His hands were still trembling, but he had changed his shirt and looked decidedly cooler than before. Spinelli and MacMurphy had been talking in low tones, but now they devoted their full attention to the ambassador.

"Gentlemen," the ambassador began, "first of all, let me make something very clear." His eyes locked on MacMurphy's. "My orders are my orders. Your orders are what I tell you to do. If you don't like my orders, you can get the hell out of my country. I am the ambassador here. I am the president's representative to this God-forsaken country, and although God may have forsaken it, I don't intend to. I give the orders here." His eyes burned, but MacMurphy held his gaze steady and remained impassive.

The ambassador broke the stare and settled back in his chair as if to say, *Now that we have that settled, we can move on.* MacMurphy sat motionless, unresponsive, while Spinelli fidgeted. Now, feeling in control of the meeting, the Ambassador continued.

"This is the situation. There are around two hundred souls left in this compound. Most of them will be evacuated by Marine CH-53 helicopters to the *Trenton* by the end of the day. Diplomats from twenty-nine countries, including Great Britain, Turkey, and the Soviet Union, and all of our non-essential personnel. That will leave a skeleton embassy staff of about thirty officers, a few locals, and your Marine security guard detachment. How many people do you have here at the moment, Captain?"

"Sixteen, including myself, Mr. Ambassador."

"So we will have around forty-six Americans, and what, another six or seven essential Somali Foreign Service Nationals, and what remains of the local embassy guard force, another dozen or so people. Around sixty-five people. Is that about right, Spinelli?"

"That's what I have, sir. And I don't think that number will change much if we stay, because the last local guard who decided to desert was shot by Aideed's men moments after he left the compound. That'll deter anyone else from trying to leave by the gates. The only way out of here now is by one of those helicopters.

"Satellite imagery indicates an attack is forthcoming. Aideed's troops are moving up into positions around the compound. We'll need to take all the remaining FSNs and security guards with us when we leave. We are burning and shredding all classified material as we speak. Commo gear and encryption tapes will be the last to be destroyed."

MacMurphy sat silently, but his mind racing. He saw where the ambassador was heading and knew that any further delay in the evacuation would end in disaster. He couldn't let that happen. If Spinelli wasn't going to confront the ambassador, he was going to have to do it.

"Sir, the security situation absolutely dictates we evacuate everyone today." He leaned forward for emphasis and locked his eyes on the ambassador's. "If we don't, Aideed's men will be coming over the walls and we'll have to start shooting people, and I don't have enough Marines or ammunition to hold off such a large force."

Sweat dripped down the ambassador's face, his eyes locked evenly on MacMurphy's. "You're not going to shoot anyone," he spat. "I will not have any shooting in this compound, no shooting, none, and that's final."

MacMurphy leaned back and stared at the ambassador incredulously. "You want us to let them into the compound? Is that what you want? They *will* come over the walls, you know." His eyes refused to let go of the Ambassador's.

"There will be no bloodshed. Not while I'm in command of this embassy. No one is going to be shot."

Spinelli leaned forward over the table, "But sir, what do you expect us to do? We have to either leave or defend ourselves. We can't just sit here and be captured. Not by that mob. We've got to get out of here while we still have the chance. That mob will hack us up like animals if we stay."

The ambassador trembled with rage. He wagged a boney finger at them and declared, "This is a fortress. We will remain inside until help arrives. When State sees our situation, they will understand and come to their senses. We cannot abandon this embassy. We will not. Not as long as I'm in charge."

Spinelli slumped in resignation. MacMurphy shook his head.

"Let me get this absolutely clear, sir. You intend to remain in the embassy with your staff, and you are ordering me and my Marines *not* to defend the compound *when*, and I don't mean *if*, Aideed's men attack. Is that correct, sir?"

"That is correct, Captain. Absolutely correct. Our country will not abandon us. We will hole up in the chancery building until help arrives. We will force our government to come to our aid. Those are my final orders."

The ambassador abruptly rose from his chair, knocking it against the plastic wall, and hustled for the door. With his hand on one of the plastic handles, he turned and glared at the two officers. "When the non-essential people and our friends have been evacuated, you will assemble the remaining people in the chancery with enough food and water to last for as long as necessary. Then you can batten down the hatches, Captain. Is that understood?"

Then he was gone, leaving the door of the bubble open behind him.

MacMurphy and Spinelli remained seated, joined in disbelief, for several moments. The silence blared. Finally MacMurphy spoke. "What are you going to do, Mr. Spinelli? The ambassador has lost it."

"I know, I know . . . but there's nothing I can do other than report this to headquarters and hope they can prevail on State to talk some sense into the moron. That's it. That's all I can do . . ."

MacMurphy stood as if to leave, and then abruptly turned back. "Maybe there's something I can do." He paused and then went on. "Let Washington know about our situation, and meanwhile I'll try to buy us some time. Either someone has to bring that idiot to his senses, or we're going to have to arrest him and take him out of here in handcuffs. Please tell your people I said that. This situation is critical."

"I will, Captain. Just don't do anything stupid . . ."

CHAPTER 3

MacMurphy walked briskly through the deserted halls of the chancery building, his mind moving faster than his footsteps, which echoed through the marble corridors. Descending the wide staircase, he hurried through the main entrance, waving at the Marine security guard on duty as he passed Post Number One. He entered the numerical code on the cipher lock at the entrance of the Marine Security Guard office and pushed open the heavy teak door.

Gunnery Sergeant Bradshaw had his feet up on his desk, talking to his staff sergeant, a short, stocky fellow named Gillis. Gillis was leaning back in a chair on the other side of the desk. He spat a wad of Copenhagen snuff into a coffee can he held in his lap and jumped up as the captain entered.

"At ease, men." MacMurphy fell into a chair next to Sergeant Gillis. "We've got a problem," he sighed.

The captain briefed the two NCOs on the events that had occurred during the two meetings with the ambassador. When he had finished, Gunny Bradshaw caressed his shaved head thoughtfully and raised his lanky frame from the chair behind his desk. He turned slowly to his commanding officer. "You have gotta be fuckin' shittin' me, sir! That dumb ass wants us to hunker down here while the skinnies out there storm the walls and take over this compound? He won't let us evacuate, and he won't let us fight. Is that the friggin' situation, sir?"

"That's about it, Gunny. Those are his . . . *orders*. But Spinelli's sending a message in his channel outlining the problem and the critical situation, so I think the CIA guys will intervene with State at the highest level. Maybe that'll help move 'em off the dime. I certainly hope so . . ."

"Let's hope someone grabs that cocksucker by his damn stackin' swivel and pounds some sense into him," growled the gunny, his voice resonating like the Parris Island Drill Instructor he had once been. He shook his head. "But I doubt it. Those State Department pogues are all alike. I've heard tell that their new hires get their gonads surgically removed during the junior officer training course."

MacMurphy smiled—the first light moment he had had all day, and it felt good to relieve the tension.

Sergeant Gillis, who had been listening quietly the whole time, flexed his powerful shoulders, spit a wad of brown juice into the coffee can, and said quietly, "There's another solution."

"Yeah, what's that, Sergeant?" asked the gunny.

"We can take things into our own hands. We can't force him to evacuate like he should, but we can defend ourselves. We can't let them bastards blast in here without a fight. And they *will* blast in here if we can't keep them at bay. But maybe we can slow them down a bit till the godamned ambassador comes to his senses or has someone slam his senses down his throat. Anyway, that's what I think."

The gunny and MacMurphy studied Gillis carefully, each wondering what the other was thinking. They looked at each other and nodded.

MacMurphy said, "That's exactly what I've been thinking, but we've got to be very careful. It's mutiny, you know . . . direct disobedience of orders. Let's head on down to the armory for a little pow-wow." He turned to Sergeant Gillis. "Assemble the detachment and meet the gunny and me down there right away. I've got an idea, but if we're going to act, we need to move fast. It'll be dark in just a few hours, and if they decide to attack, that's when they're gonna do it."

"Roger that, sir," said Gillis. He was out the door before he completed the phrase.

CHAPTER 4

The armory was located behind a vault door in the basement of the chancery building. The windowless room smelled of cleaning solvent and gun oil. Its walls were lined with racks of M-16s, Squad Automatic Weapons (SAWs), a few AK-47s, flak jackets, and various other weapons and combat gear. In the center of the room was a long, dark wood, oil soaked cleaning table surrounded by wooden benches. When the last Marine had entered the room and had settled himself on a bench with the rest of the security guard detachment, Gunnery Sergeant Bradshaw called the meeting to order.

"Where's Corporal Kelley?" he asked.

"He's at Post Number One," a Marine responded.

"Oh yeah, right. Thanks. Okay, listen up. I called you all down here to listen to Captain MacMurphy. He's going to brief us on the current situation and tell us what he wants us to do about it. Captain, they're all yours."

MacMurphy stood. "Thanks, Gunny. Have you got something I can write on, a blackboard or something?" One of the Marines jumped up, pulled an easel with a white pad of paper on it out of a corner, and set it up next to the captain at the head of the table. "Great. This'll do just fine." He used a black marker to sketch the rectangle outline of the embassy compound and its relationship to the city and sea to the south and then turned to the group.

"Okay, here we are. Afgoy Road runs along the northern side of the compound. There's not much beyond Afgoy Road in the way of cover, so I don't expect much to come from that direction. The buildings housing the Ministry of Resources, here," he indicated its position on the rough map, "and the Highway Department, here, could provide some cover, so we can't disregard the north totally, but we should consider it our least vulnerable side.

"According to our best information, including the most recent overhead from just a few hours ago, Aideed's forces are massing to the south and southwest of the compound, here and here." He indicated the positions with his finger on the rough sketch. "As you're all aware, to the south we have the ring road that runs around the compound, then a line of trees—I guess you would call it a windbreak—then the International Golf and Tennis Club sprawling out along here. Then still farther south is the heart of the city and then the coast. At the time of the last satellite pass, Aideed's main force was concentrated around here, about a half mile to the south of the club, the area between Jalle Siad Road and the club." He indicated the positions on the sketch.

"There also appears to be another troop concentration here to the southwest, beyond the Somali National University, and here along our eastern side." He indicated the positions with his finger.

"Along our eastern side, we have another tree line, which runs about fifty meters deep, almost to Digfer Road here. Backing onto Digfer Road is the Fire Brigade Compound, and in front of that is a row of low buildings . . . you know, bars and shops and restaurants, where you guys *did not* hang out just a few short weeks ago." His comment drew grins from the Marines around the table. "There appears to be about a company-sized unit bivouacked in the area just behind Digfer Road, here."

The captain moved closer to the table and rested his hands on its edge. He paused for a moment, making eye contact with each of the Marines in the room. "So, if they are going to hit us, they are probably going to do it with their main force coming at us along our southern flank. I would also expect some activity from the direction of the university to our southwest, and at least some probes along our eastern flank."

MacMurphy sat back down at the head of the table, studied his fingers for a moment, and then looked back up at the assembled group of warriors. "I see the question in all of your eyes: *So then why the hell don't we bug the hell out of here?*"

The room erupted in incredulous agreement. When they quieted down, he said, slowly and pointedly, "Because the ambassador won't let us—that's why. So we will stay until he says we can go, or until someone at a much higher pay grade than mine, and his, orders him to evacuate."

The room erupted again, this time in moans and groans. MacMurphy considered telling them about the ambassador's orders not to shoot at anyone threatening the compound, but decided against it. Telling a Marine not to defend himself was anathema to him, and he simply couldn't bring himself to do it. Instead he turned to Gunnery Sergeant Bradshaw.

"Gunny, it'll be dark in a couple of hours, so we don't have much time to spare. Pass out rifles and ammo and chow and whatever else you have in this armory of yours, and get your men deployed up on the roof of the chancery building. Set up your SAWS on the south side. Button down this building and prepare for the worst. Assign one Marine with a radio to stick with the ambassador, but get everyone else up on the roof and be prepared to stay there for the duration."

He turned to the troops. "But hang on . . . Before you're dismissed, I've got one more thing. I'm going out there to recon the area. We need to get a better idea of where they are and what they're planning for us tonight. I'm going to scout things out a bit. So keep your eyes and ears open and don't fucking shoot me."

Sergeant Gillis spoke up. "I'd better go with you, sir. I've got some pretty good experience on recon patrols, and you'll need someone to watch your back . . ."

"Thanks, Sergeant, but this is something I've got to do on my own. Our orders are to stay put, and I'm not going to ask anyone else to disobey those orders. Now, all of you, move out."

CHAPTER 5

MacMurphy sat at the cleaning table, working the bolt of an M-16, when Gunny Bradshaw returned.

"The men are in position on the roof, sir. All but Corporal Kelley, that is. He's with the ambassador, like you ordered. He's got direct comm with me, so we can keep track of what's going on. And I've got two more of these little walkie-talkie things left, one for you and one for Staff Sergeant Gillis, who's on the roof. They're really trick—encrypted, and they channel-hop in sequence. Almost impossible to intercept—unless you're NSA, that is . . . and those ignorant fuckers out there ain't even close. Got'em compliments of Spinelli. He's got a lot of neat CIA shit in that tech office of his." He handed one of the devices to MacMurphy.

"Thanks, Gunny," MacMurphy said, examining the device. It was about the size of a pack of cigarettes, with a tiny earpiece and lapel microphone attached to two thin wires.

"You put the earpiece in and pin the mic to your lapel," said Bradshaw, demonstrating. "You can whisper and still come in loud and clear. We'll have good comm."

MacMurphy slipped the device into his pocket, attached the mic to his lapel, and fitted the earpiece in his ear.

Bradshaw continued. "Don't have to do nothin' but talk when you feel like it, and we'll all get the message. Your call sign is Easy Two. I'm Easy One, Gillis is Easy Three and Kelley is Easy Four." The gunny demonstrated by calling Gillis, Corporal Kelley, and MacMurphy in turn.

"Got any more tricks up your sleeve, Gunny?"

"Sure do, Captain, sure do . . ."

He walked to a closet in the back of the room and opened the padlocked door with a key attached to a large ring of keys on his belt. He extracted a rifle and some boxed gear and laid them all out on the cleaning table. "You can put that M-16 aside, Captain. I got somethin' far better right here. You ain't goin' to be able to use that noisy sonofabitch out there with all them skinnies all over the fuckin' place."

"I've just got to make sure they don't see me. I don't want to get into a pissing contest with Aideed's militia. That's for sure."

"First of all, I've got some eyes for you here." Bradshaw pulled a pair of what looked like binoculars from one of the boxes. "It's going to be dark out there tonight. Not much moon left, and there's cloud cover, too. These night-vision goggles fit over your helmet like this, and then you just flip them up and down as you need them."

"I'm familiar with them, Gunny. Night vision will be a big help. What else?"

"Well, being that you used to command a sniper platoon, I know you're familiar with the M40A1 Sniper Rifle." He handed the sleek, bolt-action rifle to the captain. "I picked this one up during my last job at the armory at Camp Pendleton and made a few minor adjustments to improve its accuracy and allow for a suppressor and night vision scope. Doesn't have the firepower of an M-16—only holds four in the mag and one in the chamber—but you won't be needin' a hell of a lot of firepower tonight."

"Good work, Gunny." MacMurphy hefted the familiar weapon, brought it to his shoulder, and sighted along the barrel, getting the feel of it. In his mind's eye he saw the opposing troops stealthily advancing, felt himself pulling the trigger . . .

"The rifle has a heavy barrel—whole thing weighs fourteen and a half pounds, but you can shoot the eye out of a skinnie at four hundred meters. That's even with the night vision scope and suppressor. Actually, this suppressor will improve the ballistics of the rifle." The gunny was clearly proud of his creation. "It'll also increase the accuracy of the shooter by reducing flash, noise, and recoil. It's called the Thundertrap. We Marines don't have too many of them, but the Army Delta guys and the Navy Seals use them all the time over in the sandbox for their counter-terrorism shit."

He gently removed the 8.5 inch-long, 1.6 inch-diameter, black stainless-steel tube from its cushioned case and laid it lovingly in front of the captain.

"How the hell did you get hold of this?" MacMurphy hefted the artful device, gently fitted it to the muzzle of the rifle and screwed it into place.

"Told you. I was at the armory at Pendleton. I worked on this one myself and wasn't about to leave it behind for some grunt to abuse. It's a work of art."

When the Thundertrap suppressor was attached, the gunny reached for the rifle. "Wait till you see this, Captain." He opened another box, carefully removed a rifle scope, and snapped it onto the barrel of the rifle. "It's an AN/PVS-4 individual weapon night sight. It's a little heavy, adds about four pounds to the rifle, and a bit bulky, but it's also a thing of beauty. It's got a magnification of 3.6 power. Range with starlight is about four hundred meters, but with moonlight it can reach out to six hundred meters or more."

"You're full of surprises, aren't you, Gunny? I'm familiar with the rifle. We had them in my scout sniper team, but I've never used one with a suppressor and night vision scope." He hefted the rifle and brought it up to his shoulder, enjoying the feel of it against his shoulder and in his hands. "You're right—it's a heavy sucker with all this stuff attached, but still feels balanced and stable. It feels good. A Marine could do some real damage with this weapon."

"Sure could, and unless you're standing behind the shooter, you can't hear squat. They'll never know what hit'em. But you still got to be careful. If anyone gets behind you or a little off to either side of your rear, they'll hear a kind of low-pitched wail or scream when the bullet leaves the muzzle and a snap when it breaks the sound barrier. So don't let anyone get behind you.

"Now, your route . . . Since we think the main body of Aideed's troops are located near the south and southwest side of the compound, around the International Golf and Tennis Club to the south and the University to the west, I'd suggest you go out from the northeast and circle around in a clockwise direction, taking out any sentries as you go."

"Kind of like Sergeant York, right? Pick 'em off from the rear to the front." MacMurphy smiled.

"Exactly. That's the way to do it. Just don't let anyone get behind you."

"By the way, you got any high-speed ammo for this thing?" MacMurphy was sure the answer would be affirmative. He also knew the Gunny would want to tell him.

"Nothing but the best, sir. I got about a thousand rounds of M118, 7.62 NATO Match ammo. That round has a 168 grain Sierra Match bullet. It comes out of the barrel at around 2600 feet per second. That should give you enough wallop to snuff all of the skinny little motherfuckers you want, if you have a mind to do so."

"Okay, let's gather up this gear and get started. It'll be dark in less than an hour, and I want to leave about a half hour after that."

"One more thing," Bradshaw put a hand on the Captain's arm. "I want you to wear this." He picked up a flak vest with metal kevlar inserts that fit over the chest and back. "You're familiar with this. I know it's heavy—it'll add another ten pounds to your load—but you're not going to be moving very fast out there anyway. And it'll stop most rifle rounds."

MacMurphy hefted the bulky jacket. "Yeah, it's a load, all right. You really think I'll need this?"

"Up to you, Captain, but I'd wear it. You don't need to be fast, but you'll be glad you had it on if you get spotted and start taking fire out there. Our Marine Force Recon guys use'em, for close quarters combat. I think it's something you should have in this situation as well."

"Okay, what the hell." MacMurphy hung the jacket over a chair and busied himself with assembling his gear and unloading boxes of ammunition.

"Can't I go with you, sir?" Bradshaw pleaded. "Gillis was right. You could sure use someone out there to watch your back."

"No, you stay here with the men, Gunny. They'll need your steady hand. Try to keep an eye on me from the roof as best you can. Like I said, no one else will be disobeying any orders tonight. Except . . . just in case you need to hear it from me, you *will* return fire if fired upon. Those are *my* orders. Is that understood?"

"Understood, Captain. Understood."

CHAPTER 6

Two hours later, Gunny Bradshaw cracked open one of the small doors on the northeast side of the compound wall—away from the heart of the city and running along Afgoy Road—and Captain Harry MacMurphy stepped out into the night.

But the night wasn't dark for him; only for Aideed's ragtag band of militia.

He stayed close to the shadows of the compound wall, crouched, rifle at port arms, moving slowly eastward in the darkness, until he reached the northeast corner of the compound. He turned south along the eastern wall, toward the city center, which spread out along the coast. He crossed the road ringing the compound and followed a drainage ditch that paralleled the road. Deep in the shadows, he headed closer to the city and where he thought Aideed's men would be.

He moved stealthily, every hair on his body alert for the presence of the enemy. He whispered his location in his lapel mic and heard the comforting response from Gunny Bradshaw in his ear.

"Got you in sight, Captain. Watch out ahead, there's movement in those buildings about two hundred meters east of the compound."

MacMurphy scanned the row of buildings but could see no movement. A few moments later, there was a flash of light in his night vision goggles. He dropped to one knee, flipped up the goggles, and brought the rifle to his shoulder. Through the rifle scope he could clearly see two men standing in a doorway with AK-47s slung upside-down on their shoulders. One was lighting a cigarette with a match. The other was waiting for his turn at the match, cigarette dangling from his lips.

Three on a match, he thought, placing the crosshairs on the mouth holding the dangling cigarette, *but in your case, it's two.* The round struck the smoker on his left cheek, knocking him back into the doorway and blowing off the side of his head.

He quickly chambered another round, adjusted the crosshairs just left of the suddenly wide eyes of the other man, and squeezed off another round, hitting the terrified soldier in the nose and sending him sprawling in the doorway on top of his comrade. *Smoking can definitely be bad for your health,* he thought.

He chambered another round, put the rifle on safe, calmly adjusted his sights one click to the left, and flipped his night vision goggles back down over his eyes.

"Easy One, this is Easy Two, over?"

"Roger, Easy Two. Nice shooting. How's your situation?"

"Rifle shoots a little right but I fixed it. It's good now. Two skinnies down. Still quiet out here at the moment. Main force must be hanging back, but they've stationed sentries forward. Two I just took out were about two hundred meters down from the northeast corner of the compound, where you saw the movement. This is a great weapon . . . Over."

"Good work, Easy Two. We'll keep an eye on you as best we can. If you're able to take out some more of their sentries you might force them to reevaluate any attack plans they may have for tonight. Over."

"Roger, Easy One. That's the plan. I'll follow this drainage ditch for as far as I can. I've got good cover here in the tree line. Let me know if you see anything else, and try to keep me in sight . . . and make sure you've got someone posted at the closest doors, just in case I have to make a run for it. Over."

"Roger that, Easy Two. We'll keep the campfires burning. Easy One out."

MacMurphy moved in a crouch, rifle at port arms, south along the east wall of the compound toward the distant lights of Mogadishu. His senses were keen, hearing the rustle of the leaves in the breeze and listening for signs of movement just as he had done when he was deer hunting in upstate New York with his father.

He smelled the salt air coming off the ocean south of the city, and heard the horns of cars on the highway and the muted sounds of the city spread out along the coast only a half-mile away from him. The night was dark, but there was a glow above the city and the quarter moon and stars above gave off enough light to illuminate his night vision scope and goggles.

He stopped frequently to scan the area around him, paying particular attention to the row of shops and bars and two-story buildings that lined the road to the east of him, where the two smokers had drawn their last breaths of nicotine-filled air.

Needing a better vantage point, he left the drainage ditch and moved slowly and silently through the forested area to the edge of the tree line. From there he had a clear view of the row of buildings facing the road and the buildings beyond. He dropped behind a fallen tree, flipped up his night vision goggles, and brought the rifle to his shoulder.

The darkened buildings of the fire station, four hundred meters away, popped into focus. He scanned them from left to right. If Aideed had placed sentries to watch the compound, that would be a good place to station them. There appeared to be activity several blocks behind the buildings and to the south, but the area in front was dark and quiet. He concentrated on the dark doorways and shadowy areas in front of the buildings and then, seeing nothing, brought the rifle up to scan the rooftops where the initial sighting had been.

He spotted the target on the north side of the roof of one of the two-story buildings of the fire station, almost directly above and beyond the doorway where he had shot the two smokers. The sentry was fully visible from the waist up, standing on the flat roof behind the low wall surrounding it. He appeared relaxed, clearly unaware of the sudden deaths of his comrades in front of him, as he surveyed the compound wall through binoculars, a cigarette dangling from his lips.

Do all these fuckers smoke? Good thing, though, because it really illuminates the targets. He adjusted the elevation on his scope to four hundred meters and brought the rifle to his shoulder. *This rifle is really a wonder.* He placed the crosshairs high on the chest below the cigarette, released the safety, and squeezed the trigger.

The bullet smashed into the sentry's breast bone under the throat throwing him straight back and down behind the hip-high wall. *Three shots, three bad guys. Not a bad night so far, thanks to the gunny's fine equipment.*

He scanned the rooftops of the fire station and spotted two more sentries, one peering over the hip wall of the roof in the center of the building, and the other sitting on the corner of the wall at the end of the roof. He decided to take out the peering guy first, because he might have heard the last victim fall, and because he could pull back out of sight behind the hip wall at any moment.

MacMurphy had a clear view of the sentry's head peeking out over the wall and took the difficult shot. The bullet smashed through the sentry's nose and blew out the back of his head. Mac quickly moved his sights to the center mass of the fellow sitting on the corner. The bullet slammed into the sentry high on the chest tearing through his breast bone and threw him back and down sprawling on the roof.

Almost too easy. Don't get careless. Adrenaline pumping, he slipped farther down behind the fallen tree and quietly removed five more rounds of ammunition from his bandoleer, eased four of them into the magazine of the rifle, and gently slipped the fifth round into the chamber. He spent the next few minutes quietly scanning the row of buildings to seek out any new targets through the powerful rifle scope. None were visible, so he slipped back into the woods and reported in as he made his way closer to the city on the south side of the compound.

"Three more down," he whispered into the lapel mic. "No more activity visible along the east wall. Heading south. Over."

"Roger, Easy Two, keep up the good work," said the gunny.

Still using the cover of the drainage ditch, he reached the southeast corner of the compound. The area in front of him was open for about fifty meters. Next was a line of trees bordering the golf course, and beyond that the occasional lights of the heart of the city. To the right, directly across from the compound, were the darkened buildings of the International Golf and Tennis Club and the red clay tennis courts.

He crossed back over the ring road and darted back into the shadows of the compound wall. He followed the wall toward the west. At the end of the compound, lay the sprawling, unlit Somali National University. He scanned the area in front of him and to his left, looking for possible sentry locations. He knew any main-force troops would be farther to the rear, but he decided to continue to take out as many of the sentries as possible to remove the eyes and ears of Aideed's militia.

Nothing was visible on the golf course or around the tennis courts, but his attention was drawn to the clubhouse and administration buildings of the Golf and Tennis Club as likely observation posts for sentries.

He needed to get closer to the buildings, so he backtracked over the ring road and darted into the tennis complex. He moved quietly between the chain-link fences separating the courts. Taking advantage of the shadows created by the wind-netting attached to the fences, he was able to move within one hundred meters of the administration buildings. He dropped into a prone position behind a bench and surveyed the buildings through the rifle scope.

He spotted two more sentries on the roof of the administrative building and another in a tall minaret about two hundred meters farther south. He decided to take out the two closest targets first, so they wouldn't hear the sonic snap of a bullet passing overhead, and hoped that the guy in the minaret wouldn't see any muzzle flash.

He easily took out the two closer targets with perfect center chest shots and immediately raised his elevation to three hundred meters and sighted on the minaret. The sentry inside was speaking into a walkie-talkie. He decided to hold his shot and watched the guy babble into the handset while frantically looking out over the terrain in front of him. Convinced that he was reporting something, MacMurphy held his fire until the target brought the walkie-talkie down, ending his transmission. The target then turned and looked to his rear. At that point he squeezed off another round. The bullet smashed into the back of the target's head, and he went down.

MacMurphy chambered another round and continued to observe the minaret. He heard a shout, then more, coming from the general direction of the minaret. Moments later a head appeared, looking frantically out over the edge of the minaret in MacMurphy's direction. The Marine put a round in his throat, throwing him back and out of sight.

He was definitely blown by now, so he decided it was time to get out of Dodge. He slipped back into the shadows of the tennis courts and reported his situation to Gunnery Sergeant Bradshaw.

"Better get back in here, Easy Two. Your huntin' days are over for tonight. Return to the compound wall and follow it west toward the University. There's a small entry door about halfway down, and we'll have it open for you."

"Roger that, Easy One. If it's not open you'll hear me banging. Watch the area around that minaret. I think all hell is going to break out pretty soon. I'm blown . . ."

The Marine replaced the spent rounds in his magazine and retraced his steps back to the ring-road. He darted across the road to the shadows of the compound wall. There he sat with his back to the wall and directed his attention to the growing commotion taking place in front of him. He heard the sounds of Toyota-4WD pick-ups moving up and shouted commands in the distance. He scanned the area with the rifle scope, paying particular attention to the wood-line on the other side of the road. Nothing . . .

He brought the rifle up to sight on the minaret and, sure enough, two more skinnies. One was scanning the area with binoculars, and the other was talking on a walkie-talkie. He set the elevation for four hundred meters and took out the one with the binoculars first. He chambered another round for the walkie-talkie guy, but he had disappeared. He kept the rifle trained on the spot for several more moments in the hope that curiosity would get the best of the second guy, but it didn't, so he moved down the wall closer to the door and safety.

Something moved in the tree line in front of him and to his left, near the end of the tennis courts. He dropped into a prone position and brought the rifle to his shoulder. People were moving within the trees, heading toward the road and compound wall. Three of them, carrying AK-47s at the ready, had stepped out of the tree line and were visible targets.

He estimated the range of the closest one at just under two hundred meters, with the other two spread out farther down the tree line at about twenty-five meter intervals. He was still about fifty meters from the nearest entrance to the compound, and he contemplated whether to take the shots or remain motionless where he was.

He decided he couldn't remain where he was for very long with them coming out of the trees, so he picked off the nearest one with a careful shot under the armpit, chambered another round, and dropped the second one with a chest shot as well. The third started to move, so he brought the crosshairs down on center mass and squeezed off a less carefully aimed shot that caught the man in the gut, bringing him down screaming his lungs out. *Shit, that's not good.*

Inserting three more rounds into the magazine, he snapped his night vision goggles down over his eyes. No one was coming out of the trees to check on their dead and screaming comrades, but there was now a lot of commotion coming from behind the tree line all along the road.

He remained quiet in the shadows, scanning the area for a few more moments. Things were coming alive all around him, and he knew he had to get out fast before someone spotted him. At that point, the relative silence of the night was broken by the clatter of a heavy machine gun coming from behind the tennis club. He could hear the snaps of the bullets going over his head and their impact on the compound walls.

The bastards are raking the roof of the chancery. They must think the sniper shots are coming from there. Still in the shadows of the compound wall, he dropped back down to a kneeling position and aimed the rifle at the top of the minaret where he had seen the muzzle flashes from the machine gun. Two of them, one behind the gun firing in short bursts and the other feeding the ammunition belt, popped into clear focus through the night vision scope.

He remembered that his elevation was set at four hundred meters, so he aimed low on the chest of the one feeding the ammo and shot him in the throat. He took out the shooter in the same manner, the bullet hitting him high on the forehead and slamming him back against the far wall, silencing the heavy weapon for the time being.

Now I've really got to haul ass out of here. It was suddenly very quiet, except for the moans of the wounded skinny. The gunny's voice in his earpiece startled him. "Good shootin' Easy Two. Now get your ass back in here a-sap, before you get yourself killed. We're waitin' for you at the door."

Before he could respond, firing opened up from the southeast corner of the compound, near where he had taken out the guys on the roof of the administration building. He could hear the familiar bop-bop-bop automatic fire from the assault rifles as AK-47 rounds began to splatter around him. Someone had figured out what was going on.

He raised up into a crouch and, hugging the shadows of the compound wall, began moving rapidly, carrying his rifle at port arms, toward the safety of the entrance where the gunny and his fellow Marines were waiting for him.

He was about ten meters from the door when the rounds became more concentrated around him. Suddenly he felt a sledgehammer blow to his chest just below the throat that knocked him on his back in the dirt. He began to crawl toward the door with bullets impacting around him and ricocheting off the compound wall. He was hit again and then again. The searing pains in his arm and leg distracted him momentarily from concentrating on the means to escape but he knew he had to get to cover or die.

He tried to get up, but his legs didn't work, and he couldn't hold on to his rifle. Suddenly, all hell broke loose from the roof of the chancery building. Bullets and rifle grenades began raking the tree line and the other side of the road. He felt himself being tugged and lifted and dragged by two Marines, and he heard the comforting voice of Gunny Bradshaw saying, "We gotcha, Captain. Hang in there. We gotcha . . ."

And then he was safe within the compound walls with the firefight raging around him.

CHAPTER 7

He awoke the next day in the USS *Trenton's* sick bay. He felt groggy, numb, drugged. The people around him were out of focus, their voices coming from far away. He could make out the fuzzy images of Spinelli and the gunny and the Regional Medical Officer from the embassy, and a couple of nurses and some others. They were standing around his bed, looking down at him.

The RMO doctor spoke. "Don't try to talk yet, Mac. Just nod if you can hear me."

MacMurphy nodded and managed to mumble, "I can hear you."

"I told you not to talk . . . but then, you're not known for following orders, are you, Captain?" the doctor said genially. The people around him smiled. "You've got a couple of pretty nasty contusions on your back and chest, but no ribs are broken. Your body armor did its job very well, especially this one," indicating a spot just below his throat. "You also took a round in the upper left arm and another in your left leg. Both bullets passed through the muscle, so there wasn't any significant trauma to the bones. There were also some small cement fragments that I removed from the right side of your neck and face—from ricochets, I guess—but we got them out okay, and I don't think they'll mar your beauty."

The doctor reached out and touched MacMurphy's good arm. "There's one more thing I want to say, for me, and I think I speak for everyone in this embassy, I want to say thank you for what you did. I honestly think you saved all of our lives."

The sick bay erupted in applause, and the gunny let out a loud Marine "Uoo-rah!"

MacMurphy was feeling better already. He turned his head toward Sergeant Bradshaw and mumbled, "And I want to thank you, Gunny, for pulling me out of there before the bastards hacked me up, and for laying down that covering fire, despite the ambassador's orders . . ."

"Hey, Captain, I was just doin' my job, protecting my Marines. You can thank Sergeant Gillis as well. He did the heavy lifting."

Spinelli said, "The evacuation of the embassy has begun, Captain. We'll all be out within the next couple of hours. And . . . of course you were right. Aideed was planning to attack last night, and your actions, and those of your Marines on the roof, gave us enough breathing room to get the hell out of here. I will make sure your superiors know what a courageous thing you did last night. You did indeed save all our lives, and we all owe you a deep debt of gratitude for that."

MacMurphy slurred his words, "Don't forget Gunny Bradshaw and his Marines. I'd be dead meat out there if it weren't for them . . ."

"I won't," said Spinelli. "Don't you worry about that . . ."

CHAPTER 8

I t took most of the day to destroy the remaining classified information and communications equipment within the embassy, and to evacuate the remaining Americans and foreigners to the aircraft carrier *Guam*, anchored offshore. The last CH-53 helicopter touched down on the *Guam* just before dark. Neatly folded under the ambassador's arm was the last American flag to fly over the embassy.

He was still clearly in a state of shock and appeared disoriented when the *Guam*'s captain met him and quickly ushered him to his quarters deep within the bowels of the ship. The massive gray naval vessel, accompanied by the *Trenton*, then steamed north out to sea in the direction of the Arabian Peninsula, where they were urgently needed for Operation Desert Shield.

Within hours of the evacuation, Aideed's forces breached the walls of the embassy and used rocket-propelled grenades to blast down the doors of the buildings inside the compound. They sacked the buildings, removing office furniture, vehicles, and other movables. When Aideed's men were through, other looters came, many of them deserters from Siad Barre's army, and finished stripping the once-proud embassy of everything that could be removed.

The US Embassy in Mogadishu was one of the first built to a new design incorporating tightened security standards such as fewer windows and multiple walls of reinforced concrete. It was dedicated on 4 July 1989, and went into use four months later. It was abandoned and sacked on 7 January 1991.

Two days later, Spinelli visited MacMurphy in his hospital bed on the ship. He asked the nurse to leave them alone and pulled the curtain separating them from the rest of the ward. He pulled up a chair close to the bed and spoke softly. "You're looking better, Captain."

The cobwebs had left MacMurphy's brain. Aside from some stiffness and numbness, he was alert and well on the road to recovery. His left arm and leg were heavily bandaged. "I feel okay," he said, pulling himself into more of an upright position in the COS's presence. "I don't know what's worse, the pain or the pain-killers."

"I know what you mean, Mac. Having a clear head is worth a little pain. Is your head clear now?"

"Oh yeah, fog's gone now. So . . . what happened after I got shot?"

Spinelli spoke in hushed tones. "I've just been waiting for you to recover enough to brief you. You must be anxious to hear what happened after you got hit."

"What am I going to face when I get back home . . . am I going to be kicked out of the Corps for doing what I did?" MacMurphy's eyebrow rose questioningly.

"Keep it down, Mac. There's not much privacy in here, and what I've got to say is for your ears only." He scooted his chair closer. "There'll be no Court Martial of you or anyone else. The ambassador was furious when the shooting broke out and he learned that you were out there picking off sentries. He changed his tune the next morning when he received kudos from Washington for taking action that prevented an attack on the embassy."

MacMurphy closed his eyes, knowing what was coming and feeling the disgust building.

Spinelli laughed and shook his head. "No shit, Mac. He came out smelling like a rose. Apparently we got some new overhead photography that showed the massing of Aideed's troops around the compound, indicating an attack was indeed imminent. "

With a grunt of discomfort, MacMurphy painfully moved into a somewhat less uncomfortable position. "So now he's a real hero, eh?"

"You got it—he's a hero. You just saved his career, Captain. But look on the bright side, now you'll be recognized as well. He's got to say that he sent you out there to do a reconnaissance and that he instructed the Marines on the roof to return fire. All of his past fuck-ups will be quickly forgotten. He averted the attack and got everyone out of there safely. That's the bottom line."

MacMurphy shook his head incredulously. "Unbelievable." A wry smile started to twist the corners of his mouth.

"But the really good news is I wrote up a recommendation for you to receive an award for your actions that night and shoved it under his nose yesterday, while he was receiving all those attaboys from Foggy Bottom. He signed it, grimacing the whole time, and it's on its way to Headquarters Marine Corps as we speak. Who knows, you may get the Silver Star for your actions. Its high profile enough that even the Commandant of the Marine Corps will know about what you did. Congratulations, Captain."

He shook MacMurphy's good hand and looked seriously into his eyes. "And thanks again for doing what you did, despite the risks to your career, not to mention your life."

"Thanks, Mr. Spinelli. You didn't have to do that. I really appreciate it . . ."

"There's one more thing, and then I'll let you rest." The COS lowered his voice further and brought his lips close to MacMurphy's ear. "I understand you're due to rotate out of this job pretty soon."

"That's right sir. In about three weeks, actually, but I doubt they'll bother to send me back to Nairobi in this condition."

"You haven't got much time left in the Corps, do you?"

"My current tour ends in April. April Fools Day, to be exact. As far as I know I'm going to be transferred to Eighth and Eye to start pushing paper. Why?"

"Because I've got another job for you, Mac—with my outfit. I cabled them about you and they're really interested. The director of recruiting is an old buddy of mine, and as long as you don't have anything nasty in your background that would cause you to flunk the polygraph, you'll be invited to join the June Career Training class down at The Farm. What do you think about that?"

"The CIA? Do you really think so? I mean . . ."

Spinelli reached out and put his hand on the Mac's shoulder. "You're the stuff great case officers are made of, Mac. Take the job. We want you to come aboard. It's a done deal if you want it."

"Aye, aye sir," said MacMurphy. "I was wondering what I was going to do when I grew up. Who would have thought . . . CIA . . ."

CHAPTER 9

Harry Stephan "Mac" MacMurphy recovered fully from the wounds he had received in Somalia. By the time he entered the CIA's September Career Training class at CIA headquarters in Langley, Virginia, he had worked his way back to scoring 100% on the Marine Corps Personal Fitness Test. The Marine PFT had been MacMurphy's personal gauge of fitness since the day he entered OCS training at Quantico, Virginia. He believed as long as he could ace the PFT, he was at the top of his fitness game. Now he was there again.

Physical fitness was always important to Mac. He had been a "wiry" kid—a nice way of saying "scrawny." But he made up for his small size by being tough. He excelled at wrestling and boxing, and was a tenacious, never-give-up kind of kid.

41

His father, a tough former amateur boxer, enrolled him in karate and mixed martial arts classes at the age of four. By the time Mac reached his tenth birthday he had earned his black belt. He continued with his martial arts training through high school, reaching the level of a third degree black belt.

But wrestling was where he really excelled. Here the competition was real. No pulling punches and kicks and wearing heavy padding as in karate. It was all out, man against man. Only the fastest and strongest and best technique would win. He reveled in the one-on-one competition and was always the fittest wrestler of his competition.

He left high school as the New York State champion in the 147-pound weight class and went on to win a wrestling scholarship at Oklahoma State University, although as he gained in height and weight he moved up in weight class to 157 and then to 165.

The bane of all collegiate wrestlers, constantly pulling weight to get down to a lower weight class, became more and more of a challenge as he shed the scrawny kid image and developed into a strapping, athletic young man of nearly six feet.

When he entered the CIA training in September of 1991 he was back in superb physical condition and the physical challenges of the training were taken very much in stride. The mental aspects of the training were the most challenging, but he took to them with the same enthusiasm that he applied to his physical training.

CHAPTER 10

The first six weeks of his training were spent in the Operations Familiarization Course, held at a location nicknamed "Blue U" in Arlington, Virginia. The class was taught the workings of the CIA and the Intelligence Community, and introduced to the CIA's four directorates (administration, science and technology, intelligence and operations).

After that, Mac and his thirty-three classmates headed down to "The Farm"—the CIA's covert training facility—for the sixteen-week-long Operations Course.

The weeks on The Farm passed quickly for Mac, loaded with lectures, practical training exercises, lab work, and study. The mornings began at seven o'clock with calisthenics and a leisurely two mile wake-up run, which Mac would often run in his flip-flops, much to the chagrin of his less fit colleagues.

They learned basic case officer skills and practiced these skills on agent/instructors during live problem exercises. Mac excelled at agent acquisition, although others, like his more technical minded classmate Culler Santos, found this phase of instruction to be the most challenging.

The live exercises often ran late into the evenings. Afterwards, the fledgling case officers returned to their classrooms to write up their reports in order to have them on their instructor's desk by eight o'clock the following morning. Adhering to strict deadlines on The Farm developed habits that would stick with them throughout their careers.

Mac was surrounded by exceptional people on The Farm. The students were gregarious and outgoing, bright and self-assured. Most had lived abroad and spoke one or more foreign languages. Mac, for one, had acquired fluent French and German in the home from his polyglot mother, and had studied Mandarin Chinese in college.

Spinelli had lured Mac away from what would have been a great career track in the Corps and recruited him for the shadowy world of "The Company," and combat on a very different battlefield. Mac, it quickly became apparent, was born to be a CIA case officer.

CHAPTER 11

One of the highlights of the Operations Course came when senior operations officers, division chiefs or their deputies, spent the day at The Farm to sell the new officers on the merits of their respective divisions and attempt to persuade the best ones to join them. These visits were kicked off by a one or two hour talk to the entire class in the main arena, followed by another smaller session in a classroom with just those students who expressed an interest in joining the division. Later that evening the sessions were followed by an informal cocktail reception and dinner with the interested students at one of the instructor's homes on the base.

It was at one of these evening sessions that Mac was reunited with Tony Spinelli, the former COS in Mogadishu and current deputy chief of Africa Division. Mac had heard Spinelli's speech in the arena, but did not attend the smaller classroom session as he had no particular interest in joining Africa Division.

His sights were set on the China Operations group in East Asia Division. He had minored in Mandarin Chinese in college, and already possessed near native fluency in German and French thanks to his mother, and he wanted to use these language skills against the China target.

Spinelli had his own plans for Mac, and he wanted to discuss them with him. So Spinelli had asked that Mac be invited to the dinner party.

The dinner party for Tony Spinelli was held in the home of the senior Africa Division instructor on The Farm and his wife. Following cocktails with light hors d'oeuvres, a buffet dinner of venison stew was served. The Farm was infested with deer, so instructors and base employees were encouraged to hunt during hunting season to cull the herds. Base freezers were full of venison the year round.

The group at this particular dinner party consisted of two Africa Division instructors and their spouses, four students who had expressed an interest in joining Africa Division, plus Spinelli, and MacMurphy.

Conversation centered around opportunities in Africa Division for first tour case officers. Spinelli and the other two Africa hands pressed the point that Africa's relatively smaller stations meant more responsibility for younger officers, and less bureaucratic interference. Because the diplomatic communities in those countries were smaller and more close-knit than those in Europe or Asia, young case officers were generally invited to virtually every foreign embassy's parties and receptions, which meant better chances of recruiting assets within the diplomatic communities.

MacMurphy, not being one to enjoy layers of bureaucracy over his head, felt this was a good argument for selecting a smaller station early in his career. Nevertheless, he had made up his mind to join the East Asia Division and specialize in China ops.

By the time coffee and desert was served the group had broken up into smaller groups spread throughout the kitchen and living room. Spinelli approached Mac who was chatting with one of the female students in the kitchen. "We haven't had much time to talk alone, Mac, and I want to explain to you why I wanted you included in this group." Spinelli turned to the other student. "Will you excuse us for a moment?"

When the student walked off, he turned back to Mac and said, "Let's get some air."

Spinelli led Mac out through the screened porch and into the back yard. The crickets were chirping and there was a gentle breeze rustling through the trees and leaves. He said, "This is a great place. One of the jewels of the Agency. You know, we came very close to losing The Farm due to budget cuts a few years back. Thank God cooler heads prevailed and we didn't. I think I'd like to do a tour down here as an instructor myself some day. It would be a good way to decompress and recharge the old batteries."

They chatted about The Farm while walking slowly across the lawn. When they approached the tree line at the edge of the yard a deer bolted in the woods, startling them.

"You know, Mac, I still feel I owe you big time for what you did for us in Mogadishu." Mac began to object but Spinelli put up his hand. "No, I've done a lot of soul-searching since that day. You did what I should have done. You took control of the situation and acted forcefully when action was called for. I regret not having done more. I certainly couldn't have done what you did, but I should have been more forceful with the ambassador and in my cables to headquarters. I should have mutinied, or at least threatened to mutiny, to put more pressure on the powers that be to remove that ignorant SOB of an ambassador."

"You did what you could, Mr. Spinelli. Without the pressure from you on Headquarters, and then from Headquarters on State, they wouldn't have ordered the evacuation when they did. We all know that. The only accurate reporting they were getting was through your channel."

Spinelli shrugged. "Perhaps, perhaps; it's kind of you to say that, but your actions clinched the deal. I know I didn't do enough and that bothers me to this day . . . Enough said on that subject. I'm now in a position to do something for you and I wanted to discuss it with you before I put any plays in motion."

"I kind of suspected you had something on your mind. What is it?"

"I know your heart's set on China Ops, but what I want to offer you—and the China Ops people—is an opportunity to go after the

China target in an active Africa Division station where the targets are ripe and the hunting is good."

"Where were you thinking? You don't want to send me back to Mogadishu, do you?"

Spinelli laughed. "This is a little better than that. You know, we have China Ops officers in several of our larger African stations. What I have in mind for you is Addis Ababa. It's a medium sized station by Africa Division standards. A handful of case officers including the chief and deputy, and a very active recruitment program among third country dips. The Chinese Embassy there is about the same size as ours, about forty to fifty people. They have a big aid program there, and the Chinese officials in Addis seem to enjoy more freedom than most anywhere else in the world."

"Why's that?" Mac was becoming interested.

"Couple of things." Spinelli held up a thumb. "First of all Ethiopia has been a socialist country since the days when Mengistu ruled the place, so they feel comfortable there among all the rest of the former communist nations of East Europe and a lot of current ones like North Korea, Vietnam, and Cuba. Those countries still have a large presence there.

"Second," an index finger joined the thumb, "the aid projects of these countries are still very active due to the droughts and famine that continue to ravage the country, and aid workers and officials generally seem to enjoy more freedom than others. This kind of bleeds into the rest of the community.

"Third," a middle finger joined the other two, "The New China News Agency, the government controlled news service, has four officers assigned to the embassy. These NCNA guys are prime targets because they have as much access to classified information as the other embassy officials. Due to their journalist status they have more freedom of movement around the country than the others."

Mac nodded. "So there's room for a China Ops officer in the station, and there are enough good targets to justify sending one there."

"Exactly. We've never had a China Ops slot in Addis Ababa station, but I'd like to create one—tailored for you. I've talked to all parties concerned and we agree that you would be a good fit for the job. The assignment could really jump-start your career, and, well . . . you're my man, Mac. You want to go for it?"

"You don't owe me anything Mr. Spinelli. In fact, you've already done more than enough by bringing me into this outfit. I haven't had so much fun since Mom and Dad bought me my first bicycle. And I'm humbled by the quality of the people in my class. I keep thanking you and the good Lord for making me a part of this group."

Spinelli put his arm on Mac's shoulder and led him back across the yard toward the house. "Consider it done then. I'll start the ball rolling and get the necessary paperwork up to the DDO's office for his approval. You can plan on rotating out to Addis Ababa next summer right after you've completed the Special Ops Course."

"Do I have to start studying Amharic?" asked Mac, only half in jest.

"No, that's not a requirement. Your English will do quite nicely down there. And maybe your Chinese, if you get lucky . . ."

CHAPTER 12

Following the Operations Course, the class returned to Langley for two months of on-the-job training. Mac was assigned to the Japan Desk in East Asia Division. There he was involved in the support of Tokyo Station; running name traces, responding to Tokyo's operational requests for research, evaluating intelligence reports, doing file summaries, and sitting in on operational discussions regarding the station's progress in meeting it's operational directives (ODs) which emanated from Langley and set the priorities for station operations.

Due to his Chinese language skills, the station's China Branch was his main focus. He followed the early development of a fast moving case involving a mid-level Chinese MSS intelligence officer who made frequent trips outside of China to Japan. The case resulted in the MSS officer's defection to the US embassy in Tokyo.

His involvement in this high-profile case also brought him a lot of high-level personal exposure within the Agency, particularly the eye of the Agency's legendary DDO, Edwin Rothmann.

CHAPTER 13

After a final live exercise in New York City where they practiced development and recruitment, agent communications, surreptitious entry and bugging of a hotel room, and most of the other skills they had learned in the previous fifteen weeks, it was back to The Farm for another sixteen weeks of intensive paramilitary training in the Special Operations Course.

MacMurphy and his class were issued combat boots and military fatigues, without rank or insignia, for this portion of the training. The group learned infiltration and exfiltration techniques and practiced cross border operations on the river and in the woods. They were taught land navigation with a map and compass, and stream and hill navigation without the aid of a map and compass. They practiced small unit and sapper tactics to attack enemy installations and to defend friendly perimeters.

None of this was new to Mac and the other former military officers, but for the rest of the class it was, and all of the former military guys helped the others out, which added to the bonding process.

They also visited another secret CIA site for an intensive week of instruction in demolitions and explosives. They learned about roadside bombs—how to make them and how to defuse them. By the end of the week every student was a qualified sapper.

What was new to the former military guys as well as the civilians was the intensive course in interrogation techniques and resistance to interrogation. Although the students never had to endure waterboarding and other forms of physical torture, the psychology of interrogation and how to resist it was a key part of the course. It was as realistic as it could be under the circumstances—every student realized he would not actually be harmed—but it gave each of them the undisputable knowledge that the threat of bodily harm, or worse, was a very effective interrogation technique, with or without other props.

The final month was split between the Arizona desert and the Panama jungle where the class learned survival skills and escape and evasion tactics in the two very different environments. It was during the jungle phase of the training that Mac learned the most important lesson he would ever learn in the course. He would be forcefully reminded of that crucial lesson in days to come.

That lesson was: *If it doesn't taste good, spit it out . . .*

CHAPTER 14

MacMurphy hated diplomatic cocktail parties, functions given by people who didn't want to give them for people who didn't want to attend. He certainly fit into that latter category. But as a CIA case officer under official cover, he was forced to attend these boring parties.

And there was a more compelling reason that he did not want to attend this particular function. CIA headquarters, over the strong objections of MacMurphy and the Addis Ababa station chief, had instructed MacMurphy to corner one of his best friends on the diplomatic circuit in Addis, a Chinese intelligence officer, and deliver a recruitment pitch.

Huang Tsung-yao was operating under the cover of a reporter for the New China News Agency, but he was actually a very capable intelligence operative from the Ministry of State Security. Mac had been ordered to go to the party and attempt to recruit him to work covertly for the CIA.

MacMurphy and his station chief believed strongly that if these instructions were carried out, they would destroy Huang's career. They thought the approach was a dumb idea.

Mac knew his friend Huang would refuse the pitch. He and Huang Tsung-yao were very close. They had a natural affinity for one another that went far beyond their mutual interest in tennis. Although raised in different cultures on different sides of the globe, they shared athletic good looks, charm, a natural sensitivity and intellectual curiosity. They were more like brothers than adversaries. Case officers share many traits.

But he and the station had fought the battle with CIA headquarters and lost. His orders were now clear, the arguing was over; he was obligated to follow Headquarters' orders, sent under the name of the Director, even if against his better judgment. That's how things worked in the Agency, just like the military. It was time to salute.

Three years earlier, in Somalia, he *had* disobeyed a direct order. But this was different. He didn't like what he was being told to do now. But, while hating the taste of it, and wanting to spit it out, he would salute and do it.

CHAPTER 15

As he turned east from the former Revolution Square and took Dessie Road toward the Turkish Ambassador's residence, MacMurphy thought about how he would approach Huang.

He maneuvered his Toyota Land Cruiser around the bumps, potholes, people and herds of sheep and donkeys. The animals and people were in no hurry. Nor were they concerned that Mac was impatient. They all milled around aimlessly, people and animals, as they had for generations.

The ever-present surveillance from the Ethiopian Ministry of Public Security had no trouble keeping up with him. The dirty white rattletrap Volkswagen Beetle with its right front headlight hanging precariously out of its socket was close behind, as always.

It was dusk. The blue light of evening bathed the area like stage lights, and the thin air of the Ethiopian highlands was already turning cool. The dry summer season had arrived, and the city sky was no longer darkened by the thick soot of thousands of small fires burning eucalyptus twigs and leaves to keep the tin shacks and round native "tukel" huts warm.

By the time he had navigated the half-mile-long winding climb along the narrow drive from Dessie Road to the Ambassador's mansion on the crest of the hill, leaving the struggling Volkswagen panting at the bottom, Mac had decided what he would say to his friend Huang.

In the spirit of true friendship, he would deliver the recruitment pitch in such a way as to fulfill Headquarters' bureaucratic requirement, while at the same time giving Huang ample room to back out gracefully. That, at least, he could do for a man he truly considered a friend.

The affinity that had led to this friendship reminded Mac of a story by Joseph Conrad, "The Secret Sharer," he had read in college. In Conrad's tale the connection that took place on a ship between two people who had much in common was overshadowed by circumstances that imposed a barrier, circumstances which made this sense of connection and identification impossibly complicated. One of the two men had, in the end, been forced to "jump ship"—literally.

Mac had studied the remarkably detailed file that the Agency had compiled on Huang, a personality profile and operational summary that was far more informative than most of those available on Chinese intelligence officers. Even before he had met Huang, Mac felt he really knew a great deal about the real person who had been selected as his "target." There was an immediate and troubling sense that he could not simply regard Huang as a depersonalized enemy "objective."

This feeling of identification, even empathy, had been, for Mac, the foundation of something more complex than just an operational interaction.

MacMurphy wanted to preserve their personal relationship, not just because of the genuine close friendship that had developed between them, but because there might come a day when Huang really would want to jump ship. And MacMurphy wanted him to know where he could always find a sympathetic, helpful ear. Mac had both Huang's and the Agency's best interests at heart simultaneously, even if, on the surface, the two seemed mutually exclusive. Mac intuitively knew it was too early in Huang's career to make the offer.

Above all, he did not want Huang to feel obliged to report the recruitment pitch to Beijing. That was the most important thing. MacMurphy knew from operational intelligence disseminated exclusively to CIA case officers in the field that it was the policy of China's MSS to recall immediately any officer who had been on the receiving end of an operational approach from a hostile intelligence service.

The MSS's reasoning was simple: If the officer did not appear vulnerable to hostile recruitment, he would not have been pitched in the first place. So Beijing felt it was prudent to get the officer back behind the safety of the bamboo curtain before things could get out of hand. Beijing took no chances on someone who might later decide to defect, or worse, to agree to a lucrative offer to spy against the motherland as an agent-in-place.

The policy was a closely guarded secret among a few top MSS counterintelligence officers. They knew that if word ever got out that an officer would be recalled if he or she reported a recruitment pitch, pitches would quickly cease to be reported. And since counterintelligence in Beijing could usually learn about hostile approaches to its officers only through the officers themselves, they simply lied to the rank and file and told them that disciplinary action would be taken only against those officers who did *not* report hostile approaches.

MacMurphy knew all of this, but he was also quite certain that Huang did not, which complicated things further for the CIA case officer.

CHAPTER 16

A uniformed valet at the top of the hill directed the line of arriving cars to park at the end of a grass lot full of diplomatic vehicles. Mac recognized several US Embassy cars by the "4" prefix on their diplomatic tags and noticed a much larger number of Russian vehicles with the "10" prefix.

Approaching the entrance, MacMurphy passed a group of diplomatic drivers gathered in a group in the parking lot, smoking and gossiping about their bosses. He recognized a chain-smoking Ethiopian security officer in their midst—which was why CIA case officers always drove themselves. Actual Foreign Service Officers used chauffeurs from the embassy motor pool to ferry them about. It was one of the many small ways hostile intelligence services were able to distinguish the spies from the real diplomats; there were other, more subtle differences.

Squaring his shoulders and mentally girding himself, Mac entered the house. The entry foyer was festively lit and decorated. Flowers abounded, their commingled and sometimes unpleasantly mixed scents overriding even the heavy perfume of some of the arriving guests.

MacMurphy entered this olfactory war zone and joined the guests passing through the reception line. Moments later, he greeted Ambassador Zeki Gonen, a short, stocky man with an infectious grin and shiny bald head, tonight even shinier due to a coating of sweat. Mac wondered if this was an indication that Gonen didn't enjoy these parties any more than he did. Mrs. Gonen, at the ambassador's side, was a robust woman four inches taller than Zeki, decked out in gold lamé and sequins. The couple embraced MacMurphy warmly—they were old acquaintances from dozens of like functions—and Mac continued down the line to Gonen's deputy, Nail Atalay.

Nail and Mac embraced solidly, pounding each other's back with a vigor that testified to their respective physical strength. They had a lot in common. Both were in their mid-thirties, friendly but tough competitors on the tennis courts, each in superb physical shape. Other similarities included the fact that both were attractive bachelors and rapidly turning prematurely gray. Two "silver foxes" on the diplomatic circuit.

More than one female head had turned at Mac's entrance. Mac was flattered by the attention but took it in stride. He was too level-headed a fellow to let his head get blown up by the attentions of the ladies . . . even when those attentions went beyond merely being obvious in admiration of his looks and charm.

"Mac, you made it! Thank you for coming. Are we still on for Saturday?" Nail asked heartily.

"You bet. I've reserved an embassy court for eleven-thirty. You won't get a game off me this time," Mac grinned, warming to the prospect of winning on the courts. Mac liked winning in *all* aspects of his life. That's why he never gambled—he hated to lose.

"We'll see about that, my friend. We'll see about that . . . I'll catch up with you later. Enjoy the food and drink."

Nail turned to greet the next person in the receiving line, and Mac moved into the chattering mob of elegantly dressed women and pin-striped men. He maneuvered his way past the loaded buffet table surrounded by ravenous African and Middle Eastern diplomats.

Mac would eat eventually, but he had too much respect for his physical condition to over-indulge at these affairs. That was one of the reasons he remained in such superb shape at an age when many of his peers were starting to develop paunches and uncooperative muscles. He did, however, snatch a Campari-soda from a silver tray carried by a starched Ethiopian waiter.

Mac smiled and nodded at Mpana Martin, First Secretary of the Embassy of Cameroon, who was busily stuffing deviled eggs into his mouth while carrying on a rapid-fire conversation with two other wildly gesticulating West Africans.

Drink in hand, he shouldered his way through the packed dining room toward the living area of the house, nodding and waving and occasionally exchanging brief greetings with familiar people. He moved through the crowd confidently, easily, yet constantly aware of his surroundings—not so much the furnishings or decorations, nor even the abundance of food and drink, but the people. He made a mental note of who was there, memorized any unfamiliar faces . . . and searched the crowd reluctantly for his friend Huang.

The living room was less crowded, and he stopped by the fireplace to exchange pleasantries with Deuk Po Kim and Hoon Sohn of the South Korean embassy and Jinichi Yuki of the Japanese embassy. They were discussing the potential contribution of the Olympics to world harmony, debating the value—if any—that the world games offered to international relations. Mac got pulled into the conversation, but he couldn't devote his full attention to the debate at hand; a part of his mind remained occupied with last-minute revisions to the script of his forthcoming conversation with Huang.

Mac enjoyed the people he was talking with and would have lingered longer were it not for an interruption by Yuri Leizarenko, counsellor and resident chief intelligence officer of the SVR, the successor to the KGB, at the Russian embassy.

"How are you, Mr. MacMurphy, my old comrade?" boomed the sumo-sized Ukranian, pounding Mac on the back with a large, callused hand as if they were old friends. "Where have you been hiding? Have not seen you for very long time. Where have you been? In jail or something?" He laughed heartily at his own joke and didn't seem to be bothered that no one else in the group was laughing.

"Something," replied Mac, slipping into his blank, uncommunicative, boring stare routine. Mac had no time to waste on this particular obnoxious Russian. The Ukranian essayed another equally humorless joke, but Mac met it with the same glazed eyes and lack of laughter. Twice more the golem tried, and twice more MacMurphy fielded the tasteless questions with monosyllabic grunts. During the awkward silence that ensued, Mac drifted away from the group. Behind him, he heard the SVR station chief mutter, ". . . asshole . . ."

CHAPTER 17

MacMurphy stepped out onto the balcony, where it was cooler, and briefly watched one of the cooks busily barbecuing chicken wings and shish kabobs on a large grill. He couldn't resist the scent and plucked a shish kabob directly off the grill. It was difficult to eat the thing gracefully, without dripping grease on his suit, but he was concentrating on doing his best at it when he noticed the group of Chinese officials at the far end of the balcony. They were dressed alike in gray Mao jackets, keeping to themselves. Huang Tsung-yao was among them.

Even though dressed in the drab outfit favored by the late Chairman Mao, Huang stood out from the three other men. He was tall by Chinese standards, slightly taller than Mac, and his aristocratic wiry frame seemed to vibrate with barely suppressed energy. His dark eyes gleamed with intelligence and he had the bearing and presence of a natural leader. He was obviously the Alpha-male in the group.

Watching them, Mac knew that nothing was more boring than a group of Chinese diplomats at a cocktail party. They tended to huddle

together and most of them either had limited social skills or were appre-
hensive about being overly chummy with foreigners. In any event, Mac
wanted to get Huang alone, so he made eye contact with Huang and then
drifted off to the other end of the balcony to wait for him.

Mac stood at the balcony railing and looked up into the clear night.
The luminous moon seemed to take up more than its fair share of the
sky, and stars spread out over the rest of the black velvet firmament like
glitter spread by an over-enthusiastic three-year-old. Only in Africa could
the sky be displayed the way it was tonight.

As he considered with trepidation the night's recruitment pitch to
Huang, he briefly thought about other recruitment operations he had
orchestrated since arriving in the field. None had been quite like the
situation he faced this evening with Huang.

Mac had excelled during his recruitment training down at The Farm,
and he had already racked up three solid hard-target recruitments during
his first tour in Addis. And that was precisely why he did not want to
pitch Huang this evening. You needed to identify vulnerabilities or sus-
ceptibilities in your target before moving into the recruitment phase.

In Huang's case there were no such vulnerabilities or weaknesses to
prey upon. He had no children to educate. He was a rising star in the
MSS, seemed actually to enjoy the Spartan life of a third world diplomat,
and was extremely proud of his Chinese heritage. There was nothing that
MacMurphy or anyone else had found that would indicate in the slightest way that Huang would betray his country for money or anything else.

Mac had spent hours reading the detailed, thick file on Huang. It
had obviously been carefully and laboriously compiled by the Agency
over a considerable period of time. Of particular interest was Huang's
six-year long posting to the NCNA office in Houston, Texas. Huang had
been identified as a high-value target early in his career, and had been
assessed by a number of intelligence officers during his time in the US.

CHAPTER 18

Huang Tsung-yao was born in Beijing in 1962, the son of a wealthy (by Chinese standards) and privileged professor of economics at Beijing University. His father was a respected economic advisor to Deng Xiaoping, who was at the time a ranking member of the National People's Congress of the Chinese Communist Party.

The file noted that Deng and Huang and his family had been victims of the revolution. In fact, when Huang was only four years old, Mao had unleashed the chaos and violence of the Great Cultural Revolution. Huang and his family lived out the years of their exile in a squalid two-room bungalow in a small village north of Beijing.

They worked as sharecroppers on a communal cabbage farm. His father died of overwork and despair in the last year of their exile. His mother survived but her health was gravely impaired. Deng, of course, had also survived and returned eventually to the pinnacle of power in China after Mao's death.

The Agency had been able to identify Huang as a protégée of Deng and the file offered some slender information about how this connection led to Huang's highly successful career as an intelligence officer. Even the meager details represented an excellent job of penetrating the opacity of China's leadership and its intelligence service.

Like Mac, Huang had demonstrated the ability to learn foreign languages while he was majoring in political science at his father's beloved Beijing University and was fluent in French and English. And, like Mac's father, Huang had a somewhat flattened nose with a crease across its bridge. Mac was convinced that Huang had done some boxing in his youth—or engaged in some other form of orchestrated violence that could produce a nose that had been broken, probably more than once.

The file gave no indication whatsoever that Huang was anything other than a staunch patriot, and assuredly not a man who would be open to recruitment. To the contrary, Mac was sure that Huang believed China's full potential would be realized under the leadership of people like Deng Xiaoping and his own father—and wanted to become a part of that leadership. Huang was now well along his way to achieving that goal. Throwing all that away would be unthinkable . . .

But Headquarters had ordered it. Huang would be pitched tonight.

CHAPTER 19

The situation reminded Mac too much of the story, recounted to him and a small group of other students by Edwin Rothmann, the Deputy Director of Operations, the DDO.

Rothmann enjoyed legendary status among the students at The Farm. He was a frequent visitor because he viewed the new officers as the future of the Agency. He made it a point to take a personal interest in their careers.

He was a huge man in all respects. He stood six feet five and weighed over three hundred pounds. Intellectually he was even larger. Friendly and outgoing, he possessed an extraordinary memory, especially when it came to people, names, and anecdotes about them.

He was one of those case officers who bridged the gap between the heroic OSS veterans who formed the Agency, and the new Agency of the twenty-first century. His career began during the Vietnam era and took him through the jungles of Southeast Asia and sophisticated European posts to executive assignments at Headquarters and finally to the ultimate post of DDO, a position he attained while Mac was in training in 1992, and would hold for many more years to come.

Rothmann had recounted the story over drinks at the bar of the officers club during the graduation ceremony down at The Farm. The incident had taken place during Rothmann's first overseas tour in Saigon at the height of the Vietnam conflict.

CHAPTER 20

*H*e had recruited a young South Vietnamese army captain who was a genuine war hero, with three decorations for valor. His cryptonym was TURAP/1.

Rothmann had met TURAP for the first time at the Third Field hospital in Saigon, where TURAP was recovering from his eighth war injury, and there he recruited TURAP to undertake a clandestine mission to North Vietnam. The mission required TURAP to appear to desert from the South Vietnamese Army, the ARVN, hire a body smuggler to reach Cambodia, defect to the North Vietnamese at their embassy in Phnom Penh, and then to make his way into North Vietnam, where he was to organize a clandestine resistance force of his countrymen and communicate information out of the country to a letter drop in Hong Kong.

The first part of the operation went according to plan. TURAP disappeared, was listed as a deserter, spent two months in a Saigon safehouse learning clandestine communications skills, and reached Cambodia.

After that the operation began to unravel.

The Hong Kong-based clandestine support mechanism set up to fund agents like TURAP broke down due to a personal squabble between the chiefs of the Saigon and Hong Kong stations. TURAP, having run out of money, was arrested for vagrancy in the Cambodian capital.

Rothmann presented an alternate plan of funding to the Saigon station chief, a plan the COS endorsed. The Chief of Station forwarded it for approval. But Headquarters turned the plan down cold. They felt that TURAP's appearing penniless only made his cover story more believable.

Rothmann was livid but could do nothing to change it.

Three weeks after Rothmann had broadcast a coded message to TURAP telling him that more money would not be forthcoming, he received a letter with a coded message from TURAP. The message said that he was going to cache his commo equipment and try to infiltrate a Viet Cong unit to get to North Vietnam and fulfill his mission.

The hapless agent had no way of knowing that swarms of giant B-52 fortresses would soon be running saturation bombing missions all along the Cambodian border on the Ho Chi Minh Trail. The CIA never heard from TURAP again, and Rothmann never got over the guilt he felt. "I lost my cherry on that one," Rothmann had commented.

And MacMurphy was soon going to experience the same emotions. Headquarters was about to ruin Huang just as they had callously cast off TURAP. He knew this with a certainty that bordered on premonition.

CHAPTER 21

MacMurphy stood alone at the balcony railing, deep in thoughts that were far from pleasant—TURAP, and what Rothmann had inadvertently done to him. Huang, and what Mac was unwillingly about to do to him. Collateral damage in the ongoing machinations that were an inevitable part of a case officer's life, whether in war or in peacetime.

Now the unnaturally bright moon felt like a sharply focused spotlight, singling him out, making him the focal point of an unseen audience's attention. It was a decidedly uncomfortable feeling. Mac, deep in thought, didn't hear Huang come up behind him. He was unaware of his friend till Huang poked him in the ribs with an index finger, saying, "You're under arrest!"

Mac only partially controlled his reaction. His body tensed noticeably as the finger and the words found their mark. "Damn, you scared me! How are you, Tsung-yao?"

"Not too bad for an old man," responded the tall Chinese. His near flawless idiomatic English had been polished to near perfection during his first overseas tour in Houston where he had immersed himself in the American way of life. "And you?"

"Can't complain . . . nobody listens if I do." Mac smiled warmly at his friend.

"I cannot imagine you as a complainer, Mac," Huang laughed.

"I hear you've been pretty active on our embassy tennis courts lately."

Huang played tennis the way he played badminton and ping-pong, sports he had excelled at during his college years at Beijing University, with chips and spin and touch and intelligent strategy. Mac, on the other hand, played from the baseline with power and heavy topspin. Unfortunately for Mac, Huang's finesse usually prevailed when they played, frustrating MacMurphy to no end. He knew how to lose gracefully, but that didn't make him enjoy losing any the better. In sports as in his work, Mac was a man who always preferred to win and did his damnedest to see that he did.

"I, as you would say, cleaned your Ambassador's clock yesterday."

"That's not much of an accomplishment. He plays pitty-pat tennis like you do. You know, like an old lady."

"Whenever you're ready for another lesson, just name the date and time."

"You're on. I'll see if I can fit you in this weekend."

"Fit me in? Coward! Are you starting to backpedal already?"

Mac replied with an upraised chin followed by a dismissive wave.

The two friends, both experienced in the arcane art of meaningless cocktail party babble, chatted on for several more minutes. Then the perceptive Huang noticed that Mac's mind seemed to be wandering.

"Something wrong, Mac? You seem preoccupied."

MacMurphy started to speak, then hesitated. After a moment he said, "Yeah, I . . . I need to talk to you . . ."

"So talk! Tell me what is wrong. Anything I can help with?"

MacMurphy knew there was no delicate way to broach the subject. Huang was too perceptive for games. He launched into the pitch in a straightforward manner, hoping Huang would appreciate his honesty and not get too defensive or insulted.

"My people want to help you. They figure you're a good guy with a future in your service, and they think you can help create an atmosphere of better understanding between our two governments."

Huang looked puzzled. This was so out of the blue, and so out of character for Mac, that at first he didn't understand the implicit message. "What are you saying, Mac? You seem ill at ease, not at all like you."

"I'm okay," Mac hesitated. "It's just that . . . well . . . it's important that the US government has friends who can . . . you know . . . advise its leaders about the real intentions of other countries . . ."

"You mean China?" said Huang skeptically. "You need someone to tell you what China's leaders are thinking and planning?" He stared directly into Mac's dark eyes.

"That's it . . ." Mac tried to avoid Huang's unwavering gaze. "You know . . . When countries understand each other better, there is better communication and less chance that misunderstandings can occur between them." MacMurphy was on auto-pilot; he had delivered the same general spiel many times before. "Better understanding brings better relations, and both of us want that, don't we?"

"Sure we do Mac. Both our countries are already moving in that direction now that the old guard like Mao and Chou En-lai are gone . . ." The full realization began to dawn on him. Belatedly comprehending Mac's intent, Huang suddenly stiffened and backed away from MacMurphy. The smile was gone. "Do you want me to tell you what China's leaders are planning? Do you want me to tell you what is said in our classified cable traffic and pouches from Beijing?"

MacMurphy started to speak, dropping his gaze, but Huang held up his hand to cut him off. "I haven't finished . . ."

"Look, let's just drop it, okay? It was a bad idea. Washington wanted me to ask . . ." Mac's voice tapered off. He wasn't sure where to go with this next. Surely Huang deserved better than this.

"So you asked." Huang's voice was flat.

"Yes, I asked . . . Now let's just drop it and get a refill. Your glass is empty." Mac tried to divert Huang's attention toward the bar.

"Sure, I need another drink. But first let me ask you something." The Chinese grasped Mac's arm tightly. He wasn't letting Mac off the hook that easily.

"Ask me anything you like," said Mac contritely.

"Why me? I know how these things work. What did I do or say that would give you the impression that I would be a recruitment prospect? You guys are not like the Russians, who go around pitching everyone in sight on the off chance someone will say yes. You guys don't play the percentages like they do. You plan, you focus. At least that's what they tell us back home."

"You're right, Tsung-yao, you're absolutely right. You know that sometimes Washington, and I imagine Beijing as well, works in a vacuum. They don't know what is really happening out here. Let's just drop it, okay?"

"No, wait . . . First tell me why you thought I would agree to betray my country for . . . for . . . what? Money? What? What could you possibly offer me to do that?"

"I told you. Nothing. Washington just told me to ask, that's all." Mac's only concern was damage control at this point. "Now let's just forget it and get that drink."

"I can't forget it, Mac, and I don't believe you." Huang's voice was less accusatory than hurt, his tone was flat. MacMurphy started to interrupt, but Huang stopped him. "You and I are not in that vacuum you mentioned. I will tell you frankly, I feel like you have betrayed our friendship. I expected more from you. Certainly not this . . .

"When I tell Beijing about this, they will forbid me to see you any more. And I do not think I want to see you any more either. I am sorry Mac." Huang turned to leave. Mac's muscles tightened, as a mixture of sorrow and bitter regret engulfed him.

"Wait." Mac grabbed his elbow. "I'm sorry. I really am Tsung-yao. But just listen to me for one minute." Huang tried to pull away, but MacMurphy strengthened his grip. "Please don't say a word about this to anyone. No one . . . It's for your own good." Huang tugged harder and Mac blurted, "For God's sake, Tsung-yao, listen to me. I know what I'm talking about. They won't just tell you can't see me anymore. They'll recall you to Beijing. They will jerk your ass out of here so Goddamn fast . . ."

Huang jerked his arm free. "Do not be ridiculous. Why would Beijing do that? I have done nothing wrong."

"They will, Tsung-yao," MacMurphy said firmly. "I know they will. Listen to me. They always do. I know about these things better than you."

"Better than me? I don't think so . . ."

Huang turned abruptly and rejoined his colleagues at the far end of the balcony, never once looking back toward Mac. His turned back conveyed a message that burned through Mac with an intensity he hadn't felt before. Mac had done more than just fail in his doomed mission—an outcome he had expected; he had also lost a friend . . . and in the process, doomed that friend's future.

MacMurphy had lost his cherry, just as his mentor Rothmann had, more than twenty years earlier.

CHAPTER 22

Two days later, after several unreturned phone calls to Huang at the Chinese embassy, MacMurphy learned that Huang had left "for consultations" that afternoon on the regular CAAC flight from Addis Ababa to Beijing.

Huang never returned to Addis Ababa, and it would be more than ten years before he was permitted to travel outside of China again.

The system had betrayed MacMurphy as it had Rothmann so many years before, and Mac thought long and hard about leaving the clandestine service. His disillusionment sent him into a deep depression. But in the final analysis, he chalked the whole affair up to experience and carried on with his career. He had joined the Agency to serve his country, not to make friends.

At the end of his Addis Ababa assignment, he was rewarded with a promotion and a direct transfer to Thailand. He would be the deputy in Bangkok Station's Udorn base, tasked with running cross-border operations across the Mekong River into Vientiane, Laos.

He was happy with the trust the Agency had placed in him by rewarding him with the promotion and the career-enhancing assignment, but the scars left by the Huang Tsung-yao case remained. He would never again trust the Agency's management as he had in the past, and he would become more and more of a loner within the case officer ranks of the CIA.

CHAPTER 23

MacMurphy sat at his desk on the top floor of the American Consulate General in Hong Kong. His in-box still contained over four inches of morning traffic: operational cables, raw intelligence reports, and analyses of recent events in China and the rest of Asia.

He had already gone through an equal amount of priority and immediate traffic and was on his second cup of coffee of the morning. He had been at his desk for over an hour and his coffee was getting cold, but he was too engrossed in his work to get up and get a fresh cup. It was eight-thirty, opening of business, and his staff was drifting in.

As the CIA's station chief, he was charged with directing all of the Agency's operations run out of Hong Kong. The station was the Agency's most productive producer of raw intelligence on China. The operating climate was benign compared to the "denied area" character of Beijing and the rest of the mainland. Due to the importance and sheer size of the China target, MacMurphy's stable of agents spread throughout Asia and Europe.

He was going to meet personally with one of those agents in just a few hours.

Normally the COS of a station as large as Hong Kong would not be meeting agents himself. That was the job of the younger case officers, those with more energy and squeaky clean covers. MacMurphy had been a case officer for almost ten years, and his cover had eroded over those years until it was now so thin as to be practically non-existent.

Hostile intelligence services from Russia's SVR and China's MSS to Ethiopia's MPS held thick operational files on MacMurphy. They knew who he was, who he really worked for, and that his job was to recruit and handle spies within their respective governments.

So when he went out on the streets, they watched him. And if surveillance were to see him meeting with an agent, the asset would be automatically compromised; guilt through association with a known CIA operative.

MacMurphy was handling this particular agent because he had personally recruited him earlier that year—not in true name as a member of the American Consulate General, of course, but in alias and under deeper cover as French journalist Barry LeMen. Mac had taken on this particular "false-flag" recruitment task because none of his other case officers had the language ability to pass themselves off as French.

Thanks to his mother, Mac had grown up speaking French (and German) in the home, and he had continued to study the languages throughout his formative years and into college. And this Chinese journalist asset had been assessed as a Francophile, having spent a previous tour in Paris with the New China News Agency.

The operation was classic. The agent was a junior editor for the NCNA. He was spotted and assessed as a good recruitment target by another asset—a Hong Kong Chinese access agent—who had in turn introduced him to MacMurphy/LeMen. The agent was paid the enormous (by Chinese standards) monthly "consulting fee" of $500 for essentially overt information and analysis of the Chinese political and economic situation.

"Money for nursery rhymes," MacMurphy liked to say, designed just to get the development to the point where the agent becomes comfortable with the relationship and used to providing information, any kind of information, in return for money.

It had taken several months for the hook to set. As the potential agent became more and more accustomed to easy money for his "China watching" views, the case officer began allowing his cover to peel off like the layers of an onion.

First the idea of clandestinity was introduced: "We shouldn't be seen in public together. People might get the wrong idea!" Then the case officer's requirements became more narrowly focused on "privileged" information, and the concept of sourcing was introduced. "Who told you that? Information is no better than its source."

And then the recruitment pitch. "I've been passing your information to the US Government without your knowledge. They love it and want to meet with you directly. It would be a good thing for both countries. It would increase understanding and reduce friction and contribute to world peace. They're also willing to double your salary. I'm being transferred back to Paris, so you can either continue with them or call it quits."

The agent had become comfortable with the relationship and there was little incentive for him to back out of the relationship. The money was good, and soon to get much better, and there appeared to be little risk in continuing. So the agent bought it and signed a secrecy agreement to that effect.

When the recruitment was solidified and the asset had been thoroughly vetted and polygraphed, plans for the turnover to another case officer with solid diplomatic cover were put into motion. The turnover was scheduled for the first week in July, just before MacMurphy's departure from Hong Kong back to CIA headquarters in Langley.

CHAPTER 24

MacMurphy exited the Consulate on the ground floor and passed the Marine Guard Post number one at the front entrance. On his way out the door he threw a casual salute and a "Hi, Steve" to the strapping Marine Gunnery Sergeant on duty.

As a former Marine officer, MacMurphy had a special affinity for the grunts who guarded the US embassies and consulates around the world, and the Marines in turn respected and genuinely liked Mac. He had been selected as the guest of honor at their anniversary ball the previous November and had entertained them with an inspirational and witty speech on the evolution of the Corps and his experiences as a young OCS candidate at Quantico, Virginia.

As he stepped out of the air-conditioned fortress consulate building into the heat of Garden Road, the glare of the summer morning temporarily blinded him.

Mac wore tan slacks and a short-sleeved, light blue cotton shirt, yet despite his sensible dress, the heat was nearly insufferable. He had removed his tie before leaving his office and hung it on the back of his office door along with the jacket he kept for his frequent meetings with the protocol-conscious Consul General.

MacMurphy believed that jackets and ties were insane during the long Hong Kong summers. Only crazy old colonial Englishmen and some of the weirder State Department twinkies wore them in that kind of heat. He was reminded of the old Noel Coward song that posited "Only mad dogs and Englishmen go out in the midday sun." He preferred his case officers to blend in on the streets, so jackets and ties were out as far as he was concerned—at least when they were away from the strict State Department environment of the consulate. It was more than a matter of mere comfort; it was a cover issue. But the comfort element entered into it too. How could he expect his people to do a good job when they were broiling and sweating?

Strolling down the hill to the nearby Hilton Hotel, he entered through the side entrance at the base of Garden Road, went past the lobby, and back out the front entrance. There he tipped the doorman to whistle a cab for him. He knew that his surveillants—he had not seen them yet, but he knew they would be there—would have had no trouble keeping him in sight during his short stroll, and they could easily keep the cab in view during the twenty-minute trip through the harbor tunnel to Kowloon.

His training and experience had taught him that the way to handle a surveillance team was to lull them asleep. Never, ever piss them off by making them look stupid. Never let them know you are deliberately trying to shake them. There are too many ways they can make a case officer's life miserable. Better to let the team string along casually behind and lose them only when it is absolutely necessary, and only for as long as necessary—when an operational act must be committed—and then do it with finesse, so they don't appear incompetent when they submit their daily surveillance report to their superiors. If they couldn't be gotten rid of in this manner, then the operational act should be aborted.

By the time he entered the cab, he had spotted the team—three Chinese men on two small 50cc Honda motorbikes, one ready to hop off and handle any foot surveillance and the other two for vehicular surveil-lance. They were old "friends" who had been with him many times before. They were not hard to spot; short Chinese clones dressed in long-sleeved white shirts rolled up to the elbows, dark baggy trousers, one-size-fits-all belts ending at mid-back, and worn black shoes topped with droopy white socks.

Mac had nicknamed them Gimpy (for his limp), Grumpy (for his attitude), and Dopey (because he was).

His surveillance detection route through the harbor tunnel to Kow-loon was designed to draw the surveillance team through a series of "corridors" where each surveillant could be positively identified—he could not afford to be surprised by a fourth or fifth member—and accounted for before the operational agent meeting could take place.

By the time MacMurphy reached Kowloon, he was certain the team consisted of only Gimpy, Grumpy, and Dopey. He knew they were not equipped with radios, and therefore would be forced to maintain visual contact with each other. This fact was established during previous obser-vations of MSS teams by MacMurphy and his colleagues, and confirmed by operational information provided to the CIA station by a former member of the Hong Kong Special Branch, now chief of the British SIS station in Hong Kong.

Mac maintained a close liaison relationship with the Brits and knew their information came from a reliable high-level penetration of the MSS's Investigative Division in Hong Kong. It made his job a lot easier.

The taxi dropped him between the Star Ferry wharf and the entrance of the enormous Ocean Terminal shopping mall. He headed toward the mall.

Scanning the harbor area behind him as he rode up the long escala-tor leading to the upper level shops of the mall, he spotted Dopey on one of the two motorbikes, positioned to watch the main entrance of the terminal building. He knew that Grumpy would be biking his way to the Hong Kong Hotel entrance at the far end of the terminal, and Gimpy would be limping along behind him. They always gave poor Gimpy the footwork.

He knew Gimpy would hang back a good distance for fear of burning himself, but Mac would make things easy for him. He moved at an easy pace and stopped twice, once to purchase a greeting card and once a magazine, during his stroll through the mall on his way to lunch. The purchases were proof of the "rabbit's" reason for being in the building, and would serve as later justification for the team to write in their report that Mac was really there to shop, not to detect or shake surveillance. When MacMurphy eventually disappeared from sight in one of the larger shops, Gimpy would not be concerned. Who could blame him, what with so many entrances and exits; and his instructions were clear—discreet, repeat *discreet*, surveillance. Anyway, the rabbit was definitely not tail-conscious and would surely reappear at one of the main exits where one of the others would pick him up again. Gimpy would head back out to the Star Ferry entrance to join Dopey.

MacMurphy passed through the upper level tunnel, which connected the Ocean Terminal and the Hong Kong Hotel, and walked down through the hotel to the street. There, as expected, he spotted Grumpy standing casually next to his motorbike about forty meters up the road. He was in a good position to view the exit. Neither MacMurphy nor Grumpy gave any indication one had seen the other.

MacMurphy glanced at his watch. It was noon. He had spent nearly an hour on his SDR and he now knew exactly the extent of his surveillance. His meeting was in less than twenty-five minutes, and his agent had been trained to wait only five minutes before aborting. If they missed this meeting they both would have to go through the whole surveillance detection drill again before making the prearranged alternate meeting later that evening. He wanted to avoid that if at all possible. It was a *necessary* waste of time, but a waste nonetheless.

He turned into the crowd on Peking Road and headed up toward Nathan Road. He strode more rapidly now, gliding around and past slower-moving pedestrians in his desire to complete his planned path in time, yet trying not to look like he was in a hurry to get anywhere special.

He knew Grumpy could afford to hang back because MacMurphy's prematurely gray head of hair would be clearly visible above the shorter black heads of the Chinese masses who swirled around him. As he walked, he hummed to himself a fragment of a haunting popular tune from a decade earlier—one he knew well and could hum without thinking about it. In fact, he was only vaguely aware of the song going through his head at all. His mind was otherwise occupied, focused on his being seen at all the right moments—till it was time to escape his followers' view—and then getting to his meeting in a timely manner, but still undetected.

Still humming to himself, MacMurphy turned into a familiar shopping arcade. He knew he would be out of Grumpy's sight for a few moments. The arcade contained a number of shops on the ground floor and several restaurants, including the popular Lindy's, a knock-off from the original New York Lindy's, on the second level. Lindy's was well known to the team as a regular lunch stop for MacMurphy. He favored the food there as well as the service and admired several of the cute waitresses as well . . . though his admiration had never gone beyond innocent flirting. But the staff of Lindy's knew him as a regular, and so did his trio of surveillants.

Figuring Mac was going to lunch, Grumpy waited outside the arcade and positioned himself so he could observe the entrance. Watching the entrance outside in the Hong Kong heat while MacMurphy enjoyed his lunch in air-conditioned comfort in his favorite restaurant was a regular occurrence for Grumpy. This naturally contributed to the demeanor that had given rise to Mac's nickname for him. MacMurphy felt a tad sorry for the poor dude, but not at all guilty.

Once in the arcade and out of Grumpy's sight, MacMurphy darted into a stairwell, took the stairs two at a time to the next level, jogged down the shop-lined hall, circled back down another staircase, and exited out a side door onto busy Nathan Road. He looked around to make sure he wasn't being spotted or tailed, then quickly crossed the street and descended into the subway.

When he emerged in Mongkok ten minutes later, he was certain he was clean. He also knew the surveillance team would be reassembled, patiently waiting on the street outside of Lindy's for MacMurphy to reappear after lunch.

They would never risk burning themselves by going into a fancy European restaurant after a "rabbit," and they knew—or *thought* they knew—exactly where he was and what he was doing. And that's how the surveillance report would read at the end of the day. They would never know they had missed an hour of activities that needed surveillance and reporting. Precisely how MacMurphy wanted it.

CHAPTER 25

MacMurphy and his agent, Chou Hsing, made eye contact at the pickup point in front of the Hung Fat noodle shop on U Chau Street. Chou was sensibly dressed in a white, short sleeve shirt and blue linen slacks. There was a phalanx of pens jammed into the pocket of his shirt, an advertisement for himself as a busy and dedicated journalist. His shiny black hair was styled in a somewhat incongruous arrangement that made him look like a Chinese version of one of the Beetles in the 1960s. His girlfriend, Ling, thought it was cute. Mac found it amusingly adolescent.

After they'd silently acknowledged each other, Chou followed MacMurphy at a discreet distance to a small park nestled among several high-rise apartment buildings. He sat on a bench in the park while MacMurphy entered one of the buildings, still very aware of the people around him and the possibility that he might be being tailed. Exactly five minutes later, Chou followed and proceeded directly to the familiar safehouse apartment on the fourth floor.

The safehouse had been rented in alias by a Chinese/American former Naval officer whose retirement included working as a support asset for the CIA's Hong Kong station. The door to the pied-á-terre apartment was open a crack—the final signal that all was clear—and Chou slipped quietly inside and closed the door behind him.

They shook hands and hugged warmly, the case officer knowing his agent wanted to feel personally appreciated. MacMurphy led his agent to a small Formica table with a chair on either side, placed in the middle of the sparsely furnished efficiency apartment. There were just enough furnishings to allay suspicions should anyone unexpected enter the apartment.

It needed to look like someone could conceivably be living here, at least from time to time, not like the single-purpose meeting place it actually was. But it certainly lacked any homey touches. No pictures graced the walls, no books were anywhere in evidence—although a few old magazines were piled on a coffee table—and the kitchenette showed no signs that anyone had ever cooked a meal here, or ever planned to.

The two men sat across from one another and exchanged pleasantries in English, the most comfortable language for both of them to communicate in. MacMurphy positioned a yellow legal pad in front of him and prepared to take notes.

MacMurphy looked expectant; his agent looked eager. Both case officer and agent were now ready to get down to business.

CHAPTER 26

Chou Hsing's business card read: Junior Editor, New China News Agency. But in reality he was much more important than that. This fact had not been revealed by Chou—although MacMurphy and the CIA were well aware of it—until he was subjected to the intense questioning of the polygraph examination after recruitment.

Old habits are hard to break for case officers living under deep, non-official cover. However, Chou Hsing finally admitted that he was actually an MSS case officer assigned to the Hong Kong branch of the NCNA. The admission was a required part of the CIA's agent vetting process.

Like many non-official case officers working for intelligence agencies all over the world, Chou spent his evenings meeting agents and preparing reports for the MSS while carrying a full cover workload as a journalist for the NCNA during the day. The expanded access that went with the intelligence affiliation greatly enhanced Chou's value to MacMurphy's station in Hong Kong, and the CIA had rewarded this potential by setting aside a neat $100,000 per year salary, deposited in monthly increments into a stateside interest-bearing escrow account.

Chou saw himself as one of those millions of Chinese who had a flair for business. He regarded his prospects for advancement in his present career as less than brilliant. His brother, Chiang, had emigrated from China and set up a business in the Philippines, using cheap labor and equally cheap raw materials to make patio furniture for export. The quality was uneven, the designs were less than inspiring, but the price was right. Older brother Chou wanted to show that he too could be an entrepreneur.

MacMurphy had encouraged Chou to view himself as a "capitalist roader" but had his doubts about Chou's potential to become a mini-mogul. Still, you kept an asset happy; you shared his dreams and encouraged him to dream big.

The money could be used only after Chou's clandestine work for the CIA was over, however; only after he had been safely exfiltrated to the United States and resettled comfortably somewhere in the hinterland with a new name and identity. Access to that much money for an individual in Chou's position would have brought the MSS counterintelligence goons down on him immediately.

By now Chou was used to his clandestine relationship with the man he knew as Barry LeMen, and he handled himself professionally during the monthly meetings with his case officer. He came to the meetings prepared and wasted no time at all. He knew that the biggest risk he took as a CIA agent was in delivering his information to LeMen. Collecting it was the easy part, normal, but if he were caught delivering it to an intelligence operative . . . China's justice system was swift and efficient when it came to handling traitors.

CHAPTER 27

MacMurphy already had retrieved two frosty cans of San Miguel beer from the apartment's compact fridge and had placed these and a plate of assorted salted nuts on the table. The two men toasted each other with a synchronous "kam-bei" and got down to routine business.

"Any trouble getting here?" MacMurphy asked crisply.

"No, everything okay. But must be back in less than one hour today."

"No problem. Let's set up our next meet right away in case we have to leave quickly. Then we can go through your material."

MacMurphy and Chou agreed on the date and time for their next—and final—meeting. It would be in two weeks at the safehouse. Chou had been well prepared for his introduction to an American case officer. LeMen, Chou believed, would be returning to Europe.

Chou would miss LeMen and was more than a little concerned about meeting directly with an American official, but he kept his feelings to himself and displayed little emotion despite the welter of concerns that tumbled through his mind. He knew that as long as his relationship with the American CIA was kept out of sight, he would be safe, and the rewards down the road would make everything worth the risk.

Opening his leather portfolio, Chou removed six pages of photo-copied order blanks from a popular Hong Kong mail order house. He pushed them across the table to MacMurphy.

MacMurphy selected one of the pages and examined the reverse side under the glancing sunlight coming in through the window. "Your tech-nique has really improved. No evidence of any impressions on these pages at all. You must be using the #4 pencil I gave you."

"Yes, and do not press too hard like you say. It really good system. I can not see nothing on them order blanks."

"So you like the system? You like using the SW?"

"It damn better than relying on joss to get reports to you, ayah?"

"That's what I kept telling you. I couldn't understand why you were so reluctant to use SW for your reports. If you lose these in the street you have only lost blank order forms. If you lost these reports the way you used to prepare them, in clear text, well . . . I don't want to think about that."

"Me too. I stupid before. Worry too much about using 'spy gear,' you know . . . Now everything okay, ayah?"

"Absolutely. The point is you're using the methods I taught you, and your security is much better. Now, what are you giving me here?" He folded the papers carefully and placed them in the package with the purchases he had made earlier.

"You got two new *chung-fas*. Number 19 and 23."

MacMurphy knew that a *chung-fa* was a directive issued by the Central Committee of the Chinese Communist Party. Some were closely guarded secrets, which received very limited distribution among the Party elite, and some received much broader distribution among Party mem-bers. Chou had provided the gist of several *chung-fas* in the past. Provid-ing them was a standing requirement.

"Are they sexy?" MacMurphy asked, watching the Chinese man's face.

"One sexy, one not so sexy. Number 19 talk about agriculture production. You know, privatization, decentralization, incentive, and all that new crap everybody talk about. No so sexy. Everybody get copy. Maybe NCNA print whole damn thing in couple weeks. I got plenty detail on that one for you, ayah? I know you like plenty detail, ayah? You got five pages that one. Number 23 only one page, but very, very sexy, I think. Only really big shots get that one, know what I mean? It very limit. I not get much on number 23. They tell me nothing on that one."

MacMurphy tensed and leaned forward attentively. This was one of those moments all case officers cherished—being the first to hear some highly classified information from a clandestine source. "What's it about? This sounds really promising."

"Well, it call something like," he struggled with the translation, "Secret Help Iran Position." He repeated it in Mandarin Chinese and tried to convey the meaning in English. MacMurphy nodded in understanding.

Chou continued to try to explain. "That mean we gonna help Iran, but secret. You know, we gonna stick up for those guys, but keep quiet about, ayah? Understand? Like secret help. I don't know. When you read you see. Your guys translate very good. They gonna get it, no sweat."

MacMurphy smiled. "Thanks, Chou. They always appreciate the clarity of your reports. They'll get it . . ."

"Anyway, like I say, very close hold. I can't get too much. I not on distribution list. Only big shots. And nobody outside MSS. Only MSS big shots can read. Maybe ambassador, I don't know. I got to see title of Chung-fa on envelope on chief's desk. Then I hear him and Ma, you know, deputy Ma, talk about in Ma's office. Ma allas talk too loud. He is loudmouth sonofabitch. He shout alla time. Asshole . . ." The agent's voice rose as his personal feelings came to the fore, but he censored himself abruptly, sighed, and shook his shoulders. He lapsed into silence, seeming to reflect a bit, and then continued.

"Where I was? Oh yeah. So he shouting something about we help Iran, then we get cheap oil. Ma say something like: 'What about embargo?' Then chief say something, then Ma shout: 'But what we gonna do if UN find out?' I don't know what chief was saying.

"Oh yeah, almost forgot . . . Ma also say something about fifty million euros and Paris. That is lotta money, but maybe that not related to rest of talk. I dunno. But I think so . . ."

"What do you think it means?" MacMurphy leaned forward intently. He wanted to see if there was more information to be had. This business about fifty million euros certainly was intriguing.

"You want me guess?"

"Of course I do. You know I value your opinions. Just as long as you remember to differentiate between what you see or hear or read, in other words, sourced information, and what you think about it—your opinion. You know, we've talked about this many times before . . ."

"Yes, teacher," Chou nodded, a small smile playing across his lips. But it disappeared quickly as he considered his answer to the question at hand. "I think it mean China and Iran have some kind deal. Oil for some kind secret help. Iran in deep shit now. I don't think China can afford give open support Iran, but China need oil and technology bad, and Iran already saying it willing to give oil, free, to third world countries who willing break U.N. embargo to get it. And don't forget Iran buys lots and lots Chinese weapons, and lots of talk about nuclear cooperations. Lots meetings on that. China need hard currency, and Iran always pay in gold or green, ayah?"

"Makes sense."

"You bet it make sense. Don't forget Chinese leadership just like whores, ayah? Just like French—they always act in own damn self interest. Whores, all them . . ."

MacMurphy, the supposed French journalist, nodded his agreement with Chou's assessment of Mac's alleged homeland. "Anything else?" he prompted.

"Only one thing. I don't write it because I don't know if it relate."

"What's that?"

"I told you Ma say something about Paris. Well, Huang Tsung-yao's name is on summer transfer list. You know, he been head of MSS covert action section, secret propaganda section, something like that. He in Beijing long time, maybe ten years. Now he going to be station chief Paris. He's good guy. Very smart, straight-shooter type. He very well-connected. But he had big trouble during Cultural Revolution and then again someplace in Africa about ten years ago, and he not trusted by MSS ever since. They give him real shit jobs in covert action section and can't leave country. But he real smart guy and still rise to top of covert action. Now I guess everything okay again. Maybe his connections help him get rehabilitated because Paris MSS chief of station is big job. Very important job. Everybody happy for him. He really good guy, that Tsung-yao."

"Interesting." MacMurphy's mind raced to put the facts together into some kind of order. "But . . . why do you think there's a connection?"

"Maybe no connection at all, ayah? Maybe just coincidence. But Chung-fa say 'secret action' and our number-one secret action guy going Paris make me think. I dunno, then fifty million euros and Paris . . . I don't know . . . maybe nothing . . ." His voice trailed off and he shrugged, out of knowledge and out of further ideas.

"Hmmm . . . It's definitely worth looking into, anyway." MacMurphy jotted notes furiously on his yellow pad. He glanced at his watch. "Now I think we'd better break and let you get back to your office." He rose to signal that the meeting was over.

MacMurphy led Chou to the door. The two men shook hands warmly. "Take care, little brother," said Mac in Mandarin Chinese.

"You too, older brother. See you next time." They embraced and Mac checked the hallway through the cracked door and, seeing it clear, allowed Chou to slip out of the safehouse and down the hall.

CHAPTER 28

MacMurphy retraced his steps from the safehouse back to Lindy's restaurant in Kowloon. He hurried. As far as his surveillants knew, he had been at lunch all this time. But he didn't want to push his luck. Also, in reality he had not eaten a thing, and his stomach was beginning to protest that omission.

Cautiously he peered around for any sign of Dopey, Grumpy, or Gimpy. After verifying that surveillance was not at the rear entrance of the arcade, he slipped up the back way to the restaurant.

As he approached the entrance to Lindy's he checked his watch and noted that exactly one hour and twenty-two minutes had passed since he had left the arcade to see Chou. He decided ample time had passed to persuade Dopey and the boys that he had had lunch, though any more time would surely arouse suspicions. Opting to forgo what would have had to be a *very* hasty sandwich, Mac instead beat it directly back to the station.

He had exciting information—intelligence and operational information—and he was anxious to get it on the wire to Langley. And right now, that need overrode the needs of his growling, empty stomach.

Thinking longingly of a stuffed Reuben sandwich or perhaps a thick slice of meatloaf with a piled-high portion of mashed potatoes and gravy, MacMurphy exited the building sucking on a toothpick he had carried with him. As he turned toward Nathan Road, he spotted Gimpy and Dopey—Grumpy would be up the road behind him—and, despite the fact that his stomach was once again rumbling, belched visibly for added ffect.

The Chinese are certainly ones to appreciate orifice clearing—of all sorts. The team trailed him all the way back to the Consulate; Mac could have written their surveillance report for them.

CHAPTER 29

The DDO's office is located on the seventh floor of the original CIA Headquarters building in Langley, Virginia. The man sitting in the office at the moment was Edwin Rothmann.

Rothmann was a legend in the Agency. A battered and scarred behemoth of a man, he looked like an overweight linebacker or an out-of-shape body builder but possessed one of the finest minds in the outfit.

The Agency was his life, and he had held the DDO job, the head of the clandestine service, for almost as long as MacMurphy had been a member of the Agency; nine action-packed years through a series of revolving door DCIs. He was a CIA institution.

He sat behind a large table—he hated desks, not enough room to spread out—reading his morning cable traffic when MacMurphy was ushered into the office by Rothmann's widely grinning secretary. She had her arm around Mac's waist as they stood together in the doorway. "Look what I've got here, boss. Don't know how he got here or where he came from, but he says he's got an appointment. Should I let him in?" She turned and put her free arm across Mac's body as if to bar his entry.

"Where did you find this clown?" he bellowed at her. Then he hauled his great bulk around the table and enveloped Mac in a smothering Russian bear hug. Mac, although a solid 175-pound six-footer, looked like a child in Rothmann's massive arms.

"How are you, boss? It's good to see you again," said MacMurphy with genuine affection as he extricated himself from Rothmann's enthusiastic hug.

"Not too bad for a gray-haired old man. And look at you, you're getting up there yourself!" He tousled Mac's head of prematurely salt and pepper hair like a father to a son.

"Yeah, an old girlfriend used to say it made me look very 'extinguished,' Mac replied ruefully, smoothing his hair back into place.

Rothmann fondly knuckled Mac's scalp, clearly happy to see his protégé. "Come, sit down over here. We've got a lot to talk about."

They sat in comfortable leather chairs around a coffee table in a corner of the spacious, seventh floor office. The morning sun poured into the floor to ceiling windows of the room. Rothmann adjusted the blinds to shade the sitting area. MacMurphy surveyed the walls and was comforted being among the old warrior's familiar mementos.

He recognized the tattered Nazi flag Rothmann had displayed in every office he had occupied since he was a young case officer. And the French Communist Party poster that had once belonged to "Danny the Red," who led the student riots in Paris during the summer of 1968. The riots ended when French President DeGaulle threatened to shut down all the gas stations in the country so the French couldn't escape on their annual summer vacations to the "midi," the south of France.

His eyes moved over other familiar souvenirs of silent cold war espionage engagements, and of more earthy brawls and firefights fought in the jungles of Southeast Asia, and in the terror capitals of the Middle East.

Rothmann watched MacMurphy scan his treasures. He sat back, his mind bouncing from history to history, back story to back story. Every one of these souvenirs represented something to Rothmann, and he knew Mac was well familiar with many of the stories, too. Like historians and scholars since time immemorial, he used these personal "war stories" to instruct and inform younger officers of the pitfalls of being a case officer for the CIA, and how to avoid falling into them. His deep, raspy baritone voice added flavor to the stories, told with the style of a scout master speaking at a campfire.

"Remember that one over there?" he growled, indicating a poster depicting Chinese Peoples' Liberation Army troops inciting the masses to rise up against the capitalist running dog imperialist Americans. It was framed in bamboo and rusty barbed wire and displayed prominently at the far end of the room.

"Sure I do. You got that in Udorn. My old stompin' grounds . . ."

"Those were the good old days," rumbled Rothmann. He enjoyed his current position, but he missed the action of times past.

"Yeah, and I'll bet the nights weren't bad, either," replied Mac with eyebrows raised.

The pair chatted animatedly a while longer, and then Rothmann got quietly serious. He leaned over and laid a heavy hand on Mac's knee, "My boy, that report of yours caused quite a stir up here. What do you make of these China/Iran shenanigans?"

"Well, I think the Chinese and the Iranians have struck some sort of a clandestine deal—sounds like Iranian oil in return for some sort of technical and covert support. They've been dancing around for quite some time regarding nuclear cooperation as well, so that may be part of it too. And my old friend Huang Tsung-yao is being sent to Paris to help implement the thing in Europe, whatever it is. He's their covert action guru. Has been for many years. Makes sense, anyway."

Rothmann settled back heavily into his chair and clasped his hands behind his head. "That's what we think. And we think Huang may be able to give us some of the answers we're looking for. We don't know just how deeply China is involved, but we do know that Iran is becoming more and more of a thorn in our side.

"They've resumed clandestine work designed to enrich uranium, and they're testing equipment and producing hexafluoride gas." Rothmann didn't have to tell Mac that hexafluoride gas, when injected into centrifuges and spun, can be enriched to make weapons. "They've been getting hexafluoride gas from North Korea and maybe also from China. North Korea had already supplied Libya with nearly two tons of uranium before they gave up their nuclear program, and now that its market with Libya has dried up—ever since Kadafi saw the light—we think they're entering into clandestine agreements with Iran for the same purpose.

"We know for a fact that Iran is working to acquire nuclear, biological, and chemical weapons of mass destruction, as well as to build an ever-larger arsenal of ballistic missiles. And China, Russia, and North Korea are Iran's leading suppliers. This intelligence you've uncovered is a strong indication of China's continuing hand in all of this.

"But that's not all." Rothmann shifted his heavy bulk and leaned closer to MacMurphy, who was absorbing every word intently. "As you know, Iran has sent thousands of military, political, and intelligence personnel into Iraq to stir up the Shi'ites there, and more are arriving across the border every day. The Shi'ites make up more than sixty percent of the population there, you know, and Iran has a billion-dollar covert action program in place that is hugely successful in gaining their support, to the detriment of our goals there.

"The Iranian covert action strategy in Iraq since the overthrow of Saddam is to use coercion, ideology, and buckets of money to take over the institutions of Shi'ite Islam in the country. All of this runs directly counter to American objectives there. They're outspending us on covert action programs in Iraq, something I'm trying to turn around, but not having much success at thus far. The sheer mention of "covert action" these days makes those twinkies in congress cringe."

Rothmann stretched out a leg and massaged a bum knee. "Furthermore, because China has had close relations with the Iranian clerical regime for many years, Iran may have assistance from China's extensive covert intelligence resources as well. You can see where this is all leading. The combination of Iranian and Chinese political, propaganda, paramilitary, and covert action organizations working together could well overwhelm the good intentions of those many Iraqis who, with our assistance, hope to establish a stable constitutional government. We need to prevent the possibility of post-Saddam Iraq coming under the control of Iranian-backed Shi'ite extremists. That would be tragic. That would be a damn shame!

"You know this Huang fella pretty well, don't you?" Rothmann asked.

MacMurphy reflected before he answered cautiously. "Well, in a way I did . . . ten years ago. We were in Addis together. During my first overseas tour. We're about the same age. Serving in Ethiopia was no picnic in those days, so those of us on the dip circuit hung out together. An all-in-the-same-boat kind of camaraderie developed among us. The Tigreans were busy consolidating their power. We were afraid they would repeat Mengistu's terror campaigns to cleanse the country of the Amharas and former Derg members. The country was a mess, but at least the terror campaigns never occurred. The prisons were full, and a few of Mengistu's closest allies were tried and executed, but that was the extent of it."

"So you became friends." Rothmann stretched his back and neck and twirled his glasses.

"Good friends. Because Huang was under NCNA cover at the time, he had a lot more freedom than the rest of the Chinese officials assigned there. He didn't have to take all of his meals at the embassy, for example, and he had his own car to run around in. He spent a lot of time over at my house. He was good company. Very good company . . ."

"Did he display any vulnerabilities? Any recruitment handles?"

"None, sir, and believe me, I assessed the hell out of him." MacMurphy's tone was both emphatic and regretful. "We also had a thick file on him from the time he was posted in the US. He was a very successful case officer. Deeply involved in setting up dozens of hi-tech front companies, staffed mostly with Chinese Americans he recruited to assist him.

The front companies were used to collect proprietary information on US echnology."

Rothmann put a size-fourteen foot up on the coffee table and continued to massage a wrecked and aching knee. "I believe you did your homework well. You've always had a knack for recruitment operations. A dying art, I might add. So then, with no vulnerabilities, quite the opposite I would say, why did you pitch him?"

MacMurphy hesitated before responding. "I shouldn't have. I mean . . . there was a lot of pressure from Headquarters . . . I didn't want to, but . . . You're right. It was stupid. Really fucked the poor guy up in the end, too."

"Don't blame yourself. I certainly don't. Pressure from Headquarters is hard to fight. Tell me about it."

MacMurphy slid forward to the edge of his chair. "Well, as I said, we became good friends. He began breaking the rules; you know, nothing big, basically just not telling his superiors he was spending so much time with me."

MacMurphy thought back. "He used to hide his car behind a little Coptic church near my house and sneak in through the alleyway. Of course I reported the details of all of our meetings back to Headquarters. The geniuses back here really glommed on to that one. They put 'breaking the rules' together with 'meeting clandestinely' and came up with 'recruitable.' I tried to talk them out of it, but they wouldn't budge. So I saluted and pitched him."

Rothmann shook his head in disgust. "And he reported it and was immediately recalled to Beijing, where he spent the next ten years under close supervision working on covert action programs from behind a desk in Beijing."

"That's about the size of it," said MacMurphy with a short, humorless laugh. "I warned Huang not to report it . . . pleaded with him. I knew they'd pull him out if he said anything. That's always been Beijing's M.O. They figure if one of their guys gets pitched there must be a reason for it—the guy must have exhibited vulnerabilities of one sort or another. So they yanked him and screwed up his career. The poor guy didn't deserve that." Mac shook his head sadly.

Rothmann stood and worked the stiffness out of his back. He stepped over to the window and gazed out over the green woodlands that surrounded the Headquarters building. After a time he turned and said, "And you're still pissed off at the organization for making you do something you didn't want to do."

MacMurphy adjusted his position to follow Rothmann. "Sir, do you remember Bert Armstrong?"

"Good old Bert! Sure I do. Big, powerful, soft-spoken guy. Fought professionally before joining the outfit way back when. Was pretty good too. A heavyweight contender. Then he taught survival down at The Farm. What about him?"

"That's him. Bert was one of my Special Ops instructors back when I was going through the career training program. Terrific guy. He was a horticulturist, loved plants—did you know that?"

"Seems like I recall something like that. Wouldn't surprise me, anyway. He was a gentle giant. Kind of like me." He chuckled at his own joke. "So?"

"Well, Bert Armstrong taught me the single most important thing I learned during my entire twenty-six weeks down there on The Farm."

"And what was that?"

"We were down in Panama, going through the jungle survival phase of the training. Bert said you had to be careful what you ate because some things could poison you. He said if a plant didn't look edible then it probably wasn't, but the real test was in the tasting."

Rothmann returned to his chair with a knowing smile on his face.

"Have you heard this story before?"

"Maybe. I'm not sure. There are a lot of stories about old Bert. Go on." Rothmann leaned back and studied his large hands and fingers.

"So he said if you were hungry in the jungle, you should find something that looks edible and taste it. And if it tastes good you should go ahead and eat all you want. But if it tastes really bad, you should immediately spit it out because it will probably kill you.

"He said, 'God put a tongue in your mouth to stop nasty-tasting poisons from going into your stomach. So for Christ's sake, if it doesn't taste good, don't swallow it. Spit it out!' There's a clear lesson there for ife."

"And pitching Huang didn't taste good, right?"

"You got it. I should have fought it harder."

"It wouldn't have done any good . . ."

CHAPTER 30

Rothmann rose and limped over to his desk. He shuffled through a pile of cables and dispatches until he found what he was looking for. He picked up a white envelope with a bold red stripe and the words TOP SECRET running diagonally across it. He put on his reading glasses and extracted a neatly typed one-page memo and returned to his seat.

"This is from the Director," he said, tossing it to Mac. "He wants you to try it again."

"You're joking!" exclaimed Mac. He read the short memo with mounting incredulity. "This is the dumbest thing I have ever heard, boss! Huang is not, was not, will never be recruitable. Pitching him again will only further screw up his life and get us nowhere. I can't do that to him again."

Mac tossed the memo on the coffee table disdainfully. His face looked as if he'd just smelled a huge bag of week-old garbage that had been sitting out in the sun.

The DDO sat impassively across from him, allowing him to vent while peering over his glasses. When Mac was finished, he removed his glasses, rubbed the bridge of his nose with thumb and forefinger, and spoke. "Calm down, son. I agree with you—totally. However, this is a direct order from the Director. In his defense, he's reacting to pressure from the White House, Pentagon, and Foggy Bottom to find out what the hell the Chinese are up to with Iran. There's a lot at stake here, and you've opened a Pandora's Box with that report of yours, Mac."

Rothmann pondered, rubbing his chin and twirling his glasses. "But . . . while we can't ignore his order, we may be able to work out some sort of a compromise, a *modus vivendi*, that will give us a bit more breathing room."

"What have you got in mind?"

Rothmann shot Mac a conspiratorial grin—he had obviously given this idea a great deal of thought.

"The Director knows just enough about operations to make him dangerous. He's familiar with terminology and that sort of crap, but he hasn't got the foggiest about how to plan and actually run an op. All he knows is that he's under extraordinary pressure from the White House to find out what the hell China and Iran are cooking up, and that Huang, who is accessible through you, could supply most, if not all, of the answers. He put those things together and came up with this piece of crap." Rothmann lifted and shook the memo for emphasis.

Revolted by the prospect, Mac impatiently broke in. "I understand what he wants to do, boss, and why, but doesn't he realize that this kind of approach simply won't work? In the first place, Huang wouldn't be stupid enough to reestablish contact with me. He knows they'd jerk him out of there again so fast he wouldn't know what hit him. There's no way he'd let me get close to him anymore."

"I told him exactly that," said Rothmann. "His answer was, and I quote, 'You figure it out—just do it.'

"So we have a little leeway there. I'm pretty sure I can convince him to let us hold off on the actual pitch until we are able to take a new look at Huang—do a reassessment, figure out how and where to hit him again, you know . . . As long as it doesn't take too long, that is . . . The sonofabitch won't stand for any long delays . . . of that much I'm certain. Too much political pressure, and as you know he's a political hack."

"How're we going to do that? Do we have anyone close to Huang now? Any good access agents?"

"Of course not," growled Rothmann. "How could we get anyone close to him when he's been under wraps in Beijing for the past ten years?"

"That's what I thought." Mac sat back, glanced down at the memo, then back to the DDO. "So you're thinking about a technical operation—an audio op." It was not a question.

"Exactly. A successful technical penetration of his office could give us an updated operational assessment of the man and time to plan a decent follow-on operation—or provide something concrete to justify backing off the guy. Maybe it'll even give us some good hard intel we can use . . . Also, it's something even the Director would understand."

"Sounds good to me . . . reasonable. Do we have an asset out there we could use to carry something into Huang's office, or at least into the embassy?" He was gaining enthusiasm for the project.

Rothmann guffawed. "You've got to be kidding. We don't even know which office in the embassy he occupies. In fact, I don't think our station in Paris has any information at all about what goes on above the ground floor of the embassy, not to mention their COS's office.

"I've tried to get the station to do more general casing of target installations across the board, but all I get is foot-dragging. There's not much to start with. Maybe a few photos of the outside of the building, sketches and descriptions of reception rooms on the ground floor . . . things like that."

MacMurphy shook his head in disbelief. "So the station has basically got to start from scratch."

"Not the station . . . you! *You're* the guy who earned the reputation as the case officer who 'wired Paris' when you were posted there a few years back. You know the target embassy, and you're the only case officer who knows Huang. I want you out there to bug the fucking Chinese embassy, and I want it done *tout de suite* so the Director will get off my ass. *Ça va?*"

Mac stared blankly at the DDO. He had mixed emotions about returning to Paris as well as about the timing. He had served there after his Addis Ababa and Thailand tours and had gotten his fill of audio operations at that time. On top of that, he'd been looking forward to a few weeks of well-earned rest and recuperation after three stressful years in Hong Kong.

In short, he did not want to go *anywhere* right away . . . except for some R&R. He'd been very much looking forward to spending time with his recently widowed mother and friends back on Long Island where he grew up. He hadn't made one high school reunion since his graduation from Central High in Valley Stream, and now he was going to miss another one.

But he knew he could not and would not argue or whine or complain. It was simply not the way case officers responded to things. It was not in their nature—the good ones, at least. So he would salute and go where he was needed . . . especially when asked by someone like Edwin Rothmann.

The world—and the Agency—were filled with bureaucratic bunglers, chuckleheaded nincompoops . . . and then there were the Edwin Rothmanns. There weren't many of his kind, and Mac was devoted to the man.

"So that's why I'm here. You didn't just want to socialize after all," Mac smiled, eliciting a responding grin from the big man. "And what are you going to do with Burton B. Berger? Shoot him?"

With heavy sarcasm, Rothmann said, "I'm counting on you to win over the Paris station chief and make him love every moment of the time he spends supporting your operation."

"Seriously, boss, he's not going to take too kindly to someone traipsing around on his turf. He's going to want to run things himself. And frankly . . ."

"I know, I know," said the DDO, nodding his head heavily. "That sonofabitch is a real problem. The pompous ass wouldn't know an operation if it bit him on the butt. And even if he did recognize one, he couldn't run it properly because he'd be too afraid of a flap. He got where he is by talking a good line of bullshit and playing it safe, and he's not about to quit now." He shook his great head back and forth slowly.

Rothmann continued in a philosophical tone: "How bastards like him ever rise to the level of a station chief, I'll never understand. There's a whole new breed of do-nothing leadership that's taking over the Agency these days. And the bastards have a strong union, too! They protect one another. Pisses me off . . ." He fell silent and looked squarely at MacMurphy.

"Go to Paris, Mac," Rothmann said in a deep, sincere voice. "Go to Paris and get me something on Huang. Find out what the hell the Chinese are doing for the Iranians and why. Do whatever is necessary. I'll give you whatever support you need—money, people, anything—and I'll keep Burton B. Berger off your ass. *Ça va?*"

"*Ça va,* boss. I'll leave tonight."

CHAPTER 31

The flight attendant in business class gently shook MacMurphy awake as the giant 747 jumbo jet began its descent from thirty-seven thousand feet over Ireland toward Paris' Charles de Gaulle airport. Mac shook himself awake, immediately thinking ahead to the challenge that awaited him. Mac enjoyed the adrenaline rush that came with challenges, and he knew this one was going to be rough.

At that exact moment the buzz of the alarm clock penetrated the stillness of Rodney Yusef Jackson's tiny Left Bank apartment.

The man dragged his long, athletic frame out of bed, stumbled sleepily across the room, stepping on a stray high-heeled shoe in the process, and silenced the blaring annoyance of the alarm with a heavy slap.

Ever since he'd begun dating Michelle Chen, he found it more and more difficult to get out of bed in the mornings. That was why he'd had to place the alarm clock across the room—to force himself out of bed to turn it off.

He could not afford to be late for work again—he was in enough trouble with the COS already—especially on mornings like today when it was his responsibility to open the commo shack and clear the morning cable traffic for the station.

His head pounded, and his mouth tasted like a little green bug had gotten sick and died in there. He felt he could easily sleep through the rest of the day and still not be caught up. Rubbing his eyes, he stretched his naked body mightily, trying to work the kinks out of his knotted muscles. He felt like shit.

Too much cheap Marine House booze, too little sleep, and an overdose of monosodium glutamate from that little Chinese restaurant he and Michelle had eaten at the night before. The food was delicious; he overate every time. A treat, for sure, but the after-effects were a killer. And Michelle was no help, always suggesting that if it was so good, he ought to have just a little more.

Michelle, he thought, *what a number she is. There ain't nothin' to compare with these Asian chicks.* He had screwed hundreds of them over there, and now he had the best one.

He took in the sight of her, lying half-exposed in the middle of last night's rumpled playground. The morning sun illuminated one perfect breast and a sleek, tanned leg that peeked out at him from under the sheet. One almond eye opened amidst the long, silky, black hair tousled across her face. "Hmmm," she purred, arching her body seductively under the sheet.

"Ain't got time, sugar. Gotta get outahere *tout de suite*."

She slid to the side of the bed and reached out for him. He allowed himself to be drawn closer to her, and they started to kiss.

"Oh shit, Michelle," he moaned. "I'm gonna be late . . ."

"You've got time," she whispered dreamily and smiled up at him through dark, glazed eyes.

Afterwards, they lay quietly, holding each other, totally exhausted and slick with sweat. She drifted back off to sleep, but he fought the impulse. When her breathing was deep and regular, he slipped out of bed and padded to the shower.

You are one lucky bastard, Rodney Yusef Jackson, he thought as the cool spray revived him. *One lucky bastard . . .*

Indeed he was lucky. Paris was a long, long way from Cleveland, Ohio and a dead end job in an auto parts store, like the one his father had worked in for almost twenty years. Rodney had stuck it out in high school, graduated, attended community college and, lucky again, had been given a scholarship in a special program at Kent State, established for "late bloomers."

His grades had been good in the community college; more important, he had discovered, thanks to a gifted teacher, that he had a talent for mathematics and logical thinking. Even though he got bored and dropped out after two years, his partial college education had ultimately served to get him a ticket to the communications corps of the CIA and eventually to beautiful Paris.

Unfortunately, his cock started to do all the thinking when he got involved with Michelle. And his resentment at being stuck in a low-level government job, albeit in Paris, did nothing to help him think more clearly. He was smart; but his interpersonal skills were not the best, and self-discipline was definitely not one of his strengths.

None of these drawbacks had been career-enhancing. But Rodney recognized none of this. In his mind, he deserved more, and only the fact that he was black was holding him back. Racial discrimination, pure and simple . . .

How he would like to stick it to his arrogant white bosses—if only he could . . .

Rodney bounded down the three flights of his apartment building, taking the steps two at a time, and raced outside to the street, where he had parked his rattletrap Volvo. The engine started after two long, grinding tries, and he slipped an old Vanilla Ice disk into the player. The rap music blared, and he drummed the monotonous beat against the steering wheel as he pulled out into the early morning Paris traffic.

He would be at the embassy in less than fifteen minutes, which would make him only twenty minutes late for work. *Never mind*, he told himself, *or as the French say, tant pis. What can they do, fire me?* Inwardly he hoped he would get to the office before the COS and his little prick of a deputy, so his tardiness wouldn't be noticed. The bastards were obviously out to get him. *And why the fuck do they have to be such workaholics anyway? Can't they get their work done in eight hours like everyone else? Why do they have to get in so early and stay so late? Smug fuckers must be inefficient. Assholes . . .*

CHAPTER 32

Paris was already hot and sticky at this hour, promising another humid July scorcher. Traffic was light because most Parisians had already begun their yearly exodus to "*le midi*," the beaches along France's southern coast, and in the cooler mountain regions of *Provence*.

Paris was a ghost town during the months of July and August. People who lived on top of one another in the city all year long migrated to vacation places around Nice and St. Tropez and Avignon during July and August, to live on top of one another in another locale.

The wheels of government and industry simply ground to a halt. Nothing would stand in the way of a Frenchman's vacation. But Rodney and a lot of others at the American embassy liked these two months the best. They could easily find parking anywhere on the street, drive around the city without traffic snarls, and walk into most restaurants without a reservation, although only about half of them were open at any one time.

Not that Rodney could afford to go to many restaurants on his salary—communicators were among the poorest paid employees in the embassy—on the level with secretaries. And this pissed Rodney off to no end because he and the other CIA communicators were responsible for operating and maintaining all of the cryptographic equipment in the embassy.

Rodney and the other communicators were entrusted with the most sensitive classified information in the embassy. They saw everything, absolutely everything. There was no such thing as a "need to know" principle when it came to communicators. Everything passed under their eyes because it was their job to process—encrypt and decrypt and print out—every classified word in and out of the CIA station. Correspondence coming into the station was processed in the commo shack and delivered to the COS's office in clear text.

Conversely, correspondence leaving the station was prepared and brought to the commo center to be processed before being sent out to recipients worldwide. Communicators were, for every intelligence service in the world, the Holy Grail of recruitment targets.

He firmly believed that that kind of trust deserved more recognition and more money. And he was pissed off big-time that he was getting neither. Especially the money. It was a bitch to make ends meet with so little, especially in a place like Paris.

Fortunately for him, his new girlfriend, Michelle, actually preferred inexpensive Chinese restaurants and the Marine House Bar to expensive places. And Michelle's Chinese friends usually picked up their restaurant tabs, and she paid most of the Marine House bar bills anyway.

Those Chinese were very generous people—boring as hell, always wanting to talk politics and that sort of shit, but generous. So as long as they were willing to pay for everything, he put up with them. *Strange crowd*, he thought, but he could put up with a lot of their bullshit for that kind of quality pussy.

He increased the volume of the rap music, hoping to blow some more cobwebs out of his brain, and almost missed his turn onto Rue Dauphine. He careened around the corner and glanced up at the clock on the old gray stone *Conciergerie* building. It read ten past seven. He was already ten minutes late. Shit! He accelerated across the magnificent *Pont Neuf*, frightening a gaggle of street sweepers puffing on brown Bastos ciga-rettes, and sped down the *quai* toward the Place de la Concorde. He tunneled the rusting Volvo into the underground parking and jogged the remaining block back up Rue de Rivoli to the American embassy build-ing on Avenue Gabriel.

He was twenty minutes late for work when he passed the pigeon-splattered statue of old Ben Franklin in the cobblestone chancery court-yard. He pushed through the heavy oak doors into the main foyer of the chancery. The young Marine on duty called out to him as he hurried toward the elevators: "Wake up, Rotten. Your eyes look like two pee holes in a snow bank."

"Fuck you and your Marine House parties," he fired back with a grin as he entered the elevator.

He exited on the top floor and headed down the corridor past the COS's office, noting from the transome above the door that the lights were already on inside. *Fuck*, he thought. He still hoped his late arrival would go unnoticed but didn't count on it. The sonofabitchin' Berger probably checked to see if the door to the comcenter was open before going to his office. *That prick never misses a trick.*

He manipulated the combination dial on the heavy vault door and entered the commo room. Rodney thought about what excuse he would give when the inevitable chewing-out came later in the day.

Forty-five minutes later, Rodney dropped a ten-inch-high stack of precedence traffic—immediate and priority cables—on the COS's sec-retary's desk. On top of the pile was an enveloped "EYES ONLY—IMMEDIATE" cable from the DDO to the COS. Rodney had read the cable with great interest as it printed out. It was straightforward enough, simply informing Berger of MacMurphy's arrival, outlining his instruc-tions and requesting the station's support for his activities. But even Rodney caught the significance of the message, and he knew Berger would have a conniption fit when he read it. That made Rodney Yusef Jackson very happy.

CHAPTER 33

M acMurphy stepped out of the crowded metro train at the Place de la Concorde station and slipped into the herd of people meandering up through the connecting underground tunnels toward the street. Not much had changed in Paris since he'd been posted here a few years back.

Musicians and beggars still inhabited the bowels of the metro. Only their names had changed over the years; their faces and dress remained the same, and the same sounding tunes still echoed through the cavernous halls. The beggars' various pleas and ploys hadn't changed a bit, either.

He was at home in Paris. The previous day had been spent getting reacquainted with the city. Although he had passed through the city frequently on short vacations and on CIA business since his posting, it was always a thrill to return.

While the buildings and streets in a place like Hong Kong changed so rapidly that a location would often be unrecognizable from one year to the next, Paris stayed pretty much the same. Building façades and streets and landmarks almost never changed. He had worked the streets and back alleys of the city as a young case officer, and he had remained intimate with it over the years through frequent visits. Paris was his town.

The day he arrived, he had been greeted by a beautiful morning when the sun broke through the clouds during the long and expensive cab ride in from Charles de Gaulle airport, and his mood reflected the weather throughout the day. This is the way it was in Paris. There were so few gorgeous days in northern Europe that the French bloom with the sun. The rest of the time the streets were filled with long serious, dour faces of people going hurriedly about their business.

He'd spent that day of his arrival on a combination of business and pleasure, including casing for prospective meeting sites, poking around the neighborhood of the Chinese Embassy on Avenue George V, and some more general area re-familiarization.

On arrival from deGaulle, he had the cab drop him at the Port Maillot bus terminal at the western edge of the city, and then, after dumping his bags in a locker, he strolled up Boulevard Pereire into the familiar 17th *arrondissement* where he had lived during his previous tour in Paris.

He stopped for a double-espresso coffee and criossant at the Café des Ternes on the busy corner of Avenue des Ternes. He chose a small table under the awning on the sidewalk and engaged in that very *Parisienne* sport of people watching—watching people strolling by who were in turn watching people sitting in the cafés.

He focused on a handsome couple approaching along the sidewalk. The man was boring the pretty young woman in the bright orange dress with his non-stop chatter. She gazed disinterestedly past him at the people seated in the café. Then her eyes met Mac's. Their eyes locked and came alive in a flirt as she continued to walk, neither wanting to break off the moment, until the still-chattering head of her companion broke their line of sight. Then, just as the couple passed, the woman glanced back over her shoulder at the handsome man sitting alone in the café, and winked. This was Paris.

Mac allowed himself a brief fantasy. He mentally chatted up the young woman and assayed the ways to get to know her more intimately, seeing himself ensconced in her low-lit living room, a glass of wine in her hand and another in his, the bedroom door provocatively half-open . . . But even as he indulged in this delightful what-if, his eyes and his brain remained conscious of his surroundings.

A case officer could never let his guard down totally. Mac had to remain ever watchful, ever alert. And so, while part of his mind enjoyed the image of the young girl in an advanced state of being *en déshabillé*, her dress slipping invitingly to the floor, another part of his mind was watchfully checking out the faces and the actions of the people all around him.

After fortifying himself with another cup of the strong French espresso, Mac continued his stroll up the Boulevard Pereire. He turned off onto Rue Laugier and then a bit further on turned into the courtyard of a familiar small six-story apartment complex that specialized in short-term *pied-à-terre* furnished rentals.

He had rented several safehouses there in the past. The last time had been on a TDY visit about two years ago, and he hoped the concierge would still remember him. The package of alias documents and other paraphernalia he had had pouched to the Station from Headquarters would not arrive for a couple more days, and he needed a safe place to stay now. Above all, he most certainly didn't want his true name on any hotel registration slip.

He walked through the courtyard toward the rear of the complex and knocked on the door of the concierge's apartment. Mme. Fabry opened the door and squinted up at the grinning, handsome young man in the light tan suit filling the doorway in front of her.

It took a moment for the synapses of her old brain to connect, but then the flicker of recognition sparked in her eyes, and she blurted, "*Ah,*

Monsieur LeMen, comment ça va? How long has it been? *Entrez, entrez, mon vieux.*"

Mac embraced the old woman and kissed her three times on the cheeks—*trois fois à la campagne*—as is the custom among old friends from the countryside. She offered him a cup of strong espresso coffee, and he accepted gratefully. His body had not yet adjusted to the time change, nor had he slept well on the plane. He was very appreciative of the caffeine's help in staying alert.

Mme. Fabry rented him a small furnished *pied-à-terre* on the fourth floor, overlooking the courtyard and away from the noises of the bustling Rue Laugier. Mac, alias Barry LeMen, French-Canadian businessman, gave her a month's rent in advance, in cash.

Later that evening, he returned with his bags and crashed for the night. Before falling asleep, he thought about how he would handle his meeting with Burton B. Berger in the morning. But he hadn't long to think before he fell soundly asleep, exhausted.

When he slept, he dreamed not of the flirtatious young lady he had made eye contact with earlier, but of someone who had a much stronger hold on him—Wei-wei Ryan . . .

CHAPTER 34

Mac emerged from the *bouche de metro* and squinted into the bright sun over the Place de la Concorde. He crossed Rue de Rivoli and walked in the shade of the Rivoli arcade the short block to the US Embassy on the corner of Rue Boissy d'Anglas and Avenue Gabriel.

He showed his black diplomatic passport to the young Marine Lance Corporal at the entrance of the chancery. It was 8:30am, and the lobby was filled with people hurrying to their offices. He rode the crowded elevator up to the fourth floor and entered the door to the office marked "Assistant to the Ambassador."

He stepped into the room and stood quietly in front of the desk of the COS's secretary, Wei-wei Ryan. His mission was no longer the sole thought occupying his head. Wei-wei's delicate beauty had neither changed nor diminished one iota. And Mac, as a connoisseur of beauty, showed a great appreciation for the half-Chinese woman with the incredible shiny black hair who sat behind the desk in front of him.

The station communicator, Rodney Jackson, had just dropped a large stack of morning cable traffic on her desk—neither looked up. Mac stood there patiently, once again stunned by the beauty of the petite Eurasian woman as she began to sort through the morning cable traffic.

It was Rodney who looked up first and saw Mac standing there. "Hey you ol' sonavabitch, how the hell ya doin', Mac?" They greeted in a slapping high five.

"Great, Rotten. What's happening, ol' buddy?"

Wei-wei burst from her chair, almost knocking Rodney off his feet. "Mac!" She leaped into his arms, and he swung her around, her long, shiny black hair flowing outward like polished silk.

"Weren't you expecting me?" He put her down, kissed her warmly on the cheek, and hugged her once again.

"Yesterday, you dope! You were expected yesterday. What happened to you?" The darkened, worried eyes showed that genuine concern marked her question, not mere curiosity . . . and more concern than her official position warranted.

Mac put a strong hand on the back of her head and pulled her to him. Wei-wei held him tight. "I was worried about you!" she breathed softly.

Rodney retreated out the door. "Ah'll leave you two lovebirds to reacquaint yourselves. See' ya at the Marine House, Mac?"

"Sure, Rodney. See you there Friday. They still have happy hour on Fridays, don't they?"

"Is the Pope still Catholic?" Rodney closed the door behind him, and Mac turned his attention back to Wei-wei.

"I had some things to take care of before coming in, but tonight I'm all yours. You are free for dinner, aren't you?"

"Tonight and every night, sailor." She pecked him on the cheek, then again gently on the lips. "But now you'd better get in to see the boss. He also expected you yesterday, so you've got some explaining to do."

"Screw him," said Mac offhandedly.

"You haven't changed. Wait here. I'll see if he can see you now." She reluctantly pushed away from Mac.

She knocked softly on the COS's door and gracefully slipped halfway inside, holding the door partially open behind her. "Mr. MacMurphy is here, sir. May I send him in, or would you like me to set up an appointment for later in the day?"

"It's about time. Send him in," said the precise voice from within the room, "and ask Mr. Little to step in here as well."

Wei-wei backed out and held the door for Mac. "He's all yours," she said, adding a whispered "Good luck!" Then she turned and walked away, closing the door behind him.

Mac advanced into the lion's den.

Berger stood up behind his desk and fixed Mac with a superior stare. He held out a long, delicate hand to Mac. "Welcome back to Paris," he said with raised eyebrows. "I expected you yesterday. Was your flight delayed?"

Mac grasped the extended soft white fingers, shook the limp hand once in the European manner and dropped into one of the two chairs in front of the COS's desk.

He knew Berger liked to intimidate people, but like most bullies he disliked direct confrontations. So Mac decided to be confrontational until Berger backed off.

"Thanks. It's good to be back. No, my flight was on time. It landed yesterday at 9:10 in the morning."

"Then where have you been?"

"Busy . . . I had a few things to take care of, find a place to stay and all, but now I'm here. Can we get started? I don't want to take up too much of your time and I've got a long list of things we need to cover." Mac calmly pulled a small notebook and pen out of his shirt pocket and sat poised to begin.

Showing his displeasure, Berger pressed his long, thin frame back into his tufted leather executive chair. He attempted to stare Mac down, to gain control of the situation, but Mac calmly returned his gaze while motioning with the hand that held the notebook, as if to ask, "Shall we begin?"

Berger unhappily swung his chair back and forth as he regarded Mac and used a long, slender index finger to push his glasses back up his narrow nose. His finger trembled ever so slightly, displaying nervousness and pique. He folded his delicate hands gently on his paunch before responding. "We'll wait for my deputy, Mr. Little. He waited all day yesterday for you."

Mac said, "Okay," in an amiable voice that implied he didn't know he was being rebuked, which only heightened Berger's pique.

The tension in the room was broken by the arrival of Bob Little.

"I think you know my deputy. Robert Little, Harry MacMurphy," announced Berger, gesturing limply from one to the other like a priest giving a benediction.

Little, a balding, pear-shaped fellow in his late-fifties with a thin, gray mustache, scurried across the room to shake hands with Mac. He uttered a high-pitched "Hello Mac" and dropped into the other chair in front of Berger's desk.

CHAPTER 35

Mac knew Bob Little—"Little Bob," as he was called by the troops—very well. As a young, first tour officer, Little had been assigned to Siem Reap, Cambodia during the months preceding the fall of the country to the Khmer Rouge in 1975. The story of his posting there was well-known among the case officer corps within the Agency.

The danger of living in the midst of the Khmer Rouge had paralyzed him with fear. And he hated the heat, the smells, and the Asian people. All he wanted to do was return to a nice cushy post in Europe. "Europe is my specialty," he would say in his high-pitched, staccato voice. "I've got a photographic memory, two European languages, and a PhD in history from Harvard. Why should I sit in a stinking hole in Southeast Asia, dodging bullets with smelly knuckle-draggers for the sake of nasty little Asians? It's a total waste of my talents."

Bob Little never subscribed to the case officer's "go anywhere, do anything, according to the needs of the service" credo. With few exceptions—Burton B. Berger being one of them—Little was disliked and distrusted by subordinates, peers, and superiors alike. Bob Little stood out in a profession where there were very few real bad officers. But he was bright—very, very bright. And that's what had kept him afloat during his thirty-odd years within the case officer corps.

What did I do to deserve this? Mac thought. *A double dose. And I'm expected to go over them and through them and around them for Edwin Rothmann. Why is the worst enemy always us?* He sat back in his chair heavily, reflecting that the toughest part of his task was likely to be dealing with these two. His assignment vis-à-vis Huang would seem a piece of cake by comparison. He wasn't looking forward to what lay ahead . . . starting with this meeting.

"Have you begun?" squeaked Little, his eyes darting back and forth between the two men. He sat forward on the edge of his chair, feet flat on the floor, hands clasped between his knees, back erect.

"Not really," said the COS, slowly turning in his chair. "Mr. Mac-Murphy was about to tell us what he needs in the way of support. Please begin, Mr. MacMurphy." Berger settled back into the plush leather and directed his attention to his manicured fingernails.

"Is the security system activated?" asked MacMurphy quietly.

Berger glared at Mac briefly, reviled at the realization that MacMurphy had one-upped him by remembering something crucial that he himself had forgotten. He turned to his deputy, waved his hand in the direction of the back of the room, and declared: "Fix it."

Little slid off his chair and hurried across the room to a small credenza in the corner. He opened one of the draws and flipped a switch that illuminated a lamp on the top of the table and caused a slight, almost inaudible electrical hum to sound in the room.

The hum was caused by an electrical current charging through thousands of feet of copper wire running behind the paneled walls, ceiling, and floor of the room. The security system was designed to interfere with any audio signals entering or leaving the room. The lamp simply indicated the device was activated and the room was shielded from intrusive ears. It was routinely used to mask all sensitive conversations in the room, and the COS had completely forgotten about it. Mac's reminder would not help his relationship with Burton B. Berger, but the need for security trumped all in this case.

MacMurphy began. "I assume the DDO outlined for you what he wants me to try to accomplish while I'm here."

"He did," said Berger, still intensely interested in his fingernails.

"Yes," Little added, "he said you were to attempt to recruit Huang Tsung-yao, and the station was to help you orchestrate a recruitment scenario."

"May I see the cable, Mr. Berger?" asked Mac coolly.

"No need. Mr. Little knows perfectly well what the cable said. Don't you Robert?" Little squirmed and started to speak, but Berger held up a delicate hand, cutting him off. The hand gracefully turned on its wrist toward MacMurphy.

"Whether you pitch him or not will depend upon the sort of vulnerability data you are able to obtain on the man, *n'est-ce pas*? And you need the station's support to get the information you need, right?"

"Right," said MacMurphy.

"Then what do you need?" Berger did not look up, preferring to continue the examination of his fingernails.

Little fidgeted quietly, wanting to speak.

Mac crossed his legs, glanced down at his notebook, and began.

"I'm going to need an updated assessment of Huang, and I can't get it first-hand. He'd bolt at the first sight of me. You know the story about the pitch in Ethiopia. So I'm thinking about an audio penetration of his office."

"No way!" blurted Little, "Can't be done. It's too risky. We've looked at the Chinese Embassy before, and it's impossible. They've got . . ."

"Excuse me, Little Bob," MacMurphy interrupted, "I'm not asking you." His black eyes sliced into Little.

"Didn't the DDO mention the possibility of an audio op?" Mac's question was directed at the COS, and his eyes remained cold, black and unblinking.

"Yes, he did," Berger replied reluctantly, showing the first real signs of discomfort. "Please continue."

"I'll need to study everything you have on the embassy and its occupants—casings, contact reports, anything on file, including anyone with access to the embassy or any of the Chinese officials."

"No problem. You may study anything you like, just as long as you take no action whatsoever without my prior approval. Is that understood?" Berger leaned forward and placed his elbows on his desk, hands clasped under his chin, and waited intently for MacMurphy's response.

After a long silence and unblinking stare between the two men, with Little fidgeting in his chair, Mac replied. "I will adhere strictly to the orders given to me verbally by the DDO at headquarters. The same orders that are outlined in his cable to you. And I would appreciate your full cooperation in fulfilling those very specific orders. You'll be kept in the loop."

The stare-down continued. The COS leaned back into his chair and, looking away from Mac in the direction of Bob Little, said, "Ask my secretary to pull together whatever we have on record. What else do you want?"

Mac didn't hesitate. "I'll also need a couple of support assets. Guys familiar with audio ops. I had in mind TRAVAIL and GUNSHY. I've worked with both of them before when I was posted here at the station, and they're both professionals, perfectly suited for what I have in mind."

The cryptonyms did not ring any bells with the COS. He nodded to his deputy, who was itching to speak. "Impossible," Little Bob squeaked. "They've both been terminated. You can't use terminated assets."

Mac glared at Little and turned disgustedly to the COS. His eyes asked the question.

"Were they terminated with prejudice?" asked Berger.

"Um, no." Little's phenomenal memory kicked in, and he recited verbatim excerpts from the 201 files.

"GUNSHY was terminated in late-November 2002 after failing to pass his routine polygraph exam. The issue was unauthorized disclosure of the nature of his work to a girlfriend. His true name is François Leverrier, mid-thirties, French citizen, wealthy playboy. He worked for the station for about five years as a part-time investigative asset and access agent."

"And TRAVAIL?" Berger asked.

"TRAVAIL was terminated earlier the same year, I believe in February 2002. He also failed his routine poly. The issue was mismanagement of funds—cheating on his expenses. He's a real con man. True name is Pol Giroud, nickname 'Le Belge,' late forties, early fifties, Belgian citizen, unemployed. He worked for the station as a full-time investigative asset and safehouse keeper. He was on board a long time. Ten, maybe as long as fifteen years."

It figures, Mac thought. He and the case officers before and after him had always protected these two guys from themselves. GUNSHY liked to brag about his "secret agent" status. It was all he had—the only real contribution he had ever made to society. Everything else was handed to him on a silver platter by his aristocratic family. He had done great things against the North Korean target during the time Mac handled him. One of these things resulted in the bugging of the North Korean embassy, a signal achievement for both case officer and agent.

Mac and GUNSHY'S other case officers realized his need for recognition and would spend time with him, stroke him, giving him the recognition he craved, so he didn't feel the need to seek it elsewhere, like with his many girlfriends.

As for TRAVAIL, Mac and his other handlers knew he tended to pad his expenses a bit, but by keeping him on a short leash, which meant not giving him a revolving fund and reimbursing him for expenses on a weekly basis, his fudging was always kept to a bare minimum.

TRAVAIL's crafty "people" instincts resulted in the recruitment of a cleaning woman at the Vietnamese embassy while he worked under Mac's direction. Information provided by the asset, including trash and classified correspondence left lying around, resulted in reams of excellent intelligence reports. The Berger/Little management team had obviously dropped the ball on both counts and consequently lost two excellent assets.

Take away the glue and things come unstuck, he thought.

Mac directed his next question at Bob Little. "You mean to tell me you terminated two of the best support assets this station has ever had because one padded his expense account and the other told his girlfriend about his affiliation with us? What do you guys want, missionaries?"

"We certainly don't want mercenaries," spat back Little.

"Bob's right." Berger lectured Mac. "Times have changed. Under the new DCI's policies, we can no longer afford to do business with cheats and braggarts. I agree with the DCI. We must recruit patriots, not venal wheeler-dealers who are only out for themselves. But I'm sure you disagree. You would prefer to deal with low-lifes. People who sleep with dogs get fleas. But if you want them, if you want those two guys, I will not sit here and debate morality with you. You can have them, but they'll be your responsibility, not mine."

Berger brushed his fingers against each other as if washing his hands of the whole messy affair and looked like he'd just been obliged to suck on a lemon.

"Fine," said MacMurphy, surprised at the easy victory. "I'll put them on short-term contracts, two or three months, so there won't be any termination problems for the station when I've finished with them. And since they're not now working for the station, I won't be taking anything away from any ongoing programs."

"Fine," said Berger. "Get their files from Ms. Ryan." The COS turned to his deputy. "I assume the re-contact plans are in their 201 files."

"Oh yes, sir." Little brightened. He excelled at the bureaucratic aspects of case officering, and organizing the station's files shortly after his arrival had been one of his pet projects. "Every agent's 201 file has an up-to-date re-contact plan stapled in plain view on top of the left-hand side. I have personally reviewed the file of every terminated and active asset to assure there are no slip-ups in this regard."

"Good for you, Little Bob," Mac said. *God help us,* he thought.

Little shrank back into his chair, and Berger asked if there was anything else MacMurphy needed. He was eager to conclude the meeting.

"Not unless you can think of something else. Are there any assets I'm not aware of who might be able to help? Chinese access agents or anyone for that matter who has regular access to the Chinese officials or the embassy building?"

Berger looked over at Little, who shook his head. Based on his body language, MacMurphy suspected Little might be lying but decided this was not the time for another confrontation. He had enough to get started, and there were other ways to get the information he wanted out of the station.

MacMurphy stood up. "Thanks for your help so far. I'll get the files I need and spend the rest of the day reading-in if that's all right with you." He directed his remarks at the COS and did not offer his hand to either of them.

"It's fine with me," Berger said flatly. "There's an empty office across the hall you can use. O'Hara's. He's away on home leave. My secretary will show you." Without another word, the imperious COS turned his attention back to the stack of cable traffic on his desk. Little and Mac-Murphy let themselves out of the office.

CHAPTER 36

Mac walked down to the embassy canteen and got himself a cup of coffee. He struggled to contain his rage, exasperation, and contempt. What neither Berger nor Little understood—because they were both disasters when it came to handling assets—was that the very characteristics and weaknesses of both François Leverrier and Pol Giroud that they disparaged was a key part of why these two agents were so useful.

In Leverrier's case, the flamboyant "playboy" image had value as an excellent, natural cover. Leverrier was the son of parents who were minor members of the aristocracy, and he had grown up among the wealthy in St. Tropez.

His father had "retired" from the family textile business in Lyons (he had actually been pushed out by other members of the family) and moved to the Cote d'Azur, where he spent his time playing the bourse, losing a considerable amount of his inheritance, and chasing women who were much younger versions of his wife.

Marie Leverrier had been, briefly and unsuccessfully, a model and a writer for one of the more sensational French magazines until she married Alain Leverrier. François was an only child—largely because his mother found the idea of the stretch marks that came along with additional pregnancies unappealing.

Francois had grown up spoiled by servants and largely neglected by his parents. He had also become accustomed to living in a style that the diminishing family money increasingly could not support. After squeaking through college in Clermont-Ferrand, he had drifted into a job as a yacht broker. That also was not a great success. But it had led to the initial connection with Mac, during an op that required some modest maritime assets—a Zodiac and a small ketch.

François had been delighted to arrange a charter with a distinctly funny smell about it—and Mac had sensed that here was a man who needed a mission. Mac had just the right one for him. It helped that some money was involved—but the real incentive was that Mac could offer Leverrier some work that gave his life some meaning, and spiced it up with a bit of intrigue.

His ability to solve one of Leverrier's more serious problems—the death of a young lady friend who had drowned while swimming off a yacht owned by the charter outfit in Cannes, a boat which Leverrier had not been authorized to use, even for erotic adventures—had, thanks to Mac, been hushed up. Mac had his man held firmly in the vice grip of persuasion and encouragement—he could ruin him and he could pay him. And play him . . .

Le Belge was another matter entirely. His parents had been teenage members of the Resistance in World War Two. He grew up hearing accounts of heroism during the German occupation—many of which were even true. His taste for adventure and glory was not slaked by service in the peacetime Belgian army. After his military service he went to work as a line engineer on the Belgian state railroad and remained in essentially the same job until he was forced into early retirement at the age of forty.

Pol had recently married a girl he had met in the army and was thinking about starting a family, but supporting a wife and children on his meager railroad pension would be a struggle, so Pol went about looking for a new career. He thought sales would be a good fit for him because everyone always complimented him on his ability to get along with people. He had a quick smile, a self-deprecating wit, and a keen ability to quickly assess people and bring them around to his way of thinking. He was always on the pudgy side but since his marriage (Marie was a great cook) and lack of activity he began to put on weight at an accelerating rate.

Then, at a party on New Year's Eve in 1993, he ran into an old army buddy, Henri Duclos, who was visiting Waterloo from Paris. Duclos told Pol that he was doing "investigative" work there, but refused to say for whom. He said his firm was looking for native French speakers who were not French citizens and asked Pol if he would be interested in joining him. Pol, intrigued both by the chance of a respectable income paying job and the mysteriousness of the offer, said he would.

Pol was eventually contacted and interviewed by the "security firm" his friend worked for, polygraphed in Paris, and told, when he was hired, that his real employer was the American CIA.

His initial duties would be to rent and occupy a safehouse in the Marais section of Paris. He would be required to maintain the apartment and vacate it at certain prescheduled times during the week when clandestine agent meetings would be held there. That was the extent of his duties.

He would be paid a decent salary and would have free rent. He was told he could not bring anyone else into the apartment, including his wife, which meant Marie would have to remain in Waterloo. But the money was good, and the excitement of working clandestinely for the CIA, even in a mundane capacity, was very, very intriguing.

Pol, feeding his wife the cover story that he was a traveling salesman in France, remained in Paris as a safehouse keeper, commuting to Belgium on free weekends, for the next three years. Then, in 1997, he was introduced to a new case officer, "Mac" MacMurphy. The two hit it off immediately.

Recognizing Pol's crafty "people" instincts, MacMurphy began to use Pol in more and more of an investigative and principal agent capacity. Among other things, he targeted Pol against the local cleaning people who worked in various embassies. Under Mac's direction, Pol met and established rapport with a number of them, and then was able to develop and recruit two of them as agents for the CIA.

One cleaned the Vietnamese embassy and the other the Laotian embassy. Using these two assets he was able first to collect and read all of the trash from the embassies, which resulted in a number of decent but low-level intelligence reports. With his assistance, the Agency was finally able to use Pol's assets to plant bugs inside the embassies, which resulted in significant high-level intelligence.

Pol was on a roll. By the time Mac rotated out of Paris, Pol had become one of Paris Station's top investigative assets. He was also making substantially more money and Marie had given him two beautiful tow-headed daughters to dote upon.

Unfortunately, his luck did not hold. Mac's replacement as Pol's case officer was an unimaginative plodder and a stickler for scrupulous accounting. Consequently, Pol's operational performance suffered and his sloppy accounting led to his termination.

Pol found work through his brother-in-law as a sales representative for a Parisian plumbing supply company, and brought Marie and the girls to Paris to join him.

Now Mac was determined to reinstall him as an agent and bring him back into the game. They were both good men. They should not have been dismissed due to minor character flaws. That's what agent handling is all about . . .

CHAPTER 37

Mac spent the rest of the day reading files in O'Hara's office. Wei-wei brought him a sandwich and a Coke from the cafeteria, and he ate lunch at his desk. She had thought of eating with him and keeping him company, but when she saw how engrossed he was, and how much reading he had to do, she quietly slipped back out and ate her sandwich at her own desk.

Mac finally finished at seven that evening. He had taken pages of notes and had his next few days clearly planned out in advance. He waited while Wei-wei Ryan locked up the office; everyone else was long gone. They went down to the embassy lounge in the basement of the chancery and relaxed in comfortable black leather chairs over cocktails—vodka tonic for him and a kir for her—before heading off in Wei-wei's faded old blue Peugeot to dinner at a small *auberge* named Chez Fred in the 17th *arrondissement*.

They dined on escargots and veal in white wine sauce and consumed a bottle of a delightful new Fleuri. And they talked and talked and talked . . .

Afterward, Wei-wei brought him back to her apartment. There had never been any question as to where he would sleep that night. Their tempestuous affair had been raging for years, and the intensity of their affection for one another had grown rather than diminished despite the many geographical separations and reunions.

Margret "Wei-wei" Ryan was the product of the love (and marriage) between a stunning Hong Kong Chinese ballet dancer and a dashing young American Army officer who rose rapidly through the ranks of the military to eventually retire with flag rank as a Brigadier General. And she was delightfully possessed of the best that both cultures, and both parents, had to offer.

She had been born in Hong Kong, where her father had been posted to the Defense Attaché's Office at the American Consulate General. Colin Ryan was just a major at the time, but he was already what they called "an old China hand." He possessed a master's degree in Far East History from Stanford and spoke almost perfect Mandarin Chinese.

His parents had been Mormon missionaries in China so he learned Mandarin as a young boy while they were posted to Shanghai. His language skills were later honed to perfection at the Army's Monterey language school. Consequently, he spent most of his later career moving from one attaché post to another in the Far East, which suited him just fine.

He encouraged his only daughter to grow up in tune with both sides of her heritage. She attended International Schools in Hong Kong, Tokyo, Bangkok, and Taipei, as well as public schools in Arlington, Virginia, during the two tours her father was in the States working at the Pentagon.

She studied Mandarin and French and picked up some Cantonese and a little Thai and Japanese on her own. She excelled in high school, graduating at the top of her class, and possessed both book knowledge and the kind of education that comes with travel and being exposed to many facets of many cultures. She also had been gifted with remarkable poise and self confidence. Yet the most amazing component of it all was that, due to her warm personality, rather than her classmates envying her and giving her a hard time, they adored and respected her. Everyone wanted to be Wei-wei Ryan's friend.

By the time Wei-wei Ryan had graduated from high school, the family was back in Virginia. She decided to take a job as a part-time secretary for the CIA while studying International Relations afternoons and evenings at nearby George Mason University. But after completing only two years of college, she got a heavy dose of wanderlust (something else she'd inherited from her father) and applied for and was accepted for a branch secretarial position in the CIA station in Bangkok, Thailand.

It was there that she met "Mac" MacMurphy and immediately fell head over heels in love with the dashing young case officer. She didn't get to see nearly enough of him, though, because while she was stuck down in Bangkok, he was stationed up-country in Udorn, one of the provincial bases across the Mekong River from Vientiane, Laos.

They did see enough of each other to ignite a spark, though, and once ignited, the flame burned on. She and Mac had been seeing each other whenever they could ever since.

When her tour was over in Bangkok, Wei-wei Ryan asked for and received a lateral assignment to Paris to be close to Mac, who had been assigned there after Thailand.

A year later he completed his tour in Paris and left for a new assignment in Tokyo; she followed a year later. She then followed him on to Singapore and then back to Washington for a headquarters assignment.

But when Mac was selected to be Chief of Station in Hong Kong, the outfit put its foot down; no COS was going to have his girlfriend working for him in the same office—if the rule applied to husbands and wives, it would apply to "close and continuing relationships" as well. So he went off to Hong Kong, and she talked the Agency into sending her back to Paris.

There had never been any mention of marriage on his part, so she had thought this separation might just be the end of it—until now.

CHAPTER 38

Wei-wei lived on the Left Bank in a charming little one-bedroom walk-up in the 7th *arrondissement*. She had inherited the embassy-leased apartment from her predecessor and loved it. It was on the fourth floor—the walk up was good exercise except when she was loaded down with groceries—of a quaint old six-story building with wrought iron balconies. The building was tucked away on Rue Chevert, a quiet little street nestled between the Ecole Militaire and the Hôtel des Invalides, two of France's most celebrated military sites.

By the time they reached the fourth floor, Mac and Wei-wei were puffing from the walk up and flushed from the wine and food they had consumed during the evening. Mac was mellow, and Wei-wei was tipsy and feeling very loving and sexy. They entered the apartment, and she locked the door behind them. Then she turned to him, slipping easily into his familiar arms, and they kissed gently, savoring one another.

"Yum, even better than I remembered," he said.

"Must be the escargots." She gave him a follow-up peck and turned. "Fix you a drink, sailor?"

"Why not. How about a cognac? Remy if you have it."

"Of course I have it. Do you think I'd drag you all the way across town and not have a fresh bottle of Remy Martin in my larder? I know you far too well *mon petit coco cheri*."

She poured the amber liquid into two large brandy snifters and handed him one. "Here's to us," she toasted. "May this be the trip you come to your senses and decide to make an honest woman out of me."

She smiled, so it would seem like a tease and not a demand. She had never put that type of pressure on Mac, and she wasn't starting now. She knew her main competition was Mac's job, not another woman, even though her heart still ached with remembrance of the empty spot Mac's absence had left in it. They were together now, and she wasn't going to ruin the moment.

Yes, they were together now, she thought, and now her smile broadened. She had him here . . . and likely for a few months, at least. They clinked their glasses and drank. She set her glass down and turned her back to him.

"Unzip me," she purred, standing.

He set his glass down and drew the zipper down to the top of her peach-colored bikini panties. She wore no bra, and the skin of her back was smooth and flawless, an inheritance from her oriental mother's side. He slipped his hands under her light dress and rested them on the swell of her hips. The tips of his fingers reached to her pelvic bones, and he pressed them gently.

"Losing weight?" He nibbled her ear.

"Lean and mean, just like you like 'em."

He brought his hands up to the deep curves of her small waist and around and over her taut stomach and up under the swell of her breasts, which were delicate yet full and round. She moaned and pressed back into him, and her dress fell to her ankles. She turned and encircled him with her arms, and they kissed long and deeply, his hands exploring her silky back and firm buttocks.

Clutching his neck with her arms for support, she propelled her two legs off the ground and encircled his waist with them.

He carried her, legs still locked around him, into the bedroom, and they fell on the bed. They rolled back and forth on the bed, pressed together, writhing against each other, he still fully clothed. When they could stand to wait no longer, they tugged at his clothes and her panties disappeared in a kick. When they were naked, they slowed and savored each other, and their lovemaking, far from being frantic, was tender and voracious.

Later they lay in each other's arms in the darkness and let the gentle night breezes coming through the window caress their naked, satiated bodies. And then Wei-wei's fingers resumed their earlier lovemaking, trailing across Mac's strong arms and broad shoulders in after-play.

"Thirsty?" she asked.

"Dying, but leave the cognacs where they are. What I need is a large Perrier."

"Me too. Be right back."

He watched as she slid out of the bed and padded out of the room. *What a gorgeous creature,* he thought.

He had always been partial to Eurasian women—they always seemed to inherit the best of both races—but Wei-wei Ryan was truly exceptional. *Maybe I should just stop screwing around and marry her.* He had never thought of losing her before—the thought had just never occurred to him—but now . . .

She returned with tall glasses of sparkling Perrier, and he rejoiced in the front view of her beautiful body and drank voraciously of both the water and the sight. He handed her his empty glass, and she slid in beside him, insinuating her body against his till, curve to curve, they made the perfect fit.

Nestled in the crook of his arm, she yawned deeply. "Oh, Mac, before I forget, I meant to tell you that there was a file missing from that stack I gave you today."

"Really? What file?" He nibbled at her ear.

"An important Chinese case. It's RH. You know, Restricted Handling."

He frowned. "Funny, Berger didn't mention anything about an RH case."

"Well, it wasn't on the list of files Little Bob gave me to pull for you. Maybe he just forgot."

"I doubt it. Little Bob never, ever forgets anything. What's it about?"

He absentmindedly caressed her breast and again-rigid nipple, but his mind had returned to the business at hand. *What kind of crap was Little Bob pulling now?*

"Well, as I said, it's restricted. Crypt is SKITTISH. He's a young Chinese man. He's the station's only penetration of the Chinese Embassy."

Mac abruptly sat upright in the bed. "Rothmann told me the station had no penetrations of the embassy."

"I didn't think so either, but that's what Little Bob called him in the last annual review. 'Penetration of the Chinese Embassy.' That's what he wrote. I remember it because I thought at the time, how could a waiter be an embassy penetration? A penetration has to be an agent in place, right? He would have to actually work there, be on the inside, an official, to be classified as a 'penetration', right?"

"SKITTISH is a waiter?" Mac asked incredulously.

"He's an overseas Chinese who works as a waiter in one of the Chinese restaurants in town. He was recruited by a young first-tour officer— a Career Trainee just off 'The Farm.' Little Bob took the case away from the kid and put it in restricted handling channels."

"Sounds just like Bob. A young officer makes a good recruitment, and he steps in and takes the case away from the guy and takes credit for it. That's how Bob got where he is today, by stealing cases from other officers . . .

"But to answer your question, you're right, SKITTISH shouldn't be classified as a 'penetration agent.' He's an 'access agent.' He has access to Chinese officials, but isn't one himself. It looks like Bob exaggerated the importance of the case to give himself more credit. Little Bob was always better at writing about ops than actually running them."

"And that's probably why he doesn't want you to get your hands on the case."

"Yeah, that's right. But I'll fix that in the morning. If he has any potential at all to help out with this Chinese case, I want him. And the COS will have to give him to me . . ."

CHAPTER 39

Still jetlagged, Mac awakened at dawn as the morning light filled the room. Wei-wei was curled on her side, breathing deeply. For a long time, he simply watched her sleep. It was too early to get up, and he didn't want to disturb her, so he lay there watching the rhythmic rise and fall of her breasts, enjoying the closeness, enjoying sharing a bed with her again. After a while of this, he finally tried to go back to sleep.

He moved into her sleepily, fitting his body snugly against hers, spoon fashion, and brought his arm over her, resting his hand gently on her breast. She stirred in a dreamlike state and pushed back against him, arousing him. He pressed into her further and felt that familiar stirring in his groin area.

He had always been ultra-responsive to women, especially this particular woman, and neither the years nor last night's exhaustive lovemaking had dimmed his reaction to her. He didn't want to wake her—she was sleeping so peacefully—but his body had ideas of its own. He couldn't help pressing against her . . .

Wei-wei moaned and opened her eyes, realizing it was not a dream. She remained silent and pressed back into him. He maneuvered lower, attempting to slip inside her. She was moist and ready, and pushed back and he entered her easily. Her eyes remained closed and she moved with him ever so slightly at first but then she needed him deeper still, pushing back harder so as to encompass more and more of him within her. He filled her and filled her and filled her, and the fluttering began in her groin, and she let herself go . . .

He continued to move in and out of her very slowly, then more slowly, until he just rested inside her and held her very tightly against him, and then they drifted off, back to sleep again.

CHAPTER 40

The alarm shocked them awake at seven. They showered, dressed, had a cup of coffee and a couple of reheated day-old croissants, and then she drove herself to work at the embassy.

A few minutes after she left, he walked to the metro stop at l'Ecole Militaire to make his first phone call of the day at the café on the corner.

A woman answered, and he hung up.

He went down into the metro and purchased a *carnet* of metro tickets at the window and moved through the turnstiles down through the crowded corridors to the trains. He hated the metro during rush hour—people pushing and shoving like animals and the smell of French body odor. It was much too close for his tastes. Partly it was a matter of personal taste, partly it was a control issue.

As a case officer, he was used to the need to be in control of whatever situation he found himself in. Yet jostled in the metro's crowds, he felt like an animal in a stampeding herd, not at all in charge of himself or the situation around him.

So he rode the train only one stop to La Motte-Picquet and exited back into the sunlight and clean air. He crossed the street and entered a small café, stood at the bar, and ordered a large *café crème* and some change. Taking the coins, he went down to the lower level, where the rest rooms and the phones were located, and inserted a coin in the phone. The phone rang twice, and this time a man answered.

"*Allo!*"

"*Bonjour.* May I speak with Henri, please?" said Mac.

The voice on the other end hesitated and then responded tentatively. "Ah, no, ah, there's, ah, no Henri at this number. Ah, I think you must have the wrong number."

"Henri isn't there?"

"No," the voice said with more confidence now, "there is no Henri at this number. You have the wrong number, monsieur."

"Excuse me. *Merci.*"

Both hung up.

The re-contact phone signal triggered a meeting at a prearranged location, a café on the Place St. Ferdinand, exactly two hours after the time of the call. MacMurphy knew that "Le Belge," Pol Giroud, would be there—Le Belge had never missed a meeting in the two years Mac had handled him, and he was usually early.

Mac returned to the counter and finished his *café crème*. He left the café and casually began to stroll down toward the Seine. He used the quiet back streets and alleys, always heading downhill in the direction of the river so he never got turned around—he had a terrible sense of direction, and this form of "stream navigation" that he had learned as a young Marine and on The Farm served him well in cities built on the banks of rivers as Paris was.

By the time he reached the *quai* alongside the river, he was absolutely certain there was no surveillance behind him, and he still had more than an hour before his meeting with Le Belge.

He stepped into another café, ordered an espresso at the bar, and asked directions to the restrooms. He inserted a coin in the pay phone next to the restrooms and dialed a number. The phone rang four times, and then the answering machine kicked in. The voice on the recording said, "This is François. Please leave your name and number, and I will return your call." At the *beep*, Mac left a short message: "This is Georges. Please call me between seven and nine this evening."

The message signaled a meeting at the Boulevard du Montparnasse entrance of the Vavin metro station at exactly seven, with alternates at eight and nine that same evening. François LeVerrier was almost always late for meetings. That's why Mac and his other handlers always selected pick-up points at places out of doors where they could pass by at the assigned times and not be stuck sitting in a café for three hours waiting for him.

MacMurphy continued his walk along the *quai*, enjoying the breezes coming off the Seine. The river was beautiful if one did not look too closely at what floated in it. He concentrated instead on the people. While keeping an eye out for possible hostile surveillance, he also observed the people in general, playing a game of guessing at their lives, their personalities, their occupations, and their immediate destinations, and assigning names to the more interesting-looking ones.

He passed the Quai d'Orsay, where the French Ministry of Foreign Affairs and SEDEC, its external intelligence organization, were located, and grabbed a cab. He directed the cab to head back across the river to the right bank and was dropped off near where he would meet with TRAVAIL.

CHAPTER 41

In the world of corporate business, when an operation is being planned, all of the major participants are brought together in the board room to discuss strategy. Not so in the clandestine world of intelligence collection.

The concept that hampers this form of efficiency is called "compartmentation." It makes the planning and execution of complicated operations difficult—efficiency is sacrificed for the sake of security.

The "need to know" principle prevails. Only those individuals who *must* know about certain aspects of an operation in order to perform their tasks are given that information. No one, with the exception of the case officer and a few members of the operational management team, is given the full picture.

The compartmentation principle protects a station from becoming completely unraveled by the turning or compromising of a single asset. There is no linkage. The compromised asset will be able to tell his interrogators about only his own duties. The rest of the operational team is protected and remains intact.

So, it was up to MacMurphy to task his operational support assets—in this case TRAVAIL and GUNSHY—separately. They could not be exposed to one another, nor would they know the identities of the other members of the team or what tasks they were assigned. All needed to know the goal of the operation—a technical penetration of the Chinese Embassy—so they would be given this information, albeit in very general terms. Aside from their assigned tasks, they would be told very little about how that penetration would be orchestrated, or why.

CHAPTER 42

Mac found TRAVAIL sitting in a rear booth of the café in front of a huge breakfast. He was dunking a croissant dripping with butter and jam into a double *café crème*.

"*Bonjour, Pol.* I see you're still indulging in your favorite pastime, eating on the company tab."

"*Pourquoi pas, mon ami?* One could never get rich with you fellows, might as well eat well! *Comment ça va, mon vieux?* It has been a long time."

"Too long, Pol. You look good. Clearly you've been eating well!"

Mac ordered a double espresso from a nearby waiter.

Pol Giroud was a red-faced, balding, overweight, cherubic fellow in his early fifties. He blended perfectly into the French working class. He loved people, and people naturally gravitated to him and trusted him.

He could strike up a conversation with anyone, rich or poor, and they would respond positively to his unthreatening demeanor. But his real strength lay in his ability to elicit information from people and then to manipulate them into doing whatever it was he wanted them to do.

The French have a word for it—he was *"malin,"* which roughly translates as "foxy." Le Belge was indeed a fox; disarmingly honest and open on the outside, manipulative and crafty on the inside.

He smiled broadly at Mac, displaying yellow-stained teeth and flashing friendly, soft gray eyes. He patted his ample stomach and flicked croissant crumbs from his stained tie.

"Thought I would eat before you arrive so I do not spray you." He laughed roundly at his own humor, spewing crumbs across the table. "Whoops," he laughed, *"excusez moi."*

Mac flicked the crumbs from his jacket and shook his head at Le Belge. "You haven't changed a bit. I recognize the tie, too! Some of those stains date back to the days we were meeting regularly. So, how are Marie and the girls?"

"Pas mal. Marie is the same. Perhaps a little heavier. It's the cooking, you know. My oldest, Gabrielle, is almost ten. And *la petite,* she is six." Pol said proudly. *"Et toi?"*

"Not too bad. Getting older and grayer." Mac ran his fingers through his graying hair. "You know how it is; it starts up here and works its way down. First the hair, then the eyes go, then the teeth, and so on. At the moment it's right about here." He brought his hand across his waist at the belt line, and they laughed.

"Anyway," he continued, "I'm glad I could catch you on such short notice. Are you free to do some work?"

"Bien sur. My brother-in-law does not make me punch a time clock. But your company fired me. I am certain you know that, *n'est-ce pas?* It seems I failed the piece of merde box they use. They think I am liar. *Merde alors . . ."* He assumed an exaggerated pout.

"Yeah, I know. Forget about it. As of this moment you're back on salary for at least three months. If we do good work, I'll try to convince the company to bring you back on permanently. *Ça va?"*

"Oui, ça va. Does this mean I am back on expense account also?" Le Belge's eyes twinkled.

"Just don't overdo it. The guys in the green eyeshades don't take kindly to 'womb to tomb' support programs, especially for guys with appetites like yours." Mac grinned as he delivered the rebuke.

"You are a good man, Mac. How can I ever repay you?"

"You can help me get a bug inside the Chinese Embassy. Specifically, the COS's office. The casings we have on file are next to worthless, nobody's gotten above the first floor, so we have to start from scratch. You know the place, right

"*Bien sur.* Over on avenue George V in the eighth, next to the Spanish Embassy by the George V Hotel. But I've never been inside."

"Don't worry about getting inside. You'd never get past the front door. Nobody we're in touch with has ever gotten past the ground floor reception area. If we had someone who did have that kind of access to their inner sanctum, we wouldn't need an audio op. You know we only do audio ops when we've struck out—when we can't recruit a human source.

"So I'm thinking about a drilling op. You know, going through one of the common walls from one of the adjacent buildings. So let's look at common wall possibilities first. The chancery building sits smack between the Spanish Embassy on the left as you're looking at the entrance, and an apartment building on the right."

Mac sketched the juxtaposition of the buildings on a scrap of water soluble paper, paper he would later dissolve in his water glass. Pol Giroud listened attentively while searching out, with his tongue, any and all stray pastry flakes from his croissant that were lurking between his teeth. He listened attentively to Mac, the only interruption a discreet belch or two and a soft "*Pardonnez-moi.*"

"We need you to case the outside, front and back. Take a few photos that'll show us how the floor levels line up with the adjacent buildings— so we'll know the proper height to drill. The street slopes down to the Seine, and we don't want to come out in the floor or ceiling of the target office.

"And don't forget to check out the light patterns of the building. Light patterns are very important. The station chief, a tall, elegant guy named Huang Tsung-yao, is a known workaholic, so I expect his office will be lit long after the rest of the offices are dark. It'll also probably be on the top floor. You know, restricted areas are usually located on the tops of embassies, as far away as possible from public areas. These are just educated guesses, you understand, but they'll give us a place to start anyway."

"How about the adjacent buildings—do you want me to check them out as well?"

"Stay clear of the Spanish Embassy. It would be a non-starter to try and do an entry into one embassy to drill into another."

"*Oui*, but what about your liaison? You must have good liaison with the Spanish, *n'est-ce pas*? Maybe they would let you into their building to drill into the Chinese building." He sopped up the last drops of egg yolk on his plate.

Mac shook his head adamantly. "Good question, excellent question. Unfortunately, the answer is . . . no way in hell. This must be strictly unilateral. If the Spanish agreed to such a proposal, which they wouldn't, it would leak out in no time. Their service is like a sieve, penetrated by every intel service from the Russians to the MSS. We'll just have to concentrate on the apartment building and hope Huang's office abuts it. If it doesn't we're screwed—we'll have to go back to the drawing board."

Mac thought silently for a moment and then, continuing his thinking out loud, added, "Actually, it would stand to reason that the Chinese would place their most sensitive offices—commo, station, Ambassador— on the side of the building away from the Spanish. They would need what we call a 'zone of control,' in other words, an area of about ten feet all the way around the exterior of a sensitive room where no local employees or un-cleared people would have access.

"And they would definitely consider the Spanish Embassy more hostile than an apartment building. They would know full well the Spanish have the capability, and good reason, to bug them. Placing their secrets on the other side of the wall, a mere two feet away from them, would fall well within their 'zone of control.'" Mac's voice trailed off as he pondered what he had just presumed. Then he continued in a more declarative tone.

"They wouldn't do that. Let's just concentrate on the most probable approach for the time being. Let's investigate the occupants of the adjacent apartment building and collect light patterns and casings on the target building. I'll bet we find Huang's office on the top floor of the embassy. Only problem is, it'll probably be an inside room near the center of the building. That's where I'd put it. But we might get lucky. It's a narrow building . . ." His voice trailed off as he thought. "Maybe if they're cramped for space or something, they'll have broken a few rules, and we'll be able to get at him from the common wall building. Let's take a look at that first, anyway. *Ça va?*"

Pol Giroud saluted. "*Ça va, mon vieux.*"

Mac handed him a slip of paper.

"That's got our next meeting time and place on it, and our alternate. Don't forget to . . ."

"*Oui, Je sais.* I can tell by the feel of the paper. It is . . . how do you say it? Water dissolvable? Drop it in water and poof! It will dissolve. I will memorize it and flush it down, do not worry, *mon vieux.*"

Mac dunked his sketch in his water glass, and they both watched it dissolve.

"Fine, and one more thing."

"*Oui?*"

"Don't forget to take care of this." He pushed the bill over to Pol Giroud with a grin and left.

CHAPTER 43

MacMurphy took a circuitous route back to the embassy and had a light lunch with Wei-wei in the downstairs lounge. They discussed neither the wonderful lovemaking of the night before, which they'd continued in the morning, nor Mac's meeting with Le Belge, both of which topics were nonetheless very much on Mac's mind. Yet they found plenty to talk about all the same.

After lunch he accompanied her back upstairs to the station, where he met briefly with Burton B. Berger in the COS's office.

"I need to talk to you about that 'penetration asset' you have," Mac said with little preamble, "you probably forgot to tell me about him during our meeting, and I forgot to ask you about him."

He told the COS what he knew about the Chinese waiter, SKIT-TISH, attributing his information to "the desk back at Headquarters." The COS looked quizzically at MacMurphy, clearly searching his memory for details of the case. *Perhaps he really doesn't know about the case,* thought Mac.

"I'd like to use him to develop some information regarding the layout of the building, who works where, that sort of thing. I understand it's a restricted case, but it probably doesn't have to be. The guy is an access agent, not a Chinese official. I'm sure it was a mistake, but something that needs to be corrected."

Realization began to creep across Berger's face.

MacMurphy was as tactful as he could be, while at the same time leaving no doubt in Berger's mind that he considered Little Bob's manipulative act to be one of fabrication and unprofessional behavior, and that he would pursue the subject further when he returned to Headquarters.

"Go ahead and ask Ms. Ryan to give you the file," Berger said, "but first ask her to drop it on my desk. I want to take a look at it before you take it."

Mac knew that Berger, adept at playing the CYA game, would investigate the matter and take whatever corrective action was necessary before Headquarters had a chance to weigh in. In fact, despite his allegiance to Little Bob, he would probably do whatever was necessary to deflect the blame away from himself. Little Bob would be in for a very hard time. The COS would most certainly throw him under the bus, and this pleased Mac a great deal.

SKITTISH could prove to be a valuable access agent for MacMurphy's operation. So after reading SKITTISH's operational 201 file and noting down the contact instructions for non-scheduled, emergency and regular meetings with the asset, Mac returned to his *pied-à-terre* on Rue Laugier to prepare himself for his meeting with GUNSHY that evening.

He decided to put off meeting with SKITTISH until later in the week when Bob Little had a regular scheduled meeting with the asset. Warm introductions to assets were always preferable when they could be arranged.

CHAPTER 44

At ten minutes past seven that evening, MacMurphy finished his *pastis*, summoned the waiter to pay his bill, and left the café. He had been there for approximately twenty minutes, sipping his drink while observing the Vavin entrance to the metro, where he was supposed to meet GUNSHY.

Since the agent had failed to show (not a surprising eventuality for François Leverrier), he would have to kill time until the variant meeting scheduled for one hour later, at eight o'clock.

He strolled down the crowded Boulevard de Montparnasse and wandered around the narrow side streets of the Montparnasse neighborhood, once again observing the passersby and wondering about their lives. All the while he was very conscious of potential surveillance. But he detected none.

At five minutes to eight he was back on Boulevard de Montparnasse, walking east with a measured stride that, by design, looked neither hurried and urgent nor like that of a man with nowhere to go. The Vavin *metro bouche* was in sight. He timed his steps so that he arrived there at exactly eight o'clock.

Standing at the metro entrance, he looked down the steps. Still no GUNSHY. He descended into the metro and went to the bank of phones near the ticket booth. There he killed another three minutes pretending to make a phone call. Finally he spotted GUNSHY amidst a gaggle of people ascending from the train platform below.

François was nattily dressed in a double-breasted blue seersucker suit and white shoes. His longish blond hair, streaked from the sun and maybe a bottle, was combed back away from the finely chiseled features of his almost too handsome face. His pale blue eyes searched the crowd for MacMurphy, but they missed him, and he took the stairs up to the street two at a time. Mac followed close behind, and their eyes met when GUNSHY turned to look back down when he reached the top.

"*Ah, tu et là! Comment va tu?*" They shook hands firmly.

"Couldn't be better, François. And how are you? You look great."

"I feel great, too. I took your advice and started working out and running. My girlfriends love the new me. They think I have the air of an American with all my new muscles!" He flexed his arm for emphasis.

Mac laughed. "I see your ego hasn't shrunk any since the last time I saw you. And your punctuality hasn't changed any, either, by the way."

"Sorry, Mac," he said petulantly. "I didn't get back to my flat until almost six. Then I had to shower and change and . . . Ah well, I made it here as fast as I could. I didn't want you to have to hang around till nine."

"*Tant pis.* No problem. At least you're here. Let's walk up to La Coupole and get a bite to eat. Are you okay on time?"

"*Oui*, I have all night. No date tonight, *malheureusement*. What is this about? Are you here on business or pleasure?"

"Business, but it's always a pleasure to see you, François."

"*Ah oui.* I know the game. First you must, how do you say, build a little rapport, then the requirements come, *n'est-ce pas?* You are the same, *mon vieux.*" Despite his words, François could not hide his pleasure over seeing Mac again. "So we are going back to work, yes?"

"I'll tell you all about it over dinner. I can already taste that Le Coupole *filet au poivre.*"

CHAPTER 45

The famous old restaurant was already packed with tourists and Paris's beautiful people, and those who like to bask in the light of the beautiful people, but a ten euros note to the *maitre d'hôtel* got them a table by the windows without a wait.

They ordered mixed salads, *filets au poivre* with *pomme frites*, and François chose an excellent bottle of Chateau Margeaux Bordeaux to wash down the steaks. The wine cost more than the rest of the meal, but François's delicate stomach could not handle house wines, or so he claimed. "Now, *this* is wine that *soothes* the stomach, not aggravates it," he purred as he slowly savored the Bordeaux, letting it sit in his mouth before each dainty swallow.

Mac outlined the proposed audio operation and tasked François with investigating the occupants of the apartment building adjacent to the Chinese Embassy. He suggested first getting the occupants' names from the mailboxes in the lobby and then checking them out in the phone book, public records, and discreetly through François's police contacts.

Mac explained that the ultimate goal was to gain access to one or more of the apartments for a few hours for the purpose of drilling into the Chinese Embassy and installing a microphone and transmitter in the common wall between the two buildings.

"I also need you to locate a suitable listening post within transmitter range," he added. " The LP apartment will have to be no more than about three hundred meters line-of-sight from the target. Less if the signal has to pass through too many buildings."

"I have the strong feeling that this is going to interfere with my August vacation," said François with eyes raised quizzically and mouth down turned in a comical pout.

"Absolutely," Mac agreed, nodding his head for emphasis.

"*Merde alors!* Why do you fellows always pick *le mois d'août* for your operations? Do you not know that all civilized people go to the *Midi* during summer vacation time? This is not the first time you did this to me, you know. You remember that little job we did against the Russian code room a few years ago? That was in August, too. You interrupted my whole summer, and I almost lost a testicle to that guard goose that woke up too soon and bit me as we went back over the fence. Remember that one, *mon vieux*? What do you say about that? That fucking guard goose piece of shit almost castrated me."

"Something half the women in Paris would like to do to you . . . *n'est-ce pas?*"

"*Ah oui* . . . Perhaps, but what about the other half?" said François, leering.

Mac laughed. "You are a unique character, François Leverrier, you truly are. But don't worry, your family jewels will be safe and sound on this op. We don't have to put any guard dogs or geese to sleep, and we won't be jumping any fences. All you have to do is sweet-talk your way into one of those apartments for us. Do you have any questions?"

"No. *Je comprends bien.* I suppose you would like me to pay for this." He gestured to the table, where dishes and utensils and glasses and napkins were all that remained from their most enjoyable repast.

"No. I'll get it. But the green eyeshade folks are going to have a heart attack when they see the price of the wine. And, by the way, you are on expenses from this moment—that is, as long as you don't forget to bring me the receipts, *ça va?*"

François nodded as Mac drew a stack of euros from his pocket and counted out enough to cover the meal. He dropped the money on the bill and passed François a slip of water soluble paper with contact instructions for their next meeting. François glanced at the note and Mac asked, "*Ça va?*"

François looked at the note again, committing the instructions to memory. Then he assented, "*Oui, ça va.* See you then." He dropped the note into his water glass as they rose from the table. Then they shook hands and disappeared separately into the night crowd of Montparnasse.

CHAPTER 46

E arly Saturday morning Mac and Wei-wei drove to Normandy in Wei-
wei's car. They stayed at the quaint *Auberge de la Plage* in Trouville,
just across the bridge from the more famous but touristy Deauville.
They toured around the town, walked the beach and dined on *Coquille
St-Jacques, Moules Normande,* and fresh fish and shrimp prepared to
perfection.

After dinner they drank large fist-sized snifters of aromatic *Vieux
Calvados* in a neighborhood bar and took another long walk along the
beach. At night, snuggled together under the covers and drifting to sleep
in each other's arms, they were grateful for the mattress's sag that worked
to bring them even closer . . . not that they needed any outside help. They
made love over and over in the big old four-poster bed with the sag in
the middle.

On Sunday morning they drove south along the coast toward Cher-
bourg so that Mac could make another of his regular pilgrimages to the

invasion beaches of Arromanches, Omaha, Juno, Sword, and Utah, and his uncle's grave in the sprawling, manicured, US military cemetery.

They walked silently among the thousands of perfectly aligned crosses and six-pointed stars and read the dates: June 6, June 7, June 7, June 6, June 8, and on and on and on . . .

They stood for a long time in front of his Uncle Walter's grave—one of so many young men killed on these beaches on the first days of the invasion that helped to bring an end to the war in Europe—and felt very close and very vulnerable.

They finally turned, each still with an arm around the other's back, holding each other even closer now, thinking "what-if" thoughts—what if something happened to one of them? Not an unreasonable thought, given Mac's occupation . . . and even Wei-wei, working out of embassies around the world, was significantly more vulnerable than the average secretary at a desk somewhere in Heartland, USA. They left the cemetery and returned to the car, breaking apart only when it was time to get inside it, yet still not breaking their thoughtful, and appropriate silence.

Their lovemaking that evening was sweet, soulful, appreciative. They caressed, treasured each other and held each other close. Something was different between them during this whole Paris reunion. They were closer and needier than ever before. They savored each other's body and lingered long in the comfortable embrace of each others' arms.

Mac kissed Wei-wei's burnished body from the top of her sweet-smelling scalp to the tips of her dainty toes, and she caressed every inch, every cranny of Mac's strong physique. When they at last had stopped tasting of each other's satiated body, they lay in a languorous afterglow, arms entwined around bodies, enjoying the physical closeness and each thinking how much he or she had missed the other during their separation before Mac had been sent back to Paris. He kissed her tenderly and fit his body snugly into hers. "Good night, *cherie. Fait des bons rêves . . .*"

They returned to Paris early Monday morning almost regretfully. Both were refreshed and ready to tackle the week ahead, but sorry to have the weekend come to an end.

CHAPTER 47

Over the next two weeks, Mac held compartmented clandestine meetings with TRAVAIL and with GUNSHY on an almost daily basis . . . much too frequently to suit the case officer, because one of the basic rules of operational security was being bent.

The pressure to produce always resulted in sacrifice of operational security. Efficiency and production usually won over security. It happened all the time in the intelligence business, and it was the thing that "flaps" were made of. Mac was fully aware of the risks involved in meeting too frequently with his assets, but he needed his casings fast to keep the Director off Rothmann's back, and Rothmann off his.

He was also introduced to SKITTISH by Bob Little in a meeting in a room at the sprawling Intercontinental Hotel on the Rue de Rivoli. The meeting was already in progress when Mac arrived—he did not want to spend any more time in the company of Bob Little than he had to.

Little was noticeably nervous at Mac's presence. The agent was introduced to Mac in alias as Roland Petit. Mac explained that he was interested in the movements of the Chinese COS, Huang Tsung-yao, and other members of the station.

He gave SKITTISH contact instructions for their exclusive use and said he would be calling a meeting with the young waiter sometime within the next week or so. After setting up their own meeting arrangements, MacMurphy left the pair to complete their operational meeting. He could contact SKITTISH if he needed him, but was under no obligation to do so if he didn't.

CHAPTER 48

B oth support assets, Le Belge and François, had worked tirelessly, day and night, and the results of their efforts showed.

Le Belge woke up with the Chinese in the morning and put them to bed at night. His poor little dog had sore paws from all of the walking during his surveillance tours around the embassy building. He had learned that Huang's office was, as MacMurphy had predicted, indeed on the top floor of the Embassy, in the rear, and on the side adjacent to the target apartment building.

He had confirmed MacMurphy's suspicions by carefully observing light patterns in the building. He noted that by dusk, almost all of the windows were illuminated. Then, one by one, they began to go out until there were usually only two office windows above the first floor reception area that remained illuminated. One on the third floor in the front, adjacent to the Spanish Embassy, which he identified as the commo room, and the other on the top floor rear next to the apartment building.

That, he determined, was Huang's office. "It's just like you sus-pected," he told Mac. "He works late . . . on the top floor, in the back of the building. You were right on the money, Mac!"

MacMurphy had provided Le Belge with a physical description of Huang, and when the lights remained on until late in the evening in the most likely location, TRAVAIL decided to take a closer look. He accom-plished this with the help of powerful binoculars from a nearby rooftop. Ascending to the roof of the nearby building as inconspicuously as pos-sible, he gained a vantage point and discreetly trained his binoculars on the window of the top-floor office at dusk, when he was less likely to be observed himself while doing his peeping Tom routine.

There was no question in his mind that the tall, slender, balding, overworked, Oriental man who remained at his desk until long after the others had quit was indeed Huang Tsung-yao, the MSS Chief of Station.

CHAPTER 49

GUNSHY's independent reporting confirmed TRAVAIL's. He had cleverly obtained copies of the architectural blueprints of both the embassy and the adjacent apartment building through one of his friends who worked in the records section of the *Mairie* of Paris' 8th *arrondissement*.

The plans showed that an elevator shaft separated two rooms on either side of the rear top floor of the embassy, and that the building was probably too narrow for the addition of any offices to the original plan in that area.

François hit the buzzer on the door jam and entered the adjacent apartment building just once, for no more than five minutes. He swiftly photographed the locks on each apartment door, two to a floor, and made clay impressions of all the keyways.

This would help in identifying the locks in case a surreptitious entry became necessary. Some locks were easier to pick than others, but he knew that the techs would go to great lengths to avoid having to pick a lock. It wasn't at all like the movies, where the pick was inserted, jiggled around a bit, and the door popped open.

He would try to help in this regard as well, but that would come later, after the specific target apartment was identified.

He prowled the hallways at an hour just after dusk, hoping not to run into anyone. He had a close call while he was on the third floor and heard the main downstairs door open and feet begin to ascend the stairwell. *Should I brazen it out? Descend quickly and pretend I've been visiting someone on the uppermost floor?*

While he momentarily froze, debating his options, the footsteps stopped on the second floor. He heard a key turn in a lock, a door open and then close again, and then silence. Greatly relieved, he hurried through the rest of his work and re-emerged on the street undetected.

He also located a tiny *"au pair"* efficiency apartment on the top floor of a building directly behind the target. It was no more than one hundred meters away with direct line-of-sight. It would be a perfect LP from which to monitor the soon-to-be-installed clandestine transmitter. He secured the listening post apartment, in alias, with a cash deposit of five hundred euros.

When MacMurphy put the information from the two support assets together, he concurred with TRAVAIL's assessment that the top rear office was Huang's and decided to concentrate all of their efforts on that office. This meant the next step was to identify the occupants of the apartment in the building on the other side of the common wall. The building plans obtained by GUNSHY showed there were two apartments per floor in the building, and there were five floors. They needed access to the fifth floor rear apartment to gain access to Huang's office.

GUNSHY came through on this score as well. He had first taken all the names of the apartment residents off the mailboxes in the lobby of the building. Then, through selective surveillance, he had been able to follow the occupants when they left in the morning and when they returned in the evening.

He was able to put faces to apartment numbers by observing them picking up their mail from their boxes in the lobby and seeing what apartment lights went on or off when the occupants entered or left the building. By the end of the two-week period, he knew the name and face of every resident of the building, where they each worked, where they shopped, and which cafés and restaurants they frequented—more information than they actually needed.

When MacMurphy instructed François to concentrate on the occupants of the fifth floor apartment, he knew this would be a lucky operation. The occupants were a middle-aged woman, unmarried but not unattractive—she needed to take a bit more care with makeup and coiffure—and her doddering eighty-ish year old mother.

The spinster would be putty in the hands of the handsome François Leverrier. François would be in her apartment and, if necessary, in her bed in no time. Of that he was very, very confident.

CHAPTER 50

The first time François allowed their eyes to meet, he smiled shyly and the spinster blushed. It happened in the *patisserie* around the corner from her apartment while she was purchasing a baguette for dinner.

The next morning he entered the café where she and her mother usually had their morning coffee and croissants. He sat a few tables away and allowed their eyes to meet again. This time it was he who dropped his eyes and blushed. This gave her confidence, and she smiled at him more boldly, touching her hair and forcing another blush. When she and her mother passed his table as they were leaving, their eyes locked and held until she had passed him.

The next time he saw her at the café, she was alone and he said, "*Bonjour,*" and she replied. Later they started talking. He remained seated at his place on the banquette that ran along the back wall of the café, and she remained sitting a few feet down from him, behind another table.

They conversed across the empty table between them. An hour later they were still there, but sitting next to each other, and she had agreed to have dinner with him the following evening.

Collette Lebrun felt as if she had known the man who called himself Jacques DuBois for a very long time.

When GUNSHY arrived to pick up Collette at her apartment the next evening, he brought flowers for both mother and daughter. And not just flowers for each, but a different bouquet for each one. The mother's bouquet was all whites and purples, with sprays of baby's breath, while Colette received a rainbow-hued assortment, with green ferns interspersed.

The women fussed over the bouquets and placed them in vases, then offered François an aperitif. He accepted, settled back in an overstuffed old chair, and went about the task of charming the old lady while Collette busied herself breaking ice cubes from a frozen tray and preparing the drinks.

"Oh, but you have decorated your apartment so charmingly!" he exclaimed with something less than truthfulness. In reality he hated the gloomy, airless, typically French room. "And do tell me more about that wonderful antique chair," he added, pointing to an old wooden chair sitting in a corner with no pedigree at all.

He had both women fawning over him by the time they had finished their aperitifs.

Before leaving for dinner with Collette, who was looking decidedly better with makeup and a pretty new dress, cut low to display her ample assets, he asked if he could try out his new camera on the group. He then went about arranging the two women on a couch along the wall he knew abutted the Chinese Embassy, and arranged the flowers on the end tables on both sides of them.

He placed his camera on a table across from his subjects, focused, set the timer, and joined them on the couch between the two women, placing an arm lightly around the shoulder of each one.

When the camera flashed, he had an excellent interior casing photo of the common wall the audio techs would have to drill through to get audio from Huang's office.

Restoring that flowered wallpaper is going to be a bitch, François thought. Fortunately that job would fall to one of the other team members, a fact for which he was exceedingly grateful.

CHAPTER 51

The unwitting recruitment of Collette Lebrun intensified during the evening. François took her to dinner at the cozy Taillevent restaurant. It was located only a short walk from Collette's George V apartment and was the proud possessor of three coveted Michelin stars.

The atmosphere was plush, relaxing, living room style, and the food was absolutely superb. He got Collette settled in comfortably, inquired as to whether she had ever dined there before and quickly learned that she had not. He asked her, "Would you like me to make some recommendations from the menu?"

They dined on *terrine de bouchet* and *ris de veau Florentine*, accompanied by a bottle of fine white *Cotes de Beaune*. They topped the meal off with *crepes soufflées sauce Sabayon* and yet another bottle of wine; a beautiful *Chateau d'Yquem* sauterne, which further oiled their tongues and loosened their inhibitions as the evening sped by.

"And you have never married?" François asked with feigned amazement. "Such a lovely flower as you . . ." She blushed and brushed her hair back away from her face. "I am amazed! But I am also pleased . . . it is my good fortune, after all, that you are single."

"And how do you account for *your* single status?" she parried.

"Well . . . I guess I had just not met anyone as charming and . . ." François groped for a believable compliment, "down-to-earth as you."

In her forty-seven years, Collette had never been in such fine surroundings and in the company of such a handsome and refined gentleman. She was very happy and did not want the evening to end . . . ever.

François observed her as she talked and smiled and sipped the sweet nectar gracefully. Slowly he realized that he actually *liked* the plain, middle-aged woman sitting across from him.

Collette had a pleasant face and, like many French women, retained a beautiful complexion. She actually needed very little makeup. She had a certain dignity about her that is unique to French women as they age. Yes, maybe it was partly the wine and food, but he was beginning to enjoy Collette's company. He took her hand in his hand, covered it with his other hand and smiled deeply into her eyes. He wasn't acting at all.

But that would not let him forget why he was there. When she got up on wobbly legs to go to the restroom, he quickly snatched the keys from her purse, brought them to his lap out of sight of the waiters, and pressed her apartment key into the clay of the key impression kit MacMurphy had given him.

Now he could really relax. The main goal of the evening had been accomplished. From now on, everything else was topping. He could really relax and enjoy the company of Colette Lebrun now. This was indeed very pleasant work.

CHAPTER 52

They were familiar now. François had gone from non-threatening and shy during their first fleeting encounters, to protective and touching—getting her used to his touch by guiding her, hand lightly on her waist, through the crowds and across streets on their way to the restaurant, during the early part of the evening.

Now he found occasions to lightly brush her fingers and hand as they talked softly and sipped the wine.

On their way back home they held hands like young lovers, and once, after she made a witty remark, he kissed her gently on the cheek amidst the swirling crowds on the Champs-Elysées, drawing a blush made of wine, happiness, and more than a little embarrassment.

When they reached the door to her apartment, he brought her face to his with both hands and kissed her gently on one cheek, then the other, then lightly on her soft mouth. Her lips parted a bit, and she shuddered ever so slightly. She tasted of the sweet sauterne and of building desire.

He felt the familiar stirring in his own groin, but he restrained himself from letting his lust lead the way.

He let her fit her key into the lock but made no effort to follow her into the room. She sensed his reluctance and took his hand. "Come on in for a minute. *Tu veux un cognac?*" It was the first time she had used the familiar "tu" form of speech with him. "Do not worry. Mother is long asleep."

He followed her into the room and pushed the door closed behind them. She came easily into his arms, and their bodies pressed tightly together. The cognac was forgotten . . .

She could feel him through the thin fabric of her dress, and the feel of his excitement, and the sense of power she felt at knowing she had caused his condition served to generate further heat in her groin area. Her bosom swelled and pressed into him. He traced her ample but well-shaped hips with his hands and brought them up to her breasts, cupping them.

He held her tightly but made no move to advance the familiarity, even though she was clearly more than ready. "Not here," he whispered, wandering hands caressing her hips and buttocks, "not now. I want it to be perfect. Can you come away with me next weekend?"

"*Mais oui*, but . . ."

"Do not worry about your mother. She can accompany us. I have a villa in Trouville on the Normandy coast. It is beautiful. Plenty of room." His lips gently caressed her eyes and lips and ears and neck as he spoke. "I like your mother. She will love the place, and we will have plenty of time alone. You will see. *Ça va?* We will have the whole weekend together . . ."

"Of course. Of course I want to come. Are you sure it is all right? With mother, I mean?"

"*Certainement*. I would not have it any other way. I will pick you up early Saturday morning. Pack a *maillot*. We will have a swim in the moonlight."

They kissed again, long and deep and passionately. He reluctantly pushed away again and whispered "Saturday," and then he was gone, leaving her trembling and aroused. She would dream about François Leverrier, a.k.a. Jacques Dubois, every night until the weekend.

CHAPTER 53

While François's part in this complex operation was going swim-
mingly, Mac was facing a potential bump in the road. He knew
what he wanted to do, and when and how to do it, and he had all
the cogs in the machinery turning smoothly, but . . . and it was a huge
"but" . . . now he had to bring the powers that be into the loop and
obtain the necessary approvals for his proposed audio operation.

He knew that might not be so easy.

Setting up the whole complex maneuver might actually be easier that
gaining Burton B. Berger's approval for it. *Sometimes the biggest enemy
is us,* he thought. But, once again, Mac had a plan.

He had to work on two very different levels. The first was to inform
Rothmann privately of his plans and to get the DDO's support before
the official operational plan was cabled to Headquarters. This was the
easy part; it required only a short back-channel message to Rothmann.

But sending messages out of a station without the COS's approval
was totally forbidden in all CIA stations. The COS had releasing author-

ity on all correspondence going out of a station. He could, and often did, delegate this authority to others, especially when he was away, but in the end someone in authority had to release every piece of correspondence.

He decided he could accomplish this by delivering his cable personally to Rodney Jackson in the commo room. Rodney would be sticking his neck out, but he would do it for his friend.

The unnumbered back-channel, Eyes Only, cable would go out of the station to the DDO immediately, without the required release signature of the COS.

The second level required a detailed operational plan submitted through the station chief to the European Division back at Headquarters. MacMurphy spent a full day in the station composing the ops plan, crafting it thought by thought and word by word, with all the attention to detail he had ever given a major operation.

Then he spent the better part of another day defending it to Burton B. Berger over the myriad petty objections of his deputy, Bob Little, and doing rewrite after rewrite to get them to sign off on it.

When the ops plan was finally signed and released, albeit reluctantly, by the COS, approval for the operation came back to the station from Headquarters within an amazing twenty-four hours. The hand of the DDO was obviously moving the laborious bureaucratic machinery of Headquarters.

CHAPTER 54

The date set for the operation was the following Saturday. Collette LeBrun and her mother would be out of Paris in Trouville with GUN-SHY, and entry into her apartment would be accomplished with the key that GUNSHY had copied.

The entry team would consist of MacMurphy and an audio technician from the CIA's Technical Services Division. The station would provide counter-surveillance with the station's fully-cleared and well-equipped surveillance team while the entry team was in the building.

In his cable to the DDO, MacMurphy had specifically requested James "Culler" Santos, the close friend and former "Farm" classmate of Mac's, to be his audio tech. The approval to send Santos was included in Headquarters' cable, along with approval to use the new XL-79 "moon" drill. The state-of-the-art drill and Santos's other equipment were being pouched from Frankfurt to Paris. Santos would arrive separately in the morning.

The following morning, MacMurphy was in the station going over some last minute details when Culler Santos arrived . . . all of him.

MacMurphy noticed a distinct lessening of light coming through the open door and looked up to see what was blocking it. The man's bulk filled the doorway.

"Hello, you gray-haired old sonofabitch."

Mac came from behind the desk and embraced his old friend. They had been close friends since going through training together down at The Farm, learning to become case officers. But soon after completing his training, Culler decided to go into the Technical Services Division and become an audio tech. TSD was where the real action was, he used to say, and Culler Santos was certainly built for action.

Although he didn't stand much more than five foot eight inches tall, he was a solid two hundred pounds. Not an ounce of fat on him. He was one of the toughest guys Mac had ever known, and his face showed the scars of the many scrapes he had gotten into while growing up in a rough Irish neighborhood of South Boston.

But now, despite an explosive temper that he had always had trouble containing, he was—most of the time—a pussycat. He possessed an engineering degree from MIT, and he spoke with an educated South Boston accent. He was an accomplished artist, and his paintings displayed a deep sensitivity and emotions not normally attributed to strong, fiercely heterosexual men. In short, he was a sensitive, intelligent, educated thinker, locked up in the body of a street brawler.

His nickname illustrated his character. As a teenager he had been impressed by the protagonist in J.D. Salinger's *The Catcher In The Rye*, whose wish was to keep little children from falling over the cliff at the edge of a rye field. It was his way of saving the world.

Culler Santos admired it, but he had his own way of saving the world. Culler found in Salinger's protagonist something of a kindred spirit, although Culler's own mission was not to save little children. No, he had a different mission in the world.

Culler Santos wanted to "cull" the world of assholes.

"You can always spot the assholes," he would say. "Just driving down the street through a city, you can recognize the scumbags of the earth hanging out on just about every street corner. Just by looking at them, you know the world would be a better place without them."

So what Culler Santos dreamed about having was some sort of divine knowledge and dead aim with a forty-five. Then, whenever he spotted an asshole, he would blow him away with one shot between the horns, and the world would be a better place.

That's the way Culler Santos thought about life, and whenever an asshole got in Culler Santos's way . . .

CHAPTER 55

Culler and Mac chatted in Mac's temporary office until Wei-wei Ryan was ready to leave. They discussed the upcoming operation, and Culler described two new pieces of equipment he had pouched to Paris for use in the drilling phase.

The first was the "moon drill." Santo explained it had been originally developed for NASA to take core samplings of the moon's crust. It was essentially an extremely high speed, water-cooled, diamond core drill. It was capable of drilling up to two-inch holes through concrete or steel at the rate of one inch per second. It went through practically any material like a hot knife through butter. The drill replaced older model core drills that were heavy, noisy, and penetrated at a much, much slower, grinding rate.

The other piece of equipment was a new version of the old "back-scatter gauge." It measured the thickness of walls with great accuracy from only one side of the wall in only one step. Older versions required many readings as the drilling progressed, and were often inaccurate as the hole became deeper and the density of the concrete and other materials changed.

"With this baby," Culler enthused, "the hole can be drilled quicker, quieter, more securely, and with much less chance of a breakthrough into the target." His voice rose with enthusiasm and his heavy finger punched the air for emphasis. He glowed with a true technician's pride—one would have thought he'd invented the thing himself.

Breaking through into the target was the audio tech's greatest nightmare. Only a tiny pinhole was supposed to enter the target. It provided an airway to the microphone buried in the drill hole behind it. The consequences of anything larger than a pinhole, not to mention a two-inch hole, or even a three-eights inch hole, in the target's wall were too horrible to imagine.

After Wei-wei locked up the office, the three of them went down to the embassy lounge for cocktails and then out to dinner at La Coupole in Montparnasse—Mac was craving another one of their *filets au poivre*.

An observer would have thought they hadn't a care in the world. But Mac continued to observe his surroundings for any evidence of surveillance. As far as he could see, the only observers were French citizens and tourists . . . not anyone who was shadowing them. Not that he particularly expected anyone surveilling them tonight, but by habit, he was ever on his guard. The necessity was too ingrained in him for him to be otherwise.

CHAPTER 56

While Santos and MacMurphy were planning their audio operation on the top floor of the American Embassy on Avenue Gabriel, Huang Tsung-yao was being briefed in his office across town on the top floor of the Chinese Embassy on Avenue George V. The briefer was Huang's deputy, Lim Ze-shan.

Huang had barely arrived at the station when he decided to replace Lim as soon as Lim's current tour was up in December. On first meeting Lim he did not like or trust him and instinctively felt he would not be able to work with him.

Lim was a defiant, angry man. Short but powerfully built with peasant features, he was certainly bright enough, but he tended to intimidate people rather than lead them, and he resented the fact that Huang had been sent to Paris to take over the station. He thought *he* should have been named COS. He was almost five years older than Huang and had been Acting Chief of Station for almost four months while Beijing was deciding whether to send Huang or someone else.

He did not know that it was never the intention of the MSS to leave him in charge of the station. He enjoyed the power of being ACOS, and he wanted to continue in that role. But Huang's arrival had ended all of that. And he resented Huang for it.

In fact, Lim enjoyed power so much that he considered the best years of his life those spent as a youth in the Red Guards during the days of the Cultural Revolution. He was just a teenager when he and a few of his fanatic friends had commandeered a passenger train going from Tsinghua University, the birthplace of the Red Guard movement, to Shanghai, and had happily raped and beaten their way across three provinces. Lim never had much luck attracting women, but he did enjoy raping them. He liked seeing the fear in their eyes. He liked hurting them.

He liked hurting men, too. He had spent many years studying martial arts to perfect his fighting skills so he could inflict greater pain and damage on his victims. If raping a defenseless woman was his favorite thing to do, his second-most favorite was taking another man apart, piece by piece. And he was very, very good at it.

Lim was the unfortunate product of an abusive father, a submissive mother, and an older sister who received all the attention in his family. She was tall and beautiful, while he was short and squat. She was a talented dancer and bright student who was doted on by her father, while Lim got nothing but abuse from him.

Lim fell in with a bad crowd of Red Guards while attending Tsinghua middle school and this association both benefited him and hurt him. The connections helped him get into Tsinghua University where he actually excelled intellectually, but the dark side of his association with the Red Guards crippled his psyche for life.

He was thinking about how he would like to take Huang apart as he sat across the desk from him in Huang's austere, cluttered fifth-floor office. *The skinny bastard wouldn't have a chance; it would be great to make him beg and crawl.*

Huang was standing behind his desk, putting things away, separating papers, arranging his phone, pen set, note pads, and other things on the surface. His first question brought Lim out of his dream state.

"Tell me about your activities against the Americans. I have read all of the files until I am bleary-eyed, so I am fairly familiar with the essentials of the cases, but I would like you to summarize your operational planning and bring me up to date. Have you had any more success against that American communicator? Where do you think we should be headed with this case? Where do you think it will lead us?"

"Sure," said Lim, settling back and relaxing a bit. Talking about his operational successes, about his efforts against any foe, was a great pleasure to him. "As you know, we have a good, solid program against the US Embassy. We are targeted at the heart of them, and we have a couple good early-stage developmental cases. I have concentrated most of the station's efforts against Americans during the time I was acting chief of station. Beijing never lets us forget the Americans are the number-one priority. But you know this already . . ."

As he listened, Huang continued with his settling-in and unpacking. He stood up from behind his desk and began taking books out of a box and arranging them neatly in a bookshelf on the other side of the room. Lim noticed that several of them dealt with martial arts, but most of them seemed to be about philosophy and history.

"Start with your penetration operations. Tell me about your efforts to recruit penetrations of the US Embassy,"

"Well, we do not . . . not actually . . . have any penetrations . . . yet," Lim admitted. "But we have a couple of good potential penetrations. They are in the developmental stage now. I mean . . . we had nothing before I got here. Nothing . . . I must do everything myself you know. Right from scratch . . ."

"Start with the prostitute operation. The one against the CIA communicator. Tell me about that one first. They are very interested in that one back home."

"First I should tell you she is not a *putain*. She is not a whore. She is from a good family. Her father was a big Party official in Tsingtao, and her mother was Eurasian—a teacher, I think. The name she uses here is Michelle Li. She is very beautiful. Very sexy. I recruited her myself and targeted her against one of the black American communicators. Black Americans are very vulnerable—good targets, you know.

"Michelle was here with a dance troupe few years back and ran away. You know, defected. She became a naturalized French citizen. I found her and told her I would not bother her family back in China if she would do some little favors for me. She got the point right away. She is not stupid."

Lim smiled craftily as he recalled that first meeting and the way he had raped her and beaten her and threatened her into agreeing to work for him.

"First I told her to wiggle her ass at the Marine Security Guards at the American Embassy. She's got a great ass, so they flirted with her and one of them invited her to the Marine House for drinks one Friday night. It wasn't very long before she became a regular at their Friday night Marine House parties. There is where she met the black communicator, Rodney Jackson. Marines don't know hardly anything, but communicators know everything."

"He is a CIA communicator, right? Not State Department?" Huang began locking up for the evening, cleaning his desk of classified documents and placing them in a four-drawer safe.

"Right. CIA. And this guy is a great target. Much disaffection, very vulnerable."

"Like what? How? What makes you think he's disaffected?" Huang stopped what he was doing and was listening intently now, leaning on the safe.

"In the first place, I already told you he is black. His name is Rodney Jackson. All American blacks hate their white bosses. Hate the 'white establishment' that they think holds them down at the bottom of the social structure. They blame whites for everything, never think maybe it's because they are stupid and lazy that they never advance anywhere. Also, Jackson's father was a militant during the early days of the race riots in America. You know, Martin Luther King time. He was beaten up pretty bad by bunch of white guys during a big demonstration march in Alabama. He told all of this to Michelle Li.

"His job prospects are not so good either. He is always complaining about how everyone else in the embassy gets paid more than him. I have done some checking and found out he is right. The commo people are not paid very much, and there is not much room for promotion either, especially for black ones, he thinks. Rodney Jackson thinks the only ones who make it up the ladder in the communications field are white . . ."

"Sounds classic," said Huang. "You have done a good job on this case. So now you have this beautiful Michelle Li screwing the black communicator, and we are paying for his good fortune! Good for Rodney Jackson. Question is, are we getting anything out of all this? Any intelligence? Is he recruitable? That is the objective, you know. Just because he likes girls and is broke all the time and hates his white bosses does not mean he's ready to jump ship and give up all of his secrets to the Chinese communist party."

"I know," said Lim dejectedly. "But we must start someplace, eh? We do not know everything yet. He is falling in love with the girl, and we control the girl, and that will give us more control over him. It is just too soon to tell . . . But I think he would go into a huge withdrawal if we took his pussy away from him. He would beg to do anything for us to have her back."

Huang looked at Lim in a new light. *This is a damn good op*, he thought. Maybe Lim was not so bad after all.

"Thanks for being so honest with me, Lim. I appreciate that. You have done a very good job on this case. I can tell you for a fact it is considered one of the best potential recruitment operations against the Americans in the service."

Huang was warming to Lim, if not personally, at least professionally. He decided to try a little recruiting of his own.

"Why don't you put your things away and come have dinner with me over at the Mai-Lin restaurant."

The Mai-Lin was a favorite haunt of the Chinese Embassy personnel, one of the few places outside of the Embassy compound where they felt completely comfortable and safe.

"We can continue our discussion over some dumplings and kimchee and beer. Please call a driver to take us over there. I'll be done here in a minute."

"Excellent idea, it will just take me a minute to lock up." Lim returned to his office, cleaned off his desk, threw his classified material into his safe, called for a driver, and met Huang at the entrance to the mbassy.

CHAPTER 57

On the drive over to the restaurant, they spoke about the dearth of good Chinese restaurants in Paris. The fact that Paris was arguably the gastronomic capital of the world made no impression on either of them. No place—including the Mai-Lin—truly satisfied their longing for food such as they had enjoyed back home, and they lamented this lack all the way to the restaurant.

They didn't talk business in the close confines of the car, despite the fact that the driver was a cleared embassy employee from Guangzhou. The "need to know" principle applied to the MSS as well.

When they were dropped off at the Mai-Lin restaurant on Rue Richelieu, they discovered the place already full of Chinese, most of whom were from the embassy. They exchanged greetings with some and were led to a small, private table in the rear by their waiter, a personable young man named Willy Chan. They greeted Willy warmly and exchanged pleasantries.

Everyone liked Willy. Willy was bright and always remembered everyone's name. The people at the embassy treated him as one of them, although he was an overseas Chinese who had lived in Paris most of his life. Lim made a point of mentioning this to Huang. Willy could possibly be used in a support capacity by the station.

The MSS used a lot of overseas Chinese to help them operationally, and Willy Chan might also have access agent potential as well. He seemed to know everyone, quite possibly even some Americans.

Huang brought them back to their conversation. "Okay, you have our agent Michelle targeted against this CIA communicator, what is his name? Rodney Jackson?"

"Yeah, Rodney. His friends sometimes call him 'Rotten.' That is a kind of a joke nickname. I do not think Rodney likes it very much . . ."

Huang laughed and shook his head. He really could learn from Lim. "Rotten, Rodney, no matter. How close are we? Are we getting anything out of him yet?"

"Sure, plenty of good operational information. The guy talks and talks to Michelle. And she really knows how to elicit, that one. I taught her good, but she has really got a knack . . ."

"Like what? What does he talk about?"

"He does not yet give us texts of cables he sends and receives in the commo room, if that's what you mean. Not yet anyway. But he does talk about his co-workers, office routine, who is arriving and who is leaving, that sort of thing . . .

"Like he told Michelle he hates his boss. He says his boss is an imperious SOB who is always on Rodney's back. That is an American expression. It means he never lets up on him. I have Michelle working on making Rodney late for work, for example, because that is one of the things his boss hates the most. Michelle fucks him one more time in the morning and he is late! Pretty good, eh? Makes the boss really pissed off at Rodney, and Rodney moves closer to us."

"Very good," said Huang admiringly. He knew that revenge was a prime motivator for recruitment, and it was clear that Rodney Jackson would like to somehow stick it to his boss. "Very, very good work, Lim . . . "

He looked at Lim with growing respect, while Lim remained professional and distant. Lim still didn't like this interloper and wasn't going to be sweet-talked by him, even though he did enjoy the praise.

Lim continued recounting the op against Rodney. "So he's got all these problems with being black—the boss is on his back, no money, no respect, and all that, and we give him this Michelle Li super-pussy, who treats him nice, fucks his brains out, listens to him and even pays for his beer and rice."

"I'll bet she does. Go on . . ."

Willy Chan interrupted them with a tray of steamed dumplings, a dish of kimchee, and two bottles of beer. When the waiter had left, Lim continued.

"Actually, she brings him here often, and of course we pick up the bill. Several of our colleagues have had an opportunity to talk to him here and to introduce him to the Chinese way of life. These are all good, independent assessments. And they go to the Marine House often, every Friday for TGIF, that means 'Thank God It's Friday,' which gives Michelle a chance to evaluate other targets in embassy as well. It is a very good op, I think."

"Good, good. Yes, a very good op." Huang spoke through a mouthful of dumplings and beer. The restaurant was loud with chatter and the clashing of dishes. A soulful Mandarin song wailed in the background. "What kind of information is she able to elicit besides his gripes? Any intelligence?" He was eager to get to the meat of the matter. Lim's answer cooled his hopes yet didn't dash them.

"No intelligence yet . . . Maybe Rodney is too stupid to know what he sees in the commo room. But like I said, plenty of good operational stuff about what happens in the embassy. We are building pretty good dossiers on some of Rodney's colleagues, and we are identifying other potential recruitment targets in the CIA station."

"For example?"

"For example, the chief's secretary is half Chinese, half American. Rodney likes her a lot. He says she is very open and friendly, easy to talk to. I think maybe she would be responsive to some kind of pitch from us. Being half Chinese . . . I just started to take a closer look at her. I was going to target Michelle on her, actually. They could become good friends maybe. But now she is too fully occupied with some old boyfriend who just came to Paris. Michelle says she can not get close to her until he leaves. Now she spends every waking moment with him."

"What about the boyfriend?"

"He is a CIA case officer. He was posted here before. Rodney told Michelle all about him. He and the secretary—Wei-wei Ryan is her name—they have had a long love affair, more than ten years, I think. And he is hard-core. No chance of recruiting him. It would be just a waste of time. So I decided to drop any action on Wei-wei until he leaves. Rodney told Michelle he does not think the boyfriend will be here for very long anyway. Just a couple of months, so not much time will be lost."

"He's just here temporarily?"

"Yeah, temporary. He got into Paris a couple of weeks ago. Just before you got here. Rodney says he is not permanent staff here. He came from Hong Kong."

"Hong Kong?" Huang's heart jumped and his eyes widened. "What is his name?" "Um, I think . . . Mac something. Irish name, maybe . . ."

"MacMurphy?" Huang's eyes showed alarm, and he stiffened with the intensity of the emotions he felt at the thoughts that were now running through his brain.

"Yeah, MacMurphy. Everybody calls him Mac. You know him? You feel okay, Huang?"

"We have got trouble. Big trouble. Let's get back to the office. I must notify Beijing of this immediately. And I want you to contact our surveillance team tonight. Starting now I want twenty-four-hour surveillance on that American case officer. Pull the team off everything else. Now let's get out of here."

Willy Chan, known to his CIA handlers as SKITTISH, watched them hurry out the door. He began to prepare his operational report in his mind . . .

CHAPTER 58

uller Santos and MacMurphy sat talking in a banquette near the window of the Café George V, located directly across the street from the Chinese Embassy. It was a few minutes past eight in the morning.

The previous evening, Mac had rented a car in a new alias and the two of them loaded the trunk with three large Samsonite suitcases full of equipment and parked it in the underground garage just up the street from the café where they now sat.

The station surveillance team, a dozen cleared Americans—students, housewives, retired couples, and the like—was positioned around the area of the operation in pairs and singly, in rented vehicles and on foot.

Two members of the team were poised to pick up GUNSHY, Collette, and her mother, and follow them all the way to Trouville on the Normandy coast. The rest of the team were instructed to keep the two buildings under constant observation and notify the entry team inside—Santos and MacMurphy—of any unusual activities, the presence of police, anyone at all entering the building, or the sudden return of Collette and her mother, any of which might jeopardize the operation.

Each member of the foot surveillance and stakeout team was equipped with an almost invisible earphone and tiny lapel microphone to keep them in constant communication with one another, the surveillance vehicles, and the entry team.

Every member of the team knew instantly when GUNSHY and the two women exited through the front door of the apartment building and headed up the street with their luggage.

"Here they come," said MacMurphy. He shook his head as he watched them approach GUNSHY's vehicle. "Damn! He's rented a Benz! Look at that! François is running true to form. He's got a Benz. Sonofabitch loves to spend my money. The green eyeshade people are going to have another conniption fit when they see his accounting. Sometimes I think he does it just to annoy me. I *know* he does it just to annoy me! Look at the grin on his face. He knows we're watching. Son of a bitch!"

Culler laughed at Mac's exasperation. His amusement was contagious, and now the situation tickled Mac, too, and he joined in the laughter, shaking his head in disbelief. They waited until François and the two women had loaded their things in the trunk of the Mercedes and had driven out of the area, then they waited a few minutes more to be sure. When nobody returned for a forgotten suitcase or last minute "I-should've-packed," Culler and Mac left the café.

Collette appeared to have bloomed under François's attentions. She had paid extra attention to her hair and makeup today. It was going to be a big weekend for her. "The so-called 'old maid' doesn't look too bad," Santos observed as they headed down into the parking garage to retrieve their equipment. "Not bad at all, in fact . . ."

"Not bad for an ugly cuss like you, Culler, but think about poor François and what he's used to. Everything's relative, you know. And she was all gussied up too. Think what she'll look like in the morning, without makeup and her hair all a mess. François is definitely lowering his standards for the sake of the Agency. I guess I shouldn't begrudge him the Benz after all. We may have to give him a Medal of Honor for service above and beyond . . ."

Culler snorted derisively, "You're probably right. If that guy is half of what he's reputed to be, he's certainly not hurting. And I suspect he's going to make that little lady very, very happy tonight."

"Bank on it, ol' buddy! She's going to think she died and went to heaven tonight. *Mon ami* François Leverrier will see to that . . ."

CHAPTER 59

Culler Santos easily carried the two heavy suitcases. MacMurphy carried the other, lighter bag. Culler said he wanted the two heavy bags "to balance himself." He was that kind of guy.

They entered the apartment building and quickly proceeded up the stairs to the old maid's apartment on the fifth floor. Culler was puffing heavily as they reached the top. "Don't they have any elevators in these buildings?" he complained.

MacMurphy inserted the key Culler had made from François's clay impression into the lock. At first the key wouldn't turn. Mac sucked air through his teeth in frustration.

Culler took over and talked to the stubborn lock: "C'mon, baby . . ." He kept his voice at a barely audible level. He jiggled the key and pushed it in and out, smoothing some of the burrs. Culler held his breath. Eventually the troublesome key turned in the lock, and the door swung open. They were in . . .

"Sure as hell beats picking the lock," said Santos appreciatively. "Thank GUNSHY one more time for me, will you?"

"You bet." MacMurphy double-bolted the door and stood by the peephole to provide a last ring of defense from intrusion while Culler Santos set to work methodically. They were all business now.

Culler opened one of the suitcases and took out a digital flash camera. He took a sequence of shots of the contiguous wall, viewed them, and set the camera back into the case. Everything would be replaced exactly as shown in the photos when they were through.

Now Santos set about accessing the area of the wall he needed to get to. First he unplugged both lamps and silently signaled Mac to help. The two of them moved the couch and two end tables away from the wall, being careful not to disturb anything on the tables or any of the small pillows on the couch. Next he removed a drop-cloth from the open suitcase and spread it out on the floor along the wall behind the couch. Using a tape, he measured a distance of three meters from the back wall and put a small piece of black electrician's tape on the top of the baseboard.

He turned to MacMurphy and spoke quietly. "If we go in directly behind the baseboard at this point, we will come out about two feet above the baseboard near the center of Huang's office. That's because of the juxtaposition of the buildings. The land slopes down to the Seine, so the embassy building is lower than we are. That's fine for audio quality, and low enough not to have the pinhole at eye level, no matter whether people are sitting or standing. But I'd like to move over a couple of feet to the rear to be closer to this outlet, so I can tap into the AC power easier. Okay?"

"No problem. You're the tech. Sounds good to me. The less we have to disturb, the better off we are."

"Absolutely . . . And I'm really glad we don't have to go through that old wallpaper. I hate working with wallpaper; restoration can be a bitch. This baseboard looks like it'll come off easily."

Santos opened the other two suitcases and laid the tools out on the floor. One held the parts of the drill, bits, and various other tools nestled into gray Styrofoam pockets. The other held the parts of the thickness gauge, more tools, and a surgeon's green trousers and smock.

He donned the clothes, which covered him from ankle to throat, and immediately went to work gently and quietly loosening a four-foot long piece of baseboard under the electrical outlet, using a crowbar and rubber mallet.

Once the baseboard was removed, he assembled the thickness gauge—a device that looked like a pistol with a long twelve-inch aluminum barrel attached by a cord to a calculator-like instrument—and proceeded to take readings of the wall's thickness at the spot he had selected to drill.

He placed the tip of the barrel against the wall and held the trigger down until the numbers of the calculator display stopped ticking up. It read "107." He did this three more times, and each time the display read either "106" or "107."

"Close enough for government work," whispered Santos while consulting a chart. "Jeez, the damn wall is seventy-four centimeters thick! That's almost thirty inches."

"Seems about right," said MacMurphy softly, "considering there are two buildings."

"Never fear," said Santos as he set aside the thickness gauge and began assembling the drill. "This is not like the old backscatter gauge, which was hit or miss at best, and you had to keep taking readings until you were within an inch or so of the end. This gauge gives it to you one time, and believe me it's accurate to within a centimeter. It's sure reduced the number of breakthroughs."

"Well, I'm glad to hear that, because I sure as hell don't want a breakthrough on this job. We can't run around to the other side to plug up our hole in *this* op!"

"Never fear, never fear." Santos was deftly assembling his drill like a Marine with an M-16. "Now, wait till you hear this." Culler tightened a two-inch diameter core bit on the drill and pressed it against the wall. The drill gave out a high-pitched whine similar to a dentist's drill, and the bit disappeared into the wall a full four inches.

"Good Lord!" whispered MacMurphy. "That thing eats into the concrete like its cardboard."

"Thought you'd like it," Santos snapped off a four-inch core and removed it from the drill bit. He set it carefully on the drop-cloth beside him. Not a speck of dust would go anywhere other than on that cloth. "We'll be through in no time at all."

Suddenly a subdued voice spoke in their earphones. It was a member of the surveillance team. "Someone, a woman, is entering the building." Both men stopped what they were doing . . . and waited . . . and listened. MacMurphy went to the door and put his eye to the peephole. They did not want anyone knocking on the door, nor could they afford for some person unknown to them to enter the apartment with a key. For that matter, they didn't even want any neighbor to hear any sounds from within the apartment. The apartment was supposed to be empty. Pausing, listening, they waited.

When several minutes had elapsed with no indication that anyone was outside the apartment door or about to enter, the two men exhaled and work resumed. Whoever had entered the building, whether a neighbor or a visitor to a neighbor, had apparently entered another apartment on a lower floor. They breathed a sigh of relief, but tension remained high, their senses keen to any possible disturbance.

Again, some seven minutes later, the scenario repeated itself. A surveillance team member signaled an entry into the building—a man this time—and all drilling work stopped. Mac went to the door, the men waited watchfully, and when nothing further transpired after several minutes, they resumed work with relief.

"We'll be through in no time at all." Santos had seven four-inch long, two-inch diameter cores laid out on the cloth next to him. He whispered, "Now we switch to a 3/8" bit for the next few inches,"

He screwed six-inch sections of the 3/8" tubes onto the drill. He stopped when he had a thirty-inch long section fitted to the drill. He waved it around like a light saber and turned to MacMurphy with a smile, "That way the hole won't be so big if we break through."

Mac grimaced.

"Nah, you know better than that. We're in a full twenty-eight inches with the two-inch bit. That'll give us plenty of room to conceal the transmitter, switch, and masking device." He pointed to what looked like a foot-long sausage of connected electrical equipment on the floor beside him.

MacMurphy knew that the transmitter had an output of less than half a watt of power but could easily be picked up with the proper receiving equipment within a distance of about two hundred to three hundred meters; beyond that there would be nothing. It was switched, which meant it could be turned on and off remotely from the LP, and masked, which meant it would sound like static to anyone happening upon the transmitting frequency—a decoder connected to the receiver in the LP apartment would change the static back into clear audio.

"Now I'm going to mark this bit so I can stop within a half inch of the end." Culler marked a spot on the bit near the drill end with a pen and circled the spot with a piece of electrical tape. "That'll give us plenty of room for the mic to seat snugly." He pointed to an inch-long microphone, attached to the end of the transmitter sausage by a thin speaker wire.

Santos concentrated on drilling the final few critical centimeters with the 3/8" core bit. He was very careful, exceedingly precise, his whole concentration focused on the task at hand, and though he didn't betray any nervousness with his actions, the beads of sweat on his brow belied his outwardly calm composure.

Mac, despite his faith in the equipment and in Santos, was sweating so badly that his scalp itched. He didn't blink at all, just stared bug-eyed at the drilling operation, willing Culler to succeed and not break through the wall.

Culler extracted the drill and carefully snapped off the last core deep in the hole with a long, thin core probe. When he pulled the last 1-1/2" long, 3/8" core from the hole, he held it up to Mac and whispered, "*La voilà!*" The end of the concrete core showed traces of plaster from the inner wall.

Normally, the last half-inch long, pinhole-sized air passage was drilled with a device called a "grit drill." The grit drill actually eroded the material in front of it by forcing carbon grit out of a tiny hole at the end of a long, rigid hose attached to a pump. And when the erosion process was complete and resistance stopped as the grit exited through the other side of the wall, it made a "poof" sound, and the pump shut itself off. Hence the audio techs affectionately called the drill the "poofer."

But Culler Santos was a tech of the old school, and he didn't like the poofer. He thought the equipment was rather cumbersome and made too much noise—much like a small air pump—for his taste. So he relied upon the old "pin-vice."

The pin-vice consisted of an inch-long pinhead-sized drill bit attached to a long, 3/8" probe that looked like a gun-cleaning rod. The probe was inserted into the drill hole, and the tech manually turned the handle at the end. It took a little longer, but there was no noise and very little chance of a slip-up. And drilling would be easy through the soft plaster at the end of the hole.

Santos was through to the other side in less than five minutes. The pinhole was less than 1/4" long, and the tech gasped as the drill bit turned through the last centimeter of plaster and into resistance-free air. He had not meant to cut it so fine, and he did not mention to the case officer the fact that he had come very close to pushing the 3/8" drill into the target. Some things were better off left unsaid between tech and case officer, even though they might be close friends.

Santos checked to see that the air passage was clean with a device similar to a doctor's fiber optic proctoscope, and then, with a sure and steady hand, inserted the "dick-mike" into the hole with a long probe. Once the microphone was firmly seated in the 3/8" hole at the end of the tunnel, he stuffed the remaining wire in behind it and followed with the sausage-like transmitter package.

Now only two thin wires hung from the back of the hole. He attached these to the back of the electrical outlet to give the device AC power and sat back to admire his work.

"That's it!" he said with satisfaction. "Now let's check to see that all's well, and then we can backfill and get the hell out of here." Opening one of the suitcases, he turned on the receiver. He tested his equipment, first by turning the transmitter on and off several times with the remote switch, and then by listening quietly to the target room for several minutes through a set of earphones. "Perfect, absolutely perfect. We've got audio!" He gave the thumbs-up sign to Mac. "Come over here and give a listen."

MacMurphy left his post at the apartment door's peephole, slipped the earphones on his head, and listened. He heard clear, crisp audio from Huang's office. An air conditioner was running, and a phone could be heard ringing down the hall. There was no conversation in the room at the time, but the gain on the microphone was straining to pull in sounds. There was no doubt that conversations would come in loud and clear when there were people talking in the room.

He pulled the earphones off and turned to the tech. "Sounds really good. Now let's close it up and get the hell out of here."

It took another hour to backfill the two-inch-round hole with several of the four-inch cores, plaster the hole, replace the baseboard, touch it up with a quick-drying, non-smelling paint that Culler mixed to match the old paint perfectly, clean up behind them, and replace the furniture and other things exactly as they were in the photos Santos had taken before starting.

Total time in Collette LeBrun's apartment was less than two hours. No evidence of the CIA officers' short visit was left behind in the apartment. None at all . . .

CHAPTER 60

On Monday morning, Culler Santos and MacMurphy met GUNSHY in the *au pair* room they had rented to serve as a listening post.

They could smell coffee brewing as they walked up the stairs and hoped it was from the LP. Climbing the final flight, they followed their noses, appreciative that the ever-stronger scent made it plain that there was strong, hot coffee awaiting them at the top.

François LeVerrier greeted them at the door, and Mac introduced Culler to him as "Jim."

François was tanned from the weekend at the shore and dressed all in white: canvas shoes, no socks, slacks, and tee-shirt. "*Entrez, mes amis.* Pleased to meet you, Jim." They shook hands. "*Le café* is brewing, and I will tell you all about my weekend with the beautiful and multi-talented Collette LeBrun over a cup."

Mac ignored the comment and instead of responding mumbled with incredulity, "A Benz! Did you have to rent a damn Benz?" But he managed a smile when he said it. No sense damaging rapport with François.

He had done a great job getting the woman and her mother out of the way, and he did not want to put a damper on the occasion.

François responded to the rebuke with a Gallic shrug, too intent on telling his story to take offense at the comment.

The three men crowded into the tiny one-room efficiency apartment. The furnishings consisted of a small twin bed along one wall, dresser, kitchen table with two chairs, love seat, and little coffee table. The room had one window, which looked out over the rooftops of the buildings running along Avenue George V. Surely, however the rent rate had been calculated, they were not being charged for the view.

MacMurphy pointed out the rear of the Chinese Embassy to Santos. The building was clearly visible less than one hundred meters away, and there was direct line-of-sight to Huang's top floor office.

Santos looked back into the tiny room from the window. "I'd hate to have to live in this cramped space. Especially as an LP keeper who has to spend all day working in here. But it sure as hell is good from a technical point of view. You did a great job finding this place, François." He turned back to the window and mentally gauged the distance from the LP to Huang's office. "The path-loss for the RH signal between the target and here will be negligible. This is terrific."

François reveled in the praise. "I thought you would be pleased. This is not the first audio operation I have been involved in, you know. I know a little something about path-loss and line-of-sight and things like that." Directing his comments to Santos, he said, "I knew you would be pleased, Jim. You are a technician. It is Mac I was worried about. He might not understand the beauty of this place." To both of them he said anxiously, "Do you gentlemen want to hear about Collette LeBrun now?"

"You're right," said Mac to Culler, ignoring François's last remark, "we're going to have a hell of a time finding someone to man this LP."

François was pouting, but he held his silence . . . for the time being, waiting for an opportune moment to jump into the conversation with the tale of his latest conquest.

"Why's that?" said the tech.

"Cover. How are we going to find someone with a believable cover to live in this place? Whoever is going to be living here has to be able to fit in. And since this is an *au pair* room surrounded on this floor by nothing but other *au pair* rooms just like it, we're going to be more or less restricted to finding a young woman for the job, or at least a student.

"Normally we can put just about anyone we want in an LP, but not in this case. The fellow they're sending out to be the transcriber is a retired Army officer with near native Mandarin Chinese. He learned the language in China as the son of Mormon missionaries in Beijing. Anyway, I wanted to use him in the LP as well to get real-time transcriptions, but I can't use him here. He'd stand out like a queer in a whorehouse on this floor."

"You can use him to transcribe the tapes," said Culler. "I'll fix the LP up to run remotely—turn on only when conversations are taking place in the room, then off again—then you can stick your linguist in the embassy or anywhere else you want, and he can transcribe the tapes there. All you'll need is a cleared young woman to live in this place to baby-sit the equipment. She'll have to turn it on and off with the main transmitter switch every morning and night, but that won't be too hard. She won't need any LP experience at all. We don't have to worry about battery power in this case; remember, we're hooked up to AC in Collette LeBrun's apartment. We've got all the power we need to run the transmitter forever."

MacMurphy was skeptical. "I've heard about your remote equipment. Damn things work on the bench but fail in the field. They turn themselves on whenever the air-conditioner comes on in the room or when someone beeps his horn on the street below, and don't come on when a conversation takes place in the room at below fifty decibels. Bloody targets have to practically shout at one another to turn the damn thing on!"

François felt like he was at a tennis match. "Do you fellows argue like this all the time?"

"Sure," Santos responded. "Case officers are born skeptics. They have no faith in technical equipment . . ."

"That's because it poops out all the bloody time! Great op, but the equipment died! How many times have you heard that one, Jim?"

"Now, now, that was all in the past; you're a bit behind the curve now. We've made some real great improvements in the past couple of years while you were hanging out in Hong Kong. Trust me. This equipment will work."

"It had better," said MacMurphy with finality. This was the dichotomy between case officer and audio technician.

Culler began setting up the LP equipment. He moved the small kitchen table from the center of the room to the corner next to the window. Then he placed a black four-inch attaché case on the table and opened it. It was full of radio gear.

"*Alors*, you want to hear about the weekend, Mac?" François was eager to tell his story and could be put off no longer. "Everything went smooth as silk. She . . ."

Mac interrupted, "Hang on, *mon vieux*." He put his arm around François's shoulders. "The surveillance team told me that you kept Collette and her mother under wraps—so to speak—the whole weekend. That's really all that counts, and you did a great job on that score. You did your part, and that permitted us to do ours. Now let's let the audio tech do his thing. We can talk operations later." Mac's tone was jovial, but François looked like a little boy who'd just been told that he'd have to wait till after dinner to eat his giant piece of double fudge cake with chocolate icing.

CHAPTER 61

Fuller Santos sat in front of his gear, immersed in the job of setting everything up properly. He took a gulp of the strong French coffee, grimaced and added two lumps of sugar and a splash of milk to cut it.

Satisfied, he explained the operation of the LP equipment to the case officer and agent. "The antenna is built into the top of this attaché case. When it's pointed in this direction, with the open lid in line with the target, you'll get your best reception. All the gear you'll need is in this case. If someone comes to the door or wants into the apartment for any reason, all the LP keeper has to do is unplug it, stick the cord back into the case, and close the lid. *Voilà*, all evidence that the place is being used as an LP is concealed from view."

The case officer and the agent were impressed. They hunched over the tech, who sat at the table in front of the open attaché case. Santos's big hands pointed out the various pieces of gear nestled neatly in it.

"Everything's written down here step by step on this diagram." He held up a piece of paper. "But I'll run through it one time for you guys since one of you may have to train the LP keeper when Mac gets around to finding one."

"I'll find one," said Mac.

"Anyway, here's the main power supply," said Santos, "and here's the main switch for the transmitter in the target. You have to hold the transmitter switch down for at least five seconds. It sends out a tone, which the switch in the target package, you know, recognizes. When this little light comes on, you'll know the transmitter is on. This box over here is the de-masker. It automatically deciphers the encryption on the signal and lets you hear clear audio. You don't have to mess with it at all. Just make sure it's turned on and hooked up properly, or you get shit, pure static shit."

He pointed to the largest piece of equipment in the case: "This is the receiver. It's preset to the proper frequency, but this dial here will let you fine-tune a bit. The earphones plug in here." He plugged them in and placed the earphones on his head and listened for a few moments. "And now you're in business."

CHAPTER 62

The next day, Santos was not so chipper. François had delivered the first of the tapes to Mac, and when Mac played it back, he heard an hour of conversation—nothing particularly useful, as it turned out—and then a sudden silence. The silence continued. "Dammit!" he cursed. "What the hell is wrong? Why did it fail? And what did we miss hearing?"

He called Santos into his temporary office and replayed for him the portion of the tape where the audio broke off. That was the point at which Santos's usually cheery attitude turned suddenly bleak and sour.

"I don't know what went wrong," he averred. "It . . . should have, you know, worked perfectly . . . Everything checked out . . ."

"Everything checked out . . . but something failed," Mac retorted glumly. "Now we have to go back to the LP, and possibly the LeBrun's apartment again, too. Shit, shit, shit . . ."

Their first action was to return to the listening post to survey the equipment there. Everything checked out perfectly, and they found that

233

the recorder was indeed once again recording just as it should. But what had gone wrong the day before . . . and how could they be sure there wouldn't be a recurrence?

The next thing to do seemed to be to signal a meeting with François and task him with paying a visit to Collette and, while there, discreetly look around the living room for any visual indication of a disturbance. It was a long shot, but the next logical thing to try,

"But what am I to look for, *mon vieux?*" asked François when Mac-Murphy spelled out the problem to him.

"Damned if I know . . . I don't know what in blazes we're looking for, to tell you the truth. Any indication that your new *amour* or her mother might have somehow disturbed the equipment . . . see if there are signs that the couch was moved . . . anything at all that might explain the disruption. Something other than the lamp plugged into the outlet behind the sofa? Anything at all out of the ordinary. *Ça va?*"

"Your accountants aren't going to like this," François replied, smiling.

What is that roué up to now? MacMurphy raised his eyebrows and shook his finger at François. "Okay if it takes a dinner, but you don't need to rent a bloody Benz for the evening. *Ça va?*"

It was beastly hot out. Paris was sweltering under a seriously oppressive August heat wave. True, the day before had been even worse, but today was no Arctic breeze.

François phoned Collette. "I don't know what your plans for this evening are, *ma chere,* but in this heat, I think a picnic is in order. It's no weather to be indoors without air conditioning. There should be a pleasant breeze in the evening. What if I will pick up a nice picnic basket at Fauchon's for us? Perhaps some caviar, smoked pheasant, pâté with truffles, and a baguette. Oh yes, and a nice bottle of Bordeaux. Perhaps a Chateau Beychevelle. Yes that will do just fine. Chateau Beychevelle. This is no night to cook. I'll be at your place around seven, yes? And I'll bring a bottle of cool champagne as well for an aperitif." He was not going to take a no, or even a maybe, for an answer.

Collette was delighted and didn't try to hide the pleasure in her voice. The man had said, "I miss seeing you." That and his thoughtfulness at suggesting she not cook on such a hot day were enough to curve her lips into a deliciously wide smile. Her mother, seated nearby, didn't know what was being said at the other end of the phone connection but had a pretty good idea as to who it was that was putting such a smile on her daughter's face.

François arrived on the dot of seven with an overflowing picnic basket and a cool bottle of Veuve Clicquot.

While the trio enjoyed the champagne, François looked discreetly around the apartment for any clues as to what had gone wrong the day before. But everything seemed perfectly in place. He made a comment that this weather was "certainly not the time to do anything that requires a major expenditure of energy . . . like moving furniture," but got nothing but agreement from the two women, with no further comment or explication. He was almost ready to give up and declare his mission a failure.

After getting her mother settled, Collette practically fled out the door with François. She wished both to be alone with him and to escape the heat of the apartment. The hallway and stairwell were worse, windowless and enclosed as they were, and when the pair emerged onto the street, Collette breathed a sigh of relief while François did some major mopping of his face with his handkerchief.

"This heat is horrible," he said.

"And yesterday was even worse. And then we experienced a blackout."

"Blackout?"

"Yes. A main fuse in the building blew. These old buildings aren't really wired for air-conditioners, but several of the apartments have window units installed. We need to get one as well. I suppose they were running full-blast in this heat, and something got overloaded. The whole building was without electricity for most of the day. Not even a fan— nothing. It was awful . . ."

François's thoughts immediately focused on the mic that had been hooked up to the back of the outlet in the wall. *Voilla! That was what had happened to silence the mic.* He could hardly wait to report back to MacMurphy . . . but of course, he had to go through with the picnic, first. And when he thought of all the goodies he had packed in the basket, and witnessed the delight in Collette's eyes, he decided it was not at all a bad thing to spend a few hours in the park enjoying a picnic dinner with Collette LeBrun.

CHAPTER 63

MacMurphy and Santos were relieved to get to the bottom of the mystery, though nervous that there would be a recurrence of the blackout and the interruption in their electronic eavesdropping.

They paid visits to the LP three times a day for the next five days, nervously fussing over the equipment, checking the tapes, and listening to the conversations and other sounds emanating from Huang's office, but nothing of significance was recorded. Huang spent most of the time alone in his office, not communicating with anyone except for one-sided telephone conversations. The heat wave finally broke, and thankfully there were no further blackouts to interrupt transmission.

One morning Santos was sitting at the table, listening through the earphones, when he said, "Listen to this Mac—sounds like they're moving furniture around in there."

MacMurphy put on the earphones and half-sat against the edge of the table. The audio quality was excellent, but he still pressed the earphones tighter against his ears to hear better. He listened carefully. His

Mandarin was okay, but not quite fluent enough to catch every word that was spoken, and some of the conversation was in Cantonese. Several people were in the room. He strained to comprehend the conversation.

"I hope you're recording this," he said to Santos.

Culler quickly inserted a fresh cassette tape into the recorder and hit the Record button. He nodded to Mac. "I am now . . ."

CHAPTER 64

At that moment, Huang Tsung-yao was directing two heavy-set Chinese men who were trying to horse a large cabinet safe, secured to a dolly, into position against the wall in his office. "Right over there. Yes, there. Back against the wall."

The two laborers were sweating profusely as they tried to jockey the heavy five-foot-tall safe back against the wall. He motioned to his deputy, who was sitting sprawled in a chair in front of Huang's desk, leg over one arm, watching the workers. "Eyeah, give them a hand, Lim. Be useful. Help them . . ."

Lim cast a disdainful look at Huang but joined in to help anyway. They maneuvered the dolly until the safe was as close to the wall as they could get it. Then they tried to tilt the dolly down gently, but it got away from them, and the top of the safe banged heavily against the wall, digging out a chunk of plaster.

"Easy, easy, do not wreck the place," said Huang, who moved over to lend a hand himself. They finally set the safe down about six inches from the wall. The workers removed the straps that held the safe to the dolly, tilted the safe back once again, and slid the dolly out from under.

"Eyeah. That is as close as we can get it with the dolly," said one of the laborers. "Now it's going to take all of us to swing the thing into position flush against the wall."

With two men on each side, they inched the heavy safe back toward the wall, one side at a time. When they had finished and the safe was finally in position, as close to the wall as they could get it, they were all breathing heavily, and Lim's clean, white shirt was soaked through. The larger of the two laborers leaned heavily on Huang's desk, catching his breath, while the other busied himself fixing the straps on the dolly. "We will be back with the pouch in a few minutes," said the large one. "It is one big bag. Heavy. That safe there was real bitch, eh? Too big, too heavy . . ."

The laborers left to get the diplomatic pouch, and Lim excused himself to change his shirt. He was compulsive about cleanliness—one of his many foibles.

The group returned about fifteen minutes later. The Chinese workers had the large, bright orange canvas pouch bag secured to the dolly. They unstrapped it and left it, unopened, in the middle of the room. Huang attacked the wire seals at the top of the bag with a pair of wire cutters. It contained three heavy cardboard boxes stacked one on top of the other. Huang peeled the bag down away from the boxes, and Lim carried them one at a time and set them down in front of the safe. "What is in the boxes?" he asked with understandable curiosity.

"Open them and see for yourself, Lim. Close the door first. I am sure the contents will interest you." Huang watched with amusement as Lim dug in his pocket and extracted a vicious-looking pearl-handled knife. He snapped the thin stiletto blade out of the handle and carefully slit open the packing tape covering one of the boxes. He opened the lid, removed a layer of packing paper, and gasped.

The box contained tightly packed stacks of five hundred euro notes. Lim reached in and pulled out two stacks. "Eyeah," he muttered, "how much is in here?"

"Fifty million. More than either of us will ever see again in our lifetime."

"What are we going to do with it?"

"Let us first get the money into the safe, and then I will brief you thoroughly."

CHAPTER 65

"**S**onofabitch!" MacMurphy jerked the earphones off of his head and rubbed his ears. "Bastards almost broke my eardrums."

"What happened?" asked Santos.

"They just smashed a safe into the wall right above our microphone." He shook his head and dug his fingers into his ears. "Damn, that hurts."

"Safe? What safe?"

MacMurphy had not said a word since putting the earphones on, so Santos was unaware of what Mac was listening to so intently.

"Do me a favor, will you? Get me another cup of coffee and something to take notes on. I'll give you a full briefing just as soon as there's a break in the action, but for now let me listen to this. Something really strange is going on in that office." Mac held one of the earphones to his ear while he spoke.

"They're moving in a heavy safe and trying to put it up against the wall right where our microphone is located. Damn!" He jerked the earphones out away from his head and rubbed his ear again. Loud, scraping noises emanating from the earphones could be heard clearly. "Wait a minute . . . they're talking again . . . hang on."

As they talked, Mac listened. And as Mac listened, Santos watched him. His expression changed from interested to concerned, then from concerned to angry, then from angry to . . . Culler couldn't pinpoint just what it was he was seeing reflected in Mac's face. He was taking notes furiously on a yellow pad, and whatever it was, it worried him. *What was Mac hearing?*

Almost an hour later, Mac hit the stop button on the tape recorder and pulled the earphones from his head. Several pages of the yellow pad in front of him were filled with rough notes.

MacMurphy leaned back in his chair and turned toward Santos. "Huang and Lim just left the office. They locked the door behind them after Huang told Lim to activate the alarm. Probably some sort of a motion alarm system like we have in our stations. Anyway . . . where should I start?"

"How about the beginning," said Santos, motioning to the pages of notes in front of MacMurphy.

Mac put his notes in his lap, leaned back, and put his legs up on the table. "Get comfortable. This may take a while." But Mac, though he had assumed a relaxed position, did not look comfortable at all.

Santos leaned back attentively in the other kitchen chair.

"First of all, if there were any doubts before about whether we got the right office or not, they are dispelled now. It's Huang's office all right. No doubt about it. And he just took delivery of a heavy safe, which is now sitting right smack up against the wall where our audio mic is located. It's directly in front of our pinhole. At least that's the way it sounds. The quality of the audio changed, got kind of muffled, when the safe went all the way back up against the wall. And then, right after they brought in the safe, they opened a diplomatic pouch from Beijing. The contents of the pouch—get this, Culler—fifty million euros—has been placed in that safe."

"What do they need all that, you know, cash for?"

"Good question. I think it relates to why I was asked to come here in the first place. Let me just say that Huang has spent the past ten years working on covert action affairs back in Beijing. His last job before coming here was as Chief of covert action for the Ministry of State Security." Mac paused to organize his thoughts.

"A couple of months ago in Hong Kong I picked up some disjointed information. It all seems to come together now, though. Essentially, the information I got was that Huang, a covert action expert, was coming to be the MSS station chief in Paris. So the question was why send a CA expert to a place like Paris unless the MSS was considering running some pretty serious covert action operations there.

"We all know the Chinese do very little in the way of CA. But there were two other tidbits to add to the puzzle. One was that there was a large shipment of cash about to be to be shipped here by the MSS, and the second involved some sort of Iranian connection to that shipment."

"Iran? Iran and China would make, you know, dangerous bedfellows," said Santos. "What sort of connection?"

"Another good question." Articulating his thoughts to Santos served to help in the analytical process. "China remained more or less neutral throughout the Iran/Iraq war. Or perhaps I should say China did not join the ranks of those countries that condemned either Iran or Iraq before and during that war. They remained neutral or noncommittal on the outside, overtly, but supported Iran covertly, and they have continued that support through the years as their cooperation increased."

"Oil?"

"You got it. Oil. But there's more, much more. Certainly oil. In return for cheap oil, practically free in some instances, the Chinese provided military assistance and equipment. There has also been some nuclear cooperation, but I don't think anyone knows the degree of that cooperation yet. And now that Iran wants to play an influential role in Iraq to eventually drive us totally out of the country, China may now be offering its covert support."

"Iran is heavy into covert action in Iraq these days. They're actually outspending the US in this regard. I think this money might be part of that covert cooperation plan. That's pretty clear now from what Huang just said. Rothmann is going to love this."

Mac pulled his feet off the table and leaned forward to emphasize his next point. "The fact is we've just caught China with its hand in the cookie jar. Smiling at us and shaking our hand while they're giving us the finger with the other hand. They're diddling us. They are just like the French, the slimy bastards. I'm talking about their government. They'll do anything if they think it's in their own best interests. Screw the rest of the world. They're whores . . . the whole lot of them, whores . . ."

"Whew! Glad you don't feel too strongly about this, Mac. And I thought I was the one with, you know, the reputation for being a hothead! So let me see if I understand. The Chinese are supporting an Iranian CA operation to the tune of fifty million euros. Is that about it?"

"Actually, the way Huang described it to Lim just now, the Iranians supplied the money covertly through Beijing. That's why they had to bring it into the country in cash, through the diplomatic pouch. It's 'black' money . . ."

"Untraceable. Hmmm. But why cash? With the way money is being laundered these days, you know, they shouldn't have had to go to all the trouble of shipping so much cash . . . and getting a safe large enough to hold it . . . and all that . . ."

"Because it's going out in cash. Huang has a list . . . where the hell is it? Here it is . . . Huang has a list of recipients. The heat is on the Iranians and their Arab friends who actively support terrorism, particularly in Iraq, where all of them have the common goal of ousting the US from the country and indeed the whole region, so the unlikely Chinese have been tasked to distribute the money in Europe. And this is probably not all of it, just the first *tranche*. I'll bet there's plenty more to come . . ."

MacMurphy paused to find his place in his notes. "Here it is. The money will be used primarily in France—I guess because France is such a haven for terrorists and other low-lives, and so anti-American these days—but not exclusively. It'll also go to groups in some neighboring European countries like Germany, Italy, Belgium and Greece. Huang is in charge of all of it. It sounds like his station will be the main distribution center for all of Europe.

"He said about two-thirds of the money will go to advance Iranian goals, especially in Iraq, and the remaining one-third for pro-Chinese propaganda activities. To erase the stigma of the 1989 Tiananmen Square crackdown, unsafe food and toys exported to the US, and all that crap. They want to portray China as an emerging democracy with an economy to be reckoned with. Let's see." He flipped the pages of his notes.

"I can't read my own writing. Looks like most of the Chinese portion will go toward reviving European communist parties like the PCF here in France, and to buy political influence wherever they can. They are not so much interested in reviving communism, which is pretty much a dead horse, but using those communist party infrastructures and redirecting them to support anti-American political positions—especially Arab, Iranian, and Chinese political positions.

"And it gets worse . . ." He paused to study his notes and organize his thoughts. "Here it is. Huang's not too happy with this part, although his deputy, Lim, thinks it's pretty neat. Active support of terrorism. The covert action campaign for the Arab and Iranian portion of all of this includes everything from posters and rallies and articles and that sort of CA crap, to outright bomb-throwing terrorism. The Iranian clerics have finally pulled out the stops, and Iraq is the catalyst.

"Get this, Culler." He turned to the next page of hastily scribbled notes. "Cash will be distributed directly to extremist organs of Hizbullah, al Qaeda, the PLO, the PFLP-GC, the PFLP-SC, Black September, the Hawari Organization, even remnants of the old Abu Nidal Organization . . . The list goes on. I couldn't copy them all. Iran believes it is in the best position in its history to exert influence in Iraq, and it is pulling out all stops to achieve that goal . . .

"It has already flooded Iraq with its operatives and is financing the Shite insurgent groups there, and this covert action is just an extension of that effort. They want to defeat America there." He looked up from his notes. "This is scary, Culler. Real scary . . . I've got to get this out to Rothmann right away."

CHAPTER 66

Two weeks had passed since the bugging of Huang's office. The initial tapes had been fully transcribed, providing important and revealing detail to the overall plan. The tiny LP was functioning well, although the station had still not found an ideal candidate to man the tiny *au pair* room, forcing François, Culler and Mac to alternate in and out of it to check the equipment and pick up tapes to be transcribed.

Things were relatively quiet in Huang's office after the initial conversation about the covert action plan. Huang spent most of his days working at his desk in silence. The bug picked up conversations with Lim and other members of his staff and a number of short, one sided phone chats which provided unique operation information about the workings on Huang's station, but nothing more on the subject of Iran/China cooperation. MacMurphy's frustration grew, as did Headquarters' . . .

So when MacMurphy was summoned to the COS's office on Thursday afternoon, he had a strong feeling of angst in his gut. It was not misguided.

Burton B. Berger and MacMurphy sat alone in the COS's office. Bob Little, Mac was told, was summoned back to Headquarters for "consultations." The door was closed and Berger pointedly activated the anti-intrusion security system before beginning.

Berger began calmly by pointing out Headquarters' frustration over the lack of progress of the audio op in providing additional information on the Iran/China plot, or on providing an updated assessment of Huang. "It's not working. It's simply not working. You're stalling, aren't you?" He stared into MacMurphy's eyes, as if to say, *I know something is amiss here. I know what you are doing, and I'm going to nail you for it.*

MacMurphy calmly defended the operation. "I don't see why you're in such a hurry. The operation began with a bang. It provided an outline of their plans and intentions from practically the first day, and now you are telling me that Headquarters is pissing all over it because it hasn't produced anything lately? Is that what you're saying?"

"It isn't *just* Headquarters," Berger said knowingly, settling back in his leather executive chair, fixing MacMurphy with his stare. "It's the Director. He's wise to your stalling tactics. You initially did the audio op to gain assessment data on Huang that you could use to pitch him. That hasn't happened. He wants action, and he wants it *now.* He's on to the game you and Rothmann are playing. Huang is the key to all of this and he wants Huang *now.*"

Berger leaned forward and wagged a long, delicate finger at MacMurphy. "You are through playing games. You were told to bring Huang in and you refused. The Director knows you've been stalling because you have some sort of an affinity for the guy. You fell in love with your agent, MacMurphy. Something a rookie case officer would do. Huang has all the answers and the Director wants them now. Get it? Now . . ."

"What is it you want me to do? Pitch him? That's it, isn't it? I'm telling you that won't work. Huang will refuse. He's not recruitable. If you want answers, you and the Director will just have to wait for them to come to you through the audio op. That's the only way to get the answers you want. Through the audio op. For God sakes, Burton, you can't be serious. Where's the DDO in all this? He knows the deal . . ."

Berger leaned forward, elbows on his desk, glaring at MacMurphy. "The DDO, your old buddy, is out of it. The Director is running this show now. *Personally.* And you're going to do what he wants you to do or you can take the next flight out of here. Get it? The DDO and you are no longer running this op." He sat back, satisfied, and studied his fingers.

Mac had the wind knocked out of him. He was trembling with emotion and barely able to contain himself. He was back in Somalia. Back in that hot "bubble" with the Ambassador. He could not believe this was happening again. "You know its wrong, Burton, but you are going along with it anyway." He spoke softly, trying to bring the tension down, trying to make some sense out of the matter, trying to appeal to Burton B. Burger's better sense of judgment.

And then it got worse, much worse.

Berger had MacMurphy on the ropes. He enjoyed the feeling. He was winning. "So here is what I want you to do, Mr. MacMurphy. And this is straight from the Director . . ."

Berger wagged a blue striped cable in front of him and his tone was quiet and assured. He tossed his glasses on the desk, stood up and looked down on MacMurphy, gaining a psychological advantage.

"You will use the surveillance team to follow Huang. Wake up with him in the morning and put him to bed at night. And when the right opportunity presents itself . . . when Huang is somewhere outside of his embassy and accessible . . . perhaps in that Chinese restaurant he likes so much . . . the Mai-Lin or whatever . . . you will approach him and say whatever you need to say to get him to cooperate with us. I think there will be a lot of incentive for him to do it this time, because he knows he will be on the first plane back to Beijing if he doesn't."

"No! Because that's exactly what will happen. He'll refuse and he will take the first plane back to Beijing and he will be fucked and our audio operation will be fucked and we'll be nowhere. Is that really what you and the Director want? Have you guys completely lost it?"

"No, Mr. MacMurphy, we haven't *lost* it. We are totally on top of it. It's you and Rothmann who have lost it. You're dragging your feet. That's what you're doing and we know it. The Director wants action and he's right. We need answers and we need them now. We've got Huang where we want him. He has to cooperate with us. He has no choice . . .

"But . . . You see, here's the beauty of it. We will win no matter what decision Huang makes. If he decides to cooperate, we will win. If he decides not to cooperate, we will also win" Berger stepped back, proud of himself. Satisfied.

"I must be missing something, How the hell do we win if Huang is sent back to Beijing?"

Berger leaned back and put his feet up on his desk. He pondered his slender fingers before answering. "Because if he agrees to cooperate and accepts recruitment we will debrief him and we will get all of the answers we need, and if he doesn't we will snatch him off the street and still get all the answers we need. You see, it's a win-win situation . . ."

Mac shook his head, not understanding.

"You still don't get it, do you? It's time for some action, Mr. Mac-Murphy. We have a FATBOY team arriving over the weekend. They'll take care of things if he decides not to cooperate with you, or if you decide to take the next flight out of here. It makes no difference to me one way or the other . . ."

CHAPTER 67

MacMurphy left the COS' office deep in his own depressing thoughts. He passed Wei-wei Ryan's desk on the way out. They exchanged worried looks but didn't speak.

He knew something had to be done, but was unsure what he could do to prevent the unfolding of the Director's disastrous plan. This was no time to wait and be reactive, he thought. He needed to be proactive. And without Rothmann in his corner—it appeared he was no longer in the picture—what could he do?

The Director had grabbed the wheel and was driving the bus off of a cliff. Mac's only thoughts now were how to save Huang from an impending extraordinary rendition by the FATBOY team, and how to save the country from reverting back to a cold war stand-off with China. The rendition of a Chinese diplomat was sheer madness, even if the Chinese official was involved in supporting terrorism.

Mac had always been a man of action, back in his days as a Marine in Somalia and even before. And he was no less so now. But . . .

The kernel of an idea began to form and grow in his mind. And the more he thought about it, the clearer it became. It still needed a lot of refining, but it seemed that it just might be doable . . . He decided to think about it some more, and when he had everything together in his mind, he would bounce it off Culler and Wei-wei, the only two allies left.

He could not permit this disaster to occur—not to Huang—not to his country.

CHAPTER 68

Other than this germ of an idea forming in Mac's mind, the only bright spot in the entire afternoon was the news that the DCOS, Bob Little, was out of there. He was accused of fabricating a source—SKITTISH—and recalled permanently to Langley.

Fabricating a source was as bad as fabricating information. In the CIA, fabrication of any sort was *the* most egregious sin any case officer could commit.

As they say in East Asia Division, thought MacMurphy, *Little Bob is in deep kimchee*. The system had finally caught up with him. Rothmann would eat Little Bob alive this time, and this made MacMurphy very happy.

CHAPTER 69

After work, Culler and Mac joined Wei-wei in the embassy lounge for cocktails. They settled into plush black leather chairs around a polished rosewood coffee table and ordered drinks. The embassy lounge was a comfortable place to unwind, and Mac especially really needed a stiff drink after the hammering he took in Berger's office.

Mac was subdued, thoughtful, and Wei-wei and Culler gave him space to think and ponder. They didn't know what was wrong, but figured it had something to do with his meeting with Berger.

Wei-wei shot him a sympathetic smile.

"Don't worry about it, whatever it is. He's an asshole," said Santos matter-of-factly, clearly referring to the COS.

"A man of few words," Wei-wei said, pointing a thumb in Culler's direction. "So what's up? What happened in there?"

Mac concentrated on the glass he slowly turned on the coaster in front of him, but the wheels of his mind were spinning.

The idea for a follow-up operational plan had been germinating ever since his meeting with Berger, and now all of the pieces seemed to be coming together. He wanted to articulate his thoughts to his friends, but couldn't decide whether it was time. He began cautiously.

"How much longer do you plan to be in Paris, Culler?"

"A few more days. I want to make sure the LP continues running smoothly and there are no further problems . . . you know, to keep you off my back. And I have a few things to do for one of the other branches while I'm here. But I can stay, well, you know, for as long as you need me. I'll take a few days of leave if necessary. Why? What have you got in mind?"

"So you can be here through the weekend . . ."

Santos shrugged his large shoulders. "Sure. There's always plenty to do in a station of this size."

"Good. Why don't you just plan on that . . ."

Wei-wei looked at him expectantly, waiting for him to reveal what was on his mind. Santos raised a questioning eyebrow. But MacMurphy didn't elaborate on his plans. Not here. Not in the Embassy lounge. He remained thoughtful, distant . . .

Finally Wei-wei spoke up. "Look, Mac. Why don't you just tell us what's on your mind? What happened in there with Berger? We're your friends, you know, as well as colleagues." She laid a hand gently on Mac's.

Wei-wei could read Mac's introspective mood progressions. And she usually knew how to handle them. First he had to be left to think things out for himself. Then he had to be coaxed into articulating his thoughts. He was in the midst of the latter process. He had already given whatever it was that was bothering him a great deal of thought. Now he needed a sounding board.

Mac didn't immediately answer her. He was still deep in thought. Finally he said, "You're right, but not here. This is not the place to talk. Let's go get something to eat at Charlie's and discuss it there."

CHAPTER 70

Charlie's was a small grill on Rue St. Ferdinand in the 17th *arrondisse-ment*. The restaurant actually had no name. The small lit sign above the door simply said "Bar & Grill" in English. It was a neighborhood place, run by the bartender, a friendly gay fellow named Charlie, and the cook, an elderly, cherubic, round little elf named Denise. So everyone called the place "Charlie's."

The taxi let them out on the narrow one-way street in front of the restaurant. They entered, and Charlie waved at them from behind the bar, still half filled with boisterous working-class locals finishing their aperitifs before heading to the Metro and RUR trains that would get them home to dinner.

Mac demurred when Charlie offered to make room for them at the bar, where he usually liked to sit, and they went directly to one of the tables in the corner of the small dining section instead. Only one other table was occupied, and it was at the other end of the room. Mac asked Charlie to send Denise over to take their orders.

The four-foot-square grandmotherly woman waddled out of the tiny kitchen in the rear and greeted Mac and Wei-wei like family, planting a kiss on each cheek and then adding a third. "*Trois fois à la campagne*," she exclaimed gleefully.

They introduced Culler, and she shook his hand and patted him on the shoulder warmly. She announced the menu for the evening (the specials changed every night according to her whim and what was fresh at the market): Couscous (her specialty), pot-au-feu, and the old standby, filet au poivre. Wei-wei ordered the couscous, and both men took the filets served with *pomme frites*. Mac also chose a bottle of the house wine to accompany the meal.

It was warm in the restaurant, and Mac announced that he was going to get comfortable. Standing up, he removed his jacket and tie and tossed them casually over a chair at the next table. This would also serve to dissuade any new diners from choosing the table next to them.

Culler, who was feeling oppressed by the summer heat too, followed suit, tossing his jacket and tie on another chair at the adjacent table on the other side of them. He proceeded to roll up his sleeves as well.

Wei-wei looked cool and comfortable in a bright yellow summer dress with green flowers, cut low in the back—attire that complemented her golden skin and had not escaped the notice of the bar patrons as the trio passed the long bar on the way to the table.

Denise returned with crisp garden salads (Mac always insisted on having his salad first, contrary to the French custom of having it at the end of the meal), a basket of sliced baguettes, and the house wine, which she opened with a pop and set in front of them like a café waiter.

Mac poured, and they toasted each other and the success of their mission, and "whatever else that feverish brain of yours is cooking up," Santos added. There was a pause, while he and Wei-wei waited to see if Mac would finally tell them what was on his mind.

When the silence persisted, Wei-wei gave his leg a gentle kick under the table and said, "Share your thoughts, Mac. We're your friends. And we have a *need* to know. Tell us . . ."

Mac began slowly and thoughtfully. He took them through his entire meeting with the COS, from beginning to end. They listened, eyes wide and aghast. When he had finished he added, "And I can't let that happen. So I've been doing a lot of thinking. And . . . what would you think if I told you I had a plan that would on the one hand satisfy the intelligence requirements levied on us by Rothmann and the DCI, while at the same time give Huang some choice in his future and avert the extraordinary rendition?"

He tossed back the rest of his wine and sat back, obviously very pleased with himself.

The question was rhetorical, and he did not wait for an answer before continuing. Now his speech was more engaged, more rapid, more vehement. "I mean the complete picture. The whole enchilada. The relationship between China and Iran; precisely what groups, terrorist and otherwise, will be the recipients of the Iranian money in that safe of Huang's; the full extent of the funding; the goals of the covert operation; everything. All that and more . . . much more . . .

"I'm talking about a complete re-write of our National Intelligence Estimate on China. Political, economic, diplomatic, military, the whole nine yards. And don't forget the MSS. We could re-write the book on the plans, structure, organization, liaison relationships and capabilities of the Chinese Ministry of State Security." He paused, filled his glass, took a large swallow of wine, and put it down. Glancing from one to the other he asked, "What would you think about that?"

Culler answered first, "You'd have to do better than an audio op for that kind of intelligence. You might get some of that from the audio op, but never all of it. No way . . . you'd, you know, need a source for that . . ."

"He's right," said Wei-wei. "Only a very high-level source would be able to provide us with that kind of intelligence information." She laughed, "You'd have to recruit someone like Huang for that kind of stuff, and you've already admitted you can't get Huang that way and the rendition idea is too far out."

"Yes, we can," said MacMurphy. He leaned forward closer to them and lowered his voice to a whisper. "Maybe we can't recruit him in place, but we can induce his defection. We can give him some choice in the matter. We can reel him in and debrief him on everything he knows about this covert action operation with Iran, his knowledge of the MSS, and everything else he knows about China. It would be the next best thing to a recruitment in place."

"How are you . . . ?" Both Wei-wei and Santos spoke in unison. Culler nodded to Wei-wei to continue. "How are you going to induce the defection of a man like Huang Tsung-yao? Why would he want to jump ship?"

MacMurphy leaned back in his chair, stretched out his long legs, tasted his wine and savored the moment. He studied his glass a moment before looking up at his two friends. Then he spoke softly, with a gleam in his eye. "Simple. We're going to steal his money . . ."

CHAPTER 71

Culler Santos and MacMurphy sat in the café across the street from the Chinese Embassy. They fortified themselves with coffee and croissants for the work that lay ahead. "Ah, you can't beat the French at their own game," Mac said, appreciatively savoring the rich, buttery croissant. "American bakers shouldn't even bother trying."

"We're nothing if we stop trying," Santos observed sagely. "We haven't stopped, you know, trying to get the information we're after."

"And we're about to take a giant step forward in that pursuit, my friend," said Mac, bobbing his head to the left to indicate that Santos should look in that direction. When Culler looked out across the street, he saw François assisting Collette and her mother into the rented Mercedes Benz. The Benz that Mac did not object to this time.

Mac had arranged with François to take Collette and her mother back to the Normandy coast for another fun weekend, a task to which François hadn't objected in the least.

Santos's drills and equipment were packed in the same suitcases and parked, as before, in a rented car in the garage below Avenue Georges V. The only thing different this time was the absence of the station surveillance team.

That and the fact that neither Burton B. Berger, Headquarters, nor the DDO, who was effectively out of the picture for now, had signed off on it, or in fact was even aware of it. This operation was going to be a unilateral act on the part of MacMurphy and Culler Santos. And that was a frightening thought.

CHAPTER 72

Normally, the CIA's Directorate of Operations maintains the integrity of its operations by demanding level upon level of approvals for operations involving even the slightest amount of risk. Audio operations like this would normally require no fewer than eleven signatures of approval.

The approvals begin with the case officer's branch chief in the field, run up through the station bureaucracy to the Chief of Station, and then on to Headquarters, where the proposal works its way from the area desk through the branch and division and finally up to the DDO.

This case, however, was different, and the departure from normal procedures meant that MacMurphy was acting independently, like the proverbial rogue elephant the CIA was constantly accused of being. If he failed, his career would end, despite having Rothmann on his side—if indeed he would or could remain there after this—and he could face criminal charges as well. Were the personal risks worth the possible rewards for the US government?

That was a question he had still not fully resolved in his mind, despite the fact that he was sitting there now, watching the street, making sure there was no unannounced return of François and his passengers, nor any other eventuality that might interfere with their plans. Even as he mentally walked through the upcoming op, a part of his brain kept returning to the repercussions that would unquestionably ensue should the mission fail.

He took a deep breath, let it out, and said to his friend, "Let's go."

They crossed the street, entered Collette's building and climbed the steep stairs to the fifth floor. They both carried suitcases, and despite the fact that they were both in top physical shape, both men were winded before they reached the fifth floor. But they didn't dare stop and rest; they wanted themselves and the telltale suitcases out of sight as fast as possible, so no neighbor could see and start asking questions, or possibly tell Collette later on.

The key worked flawlessly this time—Culler had buffed it down back at the station—and when at last they were inside the apartment, they set down their heavy suitcases as lightly as possible, despite their great relief at being unburdened. They didn't want to tip off the downstairs neighbors that anyone was up there. Suppose the people downstairs were aware that Collette and her mother were away for the weekend and knew the apartment ought to be empty?

Mac fanned the front of his shirt away from his body, trying to stir up a breeze against his sweaty skin. The windows were open a crack, enough to let some air in but not enough to let in the rain should a downpour occur, and Mac didn't dare open them wider for fear that someone might notice. Culler wiped his forehead with the back of his left hand. They paused and listened a moment to be sure they didn't hear anyone in the hall outside. They didn't. All they heard was silence and the normal street noises from outside the room.

And they were nearly silent themselves. They kept their verbal communication to a minimum, had removed their shoes, used hand signals and gestures to communicate much of what they had to, and kept their voices to a whisper when they did need to speak. Once, when Culler had to sneeze, he stifled the impulse and sniffled instead. There was no one positioned outside this time to warn them if someone should enter the building. Having been through this once before, they worked together swiftly as a team, photographing the wall and room, carefully moving the furniture away from the wall, spreading out the drop-cloth, opening suitcases, and assembling their equipment.

Santos turned on a portable receiver and donned a set of earphones to listen to the target room on the other side of the wall. It was Saturday morning, and they expected Huang's office to be empty, but he wanted to be absolutely certain. This sort of caution was unnecessary during the first operation because only a pinhole would silently penetrate the target. Now things would be different—very, very different. An occupant of the target office would surely notice a two-inch core drill breaking into the room behind the safe, and they wanted to avoid such discovery at all costs. Santos listened quietly for several minutes.

He could hear what appeared to be the hum of intrusion-sensing equipment in the office, and street noises; nothing more. He knew the intrusion devices—sonar equipment that detects movement in the room, and sends an alarm if there is any—would not be sensitive enough to detect the slight movement they would cause behind the safe. And the fact that it was activated was a clear indication that the room was unoccupied. He passed the earphones to Mac. "Sounds empty to me," Culler observed, returning to other tasks.

While Mac continued to intently monitor the target room, the tech carefully examined the wallpaper above the baseboard that concealed their earlier audio installation. "I thought I wasn't going to have to mess with this crap." If they were forced to restore the old and faded wallpaper with a matching piece, it would require far too much time and resources.

He found a seam and traced it upward with his fingers. Then he moved to the right and found another about two feet away and traced that as well. "I think we may be able to steam the paper and roll it up about four feet on the wall. That way we won't have to cut it, and we should still have enough room to cut our hole. What do you think, Mac?"

"Where do you think the safe is?"

"Shit, I don't know. But it's sitting right over our pinhole, right? So it could be centered on our hole, or to the right or to the left. We won't know for sure until we drill a few holes."

"So let's just start from a spot directly over our pinhole and work out both ways until we see the edge of the safe. It's up to you . . ."

"I just hope I don't have to steam too much of this damn wallpaper loose." Culler picked up his steamer, unscrewed the attached jar, and motioned to Mac to fill it with water from the kitchen. When Mac returned, he reassembled the steamer and began loosening the wallpaper from the bottom where it met the baseboard. Mac grabbed both ends of a strip and carefully pulled upward, while Culler directed the steam.

Bit by bit they worked the wallpaper loose, Mac easing more and more of it out of the way, exposing the painted surface that lay below, Culler directing the steam, till finally they had almost four feet of wallpaper taped above them. Mac continued to monitor the target through the earphones, but still he heard only silence except for the low hum of the intrusion sensor.

With the painted plaster wall exposed, Culler set the steamer aside and fitted three ten-inch sections of two-inch core bits onto his "moon" drill. He knew the thickness of the wall was slightly under thirty inches, so each core would cut all the way through to the other side and stop just short of the safe. There was no need to use the back scatter thickness gauge. He positioned the bit a few inches over the baseboard, just above the original pinhole. He looked over at Mac one last time for assurance that the room was still empty. After receiving a confirming nod, Santos hit the trigger.

It took all of six seconds for him to push the drill all the way through the wall. Santos felt the bit break through into the room beyond, and his stomach did a turn. All of a technician's training taught him that breaking through a wall was the absolute worst thing that could happen, and now he was doing it on purpose. Crazy . . .

He extracted the drill, and a perfect two-inch by thirty-inch concrete cylinder slid easily from the bit onto the drop-cloth.

Mac listened with new intensity for another minute or two. Then, confident that the room was still empty, they examined the hole with a flashlight.

The dark gray rear of the steel safe was clearly visible about an inch away from the end of their hole.

Santos drilled three more overlapping two-inch concentric circles to the left of the original hole before he could see the edge of the safe within the room. He moved back to the right one circle and used a mason's level to draw a plumb line two feet up from the center of the hole. Then he continued drilling overlapping two-inch holes up the line.

The pile of two-inch by thirty-inch concrete cores continued to grow. Santos stacked the cores like cordwood on the drop-cloth beside him. He worked as silently as possible and as swiftly as he could. The sooner they accomplished their mission, the sooner any jeopardy would be behind them. Discovery was unthinkable . . .

Santos remained focused on his work, while Mac continued to monitor the audio from the next building to insure that he heard no indications that anyone had entered.

An hour later, the drilling was complete. The beehive-like concentric circles outlined a heavy concrete block within—actually two blocks loosely joined together that formed the walls of each building. Mac and Culler carefully slid out the two-feet-high by sixteen-inches-wide by thirty-inches-thick center block and laid it neatly beside the stacked cores on the drop-cloth.

By now they were both sweating profusely. Santos's shirt clung to his muscular torso, thoroughly drenched, wrinkled, and limp. MacMurphy was not in much better shape. Sitting cross-legged on the drop-cloth, they stared at the back of the safe through the gaping hole in the wall. "There it is," said Culler, matter-of-factly, wiping the sweat from his face with a cloth.

"Jumpin' Jahosaphat on a crutch," said Mac, his voice emphatic though his tones remained low. Santos chuckled at Mac's choice of verbiage.

"Now to the fun stuff," declared Culler. He asked Mac to fetch a pan of water, while he removed the thirty-inch bit from the drill and replaced it with a shorter, six-inch bit of the same two-inch diameter. He leaned through the hole in the wall and set the drill against the back wall of the safe as high up as he could reach and squeezed the trigger.

The drill sliced through the hardened steel with a low screech. Moments later Culler dropped a sizzling-hot one-inch thick steel core into the water. The interior of the safe was revealed, and the stacked money was clearly visible through the two-inch diameter hole.

"There it is," said Mac.

"Yep, now for the rest of it." Culler proceeded to drill concentric holes down in a line, revealing more stacks of money. Mac checked his watch but reined himself in from displaying any signs of his impatience. When Santos identified where the shelves were located (there were three), he proceed to widen the holes at each level to allow enough room for the stacks of bills to be pulled through. He calculated. He eyeball-measured. He focused. And he tried to ignore the growing ache throughout his arms and shoulders.

He worked more rapidly now. The awkward effort of drilling while his arm and shoulder were wedged into the hole in the wall fatigued him. He massaged his biceps and shoulder muscles between each effort, though he could not rest. He was just as aware as Mac was of the need to get finished and get out as swiftly as possible. This whole op—this whole *unauthorized* op—would be worse than failure if they were to be discovered.

At one point a noise that was not coming from the drill gave Mac a start. Santos, concentrating on the drilling, didn't hear it. Mac did, though he didn't know what it was. It sounded like it was coming from inside Collette's apartment! Had she returned? Was someone else there? Impossible . . .

Mac tapped Santos on the back to signal him to stop. Mac looked around the room, went over to the window, and saw a sparrow perched on the sill outside. The bird had evidently landed and pecked against the pane. Much relieved, he signaled Culler to resume his drilling.

Finally there were three approximately eight-inch-diameter holes in the rear of the safe connected by a slash of two-inch holes down the middle. Santos set the drill down and mopped the sweat from his face, neck, and arms.

"Move out of there," said Mac. "I'll take it from here."

Mac pulled a green army duffel bag from one of the suitcases and set it on the floor next to the concrete block and stack of cores. Then he reached through the hole into the back of the safe and began extracting packs of five hundred euro notes and handing them back to Culler, who in turn stacked them in the duffel bag.

Mac was forced to reach deep into the safe to retrieve some of the stacks of euros. As he stretched, moved around, and grabbed, the jagged edges of the beehive hole dug into his ribs, lacerating his skin. He winced but continued with his task. He hoped he wasn't bleeding on the wall, but the replaced wallpaper would cover it if he did. This was no time for medical inspections. His problem was compounded when he had to unload the bottom shelf of the safe, which was two feet below the bottom of their hole due to the juxtaposition of the two buildings. "Why didn't you make this damn hole wider?!" he complained.

"The wallpaper, my friend . . . Remember the wallpaper? You've got enough room. Quit complaining and, you know, keep the money coming. I'm beginning to enjoy this."

"You're not having your skin removed inch by bloody inch!" Mac groused, feeling the warmth of trickling blood over his ribcage on his right side.

"Just keep passing me more money," replied an unsympathetic, triumphant Culler Santos.

The packs of euros filled the army duffel bag.

The two men stood back for a moment to take a breath and admire their work. Mac fastened the top of the duffel bag and turned to Culler. "What now?"

"Now we restore the mess we made," said Culler. "There's not much we can do about the inside; not that we care much, I suppose. They'll get one hell of a shock the first time they open that safe. But we've got to make this side look like before."

"Right," said Mac. "We don't want the ladies running to the police over this. The Chinese aren't likely to advertise the fact that they have been robbed of black money they brought into the country."

"Not likely, not likely," repeated Culler. He surveyed the restoration job ahead. "Give me a hand here, will you? First pass me a few of those cores."

Before Mac handed him one of the thirty-inch concrete cores, he made sure that his shirt had absorbed whatever blood he had lost, and that he had not stained anything in Collette's apartment. Then Mac passed the first concrete core to Culler, who positioned it in one of the grooves at the bottom of the hole. The process was repeated until all the grooves at the bottom of the hole were filled with cores. Then they tackled the concrete blocks.

They lifted the first block and gently jockeyed it into position to fill the hole next to the safe, and then they positioned the second one behind it so that it was flush with the rest of the interior wall. Culler slid the remaining cores into the honeycomb holes around its sides and top. "That's the most of it," he said, stepping back. "Now I need some of that quick-drying plaster, and we're almost done. Use that pan there with the steel cores, and mix a batch. You can do that, can't you, Mr. Case Officer?"

"We're trained to do anything you guys can do," Mac laughed, though he made sure to suppress the volume down from hearty to a low chuckle. He removed the steel cores from the pan and placed them on the drop cloth. "What do you want to do with these?" he asked.

"Take'em with us for, you know, souvenirs . . ."

Mac returned from the kitchen with the pan full of plaster and placed it in front of Culler. "There you are, my friend, perfectly mixed; the consistency of heavy cream. What do you think of that?"

Culler dipped a trowel into the mixture to test it. "Not bad for a case officer." He went about plastering the hole while Mac continued to monitor for sounds of entry in the office on the other side of the wall and listening for approaching footsteps or other noises that might signal someone out in the hall and approaching the apartment. *This would be a fine time for a neighbor to come borrow a cup of sugar.* But he heard only silence in the hallway and nothing in the Chinese office on the other side of the wall.

When Santos was through, the wall was as smooth as before. He finished drying it with a hair dryer, coated it with wallpaper glue, and re-glued the wallpaper in place. Then they cleaned up after themselves, replaced the furniture, compared the photographs they had taken before they started with the way things looked now, and packed up their gear in the suitcases. They had been in the apartment for less than four hours.

Culler Santos insisted on carrying the duffel bag back to the car. MacMurphy got the heavy suitcases this time.

CHAPTER 73

The voice-activated recorder in the tiny listening post apartment remained silent throughout the weekend; no one entered Huang's office.

Huang might have been enjoying a leisurely weekend away from the office, but MacMurphy was very busy.

After leaving the apartment, he and Culler dumped everything in the trunk of the rental car and drove out of the area. They breathed easier once they had turned the corner and felt sure they had been unobserved in their work. Success! Success in accomplishing their mission without anyone any the wiser—and that included not only Huang and his people but Berger and his, not to mention the French security detail for the embassy.

Mac dropped off Culler and his gear at the embassy and then drove back to his safehouse in the 17th *arrondissement* with the duffel bag. There he separated the money into three equal piles and filled three large Samsonite suitcases. He did not want to risk being caught with all of the money in a duffel bag. Splitting it up reduced the bulk and increased the chances of getting at least most of the money to its destination.

He delivered one of the suitcases to Le Belge that same afternoon and instructed him to depart immediately by train for Bern, Switzerland. He was told to deposit the contents of the suitcase, approximately seventeen million euros, in a numbered account (Mac wrote the number on a slip of paper and made certain Le Belge tucked it away safely in his billfold) in the main branch of the Credit Suisse Bank when it opened on Monday morning. He was to ask for a Herr Merkel who would be expecting him. He was also instructed to remain in Bern for at least ten days following the deposit, and to tell no one, not even his wife, where he was.

But that last order was difficult for Pol Giroud to follow. Unlike François, Pol was a devoted family man, and he simply could not go away for almost two weeks and not tell Marie where he was going. She would have begged. She would have cried. He could not abide her tears. And it went against everything he believed. One isn't supposed to disappear on one's wife. So he did the next best thing. He told her he was going to Bern on secret business, gave her the name of the hotel where he planned to stay, and then swore her to secrecy. She promised not to tell anyone, not even the girls.

It would prove to be a fatal error in judgment.

CHAPTER 74

François returned from Trouville with Collette and her mother late Sunday afternoon. He delivered the ladies to their apartment and admired the fact that was no visible evidence of the operation. He even stayed for an aperitif just to examine the wall more closely. When *Maman* retired to her room, worn out from the trip, and Collette went to "freshen up a bit," François got up and hastily examined the wall . . . but he could not detect a sign of intrusion. *Maybe they had to abort it,* he thought.

After leaving the women, he killed some time in a café before his scheduled meeting with MacMurphy at seven.

Mac picked him up on the corner of Rue d'Assas and Rue Joseph Bara in Montparnasse. He drove aimlessly around the neighborhood while he briefed François. "That suitcase in the back seat contains one-third of the money in the safe, about seventeen million euros. Don't lose it."

"*Mon Dieu!* You did get it," exclaimed François, a wide grin spread across his face. He looked with admiration at his case officer.

"Of course we got it. What did you think we were doing in there? Holding a church service? Now, listen, I need you to take the suitcase to Bern and deposit the money in this account in the Credit Suisse branch office there. Be there at exactly two o'clock tomorrow afternoon and ask for a Herr Merkel. He'll take care of you."

Mac handed him a slip of paper with the account number on it. "Will you do that for me?"

"*Mais bien sûr, mon vieux.* May I take the Mercedes and a girl-friend?"

Mac shook his head in frustration. "You may take the rental car, but no women. Absolutely no women. Go alone, and don't tell a soul where you are going. Deposit the money on Monday afternoon at exactly two o'clock, and then get out of Bern and go someplace other than Paris for a couple of weeks."

"Villefranche? May I go to my yacht in Villefranche?"

"Perfect," said MacMurphy. "The yacht will be perfect. Go for a cruise. Get out of the area and stay away for a few days. Don't come back to Paris until I give you the okay. *Ça va?*"

"*Oui. Ça va bien.* As you know, *mon vieux*, I prefer not to be in Paris during the summer. It is too warm and boring for my taste. I am here only because you asked me to be here. *Ah oui*, one last thing . . ."

"What's that?"

"May I take a girlfriend on my yacht? It is so lonely on the water, Mac . . ."

"I wouldn't expect anything less of you, François. Just keep quiet about this Bern business." Mac pulled over to the curb to let François out. "I'll see you in a couple of weeks."

"*Au revoir*, Mac." François jumped out of the car and disappeared into the evening crowd with the suitcase.

CHAPTER 75

The third suitcase was in the trunk of Mac's rental car beside an overnight bag. He had spent Saturday evening with Wei-wei and had told her about his plans. Now he was packed and ready to leave Paris for Bern until things settled down. He promised to call her every evening to stay in touch. He wondered how long it would take Huang to discover the theft.

The voice-activated recorder in the LP apartment stuttered at the sound of a door banging open at exactly eight-seventeen Monday morning. It began recording about two hours later when Lim arrived. A rough transcript of the conversation read in part:

LIM: "Morning, boss."

HUANG: "Good morning, Lim. Sit down."

LIM: "We have some initial readouts of the surveillance on Mac-Murphy. Do you have time now or should I come back later?"

HUANG: "Now is fine. What have you got?"

LIM: "Very interesting. He has been very active over the past couple days. Back and forth to the embassy many times. Often with a heavy-set fellow. For sure another officer because he also has access to the embassy, where he stays for hours." (Long pause and rustling of papers.) "Here it is. They had dinner together several times. I mean with MacMurphy and his girlfriend. You know. I told you about her. Ryan is her name. We have her address. MacMurphy sleeps there sometimes."

HUANG: "Where does he go when he does not sleep there?"

LIM: "We do not know yet. He is very clever. Sometimes it is very difficult for the team to follow him. And you told me to tell the team not to get too close. So it's difficult for them. Very difficult . . ."

HUANG: "I know, I know. But you have the girl's address. That is good. Good start. What else?"

LIM: "We had a little luck. Remember I told you he was running around town a lot during the daytime, and our team keeps losing him?"

HUANG: "Yes. You said it looked like he was running surveillance detection routes."

LIM: "Right. Probably before meetings with his assets. Well, maybe I think we got a couple of them."

HUANG: "Terrific."

LIM: "Like I say, there has been plenty of activity recently. He runs around a lot. Not as cautious as before. You know how it is. Too many meetings, get a little sloppy . . ."

HUANG: "Yes, we all know how that goes."

LIM: "He meets one guy all the time in the Montparnasse area on the left bank. Another guy he meets in the Ternes area on the right bank."

HUANG: "Great! Can you identify them?"

LIM: "Look at these photos. The fat one is the Ternes area guy. The skinny one is the Montparnasse area guy.

HUANG: "This is real good work, Lim. Please congratulate the team for me."

LIM: "That's not all, boss. The team was able to follow the guys home so we got names and addresses too. The team says these guys are easy to follow. They are on them now."

HUANG: "Wonderful. But the question remains, what is MacMurphy up to here in Paris? Do you have any clues?"

LIM: "Unfortunately, no. But now we know those two guys, and the team is on them all the time, non-stop. We will find out what he is up to for sure."

HUANG: "Thank you Lim. You have done excellent work. Please brief me on this case every morning at this time from now on. We must find out what MacMurphy is up to."

LIM: "Okay, boss. See you later."

HUANG: "Thank you, Lim. Goodbye."

CHAPTER 76

Huang would get his answer quicker than he anticipated. At four-thirty that afternoon, two cleaning ladies arrived to dust and vacuum Huang's office. "*Eyeah*," the skinny old Cantonese woman running the vacuum cried out, "What is this mess?" She pointed to a pile of white plaster dust and chips on the carpet by the safe.

Huang looked up from behind his desk in time to see the shocked expression on the woman's face as she peered behind the safe. "*Eyeah, yamma coucho ahhh*," she wailed, "The wall is coming down! Look, look, Mr. Huang, the wall is crumbling!"

At that precise moment, MacMurphy stood in front of the young receptionist at the Banque Credit Suisse in Bern. "May I see Herr Merkel, please. He is expecting me. My name is Martin. Frederick Martin."

He had driven a circuitous route, and his car had been rented in alias. He was quite certain that there was no surveillance following him. He had driven carefully, not wanting to be stopped for any traffic infraction such as speeding. And he had worried and wondered as he drove . . . worried whether François and Le Belge had gotten their portion of the money safely to the bank, wondered when Huang would discover the theft.

On reaching the bank, he relaxed a little, but he still was concerned about his two associates and about Huang's eventual discovery of the missing euros. He didn't know that, even now, Huang was in the midst of learning the money had been filched.

"One moment please, Mr. Martin." The receptionist buzzed his office and spoke briefly into the intercom: "A Mr. Martin is here to see you sir." Then she looked up at Mac and said, "You may go right in. Second door on the right."

Herr Merkel was a spidery little man with a long hawk nose and dark hair parted low on one side and slicked over the top in an effort to cover his baldness. He wore a heavy, charcoal, double-breasted suit with wide lapels.

Merkel offered a bony hand to Mac. "Good day, Mr. Martin. I have been expecting you."

"Good afternoon, Herr Merkel. I hope my associates arrived safely with their deposits."

"Yes, yes, the second one left just a short while ago." MacMurphy felt some of the tension leave his body on hearing that reassuring news. "This is all very strange, I must say . . ."

"If you are uncomfortable, I'll deposit the money elsewhere . . ."

"No, no! No, no! It's perfectly fine. Perfectly fine. I will have it counted immediately." Merkel buzzed the intercom. "Please come in here for a moment, and bring the counting machine with you, please."

Merkel introduced his young assistant to Mac and asked him to count the contents of the suitcase. He plugged the automatic money counter into an outlet near a small desk in the corner of Merkel's office and began breaking open bundles of five hundred euro notes and feeding them into it. The machine whirred through the stacks of notes like a magician thumbing a deck of cards.

The task took almost twenty minutes. When the clerk was through, he tore the addition slip from the machine and handed it to Merkel. Herr Merkel took two identical slips of paper from his desk drawer and added the three on his calculator. "Exactly fifty million euros," he said. "Is that correct, Mr. Martin?"

"Yes, it is."

"Then if you would please sign here, here, and here," indicating places on an account form, "we will be through."

Mac signed and, with a feeling of great relief, he stood up to leave.

"Oh, there is one more thing," said Merkel, wringing his hands nervously.

Mac paused, froze. "What's that?"

"Identification. I must copy some sort of identification for your account file. You cannot make withdrawals without proper identification, you know."

"Sorry, I almost forgot." He pulled a blue US tourist passport from his breast pocket and handed it to Merkel. Merkel handed it to the clerk and asked him to copy it immediately.

"It has been a pleasure doing business with you, Mr. Martin. And you can be assured of our discretion. Your identity is perfectly safe in the Swiss banking system."

"I certainly hope so . . ."

The clerk returned Mac's passport, and Mac departed the bank, giving the receptionist a wink on his way out the door. He felt relieved of a great burden.

CHAPTER 77

ater that evening, Lim sat on the floor of the dimly lit hallway in front
of Wei-wei Ryan's apartment door, arms clasped around his knees.
He was patiently waiting for Ryan to return home after work.
Glancing at his watch, he noticed it was almost seven o'clock; he had
been there for nearly an hour. *Where is she? Did she go out for the evening? Was she spending the night somewhere else . . . perhaps with
MacMurphy? Did she somehow get home before he got there—perhaps
left work early?—maybe she was inside the apartment, locked in for the
night?*

He heard the sound of the downstairs door opening and the clump-
clump of high-heeled shoes climbing the stairs. He stood when it was
clear the woman was coming all the way up to the fourth floor.

He watched her turn the bend in the staircase and start up the final
flight of stairs to her apartment. She was carrying a small bag of groceries and a large shoulder purse and did not look up until she reached the
top step.

He startled her, and she almost dropped her groceries. "May I help you?" she asked, trying to remain calm. As she paused at the top, she should have been catching her breath from the climb but instead found herself breathing faster, while her heart pounded.

He was very polite, trying to calm her and appear as non-threatening as possible. "Please, Miss Ryan, do not be frightened."

"How do you know my name? Who are you? How did you get in the building?" She was working hard at keeping her voice calm, trying not to let her fear show, trying to gain the initiative.

His voice was low, soothing, non-threatening. "I just want to talk to you a moment. It's about Mr. Mac. We are friends, and . . ."

"Oh, you must be . . ." She bit off the words. She thought he must be the Chinese waiter, SKITTISH, but did not want to reveal the fact that she knew anything about him. "You are a friend of Mac's?"

"Yes. May I speak with you for one moment?" Lim smiled his most disarming smile, and he deliberately did not advance toward her or the apartment door.

Taken in by his deception and disarmed by his manner, Wei-wei no longer felt threatened. "Yes, come on in. We can't talk in the hall."

She dug into her deep purse for her keys and led him into the apartment. She kicked the door shut behind her and invited him to sit while she set the groceries down in the kitchen.

He was still standing when she returned. "I am Lim Ze-shan from Chinese People's Embassy," he announced. "Please, I will only take moment of your time."

Wei-wei gasped and immediately was gripped with fear. Not only was this *not* SKITTISH, it was that warped and dangerous man. Despite Lim's outward polite demeanor, she knew from Mac that Lim was prone to violence. Outwardly she projected calm, however. "How can I help you, Mr. Lim?"

He answered in halting English: "I . . . I have problem. Maybe you help me, please. I must find Mr. MacMurphy. Please tell me where is Mr. MacMurphy?" His tone was still polite, but demanding. "Mr. MacMurphy has taken something that belongs to The People's Republic of China and I must have it back . . . immediately . . ."

"I don't know what you are talking about and I don't know where Mr. MacMurphy is, and I wouldn't tell you if I did know. I am a US Embassy staff employee, and you are trespassing on embassy-protected property, Mr. Lim. I'm sure you understand diplomatic protocol. Now please leave." Her voice was firm and just as demanding as his was, and she managed to keep out of it the quaver she felt deep inside. She shuddered at the thought of having an unpredictable and volatile man alone in the apartment with her.

She started for the door just as Lim swung an arching slap that caught her full on the side of the head and face and slammed her up against the wall. She barely retained her balance, reeling at the force, and her ear rang from the blow.

"Where is MacMurphy, bitch? Tell me or I kill you, you fucking stink bitch. Is he with other two stink bags?"

Wei-wei was hardly surprised at this revelation of his true nature, but she was definitely afraid. He moved toward her, his squat frame poised to strike and his eyes focused and hard and his mouth in a tight grin. He slapped her again on the other ear and sent her flying back across the room in the other direction. Again she staggered to keep her balance. And he was enjoying the pain he was inflicting upon her.

Both ears were ringing, and she was terrified. She felt her eardrums had burst. She tried to scream, but no sound came out of her mouth. *He's going to kill me.*

She couldn't move and stood frozen to the spot, hands covering her ears and stinging face, tears streaming down her cheeks.

He slapped at the hands covering her face, first one side and then the other, not hard enough to knock her down, but snapping her head back and forth. Now she screamed, and he increased the velocity of his blows, hitting her faster now like a punching bag, enjoying the power, reveling in the pain and fear he was inflicting.

Finding MacMurphy was secondary now as he warmed to the task of hurting this woman—MacMurphy's woman.

He hated MacMurphy. He hated what MacMurphy had done, engineering the theft of the euros. He hated that MacMurphy had gotten away with it, had put one over on them, himself and Huang. He hated anything and anyone to do with MacMurphy.

Yes, it felt good to lash out at this woman, this woman he saw as a half-Chinese mongrel, daughter of a woman for whom a Chinese husband wasn't good enough. Yes, it was good to hurt her, hurt her hard, make her pay for MacMurphy's deeds. Oh, she had it coming. He would make her pay. And when he was finished with her, Mac would understand who held the upper hand.

Her hands and arms were still up, protecting her face and head, so he jabbed her in the solar plexus to lower her guard. The sharp blow drove the wind from her lungs, and her arms came down. He grabbed the collar of her silk blouse with both hands and jerked downward, popping buttons and ripping the flimsy garment down to her waist.

The adrenaline shot through her veins, and she fought back now, kicking and swinging and punching and screaming frantically. But nobody responded to her screams. Nobody came running to help her. And Lim was pummeling her, battering her, and enjoying himself immensely.

He laughed at her efforts to defend herself and easily fended off her wild kicks and blows. The sight of her swinging at him with her blouse hanging loosely at her waist and her full breasts spilling over her transparent beige bra excited him. He felt a familiar stirring, and he wanted more of her . . .

He ripped the bra from her and paused in his attack to gaze at her drunkenly. She continued to scream and cry for help but stopped trying to hit him. Instead, she focused on keeping him from touching her, covering her nakedness with her arms while backing away from him. This enraged him further, and he lifted her rigid body off the ground and flung her onto the couch. She cowered against the back of it as he lunged toward her.

He ripped at her skirt, tearing it from her body, and pulled her down to the floor. He hesitated and gazed longingly at the beautiful, defenseless creature in front of him. Nothing but filmy bikini panties covered her. The excitement was intense. She was struggling again, so he punched her hard in the face to subdue her. Blood spurted from her nose and spattered her naked breasts and stomach. The sight of her, wounded and defenseless, bleeding and exposed, only exhilarated him further.

He dropped down on his knees, straddling her on the couch, and hit her again. She stopped struggling and made her body as rigid as a mummy, arms crossed in front of her chest and legs crossed at the ankles. Wei-wei continued to scream for help frantically.

"Can't anyone hear me?! Please help me!" She yelled at the top of her lungs, but the only sounds she heard were Lim's hoarse breaths and an occasional feral growl from his mouth. No one was coming to help her . . .

He yanked his trousers open and she screamed louder. Lim pounded at her haunches and thighs, calling her a dirty slut-bitch. She screamed again with all of her strength, and he grabbed her throat to silence her, first with one hand and then with both. He squeezed and pressed his thumbs into her larynx until he felt it pop. She stopped screaming and her eyes widened in fear. Wei-wei gasped, her body convulsed, and then she went limp, eyes open and staring at nothing.

He stood up and backed away from her, zipping up his trousers. He looked down into her wide, dead, terrified eyes one final time. Then Lim turned and pulled open the door and ran down the stairs, cursing. He had failed again. He still didn't know where MacMurphy was. She was no help at all, and the bitch had prevented him from fucking her. At least she got what she deserved.

CHAPTER 78

Lim burst from Wei-wei's building. Once outside, he fought to regain his composure, slowing from a run to a trot to a walk. He noticed people staring at him, so he struggled harder to bring himself down. He took deep breaths and attempted to control his breathing. He dried his sweaty face and neck with a handkerchief and tucked his shirt back in.

After several blocks, he began to feel and look normal again. He began planning his next move. He had lost this battle, but he would not lose the war. He would find the sonofabitch and recover the money.

The surveillance team had lost François Leverrier on the *autoroute*, but Lim suspected he, too, was heading for Bern.

That was where Pol Giroud had gone. The team had had no trouble following him. One of the team simply got on the overnight train with him at Paris' *Gare de l'Est* and then got off with him the next morning in Bern. Unfortunately, the lone team member that had accompanied Le Belge to Bern subsequently lost him in the crowds of the city after observing him enter the Credit Suisse Bank with a large suitcase and exit without it.

When the news reached him about Pol Giroud making the obvious deposit, Lim knew it was too late to recover any of the money. The only thing on his mind now was revenge. MacMurphy and his two cohorts had made a fool of him and Huang, and now it was his turn to get even. And get even he would. He vowed it with a vengeance.

But he had to find them first . . .

He had failed to learn MacMurphy's whereabouts from that whore girlfriend of his, so that was a dead end. He would worry about MacMurphy later. Now he would concentrate on finding Pol Giroud and François Leverrier. He knew Giroud had last been seen in Bern, and that Leverrier was headed in that direction when the team lost him. But Bern was a big city . . .

Then it came to him. He remembered that he had both of their Paris addresses. Family or neighbors might know where they were staying. That was as good as any place to start.

He entered a café and walked directly to the telephone booths in the rear and phoned the chief of his surveillance team, instructing him to go immediately to the apartment belonging to François Leverrier. "Talk to his family, his neighbors, anyone who might know where he is. Someone must! Don't fail in this. I want to know where that stink-bug is!" His voice rose steadily until he was screaming into the phone. He would find out where LeVerrier had gone . . . and then he would deal with him.

CHAPTER 79

After Le Belge deposited the money in the Credit Suisse Bank, he stepped out into a bright, sunny day in Bern. He decided to go for a walk around the downtown area and maybe pick up a little something for Marie and the girls. He meandered through the streets and shops and chose pretty multi-colored scarves for the girls and a powder blue, sequined sweater for his wife.

He stopped in a sidewalk café and enjoyed a leisurely lunch and two refreshing draft beers. Afterward, he strolled across town to his favorite part of the city, the Casino Platz. There he checked into the familiar little *Hotel Arc-en-Ciel,* on one of the tiny side streets, and indulged himself in a long afternoon nap.

While Le Belge was napping, Lim found his way to the Giroud apartment in Paris. The apartment was located just off the Place des Vosges in an area of Paris in the third *arrondissement* called Le Marais. It had once been a run-down working-class neighborhood but was now being restored and refurbished. Consequently, chic new modern apartments were located behind newly sandblasted, restored façades.

Le Belge's apartment was in a building that had not yet been restored. The sandstone façade was black from a century's accumulation of soot and was nestled in the middle of a row of bright, new-looking buildings of similar architecture. The building belonged to Le Belge's brother-in-law, who was patiently waiting for property values to go up just a tad more before he would agree to sell.

Lim pushed open the heavy front door and scanned the mailboxes in the foyer, looking for the Giroud name. Lim found the name on the mailbox labeled "3B." The elevator was slow and creaky and cramped, but it got him up to the third floor faithfully. He exited and knocked on the door of 3B.

He was greeted by a skinny little tow-headed girl of about twelve years old. "*Bonjour petite*, is your mommy home?" he said with a broad, friendly, disarming smile.

"*Un moment, monsieur.*" She left the door open and ran to the rear of the apartment. "*Maman, Maman*," she called. "Someone here to see you."

Marie Giroud was round and pretty, with fair skin and pale blue eyes. She wore a checkered apron, and her flaxen blonde hair was pulled back into a bun. Her smile was trusting and wide, displaying clean white teeth and rosy cheeks.

This is going to be easy, he thought.

"*Pardonnez moi, Madame*," he said in halting French, "I must reach Monsieur Giroud about a matter of extreme urgency. He told me he would be in Bern, but I misplaced the address he gave me and. . . ."

"Pol gave you his address in Bern? That is very strange. He told me not to tell anyone." Marie's voice and face expressed surprise but not alarm.

Lim put on his most ingenuous mask and replied quietly and sincerely: "Your husband is in Bern on a very confidential matter that I am helping him with. But I have been very stupid and lost his address. Now I must talk to him and . . . Please help me."

"Well . . ." She paused and reflected on her husband's instructions. He had said he was on a secret mission to Bern and she was not to tell anyone where he was. *But this nice man already knows Pol is in Bern.*

"He told you he was going to Bern?" she asked.

"Yes, and I must reach him immediately. Please help me or I will look very stupid, and our business deal will most certainly fall through."

"You have business with Pol? You are working with him on this? Why didn't he tell me?"

"He wasn't supposed to tell you about it. It's confidential."

"Yes. He told me it was confidential. What is your name, please?"

"I'm Peter Chen. I am close associate of your husband. Now, please tell me where he can be reached." Lim was more forceful now. Close to the point of intimidation.

"I . . . I guess it's all right, but I should check with Pol first to be sure. He will call me in the morning and I will ask him. If he says it's all right, I will tell you where he is staying in Bern. Ça va?" She was beginning to have her doubts about this forceful stranger.

"No, Madame," he replied, "It is not all right. I must reach him tonight. Tomorrow will be too late."

"Oh dear," she said, wringing her hands. "I do not know what to do." *What if Pol's deal falls through because I refuse to help this man? It would all be my fault.* She didn't want whatever her husband was working on to come to a bad end, and she most certainly didn't want to be the cause of that failure.

Lim placed a hand on her shoulder and gave her his most comforting smile. "Do right thing. Everything gonna be fine. For sure. I need reach him right away. Please help. Monsieur Giroud will thank you."

She paused a moment and then made up her mind. He was a nice man, and what could the harm be in giving him Pol's hotel? None. "He is staying at the *Hotel Arc-en-Ciel* at the Casino Platz. Do you know where that is?"

"No Madam, but I will find it. Thank you so much." Lim turned to leave.

"Do you want the phone number of the hotel?" she called after him.

He shouted back over his shoulder as he hurried down the stairs, "That not necessary. Thank you again." He skipped the elevator and bolted down the stairs, taking them two at a time.

CHAPTER 79

Le Belge stretched and rubbed the sleep from his eyes. The late-afternoon sun penetrated the tightly drawn curtains of his small hotel room. He rolled his pudgy frame out of the bed and pulled open the curtains. The blast of sunlight forced him to squint until his eyes adjusted.

He looked down at the street and then craned his neck to check out the Casino Platz, just over the Kirchenfeld Bridge at the north end of the street. He could see that the square was filling with after-work strollers and the cocktail-and-aperitif crowd.

Refreshed from his nap, he shaved, showered, put on a clean shirt and left the hotel. He walked casually down through the now-bustling square. He meandered around a bit, enjoying the cool evening air, enjoying being part of the milling crowd, enjoying the satisfaction of knowing he had completed his mission successfully.

All was well. Nothing had gone wrong. Now he had only to wait for the all-clear signal from Mac, so that he could return to his home and family. He missed them already, but he was enjoying himself here, too. He ambled around the square aimlessly for a while before deciding upon one of the sidewalk cafés in which to have his first cool beer of the evening.

He would drink several more beers before enjoying a dinner of couscous and a bottle of dark red Algerian wine at a cozy little Middle Eastern restaurant on one of the quaint side streets.

At around ten-thirty, he weaved back to the Casino Platz for an after-dinner cognac or two to settle his bursting stomach.

Lim's SwissAir flight from Paris touched down at Bern airport at ten-seventeen. He stepped out of a cab in front of the *Hotel Arc-en-Ciel* fifty-three minutes later. A check at the hotel reception revealed that Monsieur Giroud had not yet returned for the evening.

Lim went looking for him . . .

CHAPTER 81

It was after midnight when Pol Giroud stumbled out of the Casino Stube Pub. A blast of German oom-pah-pah music and heavy cigarette smoke swirled around him as he stepped out into the street.

He stood in front of the pub for a moment, swaying drunkenly and trying to get his bearings. He located the Kirchenfeld Bridge at the far end of the Casino Platz and knew his hotel was just on the other side of the bridge. He weaved off in that direction, pleasantly drunk, full and happy. He hummed as he walked unsteadily across the darkened square back toward his hotel and a good night's rest.

He thought he would call Marie in the morning to see how she and the girls were doing. He missed them terribly.

Lim had positioned himself near the center of the square so that he could observe the entrance of Le Belge's hotel. He had reckoned quite correctly that his target would emerge sooner or later from one of the many bars and restaurants surrounding the Platz and head home.

The square was now quiet, with only a few people strolling along the bordering sidewalks, moving from one bar to another or heading home for the evening. His eye caught movement at the door of the Casino Stube Pub, and he observed the gust of smoke and sound as a rotund little man stumbled out of the pub onto the sidewalk. Lim stared. From the descriptions and photographs he had been given by his surveillance team, he was almost certain he had found Pol Giroud, but it was not until he observed Le Belge for a little longer, weaving his way up toward the Kirchenfeld Bridge, that he was absolutely positive.

Lim moved like a hunter stalking a deer, staying in the shadows well behind and off to the side of his prey, moving slowly, observing, following Le Belge's every move, calculating the risks, planning his attack.

Le Belge appeared oblivious to his surroundings. Certainly he was not in surveillance detection mode. Why be concerned with that—no one knew he was here except for Mac and Marie. He was a man with no worries, a man who was pleasantly drunk and enjoying that particular state of inebriation. Now he only wanted to get back to the comfort of the bed in his hotel.

He was an easy prey for a hunter of Lim's talents. Lim turned his attention to his surroundings. A taxi illuminated Le Belge as it passed by and crossed over the bridge, in turn bathing it in light for a moment. The Kirchenfeld Bridge was dark again, outlined only by the moonlight reflecting off the swift surface of the Aare river swirling below.

Le Belge stopped under the dim light of a lamppost at the entrance to the bridge and clumsily lit a Gitanes cigarette with a less-than-steady hand. He stood there for a moment, puffing on it, enjoying that first hit of nicotine, the tobacco flavor, the whole experience. Then, spitting out a stray bit of tobacco, he resumed his unsteady walk back toward his hotel.

Lim closed to within fifty feet of his prey and calculated an approach vector that would bring him up behind Le Belge at the crest of the bridge.

Another car drove by, forcing Lim back into the shadows for a moment. He briefly squeezed his eyes shut to retain his night vision. When he opened them again, Le Belge was about ten feet from the crest of the bridge, diagonally across the road in front of him. Lim took another last look around and, finding the bridge deserted with no cars approaching, decided to make his move.

He darted across the street behind the still-oblivious Pol Giroud and withdrew the stiletto from his pocket. He flicked the long, thin blade open and concealed it behind his leg as he closed the distance between him and his prey. He was ready to pounce when Le Belge unexpectedly stopped and turned to look over the railing of the bridge. Lim froze.

Pol Giroud gazed thoughtfully out at the water, rippling under the bridge as it flowed on its way. He slowly turned from the water and gazed at his surroundings. Lim did not think that Le Belge at all suspected his presence or the danger that awaited him.

But still the stocky Chinese man with the murderous thoughts stepped back into the shadows, lest Le Belge see him and feel the need to be on guard to danger. Better to catch him unaware.

Le Belge took a long, final drag from his cigarette, the glow illuminating his contented, cherubic face. He flicked the last cigarette he would ever smoke out over the railing and watched it tumble slowly down to the waters below. The moon glinted on the flowing water, and Pol noticed how the ripples formed patterns in the moonlight. His last thought was of Marie and the girls, and how happy they would be when he got home with gifts from his trip. He visualized the happy reunion in his mind's eye.

When Lim saw the cigarette arch out over the railing and noticed Le Belge's attention focused on the falling ember and the river below, he took the opportunity to move in for the kill. He closed the remaining distance in a low crouch, coming up directly behind and to the left of Le Belge.

The thin stiletto was held loosely in his right hand at waist level, the blade pointing out with the cutting edge up. With his left hand, he reached out across his body and grasped Le Belge on the right shoulder, turning the pudgy little man around until he faced his murderer.

Lim saw Pol Giroud's eyes open wide with surprise and shock as Lim brought the blade of the knife up and out and plunged the long, thin blade deep into Giroud's solar plexus, just below the last rib. The tip of the blade sliced into the bottom of Le Belge's heart, causing blood to gush out into his chest cavity.

Lim lifted up on the knife handle and pushed Le Belge out and over the railing. The stiletto slipped easily from the fat man's belly as Lim tipped him back and over the rail, and the now near lifeless body plunged to the waters below. There was a loud splash and then the body began its long, dead journey out toward the sea.

CHAPTER 82

Late the next afternoon Lim crested the hill overlooking the provincial resort town of Villefranche-sur-Mer. He jerked the rented Peugeot off onto the shoulder of the road, spewing loose gravel and skidding to a halt. He was bone weary.

He had been up most of the night after killing Le Belge. The combination of physical and mental exertion and the eight-hour drive from Bern was taking its toll. He knew he had to rest before continuing his mission or risk making grievous errors in judgment. He needed to be sharp before developing and executing the next step in his plan—the elimination of François Leverrier.

He stepped out of the car and stretched. The town of Villefranche spread out in a horseshoe below him. To the north was Cap Ferrat, which divided the bay between Monaco and Villefranche. To the south was the road leading to Nice and the rest of "*Le Midi*," as the French called it—the Riviera.

The barrel tile roofs of the villas and shops of the little town were nestled between the mountains and the sea directly below him, and the azure blue waters of the Mediterranean sparkled and twinkled and danced from the harbor to the sea beyond.

Lim reflected on the hours since the disposal of Le Belge. It had been an easy kill, all things considered. The man was drunk, out of shape and, most of all, had been taken completely by surprise. A good kill, clean and neat. The idiot never knew what hit him.

After the job was done, Lim had calmed himself and then had cleaned up in a café restroom. As planned, there wasn't much blood to mess up the crime scene. Most of the bleeding had been internal. That was the beauty of killing with a stiletto. You could get to the victim's heart without slashing the stupid sonofabitch to pieces.

All he had to do was wipe off the knife and wash his hands. Not a drop had spattered on his clothing. Neat. Really neat. *MacMurphy should have trained the poor sonofabitch better.*

MacMurphy would get his, too. And that sonofabitch would die slowly, very slowly. He would plan that one very carefully. But that was another matter; first he had to concentrate on François Leverrier.

After the killing of Le Belge, Lim had to kill time before the rental car agencies opened. He found a whore who took him to a cheap hotel where identification was not required. She was an ugly old *pute* with overstuffed silicone breasts and saggy skin. But all he really wanted was to get a couple of hours of sleep.

So after attempting to fuck her, he pushed her away and tried to sleep. He was still traveling on a high from the neat job he had done on Le Belge, so he didn't get the sleep he needed. He was still exhausted when he got to the Hertz counter at seven the next morning, and he was on the road headed south by seven-thirty.

He willed himself to stay awake. It would be several more hours before he could even think about sleep.

Gazing down at the town, he continued to plan. All he knew at this moment was that the surveillance team had lost Leverrier on the *auto-*

route heading toward Bern. When they later checked his apartment in Paris they found it empty—not even a maid present.

They reviewed their past surveillance reports and came up with the name of François's current girlfriend. A check with her apartment room- mate revealed that she had gone sailing in the south of France with her boyfriend. A little more investigation revealed that François Leverrier owned a ten-meter yacht named *Tout Va Bien*, and that the yacht was kept at the marina in Villefranche.

He focused on the marina clearly outlined below him. He counted a total of ten rows of slips jutting out into the harbor. Each slip moored about a dozen boats on each side, and there were a couple more dozen yachts anchored in the harbor. The *Tout Va Bien* had to be among them, and François Leverrier was more than likely on it. Locating François's ten-meter yacht among about two hundred others shouldn't be too difficult.

However, first he needed to rest, then pick up a few things. The outline of a plan was germinating in his mind.

Assaulting and killing MacMurphy's girlfriend had not been enough . . . not nearly enough. She was irrelevant. He needed to kill MacMurphy . . . and to do it in such a way that the man suffered. He was looking forward to it.

CHAPTER 83

While Lim climbed back into his car to begin his descent into Villefranche, François Leverrier was waking from his afternoon nap next to Solange Lançelot, the curvy blond sleeping peacefully beside him.

They had spent the morning swimming, baking in the sun and waterskiing. Later, they had enjoyed a leisurely lunch aboard the yacht, and then a nap. The *Tout Va Bien* was rolling and tugging gently at its anchor in Villefranche harbor. As he stirred awake among the tousled sheets of the circular king-size bed set in the center of the main cabin, Solange awakened too.

"What do you feel like doing now?" Solange asked hopefully, stretching luxuriously and running her long, manicured fingernails through the hairs of François's chest.

Feeling delightfully indolent after his nap, François suggested, "Let's go back up on deck to catch the afternoon sun with a cool *aperitif*."

Solange agreed. She jumped out of the bed and padded nude up toward the afterdeck, calling back to him over her shoulder, "Fix the drinks, Cheri. Meet you on deck."

She had a great body and loved to show it off and have it admired. She knew that he was watching and accentuated the sway of her hips as she walked aft gracefully out of the forward cabin and climbed the ladder up to the deck. She dropped into a lounge chair and let the warm sun work its way into her pores, soothing and recharging her.

François brought the drinks and plopped into a lounge chair next to her. They languished nude on the deck, luxuriating in the beneficent sunshine and watching the sun move slowly across the sky. *Just another great day in paradise, another great day in paradise . . .*

CHAPTER 84

Tim awoke at eight-thirty the next morning. He had slept well at first, the exhaustion forcing him into a deep, dreamless, coma. But in the dreamy state before waking, the nightmares returned. Ghosts from the past haunted him at night. That's why he hated to sleep. Awake, he could cope with the ghosts—asleep, they attacked his subconscious in force. He pushed them out of his mind and replaced them with thoughts of revenge and planning.

He had things to do, and the sleep had recharged his batteries. He would waste no more time in this flophouse of a hotel room. He was showered, shaved, and on the street in less than thirty minutes.

After fortifying himself with a breakfast of buttery croissants and strong coffee at a nearby café, he drove directly to the marina and found the management office. At the counter he was met by the grizzled old assistant harbor master, deeply tanned and weather beaten. He wore a sweaty white tee shirt with an anchor logo and *"Marina de Villefranche"* emblazoned across the chest, old, frayed blue jean cutoffs, and worn-out flip-flops on his leathery feet. A wet brown Gitanes cigarette smoldered from his lower lip.

He looked at Lim unguardedly. "*Oui*, can I help you?"

Lim was straightforward. Expediency was foremost in his mind at this point. Although he would have preferred to make his inquiries in a manner designed to protect being described to the police during the inevitable investigation after the hit, there simply was no time. He'd be long gone anyway, and they would never find him. He was quite sure of that. Other than his Oriental appearance, they'd have nothing to go on.

"Could you direct me to the *Tout Va Bien*, please?"

"Are you expected?" The man spoke with a raspy, sing-song Marseilles accent.

"Not until tomorrow morning, but I want to locate the yacht now so I can go directly to it in the morning," Lim backed away from the pungent odor of the smoke blowing directly in his face.

"I'm supposed to announce all visitors, so you'll have to return here in the morning anyway," the man said as his finger traced down a long index of the yachts moored in the marina. "Here it is, the *Tout Va Bien*, slip number D-19." He glanced down at the row of yachts lining the marina. "But it's not in its slip; it's gone," he announced with finality.

"That's impossible, I'm supposed to meet him here in the morning. Can you tell me where it went?"

The man assessed Lim for a moment, allowing smoke to ooze out of his mouth and billow up into his nose and eyes. He muttered, "*Un moment*," and reached across the desk to grasp the microphone of a CB radio. He triggered the send key: "Base to Line D, come in please. Over." A moment later the radio squealed its reply: "Line D, base. This is Robert. Over."

"Robert, do you have any idea where the *Tout Va Bien* has gone? And if she's due back this evening? Over."

"She's out for the day, base. Over."

"When do you expect her back in her slip? Over."

"Well, I expect her back this evening, base, but when she returns she'll probably anchor out in the harbor. When he's here the owner only uses the slip for his speedboat. To ferry back and forth from the yacht. He doesn't handle the yacht very well in the harbor, so he prefers to anchor rather than use the slip. His captain is off for the rest of the week. Over."

"*Merci,* Robert. Over and out."

The man stubbed out his cigarette. "That's it. She's here. Lots of owners have too much boat to handle by themselves, so they just hang out in the harbor when they're without crew. You'll have to take a water taxi out in the morning. Pick one up at the A row, right over there." He indicated the slip at the far north end of the marina. "They'll be able to find her for you."

"Thank you, sir. You have been a great help. Thank you." Lim pumped the man's callused hand with great enthusiasm and left the office. He was satisfied. Now he knew where François LeVerrier would be spending the night . . . his last night on earth. He also knew exactly what he, Lim, would have to do for the remainder of the day. He had some shopping to do before the stores closed for the evening.

CHAPTER 85

Lim's first stop was at a hardware store. He purchased one meter of electrical wire, a six-volt battery, a wire cutter, needle-nose pliers, screwdriver, a soldering iron and solder, electrician's tape, and a kilo of ten-penny framing nails.

He then drove up the road to a household goods store and bought a mechanical alarm clock and one box each of plastic garbage and sandwich bags. Further up the road he located a hunting and fishing outfitter, where he purchased two boxes of 12-gauge shotgun shells, a roll of strong fishing line, and a small, child's canvas backpack. While checking out, he asked the clerk for directions to the nearest farm supply store and was told it was about six miles inland on the north side of the same road he had entered the town on. "Hurry," the clerk cautioned him. "They close at five."

Lim checked his watch and saw that time was not on his side. He needed to hurry . . . yet he did not want to draw the attention of the gendarmes, nor get into an accident due to speeding. He felt caught in a vise where one side was the need to arrive at the farm supply store before five or risk at least delaying his mission, at worst failing altogether, and the other side was the need for prudence in speed. Lim cursed aloud at the situation. *Merde,* why did he allow himself to sleep so late?

He drove as fast as he dared, stopping only once, at a gas station, to pick up a gas can and fill it with a liter of diesel fuel, and arrived just as the store was closing for the day. Fortunately, the storekeeper was kind enough to permit him to make his final purchase—ten kilos of ammonium nitrate fertilizer.

He had about three hours of work ahead of him, and then he would be ready.

CHAPTER 86

Solange and François cruised back into Villefranche Bay at ten minutes to six. They dropped anchor and secured the yacht for the evening, showered and dressed casually for dinner.

They relaxed with aperitifs and hor d'oeuvres on the after-deck while watching the extraordinary Mediterranean sunset, and then rode in on the speedboat to the marina. They left the boat in its slip and strolled leisurely, hand in hand, up along the *quai* toward La Casita.

CHAPTER 87

Lim stuffed himself with Chinese food in a local restaurant and headed back to his hotel.

The ingredients he had purchased during the afternoon were spread out on the bed. Sitting at the small desk, he began removing the pellets, gunpowder, and percussion caps from the shotgun shells. Each was separated into plastic sandwich bags laid out in front of him.

He then set about assembling a primitive detonator with the caps and gunpowder. He made a tight package of the mixture with one of the sandwich bags and tape, and inserted a wire into each end. He then fabricated a timer with the clock and wired it to the detonator. Next, he wired the battery to the detonator package. He set the charge to blow when the big hand hit twelve.

Then he began working on the body of the bomb. First he lined the backpack with a plastic garbage bag and filled it with the ammonium nitrate. Next he added the shotgun pellets and nails and mixed them evenly throughout the fertilizer. He added the diesel fuel slowly and kneaded the mixture into a congealed, gooey mush, being careful not to stick himself with one of the nails. All of this was then pressed tightly into the bottom of the backpack and sealed with tape. He taped the detonator package securely on the top of the mixture.

The timer would be wired and set at the last minute.

He cleaned up the room and placed all of the remaining trash and tools into a disposal bag. He closed the flap on his homemade satchel charge and surveyed his work. The room showed no evidence of his bomb-making. Only two packages sat on the bed in front of him—the satchel charge and the trash bag. He checked his watch. It was eight minutes to midnight, and he was ready. He picked up the two packages and left the room.

CHAPTER 88

François and Solange were pleasantly drunk and full of the culinary skills of Marie-Yvonne. They stepped out into the balmy night and leisurely strolled back down toward the marina.

It was a few minutes past midnight.

CHAPTER 89

Lim exited the hotel cautiously, looking around to see if anyone was in the area. He did not want to be spotted getting rid of the trash bag. Stealthily making his way to a garbage dumpster behind the hotel, he raised the lid and heaved the bag into its depths.

Lim drove directly to the marina and parked across the street from the D row of slips. He got there just in time to observe the handsome couple weave their way down the dock, fumble with the key to open the gate, and stroll on to the speedboat tied up at slip number D-19.

Lim watched them board the speedboat on unsteady legs and settle into the front seat. He was glad to know they were mellowed by alcohol—less chance of their awareness to his eventual presence near the yacht. The engine roared to life, and the boat chugged backward out of the slip, turned away from the shore, and leaped forward. Lim's eyes followed the small craft as it sped out into the bay. Moments later, it pulled up to the side of a large white yacht, and the couple climbed aboard.

CHAPTER 90

François tied the speed boat to the stern of the yacht and turned toward Solange. He took her in his arms and kissed her gently at first, and then deeper as his passion rose. His hands traced over her hips and buttocks, and he could feel the soft, smooth skin beneath the light silk summer dress.

She pushed him away gently and purred, "Sit up top and have your cognac while I go below and slip into something more comfortable. Meet you in five minutes. *Ça va, cheri?*"

"*Oui, ça va*, five minutes . . ."

"*Je t'aime cheri. Je t'aime.*"

He gazed out over the water, but all he saw was moonlight on quiet water.

Lim was still on shore.

CHAPTER 91

im returned to his car, removed the satchel, and slung it over his shoulder. He walked back up along the *quai* to the A row, where the water taxis were docked. Several small dinghies with 10hp outboard engines and three larger motor launches were tied up along the dock, but there didn't appear to be anyone around in charge of them.

Lim found the rental office vacant and locked, although the lights were on inside. He banged on the door a few times but got no response. He stood there trying to decide whether he should just take one of the dinghies when an old man approached from the road.

Glancing toward the dinghies, Lim asked, "How much?"

"Fifty euros for the day; one hundred euros deposit." The old man lit a brown Bastos cigarette disinterestedly and flipped the smoking match into the bay.

Lim pulled one hundred fifty euros from his billfold and handed them to the old man. "I'll be back in the morning. Which one shall I take?"

The old man indicated the nearest boat. "That one's all ready to go. Do you know how to operate an outboard?"

"Of course," He climbed into the boat, set his backpack down on the seat, and set about starting the engine.

After two unsuccessful tugs on the starter cord, the old man called down to him, "Use the choke. There on the right. Flip it up."

The engine coughed to life, and the old man unhooked the bowline and tossed it into the boat. Lim backed the boat out of the slip, turned it away from the shore, and slowly headed out into the bay. He was in no hurry now. François Leverrier and his little *putain* weren't going anywhere but hell this night.

CHAPTER 92

Moonlight illuminated the bay. There was no breeze. The bay was like a sheet of glass, except in the wake of the little outboard, which chugged purposefully toward the *Tout Va Bien*.

The yacht was clearly outlined against the horizon in the distance. Lim could see lights on the afterdeck and in the forward cabin below.

As he drew closer, he could see the outline of François smoking on the afterdeck, elbows on the railing, looking out to sea. Lim slowed the engine as much as he could without stalling it and continued his surveillance while staying a good distance away from the yacht.

He watched his prey flick a cigarette out into the water and then purposefully tilt his snifter up to drain the last drop of cognac. He saw him turn amidships and disappear from view. When the lights went out on the afterdeck, Lim turned the bow of his little boat back toward the yacht and closed the remaining one hundred meters or so at idle speed.

He cut the engine a few feet from the yacht and drifted toward the white hull until he could reach out and grab the swimming platform at the stern of the vessel. He tied his boat to the platform next to the speedboat and sat quietly. He could hear soft music and voices from deep within the cabin. He was ready.

CHAPTER 93

François descended the ladder and walked forward toward the main cabin. He could hear the sound of the shower running and pictured Solange standing under the spray all wet and soapy and glistening and slick as a seal. Just that mental picture was enough to make his groin tingle and his penis swell.

He switched off the light in the hall and entered the main cabin. Her clothes were strewn upon the large circular bed that dominated the cabin. Lacy pink thong panties that were the last item to be removed had slipped off the bed onto the floor. He kicked off his boat shoes, ripped off his shirt, and slipped quickly out of his pants. Hopping on one foot to keep his balance, he hurried toward the shower, continuing to undress on the way.

He saw her blurred image through the glass shower door and hesitated a moment. The shower was tiny, with barely enough room for one person to turn around in, and when she bent over to soap her legs, her beautiful, slick buttocks pressed up against the glass and leaped into focus. He pulled open the door to the tiny shower and stood facing her. She turned toward him and squeezed the water out of her eyes with her fingers. Looking down at his erection she exclaimed: "*Mon Dieu, cheri,* you have begun without me!"

CHAPTER 94

L im climbed quietly out of the boat onto the swimming platform of the yacht. He sat down on the platform, leaned back against the stern of the yacht, and opened the flap of the satchel. He thought a moment as he examined the clock. He decided that four minutes on the timer would give him plenty of time to get out of the blast zone.

He checked his wrist watch, closed the satchel, hooked it over his shoulder, and climbed up the swimming ladder onto the afterdeck of the yacht.

At the end of the hall he could see the door to the main cabin. Light filtered out from below the door into the hall. He could hear the sound of water running from within.

He gently tried the handle on the door, but found it locked. He calculated where he was on the yacht in relation to his prey, the engines, and the fuel tanks. He figured the engines were placed amidships, below the door leading to the main cabin, and the fuel tanks were probably directly below where he was standing. If he placed the charge on the floor against the door in front of him, the blast would reach forward into the main cabin and also rupture the fuel tanks below, adding to the explosion. *Perfect,* he thought. *This will do just fine.*

He propped the satchel against the door at his feet, checked his watch, set the timer for the four minutes he had decided upon, closed the satchel, and hurried back up the ladder to the deck above. He scrambled back into his boat, scraping his knee on the swimming platform in the process and uttering a silent curse.

Haste was an issue now. After all, this was to be François's demise, not Lim's. Just François . . . and the unlucky *putain* who had the misfortune to accompany him on this vacation.

Once settled, he checked his watch again—plenty of time—untied the boat, and pushed off. He allowed himself to drift silently away from the *Tout Va Bien* for another minute before he pulled the starter cord. He tugged. He tugged again. Nothing. Now he was getting nervous. He was too close to François's boat for safety, and the damn engine wouldn't catch. *What the hell was this?!* Starting to feel a bit panicked now, he played with the choke, pulled the starter again . . . and still nothing. He smelled gas. He had flooded it. He checked his watch, felt fear flood him, and as his heart raced, he desperately tugged the starter again and again with the choke off.

Finally the engine sputtered to life. Relieved, he turned the bow of his boat back toward the shore and moved away with all due haste. His pressing need now was to get the hell out of there as quickly as possible.

CHAPTER 95

S olange and François were unaware of the sound of the little boat speeding off. They were locked in an embrace in the shower, indeed a necessity in the cramped space. *This could be the woman who ends my chase for women,* François thought.

Their passion mounted, making the couple mindless of anything else in the world, mindless of the ticking satchel, mindless of its deadly contents, totally unaware of the little boat chugging farther and farther away from the imperiled yacht, focused only on themselves and each other and the delicious sensations overtaking both their bodies . . . until he entered her with a gasp and the satchel outside the door blew them both into oblivion.

CHAPTER 96

L im watched the yacht rise up out of the water from the force of the explosion and then, an instant later, the fuel tanks erupted in another explosion, and the yacht disintegrated in a ball of flame and debris.

Bits of the yacht landed near him, and he watched in detached amazement as the bulk of it disappeared into the bay with a hiss. He was thoroughly pleased with his handiwork.

Lim drove his boat up onto the beach and walked back to his car. He didn't run, but neither did he dawdle. It wouldn't do to be seen running away. He could hear the wailing sirens of approaching police cars as he drove away from the scene and headed back in the direction of Paris.

CHAPTER 97

Three days later Huang looked up at the sound of the knock on his office door. He had been deep in thought, contemplating another inevitable exile back to Beijing.

At first he didn't make the connection between the media reports of the killing of Pol Girard in Bern and the explosion that killed François Leverrier and an unidentified woman in Villefranche—he simply didn't immediately recognize the names of MacMurphy's agents. But when the protest came in from the American Embassy about the assault and murder of Margaret "Wei-wei" Ryan by an Oriental man matching the description of Lim, things became crystal clear.

Things fell together for Beijing as well. The cable he had received from MSS headquarters that morning was scathing.

Lim appeared in the doorway, silently arrogant. He guessed that the other shoe had finally dropped.

"Get in here, you idiot. Do you realize what you have done? What possessed you? Have you gone completely mad? *Eyeah.* You stupid maggot, answer me, answer me!" Huang fired the words at Lim, splattering spittle over the papers cluttering his desk.

"They deserved what they got—all of them." Lim glared at Huang unflinchingly, displaying neither fear nor remorse. If anything, he looked triumphant, pleased with himself, and frankly surprised that his boss didn't feel the same.

"You go after his girlfriend, go on a k-k-k-killing rampage, and all you can say is th-th-they deserved it! Now I know you have gone completely mad. Do – do – do - do you not realize what you have done? What this means?" Huang sputtered, unable to suppress his rage, the veins in his beet-red face and neck pulsing.

He struggled to control his breathing, taking deep breaths to bring himself down, but then completely lost it when Lim replied quietly, "I want MacMurphy . . ."

"Get out! Out – out – out - out," Huang screamed, pointing at the door. Beads of sweat sprouted on his forehead and among the sparse hairs of his receding hairline and ran down the side of his face. His heart thundered. "You are under arrest. H-H-House arrest. Do not attempt to l-l-leave this embassy. I am g-going to have you hanged. Get out of my sight. Out out out . . ."

Lim cast a last killing glare at his station chief, turned, and slowly walked out of the office, his chin thrust up in the air, his step measured and sure, a bit of swagger in his gait. He left Huang's office door open behind him in a final petty display of defiance.

Huang collapsed back into his chair and watched Lim's arrogant retreat.

CHAPTER 98

O nce out of Huang's sight, Lim headed down the main staircase to the lobby and straight out the main doors, totally defiant of Huang's orders. Lim hesitated only momentarily when he reached the street, glancing up and down Avenue Georges V, and then purposefully turned left up the hill and hurried toward the Champs Elysées and the metro station on the corner.

Huang remained motionless in his chair, struggling to control his breathing, staring at the empty doorway. His rage slowly subsided as he concentrated on bringing his emotions down. Slowly his composure began to return. His breathing more measured. The rain of sweat from his forehead subsided. The veins at his temples stopped throbbing. He could feel the tension ever so slowly ebbing.

He was sure Lim had disregarded his orders and headed out the front door. He was equally sure he would never see Lim again. He didn't care.

Still, the full realization of what had happened left him stunned and drained and full of deep remorse for the victims of Lim's crazed brutality.

Yes, MacMurphy had been responsible, at least in part, for his being recalled to China ten years earlier, but he had to share equal blame. He should have listened to Mac and not reported the pitch. Then things would have blown over and his career would have been fine and he might not be in this position today.

And yes, MacMurphy had surely engineered the theft of the euros, which would undoubtedly finally bring an abrupt end to his career in the MSS, and maybe a firing squad—if he were lucky.

But one thing did not excuse the other. Just as there is honor among thieves, there is honor among spies as well. For some deaths, some harm might become necessary in the course of accomplishing one's objectives. But this—the mayhem Lim had wrought—was not. Huang deeply regretted Lim's most unfortunate actions. And, as well, he remembered the days when he had considered MacMurphy a friend.

Then there were the consequences he would personally face when—if—he returned to China. He imagined the impending interrogations, imprisonment, personal disgrace, family dishonor, worse . . . probably much worse . . .

He tossed his glasses across his desk and massaged the acupressure points around the bridge of his nose and temples and leaned back heavily in his chair. He stretched out his arms and brought his hands back behind his head. He took a long, deep breath and then slowly forced the air from his lungs in a relaxing, controlled exhale, which carried with it much of the tension from his body.

After long seconds of just sitting still and breathing to induce relaxation, he ran his hands back through his thinning hair, wiping away beads of sweat. There was too much for his hands alone to deal with, far too much.

Huang yanked a tissue out of a dispenser and mopped at his balding pate. The mop-up job helped calm him further down. Now, almost fully composed, he shook his head in disbelief and total resignation. A wave of emotion coursed through his body, bringing him close to tears.

Drained and trapped, he shook his head sadly, took another deep breath, and reached for the phone.

Seventeen minutes later, at exactly 2:36pm, he was met by Burton B. Berger at the Avenue Gabriel entrance of the American Embassy and was quietly ushered inside. Nobody took undue notice of the tall, tired-looking oriental man in the rumpled suit carrying the large briefcase.

CHAPTER 99

Later that afternoon, MacMurphy signaled SKITTISH, the Chinese waiter Willy Chan, by calling the restaurant and reserving a table for a dinner party of eleven people under the name Roland Petit. The signal indicated an emergency meeting at a prearranged spot in the Bois de Bologne shortly after sunset.

The two men met after running their respective forty-five-minute surveillance detection routes to assure they were clean of any hostile surveillance. Willy and Mac exchanged minimal pleasantries before getting down to business. They spoke in low tones while slowly walking along one of the many quiet paths deep within the heavily wooded park. They blended into the evening park environment by carefully dressing in jeans, tennis shoes, and tee-shirts, like many of the strollers searching for a breath of air away from their muggy flats in the hot August evening.

The hookers were out in force. MacMurphy didn't like this particular aspect of Bois de Bologne meetings because shady activities like prostitution often brought with them increased police surveillance. He didn't want to get caught up in a police net while "innocently" meeting with one of his assets.

He knew that everything in clandestine tradecraft was a trade-off, though—like a seesaw with the high side being total security and the low side being total production. Somewhere a balance had to be struck that would include just enough tradecraft to protect the security of the operation while at the same time maintaining an acceptable level of efficient production of intelligence or operational information. On balance, MacMurphy had decided that the park, with its easy accessibility to all types of people, many entrances and exits, and the cloaking of the night, was close to ideal as a venue for brief encounters of this sort.

The pair approached a particularly garish looking *putain* attempting to look seductive on a park bench. She displayed long net-stockinged legs that ended beneath a short black miniskirt. Catching their glance, she called out, "*Vous voulez, messieurs?*" punctuating the invitation by cupping enormous dark-tipped breasts and pressing them up and out to overflow the tiny, transparent white blouse she wore. The cleavage she created ran like a gash from her throat to her belly. She smiled broadly, showing long, yellowing horse teeth and repeated: "*Vous voulez?*"— knowing that they didn't but, what the hell, might as well give it a try— while grossly running a long, wet tongue over heavily glossed red lips, clearly indicating her specialty.

The pair smiled in amusement and continued walking slowly by.

"I do not know where they go." Willy Chan whispered excitedly. "All I know is they surely gone. No shit. Ambassador has whole embassy running around looking for them. He pissed off for sure. Him no like at all. Ambassador's instructions are find them and bring in."

"What about the police? Has he contacted them?"

"*Eyeah*, you must be joke! This strictly internal affair. Only embassy know. They never tell local authorities about something like this. It too much loss of face . . ."

"What do they think happened?" MacMurphy emphasized the word "think."

Willy Chan was momentarily distracted by a middle-aged man in a business suit scampering out of the bushes off to his right. The man looked furtively around him before joining the path a few meters in front of them. Then he moved up the lane happily. Fifty euros poorer, but with a spring to his step.

Smiling, Willy came back to earth. "*Eyeah*, I do not know. I only hear some things. Not everything. At restaurant I overhear one guy say there very loud shouting in Mr. Huang's office. Mr. Huang give Lim hell. Then Lim run away—he really pissed—and nobody hear from after that. Then he say Mr. Huang go out few minutes later but nobody see him anymore either. They no return for dinner or call or anything. That is very against rules, you know . . . everyone must to be back in embassy building by six o'clock unless have special permission. They gotta keep Ambassador informed where they go all times, and MSS guys not exception. That always been rule. No exception never."

"So what do they think at the embassy?" He again emphasized the word "think."

"All think they defect, that is what everybody think . . ."

"And what do you think, Willy?"

Willy Chan smiled knowingly. "I think you know about Mr. Huang."

"Don't worry about Huang. Forget about him. I'm only interested in Lim."

Willy Chan stopped walking and turned to face MacMurphy. "So Mr. Huang he defect." It was a statement and he did not wait for a response. "Okay, so Mr. Huang safe. Good for him. He is good man. Everybody like Mr. Huang. He deserve break. But that Lim is real bad prick. *Eyeah*, you guys no want him, eh? He bad news. Very bad news . . ."

"We want him all right, Willy. That is, I want him . . . I want him very, very much." Mac's eyes darkened from their usual chocolate brown to spitfire black—and the hostility that was there frightened Willy Chan. Whatever it was that he saw blazing in their depths, it boded ill for Lim and made even Willy himself feel uncomfortable and just a little bit afraid.

Willy Chan avoided Mac's malevolent glare and thought carefully before he spoke. "He got some kind girlfriend. Tall, black *putain*. Long legs go way, way up . . ." He rolled his eyes. "She work Pigalle bar scene. Not bad looking except one front teeth chipped almost in half. She fix that, she look not too bad. She real hard-core hooker, though. Real *pute*. I no understand why Lim like her, but she sure as hell all over him all times. I see them at Mai-Lin restaurant couple times. They real lovey-lovey, kissy-kissy. You know what I mean."

Mac reached out and grabbed Willy's lapel. *Where else could a Chinese diplomat on the run hole up in this city?* "Where does she live? What bar does she work out of?" "*Eyeah*, hang on. Sure, I know where you find her. She most time work from dirty bar in Pigalle near Place Blanche. Bar call something like 'Secret Place' or maybe 'Secret Club.' Something like that. I no go place like that—hate Pigalle bar scene and too expensive—but I hear them talk about."

"What about her name? Do you remember her name?"

The waiter stopped walking, stood stock still, and searched his memory. His eyes rolled around as he probed the depths of his recollections . . . but to no avail. "*Eyeah*, I no remember." Willy scratched his head and squinted his eyes tightly in an effort to recall the woman's name. "Oh yeah, but I remember they talk about manageress of bar. She kicked Lim out of place once. Say he can not just sit there without buy drinks. The Chinese people from embassy no have much money, you know. They all time broke . . . poor bastards . . . Anyway, her name Angel, good name for hooker, eh? Angel . . ."

"Good. Anything else?" Mac waited while Willy searched his brain.

Finally Willy shook his head. "Naw, that all I remember. You gonna get him? I think you gonna get him, right?"

"You bet your ass I am, but you keep quiet about it. Not a whisper to anyone. And keep your ear to the ground, Willy. Signal me if you hear or remember anything else, otherwise I'll signal you for a meeting."

Willy nodded his head vigorously in assent. "Good luck. I hope you catch bastard . . ."

MacMurphy shook hands with Willy Chan. "Thanks again, Willy." When the handshake ended, five crisp new one hundred euro notes had found their way into Willy Chan's hand. "Thanks for staying on top of this . . ." He turned and headed back up the path the way they had come, anger evident in his footfall.

Willy Chan stood for a moment watching him disappear into the night. He felt a chill, remembering the cold, hard look in Mac's black eyes.

CHAPTER 100

MacMurphy wanted to go immediately to Pigalle. He was in pursuit of his prey, and he didn't want to let the trail get cold. But he needed to do some planning and preparation before setting off.

He didn't intend this to be a seat-of-the-pants operation. His training had taught him that probably the single most important characteristic that elevates the really great case officers above the rest is their ability to "wing it" when required. Yet, even more important, the best case officers never go into a situation *planning* to wing it. They must first attempt to anticipate every possible eventuality and carefully plan their responses. Then they only have to wing it if they are thrown a really unexpected curve. All of this was second nature to MacMurphy. He was not going to wing it . . .

First he made a brief stop at his safehouse apartment on Rue Laugier. There he changed his shirt, discarding his gray tee-shirt in favor of a rather loud, touristy Hawaiian shirt. He decided the jeans could stay but substituted black silver-tipped cowboy boots for the tennis shoes.

He then took a paper clip from his nightstand, shaped one end of it into a hook, and used it to trip the hidden catch on the back of one of his stereo speakers. The top of the speaker popped open and revealed a two-inch-deep cavity, from which he extracted a mustache, a pair of heavy, dark-rimmed glasses, and a small bottle of dark brown non-permanent hair dye. He then went to work applying the items over the bathroom sink.

It was only a light disguise and wouldn't have fooled any of his friends or co-workers, but then, he wasn't trying to disguise his identity from them. It would blur his appearance enough for what he had to do in Pigalle that night.

He removed one other item from the concealment device before setting off—a unique, well-used, home-made set of non-CIA-issue brass knuckles. He had had them since he removed them from the limp hand of brawling football player after Mac had taken him down and broken his arm with an arm bar during a vicious bar fight in college.

The weapon had four heavy rings to cover the punching surface of his right hand, attached to a flat, blade-like, three and one-half inch-long hinged projection that covered the outer chopping edge of the fist. The brass knuckles were an equalizer he had never been without since that day in Oklahoma.

They were his weapon of choice in a street fight—easily concealed until the last minute and better than a knife—a knife could be knocked loose or dropped. A punch or karate chop with a set of these on the hand would crack bone—as Mac knew, having been on both the giving and receiving end of this particular weapon. And it was like riding a bike—once you learned to use them, you never forgot. They fit his hand perfectly, and he was eager to sink them into Lim's face and skull.

Lim had murdered Wei-wei and two of Mac's assets—and friends. Now it was time for revenge. This wasn't an Agency op. This was Mac-Murphy's personal vendetta.

He was also aware that Lim was no doubt out looking for him as well. Lim had struck three times already, and most assuredly he wasn't finished. But it was not self-defense that was motivating Mac. It was revenge, pure and simple. They were two deadly cobras, out to strike at each other. MacMurphy was determined to be the cobra that struck first, catching the other one off-guard. If he missed, he might not get a second chance.

CHAPTER 101

MacMurphy exited the metro at Place Blanche at ten minutes to eleven. The Boulevard de Clichy was awash in neon lights advertising cheap peep shows, strip joints, bars, fast food restaurants, pool halls, and pinball parlors. The lowlife of Paris—the people who lived in perfect symbiosis with these flashy accoutrements—gaudy hookers, slick pimps, shifty-eyed petty thieves, hard-eyed strippers—milled around aimlessly like cattle.

It was a carnival atmosphere—a carnival of debauchery. Mac took in the sights not as the tourist he was dressed as, but as the covert specialist he was. He was on guard for anything from pickpockets targeting him to a street brawl erupting around him, to the sight of Lim himself, appearing suddenly out of nowhere. Mac was ready.

He crossed to the south side of the street and headed east, planning to check every side street up to Place Pigalle and then repeat the search on the north side heading back to Place Blanche. He had faith in Willy

Chan's information and was confident of finding the "Secret" bar on one of the side streets that evening.

Treading the streets with a single-minded purpose, he was deaf to the music that blared from doors that opened, blind to the garish lights, focused on just one thing—finding Lim and exacting revenge.

It took him less than twenty minutes to find the place. It was on the Rue Froment, about halfway between Place Blanche and Place Pigalle and about thirty meters down from the corner. The cracked and flickering neon sign over the entrance announced the "Club Secret" in red letters surrounded by lots of little kissing red lips crossed by index fingers making the "shush" sign.

He pushed through the draped entrance into the dimly lit room beyond.

The first thing Mac noticed was the smell. A heavy ammonia-like stink was pervasive, and the familiar aromas of stale beer, cigarettes, and body odor combined to make it worse. He stood at the entrance for a moment to let his eyes adjust to the dim light and waves of smoke from strong French cigarettes, and his nose to the stench. *Damn, how can people live like this?*

The Club Secret wasn't exactly doing a land office business. A bored-looking topless barmaid relaxed on a cooler behind the bar, tattooed butterflies hovering over dark nipples. She could have been anywhere from twenty-five to forty years old, but one thing was perfectly clear: she had plenty of hard miles on her. Her wide mouth worked obnoxiously around a glob of gum—tongue pushing it through her teeth every few moments to make loud snapping sounds—while creating clouds of pungent smoke from the yellow Bastos cigarette she puffed on furiously. Freud would have had no trouble classifying her in the "oral" category.

She scratched her armpit inelegantly, silently watching two dusty construction workers, probably residents of the neighborhood, attempting to solve the world's political problems while hunched over beers at either end of the bar. They drank down the brew with fierce determination, not like men out to relax and enjoy the evening but like men working hard at getting agreeably drunk before going home to badly cooked meals and shrew-like wives. Mac reflected that they probably put more energy into accomplishing their objective here than they did at their labors. They punctuated their emphatic argument with fists and fingers that jabbed at the air and occasionally at each other.

But neither of them was Lim, nor did he seem to be anywhere else around. In fact, there wasn't a single oriental person in sight. Hopefully one of the girls here was "Angel."

Two of the banquettes along the opposite wall contained couples— bar girl and customer—and another far at the back was occupied by three working girls laughing and playing cards and puffing heavily on brown French cigarettes.

The entire room looked up as the American tourist with the slicked-back dark hair and wild flowered shirt walked in. The girls' synchronous thoughts were telegraphed in their attitudes: *Here comes money!* The men at the bar looked up briefly but immediately returned to their beers and conversation in total lack of interest.

MacMurphy spun into a stool near the middle of the bar and flung a cheerful west Texas "How y'all doin', honey?" to the barmaid. She slid off her perch, droopy breasts jiggling, wide smile: "*Bonsoir, monsieur.* Someseeng to dreenk?"

"You bet, sugar. Fix me a tall CC soda, would'ja, and then tell Angel to get her cute little ass over here. I wanna see if she remembers me."

"Angel," the barmaid called toward the card-playing girls in the back of the room, "someone ees eare to see you."

One of the girls answered and slid out of the booth. She wore a tight, white, sequined evening dress, which surely had fit her perfectly in the days before she gained thirty pounds. She approached the bar with choppy steps caused by the restriction of the tight skirt. Her ample bosom jiggled invitingly above the uplifting bodice—each short, bouncy step sent tiny shock waves through bursting breast tissue. Her heavy makeup concealed age lines and a complexion damaged by too many drinks, cigarettes, and late nights. But she had a terrific wide smile, which displayed a mouthful of perfect white teeth and soft blue eyes.

MacMurphy answered her broad smile with one of his own. He oozed charm and held out his hand to her. "Come on over here, you gorgeous creature, and let me take a look at you. God! You look great. And I'll bet you don't even remember me . . ."

"Sure I remember you," she lied. "'ow could I ever forget such a handsome *visage? Comment ça va, cheri?* Where 'ave you beean?"

The bargirl continued to flatter the boorish American tourist. "I thought I see you couple of weeks ago in metro. Trocadero, I think. Was eet you?"

"Just blew into town this mornin', babe. Musta been a lookalike handsome dude." He admired the way these bar girls could flatter their customers. *They're alike all over the world.* "I forget what you like to drink, Angel baby. What'll it be?"

"Tut tut," she teased, cutting her eyes at him. "*Un coup de champagne,*" she called to the barmaid.

The barmaid pulled a half empty bottle of flat champagne from under the bar and filled a flute glass with the amber liquid for Angel. A few tired bubbles drifted to the top of the glass. MacMurphy and Angel continued their banter while Mac worked the conversation around to the subject of other girls who worked in the club.

"Now does that tall black gal—what's her name—does she still work here?"

"Ah-h, you mean Kitty? She ees right over zere." She indicated the banquette at the rear where she had been sitting. She caught his sheepish smile and then grinned at him knowingly: "What 'as Kitty got zat ze rest of us do not 'ave?"

He answered her grin and replied in a sing-song voice: "She's tall, that's all . . ."

She cocked her head at him—he continued to smile stupidly. "Yeah, I bet . . . And so you weesh to buy her out, eh?"

"Why not? Life's short, and Kitty's got legs that run clear up to here!" He drew a line across his stomach. How much? I firgit . . ."

"Where you are staying?" she asked with resignation. She wouldn't have minded turning a trick with this fellow herself. He had a real nice smile. *Tant pis*, she thought. *Some girls get all the luck . . .*

"Crillon, why?"

She let out a low whistle. "Rules. We must know where zee girls are staying. Zat will be one hundred fifty euros." She was now all business.

"Why? Because I'm staying at the Crillon?"

"Okay, okay, you are *ancien* customer, one hundred, but zat's eet."

MacMurphy pulled a folded wad of bills from his pocket, removed a money clip, and peeled off two one hundred euro notes. "Never mind," he smiled. "Here's two hundred. Buy the rest of the girls a drink and go fetch Kitty for me. *Ça va?*"

"*Ça va, cheri.* I weel get her. Got to go pee-pee anyway." She pushed the two hundred euros into her cleavage and slid off the stool. "Ah well, *sois bien cheri.* Come back, okay? And . . . choose me next time, please . . . ?"

"You bet, Angel." He grinned at the way her buttocks bounced as she jiggled her way back to the rear of the bar.

Angel stopped at the booth and touched the black girl on the shoulder and spoke to her. The black girl slid out of the banquette, turned back toward the bar and smiled broadly at Mac, prominently displaying a chipped front tooth.

CHAPTER 102

She tugged at her mini-skirt, and approached the bar, boobs jiggling as she walked with a gait that was engineered to produce the maximum wiggle. She continued smiling her wide, chipped-tooth smile. *Willy Chan was right, she ought to get that tooth fixed.*

Other than that she wasn't bad looking for a Pigalle hooker—short Afro hair-do, wide brown eyes set within inch-long false lashes, and a sexy, lithe, six-foot-long body. She was dressed in a slinky wine-red mini-dress that left no doubt that only her lashes were false. Her thong panties accentuated the curves of a tight, teardrop ass, and her erect nipples punctuated the thin satin of her bodice.

She held out a hand to Mac when she reached the bar, causing one of the thin spaghetti straps to slip down her shoulder and threaten to reveal an entire chocolate breast.

He slipped off the barstool, flashed a wide grin, and opened his arms to her as she approached. "Howdy there, li'l Kitten, how y'all doin' *ce soir?*"

She pushed back the wayward strap with a thumb and smiled coquettishly. But when she opened her mouth to speak, whatever illusions he might have had about this sleek-looking French hooker were swiftly dispelled. She was pure southeast Washington, D.C. ghetto black.

"How y'all doin', sugar?" She caressed his arm and moved her face to within inches of his. He could feel her breast pressed against his shoulder. "Understan' we goin' ta have a little honeymoon çe soir." Her breath was stale with Bastos cigarettes.

"You bet, li'l Kitty." He stood and tossed another fifty euros on the bar. Now that he had found Lim's squeeze, he was anxious to get out of there.

"Aw come on, Sugar. Ain't ya even goin' ta buy me a drink?" He knew it was part of the racket, but he played the game and complied.

"Sure," he replied. He turned to the topless barmaid and indicated the fifty euro note on the bar: "Y'all take a glass of that flat champagne out of this for Kitty. She'll drink it later." He hooked his arm through Kitty's and pulled her toward the entrance. "Come on, baby, let's git outta here. We'll have our drinks at the Crillon . . ."

"She-it, never did see no one in such a hurry. Lemme git ma pockabook, will ya?" She hurried to the booth in the rear, mumbling to herself all the way, and returned with a sequined purse. "Okay, sweet talker, I's ready." She looped her arm around Mac's and led him out. "Now wha'd ya say yo name was, Sugar?"

"George," he leered, "just call me George." He gave her his best lecherous grin and hurried her out the door like a man who was extra-eager to get laid. The other girls in the bar watched jealously as they left. The black girl in the miniskirt and spike heels was inches taller than the rich tourist in the loud Hawaiian shirt. The hem of her skirt was about even with the hem of his shirt—they were comical sight walking out arm in arm. Kitty acted proud of her catch. Mac was proud of his catch, too . . .

CHAPTER 103

Mac took a deep, lung-cleansing breath when they got out into the smoke-free night air. Kitty offered no resistance as he eagerly guided her up Rue Froment and away from the noisy Boulevard de Clichy. They made small talk while they strolled along the quiet side street. Every hooker has a sad story to tell, and Kitty needed no urging to tell hers to Mac.

She had come to Paris on the arm of a lecherous militant civil rights activist almost three years ago. Then, after using and abusing her during his month-long visit, he left her behind with a chipped tooth, a black eye, the hotel bill, and no return ticket. She admitted that she had been no stranger to prostitution before she came to Paris: "Ah turned a trick or two in ma time back in Dee Cee befo' comin' ta Paree, but ah allus picked ma Johns—neva done it wit no one ah didn't wanna do."

She slipped into full-time prostitution in Paris. At first the money was good and living was grand. She was a curiosity in great demand. But recently she had fallen on hard times—a long bout with pneumonia, followed by a nasty infection after a poorly done abortion, and fewer customers.

Mac felt sorry for her—three years can put a lot of miles on a poor hooker, and the slope gets steeper as the looks continue to fade.

His compassion notwithstanding, Mac did not forget why he was there. His first goal was to get her away from the club to someplace deserted where he could interrogate her if necessary. In the meantime he would put his elicitation skills to work. Elicitation was far more preferable to interrogation. He needed to find out where she lived and whether Lim was there. This was crucial. He had to find Lim. Then he would decide the next step.

She was relaxed now and talking freely about herself. Mac turned the conversation to now: "You live around here?"

"Yeah. Coupla blocks from here. Rue Ballu. Over there." She pointed in a westerly direction and then realized she didn't know where they were going. "By the way, Sugar, where we headed?"

"My car's parked near here." He indicated the direction of her apartment.

"You gotta car! Great, ah hates ridin' in the stinkin' metro."

"Hey, I've got an idea. Since we're so close, why don't we stop off at your place for a couple of minutes and you can change clothes? How's that sound?"

"Wassa matta? You don' like my clothes? You don' like the way ahm dressed? She-it!"

"I think you're one hell of a fine-lookin' young heifer. It's just that . . . well . . . we are going to the Crillon, you know . . ."

"She-it! You sayin' ah ain't good'nuf? Fuck'em. Ah be dress jus' fine."

"Aw come on, Kitty. Gimme a break. You walk in there like that and those old farts'll cream in their jeans." He put on his most ingenuous pleading look. "Can't you just put on a pair of slacks and a shirt? Please? Pretty please?"

"Nope. No way, José. Ain't no way ahm gunna take no John ta ma pad. No way. Forgit it. We go like dis or we don' go." She stood in front of him, hands on hips, immovable.

"Okay, okay. I get it. You just don't want your boyfriend to see me. Fine. You go in alone and I'll wait outside. How's that?"

"What you know about ma boyfrien'? Who tell you about any boyfrien'? Ah didn't say nothin'."

"Damn, girl, I don't give a good rat's ass about your private life. I'm not tryin' to pry. All girls have boyfriends, and you've got a right to yours. I just want you to change your fuckin' clothes before we go to my hotel. Come on . . ."

"Well we ain't goin' ta ma pad," She stopped stock still in her tracks, planting her feet solidly on the pavement. Her face wore a stern frown.

MacMurphy thought it was about time to get rough with her, but he first had to know for certain whether Lim was in her apartment. If he was he would go after him now; if not, he would have to stake the place out and hit him when he returned. And if he wasn't staying with Kitty he would have to find out from her where he was hiding out.

Above all, he didn't want her to clam up on him. That would make things much more difficult. Putting his hands on her shoulders, he looked up into her eyes. "Look here, Kitty, I want you real bad, and I plan to give you a real nice tip in the mornin'. It don't matter to me none that you're shacked up with some Chinese dude. I don't give a rat's ass about any of that kind of shit. Now, let's go get those clothes changed. *Ça va?*"

The look of surprise on her face confirmed to him that Lim was there. *Good!* Now all he needed was her address.

"What you mean 'Chinese boyfrien'? Who tell you dat? Angel? That fuckin' big-mouth bitch! Sonofabitch. She tole you, didn't she? Fuck!" she sputtered.

Now it was time to get tough.

He grabbed an arm and spun her into a narrow alley. She tripped and almost fell over a garbage can, but he held her up by the arm and then swung her up against the wall. He held her right hand by the wrist, and his other hand squeezed her throat and pressed her head hard against the wall. His knee was under her crotch, jammed against the wall and lifting her off the ground by the pubic bone. It was a precaution against a knee in the groin from her.

But the precaution was needless. Tears welled in her eyes, and she began to shake. There was no fight in her.

"Please, please don' hurt me," she pleaded, flinching from an expected blow. "What 'cha want? I didn't do nothin'."

"No, you didn't do anything, and you won't get hurt if you just listen and do what you're told." The Texas drawl and the "George" persona were gone.

MacMurphy spoke slowly and calmly, but he continued to hold her tight against the wall. He could feel the heat of her sex against his knee as she tried to wiggle free, and it aroused him. *A rapist would experience this feeling,* he thought. He knew the bricks were digging into her skin over the low-cut back of the dress. *She was helping Lim . . . she deserved to be hurt.* And then another thought. *Was this what Lim had felt in his violent encounter with Wei-wei? The arousal . . . the belief that she deserved to be hurt . . . was this what had raced through Lim's mind and body?* The idea that he might in any way be reacting like Lim immediately doused the heat in him, the fire in him.

He slowly released the pressure on her throat and crotch, and when she didn't struggle, he loosened his grip on her wrist as well. He knew from the look in her eyes that the struggle was over, but she knew from the look in his that it could get very bad if she didn't do exactly as he said.

"Is Lim at your apartment now?" His eyes pierced into hers, seeking to gauge the truth of her response.

"Yeah," she sniffed.

"Will you take me there?"

"No . . . she-it . . . Ah can't . . . please . . . What you goin' to do to him? He didn't do nothin'."

"I'm not going to do anything to him. I don't want to hurt him," he lied. "I just want to talk to him. You can at least show me where you live, can't you? What's your address?"

"Oh shit, man, you promise you not goin' to hurt him? No shit?"
Mac nodded.

"Don' tell 'im I said nothin', okay?"

He nodded again.

"Okay, man. Fuck. Wha'd you say yo name was? George? Okay, George, ah trusts you, but she-it, you know, leave me out of it, okay?" Tears rolled down her cheeks, carrying mascara in dark, wet streams. She sobbed heavily.

"Okay, Kitty. You said you lived close by. Now, what's the address?" She still hesitated. "It's . . . it's a couple'a blocks from here. Rue Ballu. Numba 22, fourth floor, apartment D." She tried to pull away from him, but he stopped her, held her tight.

"Is that it? You wouldn't shit me now, would you?" His face loomed close to hers, fierce, menacing, eyes so intent that they scared her. "You know I know where to find you, if it turns out you're lying. I'll come back for you, and this time I *will* hurt you . . . badly. That's your address . . . straight up . . . no shit?"

"You got it all, man, no shit, now please lemme go . . . please, man." He ignored her entreaties. "Come on," he tugged at her arm. "I want you to show me the place." He tugged again. She resisted.

"Aw she-it, man," shaking her head, "you be a weird mothafucka'. You said you gunna lemme go."

"And I will. I'll let you go. Just as soon as you point out the building to me. You wouldn't want me to get lost, now would you? Soon as you show me the place, you can go." He gave her his handkerchief. "Now fix your face and let's go." His voice was quiet, calm, yet firm and insistent.

She knew there was no point in pushing it any further. She used the handkerchief to dry her face and to blow her nose loudly. He demurred when she offered to return the soppy cloth to him. Then she led him through the quiet Paris streets toward Rue Ballu, still sobbing heavily into Mac's handkerchief.

They reached the corner of Rue Blanche and Rue Ballu a few minutes later. Mac looked down the street. It was quiet, lined with low-rise apartments over street-level shops. Except for those businesses that catered to the night crowd—a café on the corner, a deli, and a small fast food joint selling crêpes and sandwiches farther on down the street—the rest were closed and dark.

Number 22 was about halfway down the block. The building was a five-story walk-up over a dry-cleaning store and an auto repair shop. They walked slowly down Rue Ballu and observed the building from across the street. Kitty reluctantly pointed out her apartment on the fourth floor. The window was open, and a light was on. The unmistakable flickering of a TV screen confirmed that someone was inside. Mac's eyes began to glow again, and his body tensed like that of a panther that's sighted his prey and is getting ready to spring.

CHAPTER 104

MacMurphy thanked Kitty for her help and apologized for hurting her. She was happy to be released, and the one hundred euro note he pressed in her hand seemed to help immensely in easing her pain.

"Now listen carefully, Kitty," he said, holding her face in his hands and looking up into her eyes, "I'm going to go up there and talk to Lim, and I want you out of the area. Go back up toward Place Blanche. When you get there, go into a restaurant and get yourself something to eat. I want you to kill at least two hours before going back to the club, understand?"

"Uh-huh," she nodded.

"Don't screw this up, Kitty, or I promise you, you'll get hurt. When you get back to the club, you can tell them you gave me a blowjob in the car on the way to the hotel, I paid you, and you returned by metro. *Ça va?*" He didn't think the threat was necessary at this point, but it didn't hurt to put a little more fear into her.

"Okay, George. No sweat. Ah'll tell'em ah got you off real fast. Can ah go now? Please . . ."

"Sure. Go ahead. But first give me your cell phone. You've got a phone, don't you? Then you can get out of here."

"Why you want my phone?" she cried, digging into her purse.

"Just a precaution. I don't want you calling anyone before I talk to Lim. I'll leave it in your apartment when I'm finished talking with Lim."

She muttered something that sounded like "Thank you" but could have been "Fuck you" and handed over her cell phone. Then she scurried back up the street in short, wobbly steps. Her head was down and she pumped her arms, determined to get out of there as fast as possible.

MacMurphy backed into a doorway and watched her retreat. When she reached the corner he saw her stop, turn, and look back down the street. Mac backed deeper into the shadows of the doorway. When it was clear she could not see him, she crossed to the other side of Rue Ballu and searched for him from there as well. She then dashed back across the street and entered the café on the corner.

"Son of a bitch," muttered MacMurphy to himself, "what the hell is she doing now?" He ran back up the street and reached the café in time to see Kitty frantically beating on the glass door of the lone phone booth in the rear of the café, trying desperately to get the woman inside to cut her conversation short. Several customers sitting at tables were watching with great amusement, as was the patron behind the counter.

Mac couldn't go after her in the café. There were too many witnesses. The only thing he could do was beat it back to Kitty's apartment and hope to get there before Kitty's warning reached Lim. If he was late, the element of surprise would be lost. He knew Lim was a very tough customer, and he wanted that edge badly.

He took off at a dead run back down the street.

He reached the entrance of number 22 and hit the buzzer hard to open the door. The door popped open, and he saw the staircase directly in front of him. He raced up the stairs taking them three at a time. He was puffing and sweating profusely now. His false mustache started to come loose and his glasses were sliding down his nose. He jerked them off and jammed them into his pocket.

His knees ached by the time he hit the landing of the second floor, and his breath was coming in great gulps. He remembered how he hated to run the stadium stairs back in Oklahoma when he was a college wrestler, but wished he were in better shape for it now.

CHAPTER 105

The woman in the phone booth finally gave up trying to carry on a conversation while that crazy black woman was screaming at her from outside the booth. How could she with this insane person banging on the booth with both fists and screaming, alternately in bad English and worse French?

Furious at the interruption, she slammed the phone into the receiver. But she continued to resist Kitty's efforts to force her way into the booth by pushing back on the door and shouting her own stream of invectives. She was too angry to give in. Kitty finally backed off, threw her hands into the air in desperation, and broke into tears.

The tears did it. The woman let her in the booth.

CHAPTER 106

Mac ran up the final flight of stairs and as he hit the landing on the fourth floor he heard a phone ringing. He redoubled his efforts and reached the door of Kitty's apartment in seconds.

The phone stopped ringing.

MacMurphy aimed at a point just below the doorknob and put all of his weight behind one mighty kick. The heel of his boot hit the door and the jamb splintered. The door flew open into the room with Mac-Murphy right behind it.

Lim stood directly across the room, eyes wide, with the phone to his ear.

The adrenaline coursed through Mac's system and more than made up for his shaky knees. He was no more than three steps from Lim. He had planned to continue the attack toward Lim, but something held him back.

It was the four-inch stiletto Lim held loosely in his other hand.

Lim calmly replaced the phone on the receiver and squared himself toward Mac. His muscles rippled under his light tee-shirt, indicating a readiness that was not otherwise apparent. "What you want?" he said calmly.

"Put it down, maggot."

"*Eyeah*, why would I do stupid thing like that," said Lim with a sneer.

"Yeah, I guess you'd better keep it. You're going to need an equalizer."

Lim laughed. "You really think Lim need this, MacMurphy? Ha-ha, that is big joke for sure. You gotta be kidding, asshole." He tossed the knife on the couch beside him and laughed again. He bent into a karate crouch, arms out in front of him at the ready.

"You surprise me." MacMurphy, though he hadn't quite regained his breath, was dead calm. Adrenaline blazed through his body. He stood in the doorway with his thumbs looped casually into the pockets of his jeans, taking quick note of the stiletto, of Lim's stance, of all relevant facets of the apartment.

"Why I surprise you, you stink shit asshole piece of puke?" Lim beamed with confidence.

MacMurphy slowly withdrew his thumbs from his pockets; the brass knuckles dangled loosely from the right one. He spoke softly. "Because I don't take you lightly, Lim. I know your reputation. Third degree black belt and all that shit. So I brought an equalizer of my own." He slipped his fist into the rings of the knuckles and held his hand out in front of him so that Lim could get a good look.

Lim leaned ever so slightly to his right, closer to the knife he had tossed aside. "You shoulda brought gun. That thing not gonna do you no good."

"I didn't want things to get that uneven. This'll do just fine." His voice was low, hypnotic, compelling.

Lim dove for the knife on the couch, but MacMurphy anticipated the move and immediately leaped to intercept Lim. He reached Lim as

Lim's outstretched fingers touched the handle of the knife. MacMurphy's right fist crashed into Lim's skull just behind the left ear.

The momentum of his whole body was behind the blow, and the weight of the brass knuckles led the way. The sound of the brass striking bone made a dull thud, and blood from the scalp wound quickly matted Lim's black hair and smeared MacMurphy's hand. Lim hit the couch hard.

Lim forgot the knife and brought his hands up in front of him to defend against additional blows. He rolled to one side and brought his knee up into MacMurphy's crotch, knocking him off balance and forcing a belch of air from MacMurphy's already-depleted lungs.

Now the two men faced each other in the center of the room. Mac's body separated Lim from the knife which lay useless on the couch. Lim struggled to focus his eyes and regain full consciousness. He shook his head and backed off. Blood blended with sweat and tie-dyed the shoulder of his light tee-shirt a sopping pink.

MacMurphy wanted to press the attack, but Lim's kick had momentarily left him incapacitated, gasping to fill his lungs, trying to recuperate fully. Both fighters glared as they moved, each trying desperately to mask the extent of the damage inflicted.

Lim crouched lower and circled. He knew he had almost been put out by one blow from the clumsy *gwai-lo,* and this forced him to become more cautious, but his head was clearing, and he knew he could still win if he was careful and stayed away from that brass-knuckled fist of Mac-Murphy's. He looked for an opportunity to slip in close.

MacMurphy also wanted to get in close enough to pound Lim again, but he respected the reach of those powerful kicks and would not get over-eager.

Lim moved in a flash. He stepped forward and spun an arching reverse kick at the side of MacMurphy's head. Mac anticipated the move, but it came so fast he could not counter it fully. He dropped his right shoulder and brought his left arm up to block Lim's leg, but the force of the blow drove through the block and smashed into the side of MacMurphy's head, sending him careening across the room.

Mac rolled with the blow and turned to face Lim just in time to see the beginning of another spinning kick being directed at his head.

But Lim was reaching too far in this attack, and Mac was prepared. His left hand went out to meet the leg at shoulder level before it had reached the peak of its power. He slapped into the ankle and grasped with all of his might, turning the leg outward and down as he moved inside the kick. With the same motion, he turned from the knees, then hips, then shoulders, and his right arm sped around and down at the end of the fulcrum like a tennis player delivering a 150mph serve.

The outer edge of his brass-lined hand chopped into Lim's shin midway between the ankle and knee. There was a sickening "crack" as brass met bone, and Lim gasped in pain as he spun out and away.

Lim was hurt badly but not finished. He stepped gingerly on the leg, but it supported him. He circled while Mac prepared himself to counter the next attack.

He didn't have to wait long.

Lim came straight in and delivered two lightning punches to Mac's solar plexus. Mac tensed his stomach to receive the blows, but they drove the air from his lungs anyway and forced him back. He struggled to defend himself as Lim reflexively swung his damaged right leg toward the side of Mac's head.

Mac was frozen in place, still gasping for breath and off balance. But Lim couldn't get the fractured leg high enough, and the kick landed low. The instep of Lim's foot slammed into Mac's triceps just above the elbow. Although the kick missed its target, and its force was weakened by the fracture, it was still powerful enough to smash the triceps muscle and tear the ligaments, causing the contused arm to drop limply to Mac's side.

Lim screamed in pain as his kick landed, but when he saw the damage to Mac's arm, he immediately pushed the pain aside and moved in for the kill.

He attacked Mac's defenseless left side and brought a brutal karate chop down on Mac's collarbone. Mac felt the bone snap and his shoulder go numb, but no pain. His right hand was already arching down toward

Lim's neck. Lim ducked into the blow, forcing it to land wide, but the brass-covered hand smashed into his back on the trapezoid with enough force to contuse the muscle and drive Lim down to his knees.

Lim screamed again as his crippled leg buckled beneath him, and he rolled out and away and up to his feet a safe ten feet away from Mac-Murphy.

MacMurphy did not press the attack. His left arm hung useless, and the whole left side of his body throbbed. He could feel the tightness of the swelling on the side of his face, and his left eye was partially closed. It was difficult to move or breathe, and only adrenaline and sheer will kept him on his feet.

Now he wished he had overridden his ego and had brought a gun.

Mac squared himself against Lim and pulled strength from deep within to face this challenge. He pushed out the pain and focused, focused, focused . . .

Lim could barely stand, and his head was cocked to one side by spasms in his trapezoid and shoulder muscles. Blood still gushed freely from the scalp wound behind his ear, further soaking his shirt and spattering the room and his opponent with each quick movement. Both men were breathing heavily. Both knew only one would walk away.

Lim moved forward, and Mac circled right, protecting his injured left side and ready to strike with a brass-encrusted fist. Lim thought he had the advantage. He wouldn't try any more kicks, but as long as he stayed on his feet he could pummel his adversary with karate punches to his unprotected side.

MacMurphy was not as well schooled in the martial arts—he was more of a street fighter who could wrestle and punch. All Lim had to do to win was stay away from Mac's right hand and set and punch, set and punch. Lim was ready to punish him—now!

He stepped in tight, feinted low and to the right, and threw a blistering backhand chop that sliced up toward MacMurphy's throat. The left-handed chop was halfway to its target when Lim released a more devastating follow-through right-handed thrust, concentrating all of his remaining power on the leading two knuckles of his fist. The blow came from low at the waist and twisted up straight toward Mac's left rib cage.

Then the unexpected happened.

MacMurphy ducked under the slice that whistled past his ear and turned the right side of his body into his attacker, causing the blow to graze across his stomach instead of crunching into his ribs. In the same motion, he swung his right leg out in a wide arch and back behind Lim's left knee, sweeping the good leg out from under him and bringing him crashing to the floor.

Keeping the momentum of his kick, Mac slammed into Lim's prostrate form with both knees, driving the wind from his lungs and snapping ribs and sternum. He brought the outer edge of the brass knuckles on his right hand down across the bridge of Lim's nose in a vicious karate chop, smashing bone and cartilage and spattering blood up into Mac's face and over his shirt.

He was in a rage and could not stop for fear Lim would hit him again. He continued to rain blows on Lim's face and head, smashing lips and scattering teeth and blood. Finally, he couldn't raise his arm to strike anymore. He slid off the body, the face caved in by the brass knuckles, to the floor, gasping for air . . .

CHAPTER 107

MACAU—MID-SEPTEMBER

acMurphy watched the speck on the horizon grow into a full-sized hydrofoil. The sleek craft arched around the breakwater and throttled back, splashing down from its pontoons onto its hull as it entered Macau harbor.

He walked slowly toward the ferry terminal and watched the boat maneuver into its docking position. He felt run down and tired, and he couldn't shake the butterflies from his stomach—that horrible feeling of trepidation. He did not like the feeling at all.

His condition was worsened by the physical injuries he had received in the fight with Lim. His left arm was held in a loose sling, and the broken ribs scraped across his lungs with each breath. The sunglasses he wore did not completely hide the ugly bruise on the left side of his face.

He wore tennis shoes, jeans, and an un-tucked short-sleeved denim shirt. He looked a mess and felt like shit.

He was also quite certain that the news the courier was bringing from the DDO was not going to make him feel any better.

Mac saw him first as he passed through the double doors of the customs area and entered the main terminal. The big man limped toward him, head down in his characteristic John Wayne saunter. He looked tired. He was dressed casually in baggy tan slacks, white shirt and a rumpled light blue sport jacket. A green backpack was slung over one shoulder. *My God*, thought Mac, *he came personally*. The news couldn't be as bad as expected—not if Edwin Rothmann was the courier delivering it.

The DDO's face lit up in a wide grin when their eyes met. He hefted the backpack on his shoulder and quickened his pace. When they met, they embraced gingerly. Rothmann pushed Mac back and frowned at his condition. "You look terrible," he growled, unable to mask his concern.

"You should see the other guy," Mac replied sheepishly, "but I guess you know all about that by now. It's good to see you, boss. Thanks for coming. I can't wait to hear what happened after I left, and . . . and what's next on . . ."

"Cool it, Mac." The big man patted Mac on the side of the head. "Let's get out of here and go someplace where we can talk. I've got plenty to tell you, and lots of time to tell it to you."

"Okay, let's go." Mac took the old man's backpack with his good right arm, slung it over his shoulder and guided him out into the late afternoon sun to the taxi waiting area. They entered the first cab in the queue and Mac directed the driver to take them to the *Pousada de Macau*.

The big man stopped and turned. "You can't imagine how sorry I am about Wei-wei, Mac. I just can't tell you . . ."

"I know, boss. It's really tough. I . . ."

"There'll be a service for her at the Trinity Church a week from today. It'll be a private thing. You should be there. You need to come home and . . ."

"I'll be there. Don't worry. I'll be there. I'll go back with you."

Talk of Wei-wei was uncomfortable for them both, so they made small talk during the short drive to the inn. When Rothmann asked about his injuries, Mac replied, "Nothing to worry about. I'll heal . . ."

Rothmann could see that the driver was concentrating on weaving his rattletrap taxi through the traffic around the gaudy Lisboa Hotel and decided it was safe to assuage Mac's greatest concern. Mac was gazing thoughtfully out the window. The DDO leaned close and spoke in a low voice. "By the way, Lim's alive; he made it—what's left of him."

After a moment Mac said, "I'm glad."

Rothmann smiled, "I somehow thought you might be. I understand." Rothmann knew that Mac had attacked Lim for his own, personal reasons. Which meant a charge of murder could have been brought by the French, complicating life for Mac and the Agency—which would not have hesitated to disavow any knowledge of Mac's actions. That's just the way things were done.

CHAPTER 108

The taxi dropped them in front of the old *Pousada de Macau*. Mac paid the driver and led the DDO up the old wooden steps of the porch, through the small entrance hall and directly out to the veranda overlooking the bay. The sun hovered only a few feet above the horizon, casting a crimson aura over the sparkling blue-green waters. *Red at night; sailors' delight,* he thought. It absently reminded Mac of a painting he had seen somewhere.

Most tables were unoccupied, and they selected one a discreet distance from the other people. A stately old waiter in starched whites arrived instantly. The DDO ordered a scotch on the rocks and Mac a vodka-tonic. When the waiter returned with their drinks, Mac lifted his in a toast to Rothmann. "*Kam-bei*, boss." The rim of his glass touched the DDO's slightly below its rim, honoring him in an ancient Chinese way, like a deeper Japanese bow.

Mac leaned forward and spoke very softly. "Soon I'll treat you to a meal of the best African Chicken and vintage Portuguese Dao wine this side of Lisbon. But first . . . let's have it . . . all of it . . . from the beginning. Start with why you came personally."

The DDO took a sip of his scotch and put the glass down. "I came because you deserve it Mac. You're one of the best case officers I've ever had the pleasure to work with. You know what I think of you. The Director wants to castrate you for what you did. No one else knows where you are and I decided not to tell them. I took leave to come here on my own because I wanted you to hear this from someone close to you, not from one of the assholes who are taking over this fucking outfit."

"Thanks for that," MacMurphy said. "Yeah, the outfit is changing. The people in charge don't want to take any risks anymore. They crept up to where they are by playing it safe, and they're so desperately afraid of losing what they have, they just talk a good show but don't actually do anything—paper ops from paper operators."

He checked himself. "But don't get me started on that one now. Anyway, go on." He had a lot of questions and he needed answers.

The DDO sipped his scotch and gazed out over the water. The hot red sun was slipping slowly into the cool and soothing sea. He reflected on the sight for a moment, then shared a memory: "When I was a little kid, I used to wonder why the sun didn't sizzle when it hit the water."

Mac smiled and nodded.

His mind returned to the present. "Anyway, I decided to come myself. The fact that no one else could figure out where the hell you had gone when you bugged out also helped a lot. You really had them doing back flips. I got the back channel message you sent via Rodney and decided to keep the information regarding your whereabouts to myself. I also wanted to gauge your mental state. You know . . . you've been through a lot and . . ."

"Well, I really thank you for that, boss. I'm okay. I'll make it okay." Mac sat back and nodded his head appreciatively. There were so few like Rothmann . . . and so many of the others.

"And I'll tell you one other thing," said Rothmann, his voice more upbeat now, "we are damn lucky Lim didn't check out, because if he had, the Director would have had an excuse to crucify me and push me out. He'd like nothing more than to get rid of me. He considers me a hair in his soup. And I hate to imagine what he would have done to you . . ."

MacMurphy adjusted his position in the chair again, grunting as one of his cracked ribs stabbed him. "So, what about Lim? When I left him, I thought he was dead. I really thought I had killed him."

"Well, from what I hear, it wasn't from lack of trying. When the police found him, he was indeed at death's door. But he survived, and the Chinese have already returned him to Beijing. Only problem is he suffered extensive brain damage from the loss of blood and oxygen and the pounding you gave him. So not only will he now be the ugliest guy in his neighborhood—I guess you really did a job on his face—he will also be the village idiot."

MacMurphy grimaced. "You must think he got what he deserved."

"You better believe I think he got what he deserved. I've got no sympathy for that SOB whatsoever after what he did. I'm just glad you're not facing a murder rap."

"What about the police?"

"It was reported as an attempted robbery." His finger spun the ice in his drink absentmindedly. "They think Lim caught someone trying to rip him off and decided to take the law into his own hands. Only problem was he obviously bit off more than he could chew," he grinned.

"And he's in no shape to tell them any differently . . . even if he wanted to . . . and from what I heard, he never will be. Actually, that's the way it is with the entire theft operation. The French know nothing and neither the Chinese nor the Agency is saying a word about the affair. But I'm getting ahead of myself." The big man threw back the rest of his drink and set his empty glass down on the table. "Buy me another drink and I'll tell you about the missing money." He smiled again.

CHAPTER 109

The waiter brought fresh drinks, and the DDO continued, feeling better now on his second scotch. "So the bottom line is the Chinese would prefer to let the whole matter drop. They don't want the news to get out that they smuggled fifty million euros into France through the diplomatic pouch, and they certainly don't want anyone to know what the money was to be used for.

"Furthermore, they are terribly embarrassed by the defection of one of their senior MSS officers and want that kept quiet too. For our part, we agreed to keep mum about it—no publicity—and to give Huang a new identity so he can live out his years in the US in anonymity. And you can be sure the Company won't be jumping to advertise the fact that one of theirs pulled a heist right under the noses of the French and then pulverized a friendly third country diplomat."

"So Huang did defect," said MacMurphy.

"You knew he would. He had no choice. Losing fifty million euros of the people's money and allowing a subordinate to run amok would not win him any medals in Beijing. He would've spent the rest of his days in whatever the Chinese equivalent of Siberia is."

"Yeah, that's about what I expected. That's what I hoped would happen. Defection's not as good as recruitment, but *Tant pis*, half a loaf and all that shit. He'll have a great life in the US. The Agency will take very good care of him."

"That's right," said Rothmann. "What we did was one hell of a lot better than kidnapping him like the Director and Berger wanted. At least Huang had a choice in the matter. And it saved the outfit the embarrassment of the rendition of a Chinese diplomat."

Rothmann thought a moment before continuing. "I'm getting a bit ahead of myself, but that's part of the message. The defection of Huang was so important, we're putting you in for the Intelligence Star. And the Director can't do anything but support it. Huang is the highest-level MSS officer ever to defect to the west. The debriefing is expected to rewrite the book on the internal structure and external operations of the MSS.

"The China Operations Group is ecstatic. They're talking about nothing else. And Huang's knowledge goes well beyond the MSS. He knows every major personality in the politburo and was deeply involved in preparing military and economic, as well as covert action plans over the last couple of decades.

"The Directorate of Intelligence is planning to rewrite their national estimates on China's military, economic, and intelligence capabilities based on Huang's information. And all of that is rather mundane when you consider what he'll bring to us in terms of Iranian plans and intentions in Iraq, its involvement in supporting terrorism, and its relations with China and other countries. Of course, there are always some operational details and other things he probably won't ever give us, but we can certainly live with that."

"I'm glad they're so pleased," Mac's voice was laden with sarcasm. "But it all didn't come without cost, you know. Wei-wei, François and Le Belge, and, well . . . Lim."

"Well, yes, but don't be too proud of yourself. The medal is just half of it—the good news. The bad news is you're fired. The Director wants you out." Rothmann looked at him levelly, watching for a reaction, but Mac didn't return the DDO's gaze.

Mac stared into his drink pensively. "Can't say as I didn't expect it. So . . . I guess it really is over . . ." His voice wavered.

Rothmann spoke softly. "Yeah Mac, it's over. At least this part of it . . ." He reached over and patted Mac's arm affectionately. "Hey, case officers like us are dinosaurs. The cold war is over, Vietnam and the rest of Southeast Asia are forgotten, and when our country does decide to do brave things like 'Desert One', the capture of Noriega, Afghanistan, Iraq, the Bin Laden takedown, and all the rest, the Agency takes all the heat if everything doesn't go exactly according to plan. We can stop a thousand terrorist attacks, but as soon as a bomb goes off somewhere where Americans are congregated, the press and Congress call it an intelligence failure, and the CIA gets all the blame.

"They castrated us through budget cuts and all the rest, and now they want to reorganize the place out of existence. It's just not the same can-do organization anymore. You said it yourself. Its time to leave anyway. It's over. Don't you think?"

"Yeah, I suppose . . ." Mac looked out over the calm, moonlit bay. Shards of silver moonlight glinted on the nearly still waters, broken only by an occasional small wave or the wake of a boat. He drained his glass and set it down. "Let's go for a walk along the quay before dinner," he suggested.

"Before we go I need to ask you one more thing." The DDO twisted his napkin and tossed it on the table. "Did you know about Rodney Jackson?"

"Rotten? What about him?" Mac was puzzled, surprised.

"Some of the first information Huang provided instigated a humongous CI investigation on Rodney. Huang says he was being developed by a female Chinese access agent who was sleeping with him. That's how Lim found out about you, which led to the murders of Wei-wei, Le Belge and François. The guys with the green eyeshades and the little ole' ladies

THE CASE OFFICER

in tennis shoes in the counterintelligence shop think Rodney Jackson was a full-blown agent working for the Chinese."

"That's bullshit," MacMurphy spat, then calmed. "No. I don't know, really, but I doubt it . . . Rodney's a good guy. He wouldn't betray his county, his friends . . . he wouldn't spy for China."

"But he might have been tricked into working for them . . ."

"Sure. That's a possibility. In fact, come to think about it, it's a very good possibility. And if that's what Huang said—that Rotten was under development—I'd believe him. Why would he lie about such a thing? Why don't the CI gurus just go back and ask Huang for the details? He'd certainly know."

"Apparently they did, but they said Huang was evasive. He admitted they had targeted him, but that's all. Maybe he's trying to protect that pretty Chinese girlfriend of Rodney's."

"Poor Rodney . . . poor guy. What's going to happen to him?"

"I don't know. I guess it'll depend upon whether he really was just duped by the girl or was a willing collaborator. Either way, he's in deep trouble. They recalled him to Washington and put him on administrative leave. He's only permitted back in the building for his interrogation sessions and polygraph examinations. He's not under arrest yet, but the FBI has been called in, and you know what that means . . ."

"That's a bitch. A real bitch . . . But I guess it fits, doesn't it? That's how Lim knew about me, and that's what led him to Wei-wei, François and Le Belge. Son-of-a-bitch . . ."

"Rodney's not the only one who will suffer over this. They're looking for heads to lop off all over the place. The last nail has been driven into Little Bob's coffin, and Burton B. Berger is back there trying to explain why one of his communicators was permitted to cohabit openly, in the Marine House no less, with a foreign national—particularly a communist Chinese one."

"Can't say as I'm disappointed over those two assholes. Whatever they get they deserve." Mac chuckled and grimaced in pain. "They created the atmosphere of hate and distrust that makes people like Rodney vulnerable, and their incompetence at not recognizing the signs ought to get them both fired."

"That's what I think. We'll nail them. You can bet on that. Now let's take that walk." He drained his glass, placed both hands on the table and pushed his bulk up into a standing position, ready to leave.

CHAPTER 110

Macmurphy paid the check and they walked slowly down to the quay. The bright full moon competed with the flashy neon lights of the distant Lisboa Casino as it danced on the bay. There was a gentle breeze coming off the water. Mac took a deep, painful breath, and inhaled the fresh salt air with a slight fishy smell. They walked silently along the gravel path on the water's edge.

Mac broke the silence. "But what about the money?"

Rothmann laughed. "Oh yeah, I almost forgot about the money. They don't want to hear about it. They don't want to hear anything about the money. As far as the organization is concerned, there is no money."

"No money? There's fifty million euros sitting in that Swiss bank!"

"Yep. The money's a definite problem. A big problem for all concerned. The Company can't return it unless the Chinese ask for it, and they won't even admit to ever having it. And we can't give it to the treasury without having to explain how we got it. So, quite simply, there is no money."

"You're joking!" exclaimed Mac, grunting again from a stab in his ribs. "Just what the hell do they expect me to do with fifty million euros?"

"Well, we just need to think about that."

"I could just leave it there," he said thoughtfully.

"You could do that . . ."

"Or I could use some of it . . . you know, to get me back on my feet—I am unemployed, and after all . . ."

"Yep, you could do that too. In fact, that's a very good idea. Get ourself established someplace. Someplace warm and close to an airport."

Mac was puzzled. "Why an airport?"

The big man stopped. "Because I'm going to help you spend all that money. Think of it as CIA money. There are plenty of things we used to do in the Agency that we can't do any more. I'll give you an example. Ever since the mid-70's when we were castrated by the Goddamned contentious Pike and Church committees, we've gotten out of the business of political covert action. You know what I mean—influencing regime change in countries that are hostile to the US and installing leaders that are friendly to the US. That's one of the three things in the original charter for the CIA. Did you know that? Collection, analysis and covert action. One, two, three. That's what we're supposed to do and we're afraid to do it any more. The covert action, I mean."

Mac said, "Sure, I know what you mean. Covert action was once explained to me down on The Farm as something between State's 'nice doggy' and the military's 'whack over the head with a two-by-four.'"

"That's right, exactly right, something between diplomacy and war. We're spending far too much treasure and American lives on foreign wars—Iraq, Afghanistan—you know what I mean. And now the whole Middle East is coming apart. Regimes are changing in Libya, Egypt, Yemen, Syria, all over the place, and the replacements—the Arab League and all those nutty jokers—look to be much worse than what we had. At least in terms of American interests, they are. And when things started to come apart in Iran, we had nothing in place to help overthrow the Ayatollahs and to install a more US friendly regime."

"And the Agency can't do this any more? Really?" Mac asked.

"Nope, we're allowed to cajole, and then when that doesn't work we're allowed to invade, but we're not allowed to 'meddle in the internal affairs' of countries any longer."

"That's stupid!"

"Of course it's stupid. But that's the way it is these days. It's a fact of life." Rothmann turned toward Mac, looked down at him and placed his large hands on Mac's shoulders. "So save that money, Mac, we're going to need it. We're getting back to the basics. We're going to do the things that need to be done, you and me. We're going to do it. Covert action and a whole range of things this great outfit used to do but won't do any more. No more timidity. We'll be bold. Just like in the old days. It's going to be just like the old days . . ."

POSTSCRIPT

M argret "Wei-wei" Ryan was laid to rest in a small, private ceremony at the Trinity Church in McLean, Virginia. Wei-Wei's close Agency friends and her parents were there, as well as MacMurphy, Culler Santos and Edwin Rothmann.

Following the ceremony, Rothmann took Mac aside and reiterated that Mac should keep the money safe in the Bern account "for contingency purposes." He added that he would be calling on Mac "from time to time to help out with some sensitive things," and the money would come in handy on those occasions.

A few days later, Mac took a leisurely drive down the Atlantic coast to Ft. Lauderdale, Florida. There Mac bought a two-story Mediterranean home on a canal in an upscale gated community, and rented a suite of offices on the eighth floor of an office building overlooking the

Intracoastal Waterway. The sign he hung on the door read: Global Strategic Reporting.

Culler Santos resigned from the Agency in characteristic fashion by flipping his badge at the Director and stomping out the front entrance over the large marble CIA insignia inset in floor.

He had a better offer which no longer required him to put up with the bullshit that had become far too much a part of his job at the CIA. He would join his friend MacMurphy at GSR in Ft. Lauderdale and embark on a new career in private intelligence.

A day after Wei-wei's interment, Edwin Rothmann visited Huang Tsung-yao at a farmhouse in a remote wooded area of Vienna, Virginia, where Huang was being debriefed by CIA interrogators.

Rothmann took Huang aside and they went for a quiet walk in the forest. He explained what had transpired and expressed his and Mac's sincere apologies for the unintentional pain their actions had caused Huang. He then presented Huang with a gift from Mac: a bank book containing a deposit of five million euros in a numbered account in Bern, Switzerland.

He also told Huang that once his debriefing was complete he would be given a new identity and a life-long GS-15 salary from the CIA. That would give him financial independence (beyond the gift from Mac) and a chance to start a new life in America.

He ended by saying that Mac was opening a business security and intelligence firm in Florida, and that there was an open invitation for him to join Mac there. After all, who could be a more effective adviser for American companies doing business with China than one of its intelligence elite?

FALSE FLAG

BY

F.W. RUSTMANN, JR.

REGNERY
FICTION

CHAPTER 1

The drive from Belmopan to the central prison of Belize in Hattieville, affectionately known as the "Hattieville Ramada," took almost two hours, mostly on narrow, dusty jungle roads. The seventeen prisoners, each one handcuffed to his seat, bounced along in an old, gray school bus with dead shocks and springs.

Culler Santos was in a foul mood. The prisoner sitting across the aisle from him, a heavily tattooed young man of mixed race named Aduan, would not stop glaring at him. Santos had heard about Aduan in the Belmopan jail. He had a reputation for being a psychopath, the worst of the worst.

Although he was only a few months past his nineteenth birthday, Aduan had admitted to killing six people, including one of his uncles. The latter murder, the killing of a close relative, had elevated him in the ranks of the Crips. Each of the murders, with the exception of the last

1

one, which landed him in prison, was recorded on his chest in a row of tattooed, half-inch circles.

The Crips and their archrival gang, the Bloods, were strong in Belize, having immigrated there from Los Angeles in the mid-eighties. And nowhere were they stronger, or more heavily represented, than in the Belizean prison system.

Santos decided it was best to ignore the kid, so he concentrated on looking out the window at the passing jungle scenery. But each time he looked over, he caught the kid staring at him.

He didn't need this. On top of everything else, he was still wearing the jeans, tennis shoes, and sweat-stained, white polo shirt he had been wearing when he was taken into custody. He had not had a proper shower or shaved in the four days since his arrest. He knew he reeked because the stench of the other prisoners reminded him of a horse barn.

The kid was dressed in rags like most of the other prisoners. He wore stained, khaki cutoffs, a pair of worn out flip-flops and an Army camouflage tee shirt. The sleeves of the tee shirt were cut off to better display his powerful, tattoo-covered arms. He sported a head full of long, filthy dreadlocks, a stringy Fu Manchu mustache, and a braided goatee.

They reached Hattieville at the two-mile marker of Burrell Boom Road. A guard walked down the aisle unlocking handcuffs. The prisoners were led out the door in single file, through the main gate of the prison and into the prison yard. It was surrounded by stained, two-story, white-cement-block buildings, which housed the cells. A chain-link fence topped with hoops of concertina razor wire surrounded the entire 225-acre plot of land. Guards armed with AK-47 automatic weapons patrolled along the roofs of the buildings and stood in towers in each corner. The entire facility stank like a barnyard.

After a short "welcome" speech from the warden, who laid out the usual warnings about the consequences of escape attempts, the group was split into smaller groups and led to their cells in the "Remand Section" of the prison. There they waited for trial. Some of them had been there for more than five years. The judicial system in Belize was in no hurry.

Santos was led to a cell on the ground floor along with four other prisoners from the bus, but not before each one surrendered his belt. All other pocket litter had been confiscated at the Belmopan jail. He assumed the belts would be added to those other belongings. After the surrender, some of the men had to walk with one hand holding up their drooping pants. Santos reflected on the "low pants" tradition that was common among young blacks in American ghettos. This is where it all began—in prisons. Why those kids wanted to emulate prison inmates was totally beyond him.

One of the prisoners in his group was Aduan. Santos cussed his luck and immediately began to think about how he would neutralize this obvious threat. Aduan was hugged and high-fived by several other inmates when he entered the cell. This macho display added to Santos's dismay.

The filthy, twenty-by-twenty-foot cell was already filled with more than a dozen inmates. Santos counted the double bunks that lined two of the walls—there were four. That meant eight beds for about sixteen smelly men. *This is going to be cozy*, Santos thought.

All of the bunks were occupied, so he looked for a place on the concrete floor where he could stake out a space. Grabbing one of the bunks was out of the question. It would have meant an immediate confrontation, and he was not ready for that. Not yet.

In one corner of the room, he noticed a plastic milk carton cut in half and realized it was being used as a toilet. *Better stay as far away from that as possible*, he thought. He found a spot near the corner on the other side of the room, plopped himself down between two other inmates and put his head on his knees.

Hurry up, Mac. Get me out of here. Please hurry...

The crowded cell was a cacophony of smells and noises. A few of the prisoners, like Santos, sat quietly with their eyes closed and arms folded around their knees, trying to block out their surroundings, submerging themselves in their thoughts.

It did not take Aduan long to saunter over to Santos's side of the cell and stop in front of him. He stood there, swaying back and forth, glaring down at the American. The cell suddenly became quiet. Three other heavily tattooed prisoners, all with long dreadlocks, moved across the room and converged alongside of Aduan.

Santos sensed the arrival of Aduan and his fellow Crips and watched them from the corners of his eyes. He sat there quietly for a few moments and then looked up and locked onto Aduan's threatening stare. He knew now that confrontation was unavoidable, but he was not afraid.

His thoughts centered on how best to neutralize the four thugs. With one attacker, it would be simple: take him to the ground and dislocate his arm with an arm bar. That was the quickest and easiest way to neu-tralize an opponent. But in this case, there were too many of them. He needed to remain on his feet while sending them all to the ground. Tac-tics spun through his mind. He knew he could beat them. It was just a matter of how.

His head rose slowly and he quietly asked, "Do you want my spot?" Aduan threw his head back and laughed heartily. He looked around at his friends and then began to reply.

As soon as Aduan's mouth opened, Santos unleashed a sweeping kick with his right leg that knocked Aduan's legs out from under him and dropped him hard on his tailbone. There was an audible thud as he hit the concrete floor, forcing the air from his lungs in a gasp.

Santos spun to his feet in one motion and caught the tall Crip to Aduan's left with a roundhouse, backhand punch to the side of the head, dropping the thug like a stone.

He turned to his right and confronted the wide-eyed, fat Crip who was swinging a lame roundhouse at his head. Santos blocked the punch with his left forearm, stepped in close, looped his right arm under his attacker's right arm and, with two hands grasping the wrist, snapped the arm down. An audible pop and a scream told him the elbow was dislo-cated. He followed up with a sharp right elbow to the temple and the Crip went down in a heap, unconscious and with his arm jutting out at an awkward angle.

Aduan jumped to his feet and attacked. Santos stepped back with his left leg to dodge a right hook, crossed his right leg over his left and launched it screaming toward Aduan's head. Santos's foot connected at the ear with a sickening thud. Aduan careened across the room, into the wall and down in a heap.

In a blur Santos spun around and delivered a side kick directly to the knee of the forth thug. The force of the kick snapped the Crip's knee backwards, dislocating it and sending the thug to the ground screaming in pain. He was no longer a threat.

Santos dodged a kick to the head from the only standing Crip and delivered two sharp blows to the solar plexus, knocking the wind from the thug's lungs and sending him to his knees. He went down into a fetal position.

Santos stood, panting. He surveyed the carnage. Two of the Crips were permanently out of commission with dislocated limbs. Aduan was unconscious and the other Crip was moaning and gasping for breath in a heap.

He stepped over to Aduan who was lying face down on the floor. He stood over him, brought his leg up high and stomped down on Aduan's right shoulder with the heel of his shoe. He heard the shoulder crunch, rendering the arm useless.

He turned to the remaining Crip, moaning and lying on his side. He brought his leg up again and brought it down hard on the femur, snapping the bone and eliciting a scream from the thug.

Satisfied, Santos surveyed the carnage he had inflicted. Now all four of the Crips would be taken to the hospital with broken or dislocated limbs, which was Santos's plan in the first place. They would be removed from the cell and no longer a threat.

Santos walked to the center of the cell, looked around at the inmates surrounding him and addressed the motionless, gawking group. "I had nothing to do with this, get it? These guys got into a fight and beat the crap out of each other. Understand? That's your story when the guards get here." He glared around the room, locking eyes with each one of them in turn.

The shocked inmates nodded in agreement, some muttering in approval and awe of what had just occurred. Santos then walked over to the nearest lower bunk, pushed aside two inmates standing in front of it, and plopped himself down.

Lying on the bunk with his legs crossed and his hands behind his head, he said, "And this is where I will spend the rest of my time here, right on this bunk. Does anyone have any objections to that?"

There were none.